Evangeline's Destiny

By

Apollonia

Bw
tanti grazie!
Apollonia

2
MOON
PRESS

MARSHALL MICHIGAN
800PUBLISHING.COM

Dedication

I want to dedicate this book to my Husband, whom is not here to see this book in its physical form, however I know he is in heaven looking down smiling upon me.

Also, to my two Josephines. My friend for life, Josephine Vitale, and my beloved mother Josephine Pizzo, who gave me the courage to get to this day. Special thanks to my family who put up with me when I talk about my characters as if they were real people.

ONE

In the sleepy little village of Santa Fara, Sicily, in1898, at the base of the great mountain, Lorenzo Rizzo sat behind a lemon tree. He was waiting for the daily procession of young girls walking from Mass to the school of The Sacred Heart.

Mother Superior led the way like a mother duck with all her ducklings following behind her.

There she was. He suddenly spotted her, *his Evangeline*. She was the most perfect person he had ever seen. Her curly black hair fell like a halo around her shoulders. Dark eyes and a heart-shaped face that always had a smile on it couldn't be ignored. He heard her sweet voice as the young students sang "Immaculate Mary" on their pilgrimage back to class. His heart skipped a beat every time he saw her. Evangeline noticed him too, when he tipped his hat to her as he had for the past month. He had to be careful not to let Mother Superior see him. If that happened, Evangeline's father would have to be notified and then there would be hell to pay.

Lorenzo had learned several young townsmen, even those from good families, were sent away by her father when they asked to be introduced to Evangeline. She was still a baby in her Papa's eyes and he wasn't going to part with her yet. In fact, he didn't think he would ever be ready for that. The sisters had high hopes for Evangeline too. She was their star student and they wanted her to become a teacher and stay at Sacred Heart. They certainly didn't want the likes of Lorenzo hanging around her.

He left his mark on the school during his time there and they were glad to be rid of him. He was absent most of the time anyway. His excuse was that he was sick or that his father needed him home for the day.

Mother Superior called him to her office when he arrived at school several hours late one day.

"Where have you been, Lorenzo?" she asked.

"Helping my Papa," he said.

"Come here, son," she said.

When he got close to her, she licked his face.

What is she doing? Lorenzo thought with total disgust.

To his surprise, she guessed correctly that he was swimming in the Mediterranean Sea. She tasted the salt from the water on his skin. He had to say ten Hail Mary's and ten Our Fathers for lying to her. He prayed a lot in those days.

Lorenzo's family was poor and at the lower end of the social class of Santa Fara. They lived at the edge of town near the crest of the great mountain. His father was a shepherd and also raised a few pigs and a couple of horses that he rented out once in a while to make some extra money to support his family. The house was a little more than a shack, but it was theirs.

His older sister, Maria, ran off with Nicolo Romano, got married and sailed to America. The family was very upset with her because they depended on the few lira she brought to them with her needle work. Lately she was helping by sending them money from her job in New York City. It was such a relief for her mother and father. Lorenzo wished she had taken him with her, he envied her so. Maybe someday he and Evangeline would go to America and send home money; and then her Papa will be so proud that he is his son-in-law.

"Wake up Lorenzo, come out of that silly fog you are in, " said Franco, his boyhood friend. "Get away from that girl, she is more trouble than you can imagine."

"Shut your mouth, you dog face. She is going to be my wife someday."

"Yes, yes you are right," replied Franco; "If you can steal her! Come on you thief, I know a lemon tree that is ripe and you can have all the fruit you want. The owner has gone to Palermo for the day and if we must steal something this is our chance."

The two ran off with a flour sack in hand to help themselves. The idea was rattling around in Lorenzo's head. *What if he did steal her? Oh my God, what an upheaval that would make,* as he pointed his clasped hands to the heavens. All he could think of was Evangeline and that he loved her and had to have her. Later that night when he and his friends were together, they could make a plan.

Georgio Como, Evangeline's father was the town's mayor. He was a highly respected man and they lived in the nicest part of town. Lorenzo knew he would never be welcomed or even invited to one of the many receptions the mayor and his wife hosted. How was he going to get a proper introduction to the fair Evangeline? Lorenzo and his friends had a reputation of being the *bad boys* of the town and that was a big strike against him. It was no secret that they took many trips to Palermo to visit a brothel or two. His tall thin body and charming gift of gab didn't go unnoticed. In the eyes of the beautiful girl, however, her admirer was misunderstood.

She was ignorant of Palermo brothels; in fact she didn't know what a brothel was. She was so young and innocent she didn't understand the feelings she had when he brushed against her in the market place or when he glanced at her at Mass. All she knew was those dark brown eyes that winked at her when they passed on the street always made her melt. Although never a word had been spoken between them she knew in her heart that he would be her destiny.

"Stop mooning over something you can't have, Evangeline," scolded her older sister Felicia. "Don't let the people talk. You are an evil child and an ungrateful daughter to have such ideas. Lorenzo Rizzo is a low life and a thief. Papa would kill him if he knew he was even *looking* your way."

"Please Felicia, don't tell mama or papa. I will die if they know."

Felicia was jealous of her beautiful little sister with her pretty eyes and dark brown hair. Unlike Evangeline, she had been born with eyes that crossed and hair that was somewhere between red and brown and totally unmanageable. No creamy skin for Felicia, no, hers was splotched and considered very odd. Growing up in the shadow of Evangeline's looks had given Felicia what the Sisters termed a bad temperament.

She knew she was headed for a life in the church: No man in Santa Fara was ever going to ask for her hand in marriage. Going to the convent in the city would be the best thing for the family as no family wanted to be strapped with an old maid daughter. Certainly not her father, who while he had some stature as Mayor, was still a man of limited means and could not afford the immense sum required to dower an ugly daughter. Nor could he donate a huge sum to the convent which, Felicia knew, would mean a lowly stature there as well. In-between the required praying, she would also be required to scrub floors, clean chamber pots and do laundry.   Felicia put it in God's hands and prayed every day that something better would come along to save her.

Springtime brought about the annual festival of the Blessed Mother. Sacred Heart church celebrated the mass in the morning followed by a procession of the Statue of the Virgin carried by several young men of the town. Little children in their First Holy Communion garb would lead the way. The men that belonged to the Society of the Blessed Virgin came next followed by the sisters, novices and priests. Later the festivities with food and sweets of various kinds were spread out in the plaza. Dancing, singing and fireworks finished off the event. The villagers looked forward to the festa all year. People came from other small towns and reunions of families and friends were in many households. When it came time for the musicians to start the music, the single young girls were seated in one area of the square during the evening dance. They were dressed in their finest attire to perhaps attract a suitor.

Weeks of planning went into the color and style of their dresses. The girls whose fathers were better off, got copies of the style of the day from Palermo, and were sewn for the occasion. Of course, their mothers or chaperones were seated next to them or at least nearby. This was one of the rare occasions when a single male could ask a girl to dance with him. Under the watchful eye of Evangeline's mother, Lorenzo gained enough nerve to ask her to dance.

Alicianna Como secretly wished someone was going to ask Felicia to dance. She got a little excited when the boy came in their direction. She said yes before she even knew which daughter he was asking for. Evangeline thought the wind had been knocked out of her when she saw her mother nod yes. Lorenzo felt a little electric shock when he took her hand and it made them both laugh.

Evangeline had never danced before and Lorenzo wished he were better at it. He held her at arm's length and felt like a hundred eyes were on them. The music was a waltz and they were a little clumsy at it. At one point his left foot got in the way of his right and he fell forward against her. He had the funniest look on his face. He couldn't believe their bodies had actually touched.

"Excuse me" he said, but it only made Evangeline laugh. The music ended much too soon for both of them. He took an extra second to look into her eyes. His heart was pounding double time by now.
    "Thank you," Lorenzo said, when it was over, she replied quietly, "You're welcome."

He escorted her back to her mother and bowed politely. He then ran back to his hoodlum friends who were laughing and teasing him mercilessly.
    Felicia gave Evangeline a dirty look when she returned with Lorenzo.

"You should have said no to him," she insisted. Papa would never have allowed you to dance with him.

"Stop it Felicia," Evangeline said, "Mama said it was alright, and besides, it was only a dance." It was a good thing no one could see her heart jumping inside her chest. *It was the best moment of her life,* she thought.

Later that night the plan to kidnap Evangeline was worked out. It took some convincing to get the guys to go along with him. Franco, Masi, and his brother Carlo weren't sold on the plan, but the idea of the kidnapping intrigued them.   After all, they figured, he was going to marry her so what was the difference.

'Listen amici me, this is very important," said Lorenzo. "My whole life is on the line. I'm sure she will come along willingly."

"What makes you think so?" *asked,* Carlo.

"I could feel it when I danced with her tonight," Lorenzo said assuredly. "It should only take a few minutes to grab her and put her on my father's horse. There is a rose trellis next to the balcony where her room is located. I have been watching the house for several nights now and I even saw her on the balcony once."

Franco was worried his friend didn't understand the repercussions this kidnapping could have. He knew he would have to marry the girl once he took her out of the house, or suffer the consequences. No respectable family would have her; she would be tainted goods.

Late that night after the crowds went home, Lorenzo knew her father would be tired and a little drunk from all the festivities. When the lights were out, the tranquil darkness of the night assured them the family was asleep. Only the lace drape that covered Evangeline's doorway stood between Lorenzo and his love. The kidnappers climbed the trellis and stood on the balcony to assess their next approach.

"Gee, Lorenzo why didn't you say anything about the thorns?" complained Carlo.

"Quiet Carlo, you idiot, do you want to wake up somebody? "

Lorenzo whispered. The fragrance of the roses, not the sharpness of the thorns, was all Lorenzo was thinking about that moment. Their perfume reminded him of his love and the sweet life they would have together.

The kidnappers easily broke into the dark room. Lorenzo wondered why Georgio didn't have a door installed to secure her room from the balcony. Mayor Como is just looking for trouble to leave his daughter so unprotected, he thought. Lorenzo always had a way of justifying his antics. Carlo stood at the door that led to the hall where her parents were asleep. He was the look out and urged them to hurry. Perspiration was pouring down Lorenzo's face. He had never been in the personal confines of her space where all her belongings were scattered around the room. Lorenzo was a little distracted when he saw pictures of her family on the wall and a little doll on a shelf that she must have caressed as a child.

"There she is," he mouthed to Franco, "Don't hurt her. " Franco covered the girl's head with the same flour sack they used to steal the lemons, and wrapped her in a blanket. They tied her up with Lorenzo's belt so she wouldn't kick them too hard. She had been still up to that point and in a deep sleep. Franco's hands were shaking like a leaf. *What were they doing?* he questioned himself? He was second guessing his decision to go along with this crime. They recklessly took Evangeline from her home like she was the sack of lemons they stole the other day. Lorenzo took some pillows and a blanket off the other bed in the room and made it look like Evangeline was asleep. Lorenzo's victim didn't know what was happening to her, she thought at first she was dreaming. The pain she felt when Franco tied the belt around her legs let her know she was awake. She panicked when she realized something was over her head and she was having trouble breathing. She fought with all her might, but to no avail.

The air was getting thick like it did when a storm was about to strike. It made Lorenzo breathe heavy, too. Lorenzo climbed down the trellis first to make sure Masi had the horse settled. Franco draped her over his shoulder and dropped her as he shimmed down the trellis. Fortunately, Lorenzo caught her.

"Careful!" Lorenzo scolded! Franco swore some choice words

because the thorns cut him on his hands and arms.

What are they going to do to me, she wondered. *Who are these people?* She couldn't imagine why she was being kidnapped. Her screams were muffled, but she kicked like the devil. She almost kicked the blanket off, but the boys had her tied up tightly. Lorenzo was a little shocked to hear some of the obscenities that came out of her mouth; he couldn't imagine the beautiful voice he heard sing *Immaculate Mary* using such bad words. It took Lorenzo and the two others just to put her on his father's horse. Carlo used a rope they stole from the cow barn that belonged to one of the neighbors to tie Evangeline on the horse. The poor girl was weakening from the manhandling she was getting to secure her to the animal.

"I'm sorry, Cara mia," Lorenzo kept telling her, "It will be fine, I promise. " Lorenzo, with one arm holding her down and one hand on the reins, rode the horse to the cabin in the mountain they had agreed on earlier. It was a place the shepherds used to watch after their flock. No one would be there at this time of the year because the baby lambs had been born a few months earlier so it was abandoned.

The boys arrived a few minutes later after running all the way. They helped him carry her into the cabin and put her on a dirty cot that was left inside. Lorenzo told his companions to leave them and tried to quiet her. He left the flour sack on her head so her screams wouldn't arouse anyone nearby, besides he was having thoughts of remorse for what he had to do to her now. He didn't want to face her or look her in the eyes, the eyes he fell in love with. He probably wouldn't have been able to see those eyes because the cabin was dark as pitch. There wasn't a star in the sky and the moon had disappeared. He begged her to forgive him, but he saw no other way.

"Please don't be afraid Evangeline I promise not to hurt you, "He was sorry he had to put her through this. "I love you so much, we will be married in the morning, I promise." Lorenzo untied the ropes Carlo tied so well and threw them on the floor. He pushed her nightgown over her hips and tugged at his own trousers. He felt himself arouse with every twist and turn of her body. She fought to get him off her, but against all of her efforts he managed to enter her; and the pain soared through her like fire. Blood was everywhere. *I've killed her,* thought Lorenzo.

He's killing me, she feared, as she felt the blood on her legs. The poor girl was exhausted and scared to death. She passed out from the trauma. During a deafening boom of thunder and a blinding flash of lightening he abruptly unveiled her. The room glowed as though lit by the flame of a thousand candles. The clamor woke her up and the light shown on her face. To his complete horror, he found that he had kidnapped the wrong sister. Another rumble of thunder shook the little cabin and welcomed Lorenzo back to his senses. It was Felicia who lay there weeping uncontrollably, not Evangeline. The storm that seemed to come out of nowhere brought down torrents of rain.

      This can't be true! What kind of cruel joke was this? He yelled for his friends to come to his rescue. "Franco, Carlo, Masi, come here, now! Something wicked has happened!"

The boys were sheltering themselves against a lean-to to stay out of the rain, trying to keep the only cigarette they had between them dry. They were discussing how stupid they were for getting involved with Lorenzo again.

      "I always get in trouble from my Pa when I get home," complained Franco.

"The last time I got a strap from my Ma because we took the fish from the fisherman's boat, remember Masi?" Carlo complained.

      "I run faster than you do," bragged Masi, "Ma can't catch me." When they heard Lorenzo's piercing cry they ran for the cabin and realized the unforgiveable mistake. They were awestruck. The terrified Felicia sat up on the cot breathing hard and trying to cover her legs to ensure some kind of modesty.

      "Lorenzo what are you going to do now?" Franco asked with concern. "You have to take her home it's only right."

      "No!". screamed Lorenzo.

      "Yes." said Franco. "You made a mistake; now this girl will have to suffer for it all her life. Do the right thing, you are a little bit crazy, but you are not a bad person. Maybe her family will have mercy on you. Come, we will help you get her on the horse."

Lorenzo saw his life flash before his eyes. His life was over, as far as he was concerned, if he lost Evangeline. They put the shaking girl on the horse and the friends ran all the way back to town trying to shield their bodies from the force of the rain.   Masi saw the anger in Lorenzo's eyes and ran the fastest, he had seen Lorenzo's temper before and it wasn't a pretty sight. Franco felt sorry for his best friend, but he knew Lorenzo had to marry Felicia now.   On the way down the mountain Felicia finally found her voice.

"You cretin, my father will kill you, you know. My mother will cut your heart out and feed it to the dogs. My sister will spit on your memory forever." He couldn't speak, he could only grunt.

The thunder that woke Felicia also awoke her mother. She got up to see if her daughter was alright. Sometimes, when it stormed hard, the lace on the doorway wasn't enough to keep the rain out. When Alicianna Como looked in the room something didn't look right to her. She went to the bed and found only bedding there.

"Georgio! Georgio! " She screamed at the top of her lungs. "Felicia is not in her bed!"She noticed the drape on the doorway was torn down. When she went to the balcony, she saw that the roses were smashed and the trellis was broken.

"Someone has taken her!" she screamed.   Georgio couldn't believe his eyes.

"Who would have done this?", he exclaimed.   "I will go to the constable immediately. Get dressed Alicianna, we are going to find our daughter." Within an hour a search party was formed. Some with lanterns and some on horseback, the men started out of Santa Fata in search of Felicia. It didn't take long before they stumbled on Franco, Carlo, and Masi, who looked like drowned rats.

"What mischief have you boys been up to tonight?" the constable asked.

"We were up at the shepherd's cabin, sir."

" Have you any information on the whereabouts of Felicia Como?"

" Yes," spoke up Franco, "she is coming down the mountain with Lorenzo Rizzo. They should be right behind us, he is taking her home." Shortly Lorenzo and Felicia, seeing the light from the lanterns, knew the town folk were looking for her. Felicia screamed for her father. The men ran to them and dragged Lorenzo off the horse. The constable told Georgio to take his daughter home and the boy would be taken care of. Felicia went home immediately to a hot bath and clean clothes. Her mother screamed when she saw her. The blood on her nightgown told her all she needed to know.

"Can you walk Felicia?, she asked .

"Yes Mama, help me," she cried, "I am ruined!" She told her mother what had happened and cried until she fell asleep in her parents' bed. Alicianna was thinking of a way to keep her daughter out of that convent. She went to her husband and tried to reason with him.

"If he has already taken her virginity what else can he do but marry our poor daughter. She was doomed to live in that convent; don't you see how this can work to her advantage?"

"Do you think Felicia will go along with this idea," *he questioned?* "I just want to kill him right now," he hollered!

"Let's wait until tomorrow, when cooler heads will prevail," the mother said. "Our daughter is alive, we have to be grateful for that"
He agreed adding, "I will go out and talk to the constable, I'm sure they have all had their turn with Lorenzo already. I hope he is still conscious.".

Evangeline wasn't home at the time of the abduction. After the festa she was helping the nuns with some of the cleaning at the church. The vestments had to be properly put away and the alter clothes had to be washed and ironed for mass in the morning. Her father never allowed her to sleep anywhere but in her own bed. But one day a year he allowed her to help the nuns. They worked late into the night so she slept at the convent in a little cubicle of a room and came home after mass the next day. She couldn't believe her ears when her mother told her of the debacle.

"Once a year, once a year," Lorenzo kept repeating over and over with his hands over his ears, as if he were in shock. He had just learned that

Evangeline spent the night at the convent and her dad only allowed it once a year. In order to save his skin Lorenzo agreed to the marriage. The price he had to pay for his stupid mistake was that now he must call his beloved, sister-in-law.

When Evangeline saw Lorenzo later that day she couldn't look him in the eyes. Her disappointment in him was heart breaking. Was this the man she thought the sun rose and set on? He looked like a beaten dog. When the search party found them they roughed him up quite a bit. He had a black eye and a swollen lip. He limped a little and his clothes were torn. His father and mother were begging forgiveness for their son's folly and the shame he brought to their family. Both mothers were crying and the fathers had stern looks on their faces. Lorenzo's mother tried to explain how her son always jumped before he knew where he was going to land. That same morning the parents took their children to Sacred Heart and the priest waived the banns and performed the marriage. No white gown, no candy almonds and no musicians to serenade the couple as they walked back home. Evangeline had to sign as witness on the marriage papers. *This is the worst wedding I have ever seen,* thought Evangeline. Lorenzo just went along as in a daze. Every bone in his body was aching; he was bruised all over his back and ribs. *Why didn't they just kill me,* he wished? When they were leaving the church, Lorenzo spotted Franco, Carlo and Masi standing behind an arched column in the church gardens. Their faces were somber and a little bruised also. They too, had gotten a beating for their part in the travesty.

"I told you, "Carlo said, "every time we get involved with Lorenzo we get in trouble."

"We aren't in as much trouble as Lorenzo," Franco said.

"Being married to Felicia should be enough penance for the rest of his life. " Masi cried. "Did you hear some of the words that came out of her mouth? I thought good girls didn't know that kind of language," he questioned. "I know my sister doesn't, she is a saint," he said defiantly.

Alicianna Como was secretly relieved that her daughter didn't have to go to the convent in Palermo and had a husband to boot.   Felicia had a husband, and was expecting a baby, but she couldn't have been more miserable. She heard him profess his love to Evangeline on that fateful night over and over. Felicia made Evangeline's life a living hell.

"My feet are so swollen, come and rub them Evangeline," Felicia ordered. "Bring me a cool drink of water sister," Felicia demanded; there was no end to her requests.

Evangeline secretly imagined what it would be like if Lorenzo hadn't been so stupid and kidnapped her instead. She wished it were she carrying Lorenzo's baby, but would die if anybody actually knew that. Would Lorenzo rub her feet and fetch a glass of water for her? He was an absentee father and husband, would he be more attentive to her, she wondered? I *guess it doesn't matter*, Evangeline thought, *what he did to Felicia was unforgivable.*

Lorenzo and Felicia settled down in the Como residence. Evangeline had taken the space under the stairs for her new bedroom. Georgio got Lorenzo a job cleaning the stables for the constable during the day and he came home to Felicia every night. Lorenzo put up a door that led to the balcony in Felicia's room as a reminder of his guilt. He went through the motions of living, but inside he felt like he had died. Evangeline was a slave to her sister during and after the pregnancy.

Nine months to the day of the abduction, a boy child was born. Felicia's labor was intense. She was in labor for two days. The midwives, Alicianna, Evangeline and several neighbor ladies were there around the clock. She walked and pushed and walked some more. Lorenzo's mother Elena came with the same birthing ropes that brought scores of babies into the world. They tied the ropes to the bed posts and Felicia pulled with all her might. Finally the baby broke loose from her body and gave out a healthy yell.

"It's a little boy," Alicianna told Felicia.

"Thank you, God" Felicia prayed and fell sound asleep. To her delight she gave birth to the most beautiful baby in Santa Fara. He was baptized Michele after Lorenzo's father and Evangeline and Franco were his godparents. Evangeline was the constant caregiver for the baby. She only gave him to Felicia to nurse. Felicia was proud of the fact that she had an abundance of milk and only she could give him such a good start in life.

The labor and birth were so hard on Felicia she couldn't stand for very long nor walk at all. She slept for long hours at a time and had to be awakened to feed the baby. Knowing how her sister's heart was breaking, Felicia gloried in the fact that at last, she now had the upper hand. Lorenzo was no prize to her, but it was better than the slave labor she would have performed in the convent.

Lorenzo was very distraught about his mistake and after a few weeks of fatherhood he made a decision.

"Felicia," he begged, "let me go to America. I can find my sister Maria and she will help me get a job. I will send for you and Michele as soon as I can."

" No," she argued, "you will leave and never come back or send for us. Do you think I am as stupid as you? I know you Lorenzo. You will go to America and think you will be free of us, but I have news for you, you never will, God will see to it. I've heard of many men who left their families never to be heard of again, some even get new families, besides, I don't want to leave everyone here in Santa Fara. "

" We can bring Evangeline with us," he said with a grin when his back was to her. That only infuriated her more. "Maybe she doesn't want to go either, you idiot. I happen to know she has her eye on one of the DiMaggio boys," she lied.

"I don't know how any man could court her with Michele in her arms all the time," he argued. "She never puts that baby down," he exclaimed!

"Oh go on to your precious America, Lorenzo. I hope you never do come back here!" If he left, at least Evangeline would be out of his reach, she imagined. She knew that was the worst thing that could happen to him.

Trying to see Evangeline by herself was impossible. He wanted to tell her how sorry he was about what happened to Felicia and his plans for America. Mayor Como watched him like a hawk, Mrs. Como watched him like a hawk, and most of all, Felicia watched him like a hawk. Evangeline ignored him the best she could; she was afraid he would talk her into something she would regret. She was still attracted to him in an odd way and it bothered her very much. When he couldn't stand it any longer, Lorenzo sold everything he had or could steal and bought a ticket to America.

By 1899 almost ten million people had left Italy in hope of a better life in the United States. It was said that more Italians lived in New York than in Rome. Lorenzo read those words in a newspaper article on his way to Naples to purchase his passage across the Atlantic. The trip would take twelve long days from start to finish. He had a lot of time to reflect on the mess he made of his life. His mother always told him, *Lorenzo, you always jump before you know where you are going to land*. He knew she had been right, but he never seemed to care. He studied the look on her face, tried to remember every wrinkle as he wiped the tears away.

"Don't worry Mama; I'll see you again someday soon," knowing he was probably lying to her.

"Lorenzo, give Maria our love. Fighu mio, please be safe and don't do crazy things." He laughed and kissed her and his papa one last time.

"Paesano," said Franco, "don't forget me when you become a big shot in New York. Maybe I'll come and find you someday." Franco wanted to cry, he knew he would miss his friend so much. He bit his lip and ran off before Lorenzo could see his face.

Lorenzo and the other Italian passengers were booked in steerage'. The pungent odor of the many people in tight quarters was sickening. Lorenzo dreamed of the lemon blossoms and the olive groves near his home. The straw filled sacks that served as mattresses were lumpy. The food they served was something his father fed the pigs, he thought as he picked through it. The tobacco and papers Franco gave him as a going away gift made his seasickness unbearable; he threw them overboard the first chance he got. His taste for tobacco never appealed to him again.

On the twelfth day with his clothes wrinkled, and needing both a bath and a haircut, Lorenzo and the others looked over the bow of the ship. They were in the Verrazano Straits of New York when suddenly Lady Liberty appeared. He didn't know if he had arrived in The United States or fallen off the edge of the earth.   With a flick of a stranger's pen, he was allowed through the gates at customs and several hours later he was in the arms of his sister Maria. He was 19 years old, barely a man, but that moment, he felt like a little boy with all the emotion that comes with youth. They both cried, he with exhaustion, she with happiness.

"My sister," Lorenzo cried when he saw her. She looked a little older, but she looked a lot like Ma. "I'm so tired," he told her

"Don't worry, Lenox Hill is not too far. You can have a good rest when we get home." *Home* thought Lorenzo, *how odd to think of America as home.*

Nicolo was happy to have another family member in America. He said America is so big there is enough room for everyone. He was a simple man with a huge heart. He and Maria had no children so Lorenzo would be like a son to him. The Romano's had been in New York for several years and worked for a wealthy family in the city.

TWO

The Winston family owned a steel mill and had business affairs all over the world. They agreed to hire Lorenzo on his sister's recommendation. Mrs. Winston had become quite fond of Maria. She thought of her not only as an employee but as a friend. It was breaking one of the first rules of employer, employee relationships, but Mrs. Winston was a liberal woman and didn't put much stock in such things. Lorenzo was to work in their stable and care for the fine team of horses. They gave him a spot in the loft for his room and he had kitchen privileges with all the food he needed. Lorenzo had taken care of his father's horses in Sicily, and took care of the constables horses too, so Maria was sure he would do a good job for the Winston's. He had never seen such a fine carriage before. He was used to the little donkey carts people in Sicily used.

"Che bedda," he exclaimed! "Nicolo look at that rig, I have never seen anything so beautiful." He was walking around the buggy as he slid his hands over its seats. *How much does something like this cost,* he wondered? He was proud to have been given such a big responsibility.

"Take good care of them little brother, Mrs. Winston is very particular about her horse's and carriage," warned Nicolo.

Lorenzo was overwhelmed when he saw the size of the Winston Mansion. He didn't know a house could have so many rooms. The mansion was located on the upper east side of the city in a place called Lenox Hill, where all the homes were mansions, one bigger than the last. *If only Evangeline could see this place,* he thought. The house itself was in the Greek revival style. Towers, domes, iron fret work decorated the exterior. There were scrolls, brackets and balconies with cornices everywhere. *This must be what Rome looks like,* he pondered. Inside the Persian carpets and floral patterned "art glass" windows were in every room. The domed crystal chandelier that adorned the main hall entrance was fit for a palace. He thought of the small house where his mother lived and raised a family. She *would get lost in here,* he laughed to himself.

"Maria," he said, "can you see mama in this place?"

"Don't make me start to laugh Lorenzo; she would think it a terrible extravagance. I can see her saying her rosary to pray for the people who had so much when so many had so little. This is America Lorenzo," Maria told her brother. "It's the land of opportunity they say. As long as you are willing to work hard you too, can enjoy the fruits of your labor."

" I'm going to remember that Maria and someday I too will have my own home. "

"Good boy Lorenzo, remember what mama always tells you, look before you jump and you can see where you will land.

"Lorenzo," Maria asked, "will you tell me what happened in Santa Fara that made you come here? Mama's letters are so hard to understand sometimes, she doesn't know how to spell many words. She never went to school you know."

"I'm so ashamed of myself Maria. I did the unthinkable to a good girl and was forced to marry her. The irony of the whole thing is that I mistook her for her sister and ended up with a son and a wife for my crime."

"How could you make such a mistake?" she questioned.

"My friends and I kidnapped her and put a sack over her head, it was dark, Maria and we got the wrong girl," he confessed. "I'm still in love with Evangeline, that's her name, "he told her. "I will love her till I die. I couldn't stay in Santa Fara and watch her marry one of the local boys and not want to kill him.

"Ok Lorenzo, don't tell me anymore, I might start to cry. I'm sorry you are so unhappy. I love Nicolo more than anything in the world; I can't imagine what you are going through. But, my darling brother, Mama was right about you, you need to look before you leap," she tried to tell him.

"What are you going to do about the boy," she asked?

"He is better off without me and my mistakes. He has people who will make sure he is taken care of. Mama and Papa are there too, I'm not worried about that," he told her.

"Did Franco Valio have anything to do with this tragedy?"

"Why?" he asked.

"Just curious," she said, "just curious."

In Sicily, in 1901, a terrible influenza epidemic was taking place. It wiped out 10% of the population of Santa Fara. People were in shock for months. Families had two, three, four members die within weeks of each other. It was the worst thing to happen to the village in years. Georgio and Alicianna Como both had taken to their bed with severe fever and pain. Felicia who was already weakened by the birth of the child was in the worst way. Evangeline was at her wit's end, she couldn't get help anywhere. People were either ill themselves or taking care of their own families. The medicine that the government rationed out to the town folk either didn't work or wasn't available. She thought Lorenzo's family might take the baby, but they were in the same shape as her parents. Evangeline was grateful that she hadn't gotten sick and Michele seemed to be healthy, but she watched him carefully. He was almost three now and was a happy, chubby little boy. He had Lorenzo's eyes and was developing his own personality.

"Evangeline?" whispered Felicia.

"Yes," the younger girl answered.

"Come closer, I can barely hear you," said Felicia.

"What is it, sister?"

"I'm dying and you have to promise me something. "

"Anything, Felicia, but I think you are getting better," she voiced the lie.

"Take care of Michele for me when I'm gone. You are a better mother than I am. I have been ill all his life and haven't been the kind of mother I wanted to be."

"Don't be silly Felicia, he loves you very much."

"Yes, but he calls you, mama. I've heard him say it," she cried.

"Lorenzo loves you not me, she continued." "I was the mistake. I heard him call your name the night he took my virginity. Didn't I tell you years ago that he was a thief?" Felicia gasped for air and then said, "Don't let Lorenzo take Michele away from you. Remember, Evangeline, remember," and with that she mercifully died.

The Como's took the death of their daughter as a sign that their deaths were inevitable. Evangeline kept a tighter rein on Michele. She went through the motions with the help of the nuns on their daily administering to the sick.

A funeral was impossible at this time. The priest was so busy tending to others and giving last rights he would hold mass funerals once a week. Felicia had a temporary grave and a tag number for identification. Evangeline had promised her sister two things, a proper burial and good life for her son.

A week later Evangeline's parents suffered the same fate. While on his death bed, Georgio Como held his daughter's hand. Using the last bit of strength to hold on to his loving child, he gathered just enough breath to share with her his final thoughts.

"Evangeline, my beauty, I never dreamed this disaster could happen to us and to so many of our friends. You are strong, and smart, take Michele away from this place of sickness and death."

"No, papa," she insisted, "I must stay and take care of you and mama."

"There is nothing you can do for us now, it's up to God. Please, the child has his whole life ahead of him; don't risk the chance that he, too, can get sick. He is so small and innocent; his mother would want him safe. Go, Evangeline, the nuns come every day to check up on us. Please grant me this last wish."

The tears were streaming down her face as she said her good byes. She grabbed a satchel, filled it with the child's belongings and ran out of the house. She started running, holding on tight to the only thing that mattered. The toddler squirming in her arms, sensing that something was wrong,screamed as she ran for their lives. She didn't know where she was going. People were dying in every direction. She ran down the Main Street and straight to the mountain that seemed to give the locals solace in their time of need. She stumbled upon a shepherd's cabin and found the door ajar. Ironically, it was the same cabin that Michele was conceived in. It started with his life and now it would save his life. Fortunately, the epidemic hadn't reached some of the farmers that high up the mountain. She was able to get milk for the baby and some vegetables for herself.

Please, God, let me take care of him and protect him from harm. She stayed at the cabin for two weeks before she ventured back down the mountain. Miraculously, the epidemic had subsided and people were getting better. Some were left with poor breathing, others with paralysis. The young and strong were left with little side effects. The daunting task of burying the dead was left to them and the *uomo di la morte* from the prison in Palermo.

It had been raining all day. The gray skies were uncharacteristic of Sicily. Evangeline wrapped a shawl over her head and put a jacket and hat on the baby. She felt chilled all day; she hoped she wasn't getting sick too. The first thing she did was rush to her father's house to see if they were still alive. She was greeted with a notice on the door to the next of kin; the family was buried in the local grave yard with the plot number attached. Evangeline got sick to her stomach. She didn't expect any different, but the realization was numbing. Evangeline went to the cemetery with Michele in tow. They sat at the graves and told her family how much she missed them and that they would never be forgotten.

"Mama, Papa, what will I do now?" Her words screamed out ringing with utter fear. "I am a child myself; I don't know the ways of the world. I was always kept under your skirt, mama or under the skirts of the nuns. "

Please God, show me the way to live through this, she prayed. *Michele is all I have left, help me take care of him,* she begged. She was barely able to hold the boy and laid him down. Her tears were salty and her blouse was wet from wiping her face. Evangeline was crying with her head buried in the shawl, when the sleeping Michele, lying on the stones, started to stir. Suddenly she felt warmth on her shoulders. She looked up and the sun came out. The sky lit up like it always did in Santa Fata. She felt a strange feeling of well being. Whenever she had a problem she couldn't handle, her mother would tell her to give it to God. He will always help you through it, she assured her. Did He hear me so soon, she wondered? When she pulled herself together, she took Michele to the church to see if some kind of Mass would be said for her parents and Felicia. The Mother Superior put her arm around her and told her not to worry. A mass for the dead was said everyday at daybreak. The epidemic left so many people alone and stranded with no place to turn, the church was the logical refuge for the people of Santa Fara. If Evangeline was able to help out with the cooking and serving the dinners they offered, she and Michele were welcome to stay with them at the convent. She was so grateful for the familiar hand to hold on to, it calmed her fears immensely. She also thanked the Lord for coming to her in her time of need so quickly.

As was the custom of the country, the eldest son inherited all the worldly goods of the father. Evangeline had an older brother, Antonino, who lived with his wife and children in Palermo. When he was born his mother died and several years later Georgio married Alicianna. Evangeline and Felicia were the only other siblings he had. Antonino Como was a kindly man who already had four children. He worked as a baker in Palermo for his wife Luna's family. He didn't want to raise any more children especially since Michele had a father in America.

"I heard my sister hadn't gotten a letter from her husband in months," he complained to his wife. "Sounds like he is enjoying his time in America and doesn't remember he has a family in Sicily."

"Remind him," Luna offered her opinion, "Send him a letter and tell him of his obligations."

A few weeks passed when Lorenzo received a letter from overseas. He didn't recognize the handwriting and was curious to its contents.

Dear Brother-in -law, I am sorry to inform you that your beloved wife Felicia has passed away from the flu epidemic that devastated the Island of Sicily last month. Our parents were also taken by this menace. Evangeline and Michele were spared, thank God. The church has taken them in, but it is only a temporary situation. Lorenzo, you must step-up now and take care of your son. I'm sorry but Evangeline is also part of the arrangement as she cannot be separated from the boy.

Lorenzo put the letter down in disbelief. He didn't' know if he should laugh or cry. He continued to read the letter. Michele and Evangeline would be sailing to America as soon as he can sell the house in Santa Fara and get the money for their fares; that was the best he could do. Lorenzo was overjoyed. He told his sister Maria to get a place ready for Evangeline and his son. He had been so sure that Evangeline was married to someone else by now, he tried to put her out of his mind. The letter said Evangeline was the total caregiver of the boy and how well she took care of her parents and Felicia. Antonino also threatened to make Lorenzo pay if Evangeline wasn't taken care of in any way but royally. She was so special and deserved nothing less. Lorenzo was thrilled by the open door he was invited into; of course he would do anything for his love, especially since finally now she would be his wife.

It was with a heavy heart that Evangeline, little Michele in her arms, watched the steamer ship leave the dock in Naples. Antonino had taken them north, to catch the German-line steamer to America. He purchased tickets for them that were priced better than steerage hoping it would be more comfortable for her and the baby. When the ship arrived two weeks later, her ordeal at Ellis Island was frightening. The nick-name "Island of Tears" wasn't far from the truth. Many people were turned back to repeat the horrific trip because of certain diseases.

As they were attended to by the island doctors and nurses, they were humiliated beyond belief, they were prodded and poked in the most private of places. Because of the many dialects in Italy, the interpreters weren't familiar with all of them. Some sounded like different countries altogether, not even Italian, and the translators considered the travelers illiterate. With twelve to fourteen days of lack of water to wash with, they also came across to them as filthy commoners.

How ironic it was that these American inspectors didn't remember that this country was named and discovered by Italians. Evangeline was terrified when they took Michele away from her to check him over and to take her to an examination room. They stripped her down and examined her head to toe. *What am I doing here?* She thought, *I never wanted to come to America.* She was safe in Santa Fara with the care and help of the good sisters at Sacred Heart. Oh, how she hated Lorenzo for putting her in such a situation. In an hour's time she was reunited with Michele and she could breathe a little easier. She waited by the gate with the others who were waiting for their family members to pick them up when she saw Lorenzo. He was smiling from ear to ear when he came running to her. *Damn him,* she thought, *he was better looking than ever.*

"Evangeline, Michele, I'm so happy to see you," he said as he wrapped his arms around them. Michele took one look at him and let out a scream; he never acted like that, even when the attendants took him away on the island.

"Don't cry, my love, this is your Papa," said Evangeline. "He has come to take us to our new home."

" No!" screamed Michele. "No! No! "

" I'm sorry," Evangeline apologized, "no seems to be his favorite word lately. "
Evangeline put the boy down on the grass and let him walk on his own. He soon calmed down.

"I don't think he has ever seen grass like this before," she told Lorenzo..

"Where we are going, he will see grass everywhere. The gardens at Lenox Hill are breathtaking," he promised. Lorenzo thought Evangeline looked thin and pale. She seemed a little cold and distant towards him, too. *It must be the effects of that horrible trip.*

"Did you have a bad time with the voyage Evangeline,?" he questioned. She wouldn't give him the satisfaction of knowing that several times she thought she would die of the sea sickness. "It was fine." she answered curtly.

"I think I would recognize Michele in a crowd." he said, "It's like looking in a mirror. I just didn't think he would be such a big boy."

"Three years is a long time Lorenzo, we haven't heard much from you in all that time," Evangeline said sarcastically. Little did Lorenzo know, but his love had lost the luster she once had for him. She was upset when he left for America and abandoned his wife and son. And the little interest he held for them for the past three years showed her the quality of man he was.

"I'm sorry about the family, Evangeline, I hope they didn't suffer too much. Thank you for taking such good care of my son," he said. She remembered what Felicia told her about not letting Lorenzo take the boy away from her. "I think of him as my son, Lorenzo, he calls me Mama. Can you be in agreement with that?" she asked him. *Why shouldn't he*, Lorenzo thought, *when we get married you will be his Mama.* He didn't want to bring up the subject yet so he just said, yes of course.

Lorenzo knew his life in America would have to change since his love and the boy were here. His job as stable manager for Mr. Edward Winston would have to be enough for a wife and child to live on. Maybe Mr. Edward would give him a raise in pay. He never spent many nights alone in New York, but now he would have to become respectable. This to the dismay of Elsie, his bed partner for the past two years.

Elsie Zender was a chamber maid for the people who lived in the mansion next to the Winston's. She came to America from Germany and was on her own. She was sure that Lorenzo would marry her someday, especially since she kept his bed warm and interesting. When she heard the news of Evangeline and the baby, she was curious.

"Who was this girl anyway?" she asked.

"She was my late wife's sister," he told her. "I understand she took Michele as her own when her family died. She has taken good care of him with the little she had. Elsie, I owe her so much for protecting my son all this time."

"Why haven't you told me about the baby sooner?" she asked.

"I truly thought he was better off without me and that was the truth," he admitted. Lorenzo always knew he wasn't going to make much out of his life, trouble always seemed to find him somehow. Elsie loved Lorenzo and thought he was wonderful, why would he think anyone would feel differently?

When Lorenzo arrived at the mansion with his little family, a room had already been prepared for them. The Winston family was happy to receive them because they had become fond of Maria and Nicolo. Lorenzo was a good worker and their stable never ran so efficiently. The work ethic of the Italians was admirable. They went to work in the morning and usually went right home to their families afterwards. Mrs. Winston was hopeful that Evangeline would stay on as nanny for her daughter who was four years old. She wanted the child to become bilingual and Maria said Evangeline was a star student in Sicily.

On their first night in America a welcoming get together with the Winston's to introduce Evangeline to the family was at hand. The Winston's had three sons and daughter, Larissa. Chance, their eldest son, was 21, and 14 year old twins, Mark and Matt, gave their parents plenty of aggravation. It only took Chance Winston five minutes to become totally swept away by Evangeline. She was so lovely and bright, he couldn't help himself. The obvious attention Chance placed on Evangeline infuriated Lorenzo, but he had to hold his tongue for fear of all the family losing their jobs.

When he had her attention, Chance asked Evangeline, using Maria as an Interpreter, if she left a boyfriend back in Sicily.

"Life has a lot of twists and turns, Mr. Winston," she said as she stared at Lorenzo. "I didn't have much time for such a luxury. My sister was very ill after the baby was born and I had to attend to them both. Since her husband was here, she had no one else to depend on. As you can see the baby is very attached to me." Michele was crying. He tried to wiggle out of Lorenzo's arms and lunged himself toward Evangeline.

"When the horrible epidemic came to the island, my family became very ill and then they died. The next thing I knew, I was on a ship headed to America."

" My dear Evangeline," said Chance, "I hope we can help make your life here at Lenox Hill happy for you."

"Thank you Mr. Winston, I appreciate that."

"Please call me Chance," he said. "I feel like you are referring to my father when you say Mr. Winston." Evangeline smiled and reached out to rescue Lorenzo from the crying baby.

"Evangeline," Lorenzo scolded, "don't become too friendly with the employers." He hated the way Chance was playing up to Evangeline. Maria, who was very friendly with Rosalyn Winston, paved the way for Evangeline. Maria was Rosalyn's right hand in handling the household. Maria gave Evangeline and Michele a very nice room next to hers. This way she could help her with the baby if he cried in the night. Michele reminded her so much of his father, at that age, it gave her a feeling of homesickness. That night, Maria sat down and wrote a letter to her mama, to let her know that the family would all be sleeping under the same roof tonight. Lorenzo's room was over the stable, so it was technically under the same roof. She also slipped a couple of dollars in the letter like she always did. The flu epidemic hit the Rizzo family hard, but no one died. Life in Santa Fara was getting back to some kind of normalcy.   Life in America it seemed was far from normal for Evangeline.

Later that night when Elsie climbed into his bed, she thought Lorenzo would be in a better mood.

"What's the matter my dear?" she asked, "I was sure you would be happy because your son is now with you."

"He hates me, Elsie," he cried, "he won't let me hold him or play with him, he just screams. He is probably afraid he will grow up to be just like me," he pouted.

"Don't be silly," she laughed, "he's just a baby. He doesn't know you yet. Come here, I'll make you feel better," as she caressed his chest. *How can I tell her we can't see each other like this anymore,* thought Lorenzo? *Oh well, she is here now I might as well make the best of this night. I can figure it out tomorrow.* He reached over, held her close and they made love into the morning.

Elsie Zender was a tiny blond with ruby red lips and a thick German accent. Elsie came to America with a group of immigrants from her home town. Her father died and left her mother with five children to care for. When the opportunity came to be, that people of stature in America were looking for domestic help, she jumped at the chance to seek her fortune. Her mother would miss her terribly, but was relieved to have one less mouth to feed. Elsie was fourteen years old when she was employed by Mrs. Mitchell. Chamber maid was her title, but Mrs. Mitchell used her in other capacities as well. The Mitchell's had two grown sons who had married girls from tobacco families in the South. They lived in Savannah, Georgia and only came to New York at Christmas or other special occasions. During the rest of the year the house was pretty empty. Mrs. Mitchell only entertained once a month for her suffragette meetings. Elsie had some time on her hands, so her employer lent her to her neighbor, Mrs. Winston, who was giving one of her grand parties. Her eldest son Chance had finished his studies at the Naval Academy at Annapolis in Maryland.

Elsie heard the gossip among the other servants that the Italian couple next door had a relative hired as stable manager. She was curious to meet him; rumor had it that he was extremely handsome. Lorenzo Rizzo pulled up the horses and the open air buggy to the back door of the kitchen. He was asked to pick up Elsie and her few bags as she would only be staying a short time. When she boarded the buggy, Lorenzo smiled at her. His good looks were far better than the others said they were. He seemed a little shy, she thought, because he couldn't speak a word of English. Soon language wasn't a problem.

Lorenzo thought she was quite pretty and very willing to accept his advances. Of course she wasn't Evangeline, but he was sure he would never see his love again. It didn't take long before he was welcomed into Elsie's bed in the maid's quarters of the Mitchell mansion. Besides English, the other problem he had was Felicia and Michele. He had no intention of bringing them to America, they were better off without him, Elsie didn't need to know of his family in Sicily for he could never be serious about her. If he ever did marry again, it would have to be to an Italian girl from one of the immigrant families in New York. But for now, Elsie kept him warm at night and he was probably doing her a favor since she was alone in the city.

The Winston's were very nice to Evangeline and the little girl, Larissa, was mesmerized by her. The other member of the family who was mesmerized was Chance. He took every possible occasion to speak to her.

He asked if he could help her with her English lessons, carry her books, bring her a flower, anything to get her attention. She did take him up on the English lessons though and she learned the language quickly. He was enchanted by her infectious accent and the way her mouth pouted when she tried to speak the English words. Mrs. Rosalyn Winston shared in the enchantment as she saw how her beloved son was undoubtedly falling in love. Evangeline, too, was being swept away by his boyish good looks, charm and education.

Chance was Rosalyn's special gift from God, especially by the way he came into the world. Edward Winston was her second husband and she was fortunate to find a man who truly loved her and her infant son. Her upbringing was typical for a young English girl of her class. Her father was Earl Marcus Thornton; he married Laura Sherwood a commoner. He married her for no other reason than they were in love. His family wasn't happy about the union, but Laura was a wonderful daughter-in-law and they in turn loved her too. Although they were children of wealth, Rosalyn and her siblings were brought up to do chores. *Duty to the home and family* was her father's motto. When her two brothers were eight years old, they went to Eaton. All the girls stayed at home and were taught by a governess. Rosalyn was a watercolorist and any window was her subject. She also excelled at the piano and the languages of French and German were second nature to her. Archery was her sport and she was trained to be a wonderful horse woman. Horses were very important to her, but she would tell you that her children were her real prizes. Rosalyn was a pretty girl, small in stature. Her golden red hair and green eyes set her apart from her blond, blue-eyed siblings. Her father would tease her and say she was found in a basket behind the pantry door. It made her laugh because she knew she looked just like her mother. Her Papa loved her beyond belief, he was very careful to pick the right husband for her.

"Rosalyn my dearest, I have the best possible news for you," her father had announced. "I have found a suitable husband for you. You remember Lord Hennessey don't you? Your uncles and I have made a deal with the Hennessey representatives and a wedding will be sometime this summer."

"No Papa," she implored, "I'm too young, I can't leave you and Mama yet!"

"Your mother was younger than you when we were married, it will be fine I promise you," he insisted. Lord Hennessey was ten years older than she, but would make a fine spouse for her, Marcus decided. The property the family would gain from the union would bring great wealth. He would never know how Hennessey's secret would change the course of life for Rosalyn. The poor girl was devastated when she found out that she was betrothed to Lord Hennessey.

No one knew that she had given herself body and soul to Chance, a Page in the Queen's Court. Chance and Rosalyn met at a party the queen was giving for one of her nieces. Many young people were in attendance. Chance had a smooth way about him and Rosalyn fell head over heels in love with him. He had fair hair and blue eyes just like her brothers. He would sneak into their summer house on the property and she would meet him there almost every day.

"Chance, we have to be careful that the gardener doesn't find us here," she told him. He made her laugh when he picked up a rake and pretended it was a sword.

"I will defend your honor my lady," he said. "Rosalyn I want to marry you; but it may take a while; I have to work my way up the ladder from page to house man to earn enough money to take a wife," he informed her. They spent a lot of time kissing and exploring each other, which seemed innocent enough. One day things got out of hand and they made love: it was totally unexpected and totally mutual. They were hungry for each other and their love making was all they could think about. Rosalyn had no idea of the consequences of her actions. No one had ever spoken to her about the fact that she could have a baby.

"Rosalyn, we shouldn't do this anymore," Chance told her.

"Why, don't you love me?" she cried.

"No, my darling, that's not it. What if you conceive a child?" he asked her. She was unaware of such things as no one ever talked to her about it. Before she had the chance to casually ask her mother about it, her father dropped the news about her upcoming nuptials. Her wedding day arranged by her father and uncles, was the worst day in her life. Many slaps on the back between her father and his brothers were given, for they had just acquired much land in the deal. She could tell no one about her young Page and when her husband found out she wasn't a virgin he would send her right back to her father. *Oh, what a scandal this is going to be,* she feared. On her wedding night, to her relief and confusion, her husband could not consummate the marriage. He cried and told her he was sorry and so ashamed.

"Please keep my secret," he begged.

"I will Sir," Rosalyn assured him, "if you will keep mine." She told him about Chance and that they had planned to be married someday. She also confessed that she wasn't a virgin.

"Don't' worry Rosalyn I have a plan. My family insisted that I be married to sire an heir. Since that is something I cannot do, I will find your lover and bring him to you. He will sire the baby and my family will have their heir." The next day the boy was found and brought to Rosalyn. They couldn't get over their good fortune that they could be together without fear or interruption.

"What stroke of luck is this!" Chance exclaimed. "When you told me you were to be married, I thought my world ended," he confessed.

"I was happy you agreed to come to me," Rosalyn said, "I love you so much". How naive they were, for as soon as Rosalyn conceived, her lover disappeared. He was never to be heard from again. Lord Hennessey had an evil streak in his nature. He couldn't trust that his secret would be safe, so he had the boy killed. Rosalyn was grief stricken when he didn't return to her; she didn't understand what could have happened. Morning sickness was blamed for her not leaving her bed. When she asked her husband what could have happened, he said that Chance wasn't mature enough for such foolery. *Foolery,* she thought.

"Chance and I were in love with each other," she insisted. For the next six months Rosalyn moped around like a sick puppy. Her family was worried that something might be wrong with the baby. One month before the birth, Lord Hennessey was found dead in a back alley in a questionable part of London. Some people said that his lover found him with another man and shot him in the head.

Rosalyn didn't know how to feel when she heard about the death. There was little feeling for this man who left her alone most of the time, but his kindness in allowing Chance to be with her was more than she could hope for. She never learned the truth about Chance's disappearance, which would have been the end of her. The next month her son was born and had inherited millions at his birth.   Hennessey had put the baby in his will, before he was born, to be sure he, or his mother would never want for anything.   At his christening, the priest asked,

"What is this child called?"

His mother spoke up,

"Chance." - she could think of no other name.

THREE

Rosalyn, Laura, and the baby were sent to America to pass her mourning period. The families felt she would heal faster if she wasn't around the reminders of her marriage. It couldn't be truer; she just wanted to be away from anything that reminded her of the past year, period.

"Thank you, mother for taking me out of London," she mentioned, a few days after she arrived in America. "I couldn't breathe there anymore."

" My poor daughter," Laura cried, "a wife, a widow, and a mother all in a year's time. No wonder you are so upset. Your aunt is having a tea this afternoon. Maybe that will make you feel better," she added.

"Do I have to wear these widow's weeds," she asked?

"Now don't disgrace us all, "Laura chastised her, "of course you do."

"I hate black, it makes me look terrible," she insisted. The New York season was in full force. Many parties and balls were the elite societies' way of young people getting to meet each other. Because Rosalyn was in mourning, she couldn't attend the festivities. Her aunt's afternoon tea was for some people involved in the steel business. She was invited, but hated her black dress and wasn't in the mood to see anyone. After a little coaxing from her mother and aunt, she pacified them and agreed to meet the guests. She was introduced to Mr. and Mrs. Winston and their son Edward, owners of a steel mill on the East River.

Edward Winston was a pleasant man with a quiet temperament. The Winston's were from old money and they could trace their heritage back to the Mayflower. Their stately mansion was at Lenox Hill on the Upper East Side. Edward didn't want to be at the tea any more than Rosalyn but he only came along to satisfy his mother. Edward was an only child and his parents were considerably older than most. His mother liked to show him off to her friends.

"I hope I grow out of that someday," he teased his mother. His father walked with a cane and was very hard of hearing. His mother had to shout a lot during conversations and sometimes it was very amusing. Edward loved them dearly. When he was introduced to Rosalyn, he decided he needed to know more about the beautiful girl in black. Rosalyn begged to be excused and walked into the flower garden.

"Excuse me, Mrs. Hennessey, is it?" Edward asked. He knew darn well what her name was, but he didn't know how else to approach her.

"Yes," she said, "Mr. Winston?" She knew his name too, but didn't want to seem too forward.

"Would you like me to bring your tea outside for you to enjoy?" he asked.

"Will you join me?" she offered.

"I would like that," he agreed.

"So would I," she smiled. They talked for what seemed like hours. She told him about her baby and how much he meant to her. Edward asked to meet him and she agreed on a time to meet in the park the next day. They met on Columbus Circle and Rosalyn wore a pink dress, Edward followed her in the garden that day and hadn't left her side since. They were married later that year and she never returned to England again.

Chance had his inheritance from his late father's estate in England. On the twenty fifth year of his birth; he would be awarded the bulk of the money from the sale of the land around the estate. He was a very rich man on his own, but he also was in business with Edward in the steel mill. Now that he had fallen in love with Evangeline, he wanted to marry her and build a grand estate for her. Since she had no family in America, Lorenzo seemed the most logical person to announce his intensions to. When he approached Lorenzo with his proposal, he was shocked at his reaction. Lorenzo flew off into a rage. He claimed Chance had only known Evangeline for a few months. Then he accused him of taking advantage of her innocence and in time he would drop her for a worldlier woman. Then he called him spoiled because he came from rich people and he thought he could have whatever he wanted. Lorenzo went on like a mad man for much too long, Chance was thinking. He was so insulted by his words he threatened to fire them all. He thought better of it for fear that Evangeline would go away with her family. Chance didn't understand the Sicilian man. He had no idea of Lorenzo and Evangeline's past. Chance left the stable in a state of confusion. Why was Lorenzo so upset he wondered? I certainly can give her anything she wants. He must be insane; I shall talk to Nicolo about him.

"Sicilian men were jealous of their wives, sisters, and daughters," Nicolo told him when he was asked about it. "These women have to walk the straight and narrow with never a hint of shame. Their virtue was of the utmost importance. No man should speak to her in any intimate way before he married her. Most of all she should never, never be left alone with him." Chance thought that was a terrible burden to put on a woman. He had heard of some countries who had such ideas, but that was in the Far East.

"I'll try to be more understanding," said Chance, "for Evangeline's sake. " Elsie was sick of Lorenzo ranting about Chance. What was so special about Evangeline any way? She was tired of hearing Lorenzo talk about how chaste and innocent she was. Why? She was a woman too, wasn't she? Lorenzo found no problem bedding her down. Elsie was disappointed that she hadn't given Lorenzo a son by now. They had been together for two years, and surely he would marry her if she was going to have a baby. One night in his bed, Elsie told Lorenzo that she had a secret to tell him. She confessed that on one of her errands to the Winston mansion she saw something that had disturbed her. Her mistress asked her to deliver some homemade jam to the cook. She went to the kitchen by way of the stable and she saw Chance and Evangeline in a compromising situation. He was supposed to be giving her an English lesson, but he was teaching her something else.

Of course Elsie lied through her teeth to make Evangeline look bad in Lorenzo's eyes. Lorenzo flew out of the bed in a violent rage. "I will kill him with my own hands!" he kept saying over and over. He quickly got dressed and ran to the main house and pounded on the door. He demanded to see Chance and seek satisfaction for his actions. As usual, Lorenzo jumped before he knew where he was going to land. All he did was force Chance to marry Evangeline. Chance couldn't have been happier and neither could Elsie.

Once again Evangeline's life was in the hands of others. She tried to convince Lorenzo that nothing had happened in the stable.

"Don't cover up for Chance," he told her. "He has been after you from the beginning."

"Why do I have to marry him she pleaded? I can't be the kind of wife he deserves," she cried.

"It doesn't matter now", said Lorenzo, "the rumors are already out there and I will not have you known as a loose woman."

"I think you know better Lorenzo, I am terribly offended. You must know that Elsie lied," she begged. He couldn't be convinced, but his heart was breaking. *I'm losing her again*, he thought. *I'm going to stay close to make sure Chance Winston doesn't hurt her in any way.*

Chance made a big production of the engagement as he was inclined to do. He got all the families together as witnesses to his intentions. He bought her a three carat diamond ring with rubies as accents. Ruby was her birthstone, as well as his. He got down on one knee and asked if she would honor him and be his wife. She felt like she had no choice but to say yes. When they were out of ear shot of the others, she expressed her fears to Chance.

"What makes you think I will be a good wife for you?" she asked. "I don't speak very good English, I don't know my way around the block, I have nothing to offer you and where I go, so goes Michele."

"First of all, Evangeline, I'm crazy about you, I understand all I need to know when you speak and all I need is you, nothing else. As far as Michele is concerned, I promise to love and care for him as my own. Edward Winston isn't my biological father, but he couldn't treat me any better than if he were. He has three sons and that is just the way it is. I hope to follow in his example and when we have our own children, nothing will change. I promise. "

Evangeline knew Lorenzo wasn't the father figure she hoped he would be.

Michele and Lorenzo hadn't bonded at all. In fact Michele cried every time Lorenzo came near him. How could she leave the little boy that she loved so much, with this man, who was like a child himself? Evangeline told Lorenzo she would not marry Chance unless she could keep the boy. Michele already called her mama and she would die without him. She was relieved to know Chance was willing to spend his life with the both of them Lorenzo, in his simple way, thought so much shame would come to Evangeline from the Sicilian community in New York, if she didn't marry Chance, that he agreed to let them raise Michele. *Besides the boy brought back awful memories of Felicia and how he was conceived.* Chance secretly loved the idea, that he would be raising the boy. He knew it would be a slap in the face to Lorenzo. The two men had grown to dislike each other very much.

Evangeline's wedding day came to be. Her mother-in-law planned a beautiful church wedding. The Winston's were Catholic also, and they had their friend, Monsignor Kelly, celebrate the wedding mass at St. Patrick's Cathedral. Rosalyn had the fine lace and silk imported from France for Evangeline's gown. It was the highest of fashion for the day. Tiny seed pearls were encrusted to bring out the design of the flowers on the lace. Each pearl was sewn by hand by the most premier seamstresses of New York. The train was ten feet long and started from the dropped waist of the gown. Evangeline was taken by surprise by the extravagance of the whole wedding. The thousands of dollars spent on the gown alone could have fed the whole town of Santa Fara for months. She couldn't forget about the epidemic and how she had to beg for milk for Michele. Rosalyn insisted on the Chantilly lace edging for the cathedral veil and blusher. She said the gown wasn't finished without it. Evangeline wished her mother was here to see her baby girl get married in such a fashion. Felicia got married in the brown cotton dress she wore the day before at the festa. *How did Michele and I catch the golden ring* she wondered? *This is something I had never envisioned or even knew existed,* she thought.

Set designers from the Theatre District were hired to decorate the Grand Ballroom. They hung garlands of Ivy and white roses from pillar to pillar. Satin ribbon bows seemed to adorn every inch of space in between.

Flanking each doorway were golden candelabras with their white candles standing like soldiers in their little golden cups just waiting for the bride and groom to be announced. Fifty tables were dressed in white cloths with golden chargers under the beautiful white china. Each table had a centerpiece of white roses and green ivy with white satin ribbons that matched the spray on the bridal table.

Maria was matron of honor and two of Chance's cousins, dressed in lavender water moiré taffeta attended the bride. Michele and Larissa were ring bearer and flower girl respectively. As the twins, Matt and Mark ushered in the guests, Lorenzo and Elsie sat in the back pew of the cathedral. Lorenzo, with a sour look on his face, refused to speak to anyone. Elsie was overjoyed and prayed Lorenzo would soon forget about Evangeline. After all, she was Chance's problem now. She was so happy, she bought a new dress and hat for the occasion. All the upper crust of New York was in attendance, Rockefellers, Ansonias, the mayor and his group of socialites, friends of the family, and the few family members in America. Evangeline knew none of them, only Maria and Nicolo, Lorenzo and Elsie and of course the Winstons.

Chance sat nervously in the church sacristy with his military school friend, John Lee. John was the obvious choice for best man as, his mother used to say ,they were joined at the hip.. The Lee's were distant cousins to General Robert E. Lee and they were proud of the fact. Chance and John had spent several days together before the wedding. They went fishing and riding and talked about old times. John reminded Chance that his old girlfriend Rebecca Clay was back in New York after her World Tour. Chance knew he'd have to see Rebecca before the wedding.

Her trip to Europe had ended the previous week and she had been shocked to hear of Chance's engagement. She had always believed Chance and Rebecca would be the names engraved on the wedding invitations. She wasn't sure how, but she wasn't going to let Chance Winston slip through her fingers.

Chance paced back and forth in front of the brownstone townhouses on 5thAvenue. He finally got the nerve to knock on the door and ask for Miss Clay. When she entered the room, the maid was dismissed and Rebecca ran into Chances arms. He tried to explain how he met Evangeline and how she just seemed to enchant him. "It's your fault," he blamed Rebecca, "you had to go traipsing around Europe and you left me here alone."

"What a coward you are ,Chance Winston, putting this all on me. I told you I would be back in one year. I couldn't disappoint my mother, you know that," Rebecca pouted. "Chance, leave her, she can't mean that much to you; stay with me, my parents are still in Europe, we have the whole house to ourselves."

"It's too late Rebecca, the wedding is tomorrow."

"Chance, I love you, and I want you to know I will always be available for you."

And in the years to come Chance would take Rebecca up on her invitation many times.

The day of the wedding couldn't have been more beautiful. The sky was clear and blue as can be. The organist started the wedding march. Chance watched as the cousins walked down the aisle, Larissa dropping rose petals and Michele carrying the rings came next. He was so little, he wasn't sure what he was supposed to do, but as long as he could see Larissa he was fine. He didn't remember life without her and she adored him.
As the double doors opened at the end of the aisle, Evangeline, with Nicolo at her side looked like a vision; an angel wrapped in layers of netting. Her face was barely visible, but he melted when he saw her. He was sure he had made the right decision to stay with Evangeline and make a good life for them both.

Evangeline's mind was spinning like a top. She was sure Chance would be a good father to Michele; he certainly had the means for him to go to the finest schools. Evangeline thought about her parents and sister she left in their graves back in Sicily. She couldn't imagine what her father would think about this union. Then she gave a thought to Lorenzo as she spotted him in the last pew. Five years earlier she was sure she believed the sun rose and set on that man. How foolish she felt that she fell for his good looks and charm. The brown eyes she fell in love with she now saw in her beloved Michele. Evangeline knew for sure Chance was not the love of her life, but she believed him when he said he loved her, and that would be enough. Before she knew it, the monsignor was pronouncing them husband and wife. The smiles on their faces satisfied everyone at the wedding that this was indeed a happy couple.

In the year 1905 Chance built an enormous house for his wife. It was across the East River at Hunters Point, Long Island. Many prominent families were building mansions in that area too. Evangeline thought it was too far away from her loved ones, but at least when they came to visit, they could stay as long as they wanted because the house had ten bedrooms: plenty of room for everyone. The new expansion bridge that connected New York and Long Island was in progress. It had been started a year ago and it should be finished soon. The ferry transport was sometimes burdensome to carry the horses and wagons and in the winter the ice caused a problem if it jammed up on the river. Hunters Point was actually only a few miles from where Edward's stately mansion was located.

"Why can't we live closer to your parents?" Evangeline asked Chance.

"Why it's the up and coming place to live, Evangeline," bragged Chance. "It's a good investment and the new bridge is going to make the company a fortune," he continued. The property was settled nicely on a small lake which was a great place for rowing, the twins favorite sport. Chance could hunt pheasant and rabbit in the vast woods behind the house. There was plenty of room for Larissa and Michele to run and play on the grounds. Evangeline still gave Larissa Italian lessons, but Michele didn't want anything to do with the language. He was American he would tell Lorenzo and his father would beam with pride. That's right son, he would say, you are an American now. It bothered Lorenzo a little that Chance was the one to give him all his opportunities. Michele was so smart he didn't want his chance for an education to go to waste. The new house had a school room set up for the children and when Larissa was at the house they would get their lessons together. Next year they would be going to St. Mary's school on Long Island for their elementary training. Evangeline checked out their credentials and they were perfect for the two of them. They would get their religious training along with their academics. They would be making their First Holy Communion next year too, so it was perfect.

Rosalyn and Evangeline spent the better part of a year with decorators and decisions about paint and fabrics. Chance gave her full reign and a large allowance and the end result was fit for a Queen. Rosalyn and Evangeline were very proud of themselves and the mother-in-law, daughter-in-law team got along so well that people were amazed. But then again, both ladies had the same mind set and that was the care and welfare of their families.

Chance's allowance for Evangeline was so generous that she sent a gift to the nuns at Sacred Heart in Santa Fara every month for the upkeep of her family's graves. She had a mausoleum built with the name COMO across the top and Georgio, Alicianna and Felicia Rizzo inscribed across the bottom. She had them entombed there and the nuns looked after it. The money was enough for the sisters to buy food and clothing for the poor also. Lorenzo's family kept an eye on it too and Maria got updates from them often. Michele and Elena Rizzo were so grateful that Lorenzo didn't go to jail for his crime, looking out for their graves was the least they could do for the Como's. The Rizzo's were good people and it put Evangeline's mind to rest that her family wasn't forgotten like she promised years before. Evangeline was becoming somewhat of a social darling. She was interested in the idea that women had the right to vote in America. She, herself, had not become a citizen, but her marriage to Chance gave her citizen status. It saddened her that Elizabeth Cady Stanton died the year before. She was sorry that she never got the chance to hear one of her speeches on women's right to vote. Evangeline had The Women's Bible in her dressing table that Elizabeth had published seven years earlier. She kept it under her hankies so no one would see it.

The suffragette movement was frowned upon by her husband. All her life she listened to the men who seemed to own her. Her decisions were made for her or she had been convinced to do what was best for her. Her intention was to make women accountable in their own lives. In the case of a husband's death, if there was no money for the wife to live on, she was at the mercy of her family. If there was no family, she had to fend for herself. Elderly women were said to have died of a broken heart, when the truth was, they probably died of starvation. She wanted women to be educated in practical things, not how to hold your tea cup. She had been through it and she knew the pain of it. Chance thought it amused her, this suffragette business, so he let her have her fun.

Georgio Como, her beloved father, had been a politician in Sicily. Evangeline always wished she was born a boy so she could work for the people like her father.   What a scandal, if she had ever tried such an unfeminine thing.

A woman's place was in her home. Taking care of her family was all that was required of her. Of course being submissive to her husband was a natural thing in their minds. A slap in the face was acceptable to keep the wife in line and she would have no recourse. Chance never laid a hand on her: she gave him no reason to.

She was getting used to the submissive part of the marriage. Her husband had a veracious sexual appetite, and she wasn't sure if this was normal. Maybe she wasn't normal, she didn't know. No one spoke a word about what would happen on her wedding night. She had no mother to ask and any respectable woman would never speak to another woman about such things. It certainly would have been awkward for Rosalyn to mention her wedding night. So much for being chaste, she thought. All it does is leave you in the dark. Sometimes she wished she could ask Elsie a few questions. *I bet that one would tell me,* she thought. She also knew Elsie would tell Lorenzo and God knows what he would do with that information. So she went through the motions without any passion or emotion, knowing Chance was getting irritated with her. She knew she had to keep him happy enough for Michele's sake, he was her first priority. Elsie was happy when Chance and Evangeline moved to Hunters Point.

They were far enough away that Lorenzo had to make a special trip to get there. It really didn't do much good though. Lorenzo couldn't be away from Evangeline for more than a week. With the excuse of seeing Michele, he would spend every weekend at the new house. He stayed out of the way of Chance, but lately, Chance spent a lot of time in the city. Elsie was livid when Lorenzo told her he was off to see Michele again. She knew Evangeline was the reason for his trip and she told him so. Lorenzo told her that she was not his wife in the iciest tone he could conger up. So he rode off to see the one who was his wife in his heart. He hated to hurt Elsie like that, but sometimes she brought it on herself.

Chance was busy with steel mill business all the time. He started to spend more and more time in New York. Evangeline knew the rejection of his sexual advances toward her made her husband furious. She actually didn't mind when his working schedule kept him overnight in the city. Lately, she wasn't feeling very well and was sick a lot in the morning. She remembered Felicia had the same feeling when she was expecting Michele. Eight weeks later she knew her suspicions were true: she would be having a baby in seven months.

Chance was elated when he heard the news. He also knew that now his wife would have a reason to reject him further. He worried about having a little one and could he be as good a father as Edward. He expressed these feelings to Rebecca one morning when they were lying in bed together. Rebecca hated when he spoke of his wife, but he always used her as his sounding board. She had promised to be there for him whenever he needed her, but she also knew divorce was out of the question. Rebecca was giving up her youth for Chance, but he was worth it. Chance was a powerful respected man, but he could relax and be boyish around her.

"Don't worry darling," she told him, as she stroked his hair, "you will be a wonderful father. " He snuggled up against her and fell asleep in her arms again.

Rosalyn and Edward were looking forward to being grandparents. Baby furniture was imported from Italy and England. The layette was being stitched by the finest seamstresses in the state. Larissa's nursery was redecorated with fresh paint. Murals of nursery rhyme characters painted by artisans were decorating both houses. Characters from Miss Beatrix Potter's books covered the walls on the new house. Evangeline thought it was a bit over the top, but she enjoyed watching Rosalyn and Edward fuss over the blessed event.

Edward hadn't been well in the last few months and Rosalyn was worried about him. His doctors told him to cut back on his work, which he did. His free time was spent under Rosalyn's feet, and although she complained, secretly she loved having him around. With Edward out of the office Chance spent even more time in the city. On a few occasions Evangeline was taken to New York to have lunch with her husband.

Lorenzo was the only one trusted to get her there and back safely. Of course he was happy to oblige because then he could spend time with her. Lorenzo needed to speak to her about his future employment. The gasoline car was all the rage and soon Mr. Edward would want one. Lorenzo was pretty handy around the house repairing some of the mechanical conveniences. He wanted Evangeline's opinion about him learning to repair these new vehicles. She was very proud of his ambition.

"Lorenzo," she said, "an education is something no one can take away from you. That is what I hope for when Michele gets older. If it doesn't work out for you, what do you have to lose?" Lorenzo was happy to see Evangeline so pleased with him. It had been a long time since she even smiled at him. Lorenzo dropped her off at the restaurant and went to the Sons of Italy hall to catch up on the events of the day. He would pick her up in a couple of hours to take her back home.

Chance was waiting for his wife at his favorite restaurant in Central Park, Tavern on the Green; it was the best place for lunch in his opinion. Besides he had never taken Rebecca there, so no one would question Evangeline's presence. He could see how her blossoming belly was becoming laborious for her.

"I don't think you should come into the city any more Evangeline, I can see it's getting harder for you. "

" I think you might be right," she agreed. They talked about the baby and the school she wanted Michele and Larissa to attend next year. Chance told her about the trouble in Europe and how his business might be involved with the government. She told him about the ladies she befriended with Mrs. Mitchell and the meetings she attended with her.

"They call themselves Suffragettes and they think they deserve the right to vote in elections," she said excitedly. He gave her a dubious look so she changed the subject. Evangeline would never mention them to Lorenzo. He would have no patience for such talk. She could hear him say," What are you talking about Evangeline, go take care of your family." She wasn't sure if Chance would forbid her to attend these meetings; she knew some women had to hide the fact from their husbands. Respectable women didn't associate with the likes of Susan B. Anthony, and other radicals of the movement.

Chance was right about her trips to New York, six weeks later she gave birth to Alicianna Rose. The baby was perfect and her labor was quite easy for a first baby. Her husband had been right by her side during the labor, but was rushed out of the room for the birth by Rosalyn and Maria. Edward, Chance and Lorenzo were toasting the baby for the fifth or sixth time when Maria came out and announced it's a girl!

Evangeline was exhausted when they handed the swaddled baby to her so she could nurse her. She held her daughter and whispered to her that her fondest wish was that she had the freedom to make her own decisions in her life. At one point Evangeline would have liked to name her Susan after her suffragette hero, but knew Chance would have thought her insane. The baby was named instead for both her grandmothers and christened two weeks later. Maria and Nicolo were her Godparents and Michele beamed with pride over his baby sister.   Evangeline and Chance had been worried about how Michele was going to react to the baby. Evangeline was his whole life and what if he was jealous of Alicianna? Thankfully, he adored her and told his parents that he had to go to school now and mama needed a baby to take care of. The boy was proud to be the big brother and he would always watch over her.

Michele had changed his name to Mike Winston when he went to school with Larissa. He liked the American version of his name better. His name was pronounced Mi gay li, sometimes people mispronounced it and Michelle or Michilli came out. He thought a name was important and he didn't want his slaughtered like that.

Mike looked so much like Lorenzo. His straight dark hair and beautiful brown eyes were the opposite of Alicianna's blonde curls and ocean blue eyes. Although she looked more like Larissa than Evangeline, she didn't have Larissa's mild temperament. The baby had a bit of colic and cried for two hours every night. Evangeline was so tired but it didn't bother Chance. He was back in New York in Rebecca's frilly bed in the brownstone. His excuse was the baby kept him up and he had to go to work in the mornings so he was going to sleep at the Men's Club.

Evangeline was happy to be a new mom; although she took care of Mike since birth because Felicia couldn't, this baby was her own. Her other new passion was her flower and vegetable garden. She spent hours with the gardeners arranging the flower beds and vegetable beds. Alicianna played in her English Pram and prospered like the gardens in the fresh Long Island air. Larissa Winston was now eight years old and happy to be on vacation from school. Her baby niece was all she cared about that summer and she was a big help to Evangeline. She was a little confused about the relationships between all the people in her life.

"Evangeline," she asked one day while tending to the baby. "is Mike your son?" Evangeline was so surprised by the question.

"Why do you ask darling?"

" If he is your son, would he be my nephew,?" she questioned.

"No, you see, his mother died when he was a baby. His mother was my sister. Do you understand? We came to America from Sicily to be with Lorenzo; he is Mike's daddy. Chance is the father who takes care of him and is married to me. I know this is hard for you to understand Larissa."

"Evangeline, my daddy takes care of me, why doesn't Lorenzo take care of Mike?"

"Lorenzo was very generous to allow Chance and I to take care of Mike," Evangeline explained.

"Then is Alicianna his sister?"

"Well yes, in a way she is, she is his sister in his heart. He calls me mama and so will Alicianna."

"Then is Mike related to me?" she asked.

"Not by blood, but we are all related in our hearts. Lorenzo was married to my sister and Maria is Lorenzo's sister. We all love each other very much don't we?" asked Evangeline.

"Yes we do," said Larissa. In her heart she loved Mike related or not. That was her special secret and no one needed to know about it for a long time.

On March 30 th.1909 the Blackwell's bridge finally opened; it had been seven years in the making. It made life so much easier for the people who lived on Long Island. Now it only took minutes to get from Lenox Hill to Hunters Point. Some people thought it would never be finished. There were so many workers who were treated unfairly by the owners, and so many labor problems. A terrible wind storm tried to collapse it, and someone tried to blow it up once, but the bridge seemed to have a will of its own and it survived. To the relief of many it was finished and a beautiful spectacle to behold. Chance and Edward's steel mill made millions on the bridge, so no one was happier than the Winston's that the bridge was completed. The big market place at the foot of the bridge was also a handy convenience. Farmers from Long Island brought their wares there to sell; beef, lamb, pork, wild game. Vegetables of all varieties made the cook's life easier. Dairies brought milk, butter, and cheeses. The cooks and maids gathered on market day to shop and gossip about the rich people they worked for. Lorenzo and Elsie were always a topic of conversation too.

"When was that good looking Italian going to marry poor Elsie?"

"She is so in love with him, he should make an honest woman out of her."

It would have landed on deaf ears if Lorenzo had heard them. Evangeline was the only women for him, and his punishment from so many years ago was that he could never have her.

Lorenzo had been learning about the new car Mr. Henry Ford was building. The year before in 1908, his assembly line was turning out many cars. Lorenzo thought someone had to repair them when they break down. Mr. Edward wanted to buy one for quite a while now, but Mrs. Rosalyn was happy with her team of horses and didn't trust those monsters of the road. But to her chagrin, Mr. Edward came home with his precious Tin Lizzie. He didn't know how to drive so Lorenzo was his chauffer. He also gave Lorenzo free access to it whenever he needed it.

"Take it my boy," Edward offered, "you go more places than I do. Just get me to and from the office occasionally that will be fine with me." Driving on the bridge made it so easy to get from Lenox Hill to Hunters Point every day too. Lorenzo said,

"Driving a car and repairing them was not the same thing. Cars and horses were different too; horses didn't have a clutch or a gas pedal. Horses stopped when you said whooh and pulled on the reins" That always made Edward laugh. Other car manufacturers in Europe built heavy, fully loaded machines. Mr. Ford wanted a more affordable car that the average working man could afford. Lorenzo's little business of going to customers with broken down cars and repairing them with his little tool box was taking off pretty well. The work was becoming overwhelming and he was exhausted every night. One evening after dinner, when Lorenzo and Nicolo were enjoying their wine and cheese, Nicolo remarked, "Wouldn't it be nice, Lorenzo, if people could come to you instead of you going to them to fix the cars? You are so tired everyday working with the cars and working for Mr. Winston's horses too. "

"Nicolo, how did you get so smart? You don't have an education like my son Mike, yet you can have such a good idea. God gave you a good brain; he put his hands on each side of his head and squeezed his cheeks."
Lorenzo stood up and started pacing the floor.

"How can I get a place? I have a little money saved, but not enough to buy a garage. I can buy the tools I need, but not the building. I know, I will ask Evangeline, surely she will help me. You know how she is about people bettering themselves. I'll ask her first thing in the morning."

Early the next day Lorenzo drove Mr. Winston's car to Long Island to talk to the only person he truly trusted in the world. Evangeline poured him an espresso coffee. "Okay, Lorenzo what has you so excited? Did you hear about Mike being on the honors list?"

" He surely didn't get his smarts from me," Lorenzo admitted. "Evangeline, I need your opinion. I have an idea that I think will make me a wealthy man and perhaps Nicolo too."

"Wonderful, Lorenzo, how can I help?"

"You know how I repair the new cars Mr. Ford builds in Detroit? I go from one house to another to help the owners repair their automobiles."

"Yes, and I am so happy you have come so far in your work. How can I be of help?" "Well if I could have a building where the owners could come to me, I could double my business. I could train Nicolo and maybe other men to help me as mechanics."

"What a wonderful idea!" Evangeline exclaimed. "But let me ask you again, what do you want of me?"

"Do you or Chance know of a building I could use to put my shop in?" He hated to ask Chance for anything but how else could Evangeline find him a shop.?" I am willing to rent someplace or if the price is right I might buy it. My savings will cover the tools ,but I need a place to put them." Suddenly Evangeline felt a wave of excitement, "Lorenzo, will you let me be a partner in this venture?"

" Evangeline, you are a woman," he said in disbelief.

"Yes, a woman with money," she reminded him. "Okay then, I will be a partner that no one knows about, how would that be?" she suggested. *If people knew his partner was a woman he wouldn't be taken seriously, he was sure.*

"Well do you know of a place where I can set up shop?"he asked.

"What about Edward's stable, it's close to the city where more people have these vehicles. We can build on the back of it to give you more room," she said excitedly.

"No," said Lorenzo pensively, "those noisy motors spook the horses."

"Then we will find property and build a new one," Evangeline said with determination. "Don't worry, Lorenzo, you know if I put my mind to something it gets done. Now sit down and let me tell you about the suffragette movement, women have good minds and should be allowed to speak them."

He spent the next hour listening to her rant on about her right to vote.

"Did you know," she said, "the emancipated African American man could vote in 1870, but the women who helped them get the vote cannot," she sputtered? As much as he respected Evangeline, he thought she was wrong on this issue. Women should take care of their homes and children, not carry signs in protest. What a *disgrace,* he thought. He had seen some of the parades in New York with women waving signs and screaming like crazy. *Where were their husbands,* he wondered? *How could he argue women's rights with her today? She had just offered to be his partner in the auto shop. Evangeline was an amazing woman. He came looking for a place to put his business and not only did she figure out where, but became his partner too. What a woman,* he said to himself. By the next month a brand new brick building was erected on a corner lot in New York City. "Lorenzo's Auto Repair Shop" read the sign in red, white and green paint, same as the Italian flag. The lawyers had the papers ready to sign. Evangeline was the silent partner and Lorenzo had all the rights as to how the business was run. *Here we go again,* thought Evangeline, as she signed her name; another man controlling my destiny.

In January of 1912, Lorenzo received a letter from his best friend Franco Valio. Franco, his old partner in crime, seemed to be just that. He was in trouble with the law in Santa Fara and needed to get out of Italy quickly. It seemed because of the assassination of Franz Ferdinand the Archduke of Austria, pockets of resistance were popping up all over the world and Franco had gotten himself mixed up with the wrong people. He escaped to London to elude his enemies. Franco asked Lorenzo to sponsor his voyage to America. The new ship, the grand *Titanic* was to depart in April and Franco wanted to be on it.

Lorenzo was very excited to see his old friend again. Franco and Lorenzo were seldom apart in Santa Fara. They would bring the good sisters of the Sacred Heart to tears with their antics. Once they slipped a frog in the desk drawer of Mother Superior and when she opened it, her screams could be heard all over Santa Fara. Numerous Hail Mary's were recited after that, remembered Lorenzo with a smile on his face. Franco was one of the kidnappers on the fateful night Mike was conceived. Franco had called him every name he could think of because of his stupidity. Suddenly a chill ran through Lorenzo, he didn't know why, but he had an uneasy feeling in his stomach. He shook it off by thinking of how much trouble they could get into in America. Lorenzo wired Franco the money for a first class ticket. He didn't want his friend to suffer the way he had on the ocean.

The headlines in the New York papers read "Titanic's maiden voyage ends in tragedy". Lorenzo was inconsolable. He rushed to the port authority to see if Franco was one of the survivors. His name was nowhere to be found. He waited around for days in case his name showed up on any of the lists the authorities had, but to no avail.

Everything is ready for him, Lorenzo thought; a job at the auto shop in New York, and an apartment that he could share with one of Lorenzo's employees. Most of all, the plans he had to rekindle their friendship. Elsie had never seen Lorenzo cry. Not even at the news that his parents had died. He blamed himself for agreeing to be Franco's sponsor. Why didn't he just say no to him, he wondered? He remember the uneasy feeling he had when he received Franco's letter, he knew there was a reason for it. Lorenzo wore a black arm band for months. He was only consoled by the fact that Franco didn't have a family. He never married and his parents were gone. He left only a few cousins back in Santa Fara.

"It's like a book that has been closed on a life that wasn't finished," he told Elsie. Lorenzo sank into a depression. Every time he read the obituary in the newspaper of a Titanic victim, he sank deeper and deeper. He started drinking too much and spending too much time in bed. He neglected his business which put too much burden on Nicolo. Elsie was beside herself, she went to the only person, she was sure could help him. Evangeline went straight to the stable apartment and pulled the covers off Lorenzo and demanded that he get up and snap out of it.

"It was Franco's destiny," she told him, "you can't change destiny. It's not your fault; Franco could have married a nice Santa Fata girl and had a family and a safe life. But, No, he chose the life he had. No one chose it for him. He was a man in control of his life; not like a women, she has to listen to her brother, father, uncle and especially her husband." He had never seen her like this before. She was livid.

"Get up, Lorenzo, and get on with your life," she screamed at him. "Instead of burying yourself in place of Franco, honor his memory and do something positive with it." Lorenzo got up washed his face and went to work.

"Evangeline blamed everything on destiny," he grumbled. *She should have it engraved on her forehead,* he thought.

Apollinia   ------   Evangeline's Destiny

FOUR

For the next five years, Lorenzo's dream came true: he had ten workers in his city building and he built a new one on Long Island where six mechanics took on the job for him. He put up a plaque in Franco's honor so he wouldn't be forgotten. He was finally coming to grips with the fact that Franco was gone. He spent most of the time at the Long Island location. He told Elsie he had to be near the new shop to be sure it got off to a good start. Nicolo was in charge of the New York shop and was doing a great job. Elsie was no fool. She knew Evangeline was the real reason. Evangeline wasn't that much of a threat to her. She knew Evangeline only considered Lorenzo as family and not in a romantic way. Elsie had spent fifteen years with Lorenzo and she wasn't getting any younger. She would be thirty one on her next birthday and her child bearing years were getting short. If she couldn't' convince him to marry her soon, she would have to resort to drastic measures. Lorenzo was the only man she had ever been with, yet people looked down their noses at her. Her mistress, Mrs. Mitchell told her that what happened outside of her residence was none of her business, as long as she didn't bring shame to her family. Mrs. Mitchell chose to ignore the fact that Lorenzo spent many nights in Elsie's room; she was a modern day woman in many ways. Elsie's goings on with that Italian boy was none of her affair. She knew Elsie was in love with Lorenzo and eventually he would marry her. Mrs. Mitchell was completely involved with the suffragettes and spent all her energy in that direction. Mrs. Mitchell was Evangeline's companion to suffragette meetings on Wednesday afternoons while her husband thought she was going to bible study. Like many men, as long as she didn't bother him with her whims, it was all right with him.

In late 1914, while accompanying Mrs. Mitchell on a visit to her friend's home, Elsie received the shock of her life. Mrs. Mitchell's friend had just moved into one of the brownstone row houses on 5th. Avenue. While they were walking up to ring the bell, someone stepped out of the house next door. To her amazement she recognized Mr. Chance Winston. As he kissed the woman good bye and turned to walk away, his eyes fell on Mrs. Mitchell and Elsie. He didn't know what to do so he simply pretended they were invisible. Mrs. Mitchell needed smelling salts when she entered into the house, but Elsie couldn't wipe the grin off her face.

When they enquired about the people next door, they were told they were a nice couple and since they had only just moved in themselves they didn't know much about them, other than the name on the mail box read, Clay. When Elsie told Lorenzo of what she saw, she saw his face grow red as a pepper. *Oh dear, what have I done, she feared, what is he going to do now? His precious Evangeline is going to be hurt and he won't have that. Maybe if I tell him my news, his mind will be distracted and Evangeline won't matter?*

"Calm down Lorenzo, I have something important to tell you," she insisted.

"What is it?" he said, with clenched fists

"I'm going to have a baby," she said calmly. This was too much for Lorenzo to take in and he fainted on the spot.

Mrs. Mitchell didn't know what to say

"Should I mention this terrible news to Evangeline, or not?" she asked her husband for his advice.

"Forget all about it. A man has a right to his privacy, why should a meddling, old woman, ruin his reputation? Think of Evangeline," he said," what good would the truth do her?" She agreed with him, but why didn't Chance think of his reputation before he had this affair. In the back of her mind, she wondered if her husband had a secret too. Men had all the rights, she thought to herself, it just made her more determined to fight along with her suffragettes.

Evangeline didn't need anyone to tell her of her husband's indiscretions, a woman knew these things: The lip rouge on his handkerchief, the smell of her perfume on his shirt, the many nights way from home. Evangeline never mentioned it to him, partly because their sex life was so disappointing, and partly because she didn't want to upset Rosalyn. She had been told that a man had to take out his frustrations on a paid-for women and leave his wife alone. , She was thinking about her children and how disappointed in their father they would be. Chance gave her the gift of her beautiful Aliciana, and he was the most dotting father.

He let her have whatever she wanted for Mike, and his studies were coming along so well. He was fifteen already and they were thinking of universities. So rather than rock the boat, she kept her silence. She was very curious though, she was a woman after all. Several years ago she had Patrick Ryan, an investigator track Chance's comings and goings and he reported to her that his paramour was a certain Rebecca Clay. She paid him well and thanked him for his services, but that was all she needed to know. Evangeline never laid eyes on the woman and didn't care to.

Lorenzo wasn't as discrete as Mr. Mitchell. When he saw Chance in the study the next day, he punched him right in the nose. He told him his secret was out. Elsie was forbidden to speak to Evangeline and Mr. Mitchell took care of his wife's part in it. No one wanted to hurt Evangeline.

"He was a lucky to have such a beloved wife," Lorenzo warned Chance. "Whatever nonsense you and Miss Clay have been up to, keep it away from Evangeline. If Evangeline gets hurt over this, Chance," he said with his teeth clenched, "I won't be responsible for my actions,". Lorenzo knew some scary people in Little Italy. Some of them had to disappear from Sicily quickly; some even had to change their names. Chance knew what he meant and decided to spend more time at home for a while, at least until this blew over.

Lorenzo had his own troubles to deal with. With a baby on the way he had an obligation to marry Elsie. A wedding and a baptism would be on the agenda. When Maria and Nicolo heard the news, they couldn't have been happier. Mrs. Mitchell was relieved because she had grown to love Elsie and she knew how much she wanted to marry Lorenzo. Mike was happy to have another sibling; he just wished it was closer to his age.

"Elsie," he asked, "couldn't you have had this baby years ago? I would have loved to have a brother my age." Alicianna was the most precious thing he could think of, so another sister would be fine too he told them. Elsie thought to herself, if you only knew how long I tried to have Lorenzo's baby, but it was here now and life would change for everyone.

Elsie went shopping for houses on Long Island. She found one that was not too far from Evangeline's that would suit them fine. It was a cozy little cottage near the village that Lorenzo could afford. His auto repair business was prospering and she would have to give up her job with Mrs. Mitchell, now that the baby was coming along. The previous year, Maria and Nicolo left the Winston's employ and bought a little cottage in the same area. Elsie wished she could find a house on the moon rather than one so close to the Winston's of Hunters Point. Lorenzo wouldn't hear of anywhere else, his excuse was that he needed to be near Mike.

November, 1914 was a rather mild one with the temperatures in the 60's. This would be their first Thanksgiving in their own house as a married couple. The wedding was a quiet affair, with only Maria and Nicolo as witnesses and Mike in attendance. Father O'Reilly was a crotchety old man with very strict morals and didn't appreciate the situation of the couple. The ceremony was performed in the rectory without a mass. Elsie didn't care, she was Mrs. Lorenzo Rizzo and that was all that mattered to her. Lorenzo bought two gold rings, a flower for her to hold and one to put in his lapel. *What made her stick by him for so many years?* he wondered? *What made him stay with her? He never strayed in all those years.* He always thought it was because of Evangeline. He didn't want her to think less of him if he was with a lot of women. He realized a long time ago that Evangeline didn't love him, not in that way. She cared for him because of Mike. She did everything for Mike. She gave up her life for Mike. She had an unfaithful husband, but kept up the charade because of Mike. Lorenzo's stupid idea so many years ago in Santa Farahad affected so many lives. Evangeline's, Felicia's, Chance, Mike and especially his. Mike is my son, he calls me Papa, but he calls Chance Dad, it's so confusing for him. I vow to do better by this child, he promised himself. He or she will have a Mama and a Papa who loves it. Elsie never looked as pretty as she did on her wedding day. Her pregnancy wasn't showing yet and she hadn't been sick at all. She knew she was getting a little plump because she was hungry all the time.

Elsie felt in her heart that once she and Lorenzo had their baby and moved into the new house, all would be well and all her dreams would come true. Lorenzo was now 34 and had matured a lot. His good looks had only intensified with age. He was getting grey around the temples and his slim body had filled out a little, but it was only befitting a man his age. After a few weeks, their house was ready and Lorenzo carried Elsie over the threshold.

"I love you, Lorenzo" she whispered to him.

"I love you, too, Elsie," he said.

The war in Europe was raging on. America wasn't committed to the cause yet. Chance's business was growing by importing steel to build railroads, bridges and guns. His business partner on one of his ventures was Joe Cross. Joe was involved with the Italian government; rumor had it that Joe was attached in some way to the Italian resistance league and came to New York in a dubious fashion. It was only a rumor and Chance wasn't interested in rumors.

After working all day on some important business, Chance brought Joe home to have dinner with the family. The next day they were going to try their luck at the horse races at Belmont Park. Joe was very impressed by the huge home and grounds. Chance truly was a lucky man, he thought. Joe was alone in the world and envied the way Chance lived. That night Joe met Chance's parents, brothers, sister and children. He couldn't take his eyes off Evangeline. The twins, now 26, were anxious to hear any news of the war overseas; they had graduated from the Naval Academy several years earlier and had the Navy in their blood.

Chance had put them to work in the business, but they wanted to stay in the service. He promised if war broke out in America he wouldn't stand in their way. Not that it mattered too much to the boys, but their mother wouldn't hear any of it. She had her hands full with Edward and wouldn't have her boys in some far away war. Chance had attended the

Naval Academy himself, and had no interest in the service; business was his forte. He had his inheritance from England and the steel business was doing quite well. Since Joe had just arrived from England, he told the family all he knew about the going's on overseas. He said the war itself wasn't his business but Chance had directed him in some lucrative railroad dealings for the government.

Evangeline wasn't so sure about this Joe Cross. His thick Italian accent wasn't befitting an English business man. She recognized his accent to be from southern Italy-- around the boot, she thought. Not that she herself had ever been there, but she recognized the same way people from that area spoke at The Sons of Italy festival on Mulberry Street.

"Mr. Cross," Evangeline asked, before the second course, "where do come you from?"

Joe was taken by surprise by the question. He couldn't tell her the truth so he just said, "I've been living in London for several years now, and I feel very much at home there."

"Oh," Evangeline said, "I wondered about your accent, I thought I recognized it." Joe tried to change the subject and said, You have quite an accent yourself, Mrs. Winston." Evangeline smiled but couldn't stop thinking about Joe Cross all night. His blue eyes were mesmerizing when he looked at her, she thought he could see right through her. Later she asked Chance what he knew about him and he said that he was a business associate and he had a lot of good connections.

"Really that's all I know, do you have a problem with him, Evangeline?", he asked

"No, I suppose not I was just curious that's all." Evangeline decided it was all in her head and tried to forget about it, but she couldn't shake that uneasy feeling toward him.

Late that night, alone in his room, Joe reflected on the last ten years. His involvement with the Italian Resistance Movement had gotten him in a lot of trouble. He was trying to save his country from the ravages of war and he had to give up his identity to do it. At that time Greece hadn't given allegiance right away to either side and they were cut off from the rest of the world. The resistance was smuggling arms into Greece from Sicily.

Giuseppe Croce was leading a group of rebels with a boat full of guns. That night, the smugglers were caught by government soldiers, arrested and taken into custody. Following negotiations between the resistance and the government, they were released.

He was sent to London and given a new identity, and set up as an agent for a steel company in the U.S. His death had been staged to protect him from the enemy. He was lucky to be alive because smugglers were usually shot on the spot. Fortunately, at that time, the war was years away, but the wheels were turning in that direction even back then. He gave up the information for his life. The heartbreak his young wife and parents endured was pitiful. He was taken to London but kept under wraps. He couldn't go back to Italy. His wife, son and possibly his parents were in danger. He always knew where they were and eventually his wife Margarita remarried. She was living a good safe life and his son was taken care of. This secret must be kept, it was imperative to their well being.

The next day Joe, Chance and Edward drove up Long Island to the horse races at Belmont Park. Joe had never been to a race in the states before. His doings in America were always work related. It was nice to have a friend like Chance who took such an interest in him socially. Edward was very amusing in the way he coaxed his horse to win from his seat. Get along you old bastard, he would yell. He could use crude language when Rosalyn wasn't around. If she were there she would say, Edward darling that's not language a gentlemen would use. The Winston's owned a set of box seats at the track. They were served lunch and drinks without ever getting up; although they did go to the windows to place their bets. Joe didn't do so well, Edward said he broke out even, but Chance came away with a fist full of money.

"Are you lucky in everything you touch?" teased Joe.

"Why, I suppose I am," pondered Chance, while he stroked his chin.

"I know you are lucky in love, my friend," Joe remarked.

"Oh, you mean Evangeline?, Yes she is a beauty and smart, too. I am very fortunate to have her."

You don't know the meaning of fortunate, Joe thought to himself.

In December 1914, Rosalyn planned one of her famous Christmas parties. Her English upbringing had always come through her planning of these affairs. Since she was brought up in the Victorian Era, the Christmas tree was the centerpiece of the ballroom. Prince Albert, Queen Victoria's beloved husband, brought the Christmas tree to England from his native Germany. The tree was decorated with silver and gold tinsel as well as candles that were lit on Christmas Eve. All the children had presents under the tree and wore their finest outfits to the party. The children of the servants were also included in the gift giving so no one would be left out. The ladies and gentlemen were treated to a fine dinner of hams, beef, turkey, salads and Christmas pudding. Special rums and punches were also on the menu.

This year the festivities were going to be of a grander scale, the guest list would include Evangeline's brother and his family who just arrived from Palermo. Recently Evangeline received a letter from her half brother Antonino Como. It read that he was coming to America with his wife Luna and two daughters, Mona and Mariella. Luna had a brother, Vincenzo, in New York that had a bakery and wanted Antonino's experience to help him expand the business. They would be there just before the holidays and were looking forward to seeing her and Mike. His daughters were so anxious to be in America, it was all they talked about. Mona and Mariella were 19 and 20 years old now and had just finished their studies in Palermo.

The war was getting very close and Antonino wanted to get his daughters out of Sicily. Many young women were taken by enemy insurgents and raped and left for dead. It was a terrible thing to endure for the families of these poor girls. Evangeline was delighted to think her family would be together for Christmas. She knew her father would be smiling down on them from heaven. Forever the optimist, Rosalyn was happy the girls were around the same ages as Matt and Mark.

"Wouldn't it be wonderful, Evangeline, if I could get a daughter-in-law or two out of all this?" she wished. "Maybe a romance will be in the cards for my boys.". Lately Rosalyn had been seeing a spiritualist with Mrs. Mitchell and some of her lady friends. Evangeline thought she should go to mass more often, but Rosalyn was having a good time with Madam Sasha and didn't think it would hurt anyone.   Sasha Comanink was a refugee from Romania. She had a flair for the theatric and she needed money to support herself and her mother. Her only source of income came in the way of the spiritual world. She did card readings and other tricks of the trade. She liked to shock people in the way she dressed and wore lots and lots of costume jewelry. If you didn't know better you would think she was your best friend or close relative. That's how personable a lady she was and Rosalyn got the biggest kick out of her.

"Don't underestimate her," Rosalyn warned, "she has the gift. I think I will ask her to come to the party and entertain my guests."

"Whatever you think darling," Evangeline agreed. "Don't forget those boys of yours are as different as day and night, and I'm not so sure they are looking for wives just yet."

"You never know. Madam Sasha told me she saw a wedding in the future that I will attend," Rosalyn said.
Evangeline rolled her eyes and said, "how nice for you, will you be buying a new dress?" Both ladies started to laugh at the way this conversation was headed. Just then the butler brought in the morning mail.

"Look at this." Rosalyn said with excitement, "My goodness, it's a wedding invitation!" One of the Roosevelt daughters was getting married next month and Rosalyn and Edward were invited to the wedding.

"Wait until I tell Madam Sasha!" she exclaimed. Evangeline laughed at the coincidence and how fast her mother-in-law ran out of the room to call Madam Sasha. Everyone knew the couple had been engaged for several months, and she expected Madam Sasha must have heard the news too. Evangeline was right about the boys; they were more interested in the war than in getting married. They had a lot of girlfriends and promised nothing to anyone of them. They were the best catch in town and many a mother had their eyes on them for their daughters. Rosalyn was sure that was the reason her date book was full with invitations for lunch, fashion shows, teas and cards. It seemed to her that every one of them had a daughter to marry off.   That was fine with her, though she knew

Evangeline was the best daughter-in-law she could ever ask for. Rosalyn mentioned the visitors to the twins in hopes of getting a reaction from them, but they weren't interested. Matt was such a serious fellow and Mark was much more flip. Mark could make his mother laugh with his jokes and little pranks; he was such a joy to her. Matt was the accountant in the family. Chance took advantage of his abilities and put him to work in the office making sure the books were always accurate. Matt was very proud of his work and his mother was very proud of him.

Antonino Como was very strict with his daughters. There was no courting allowed. They were chaperoned to and from the school which was run by nuns. They were sheltered from the evils of the world, and never strayed far from their mother. To the girls, America was golden staircase and velvet draped grandeur that their aunt Evangeline lived in. When they got to New York they found that their lives would be very different from that dream. They wouldn't be living on Long Island, but in a tenement apartment in the city. There would be a bakery on the first floor and they would live a long flight up a wooden staircase above it. When the family arrived in America they were taken to the apartment. They couldn't get over how the people lived. They were used to city life living in Palermo, but so many people in one place overwhelmed them.

Later that week Evangeline and Mike went to the city to bring the family back to Hunters Point. Tears of joy flowed when the relatives saw each other. Mike just smiled. He didn't know any of these people. He was only three when he left Sicily and they lived in Palermo not Santa Fara. But his mother was happy and he would do anything to keep her that way, so he embraced his Aunt Luna and Uncle Antonino and had no problem being fussed over by the cousins.

His English was perfect because he was educated in America. He was amused by the broken English his cousins spoke. They had some English classes in school at the University in Palermo, but never had the chance to use it. His aunt and uncle had a different dialect than that of Santa Fara, it was almost a sing song sound and it made him laugh. The ride back to

Hunters Point in the motor car was rather chilly. In December, New York weather was quite different than the warm temperatures of Sicily. The family snuggled together and it made the trip tolerable. Anything was better than the twelve days crossing the ocean. When they arrived at Hunters Point, the girls' dreams were met when the house came into view. Mona was impressed, but Mariella decided then and there that she was going to live like her Zia Evangeline.

"Welcome to my home," Chance announced as he walked into the room. "We are so glad to have you here for the holidays." Chance very much liked Evangeline's brother Antonino. He thought his jolly laugh and robust stature was very pleasant. The way Antonino flung his arms around when he spoke made Chance laugh even though he didn't understand a word he heard spoken.

The Comos were amazed to see Evangeline's home. Two bedrooms were prepared for them and a servant to see to their every need. Six year old Alicianna Rose was fawned over by all after she performed a little song and dance she'd prepared for her relatives. Antonino commented that Alicianna didn't even look like an Italian child at all. Everyone thought the Como daughters resembled Evangeline with their sweet faces and beautiful curly dark brown hair. Their father teased that he had nothing to do with it, and gave all the credit to his wife.

Luna Como came to America with a heavy heart and an album full of pictures. She left two married sons and four grandchildren back in Palermo. She was so worried that the war would be terrible and prayed that her family would be safe. She and Antonino hoped they would come to America and work for the bakery soon. Chance was happy to see Evangeline smile and busy herself around the house. Lately he'd felt a chill in the air around her. It was the same sensation he noticed when Lorenzo was around Evangeline. She was never harsh with him, but the look in her eyes was icy cold and it made him sad. He wasn't sure if she knew about Rebecca Clay or not. It was never ever mentioned.

Christmas Eve was like a winter wonderland with a light sugaring of snow. The Como sisters had never seen snow before. The mountain in Santa Fara had some snow at the top but the girls had never gone up that high, they never had an occasion to climb a mountain. The ballroom at Lenox Hill looked even more beautiful than it had for Chance and Evangeline's wedding. The Christmas tree brought down from a tree farm in Albany was bigger than the year before. Rosalyn had some ornaments shipped in from Spain and they hung with flair among all the old toys and balls she had purchased over the years.

The guest list was quite extensive this year. It included the Mitchells and their sons Ronald and William, their wives and children. The Como family along with Maria, Nicolo, Lorenzo and Elsie, were always on the list. John Lee and his family looked forward to an invitation although his wife had just given birth so only John and little Andrew accepted. Of course Evangeline and Chance along with their children finished the list. There was a surprise guest that Chance invited at the last minute. His name was Joe Cross, but he had not arrived yet. Joe gave Evangeline a funny feeling, although she wasn't sure why. Edward made a toast and welcomed all their friends. He wished everyone a Merry Christmas and a prosperous new year.

Just before the dinner bell rang Joe Cross was announced. He begged his pardon and was seated at the table next to Evangeline. Joe blamed his tardiness on business and asked for her forgiveness. Evangeline told him her mother-in-law was the hostess and perhaps he should explain his story to her. She knew she sounded curt and wished she hadn't been so rude to him. Every nerve in her body tightened when he sat down next to her. When he brushed his arm against hers it almost took her breath away. She felt like a school girl. *Pull yourself together, Evangeline,* she said to herself.

Joe was a rather large, muscular man and was the tallest man in the room. Joe Cross was handsome in his own way with salt and pepper hair and thick eye brows. His voice was deep and she swore the walls shook when he spoke. When he looked at her with those uncommonly blue eyes, he really made her uneasy and she didn't like it. Lorenzo was also considered tall, his thin body filled out over the years and Evangeline still thought him to be the handsomest, man with Mike following in his footsteps. Chance's boyish looks hadn't ever left him. His blonde wavy hair would never have a salt and pepper look she imagined.

Chance was very happy to see that Joe could make it to the

festivities. He made arrangements with the housekeeper to prepare a room for Joe so he could stay over for a few days.

Matt and Mark had forgotten that Evangeline's nieces were in town. When they finally arrived, their Mother scolded them for not appearing earlier in the evening. She wanted to introduce the girls to them. They were pleasantly surprised when they did finally meet them. They knew about Sicilian girls and how their fathers were so strict with them. They weren't allowed to court a young man even with a chaperone. The chaperone was reserved only for an engagement. Fixed marriages, like that of Rosalyn's, were normal for that culture. With small towns all around the Island of Sicily children grew up together or went to the only school in the town. The families knew each other and usually a match was made in their early teens.

Now that they were in America, some fathers lightened up a little, but not Antonino Como. He wasn't having any of it. He told Evangeline his daughters were virtuous and these American boys better leave them alone. Evangeline explained that Chance had given her and Mike a good life and he would be lucky to have a Winston as a son-in-law. Mariella held the same sentiments as Evangeline. She was going to get out of that apartment in the city come hell or high water and she didn't care who she had to step on to do it. Her sister Mona might have been content to sit by and let her father dictate her destiny, but not she.

One evening shortly before the visit to Evangeline's home, Antonino invited Vincenzo, his brother-in law and family over for coffee and a visit. Salvatore and Mamie Ricci still had a large family in Palermo and wanted to catch up on the news from there. They brought along their son Roberto to meet the girls.

"No way is this going to happen," Mariella complained, and behaved badly at the introduction.

"Mariella, this is my nephew Roberto," her uncle Vincenzo announced, "he has a bakery not too far from here."

"How nice for you," she said, and walked away uninterested.

"Nice to meet you," Roberto said with a grin when he realized he was talking to her back. *I don't think she is my type* he thought to himself.

Then he noticed Mona. *Wow, now she's beautiful* he thought. He motioned to his uncle that he would like to meet the other sister. Happily Vincenzo made the introductions. This time it just felt right to him. People always told him that he would know the right girl when he saw her, and he thought he'd just seen her. Mona was much more gracious and she and Roberto seemed to click right away.

FIVE

When Mariella met the Winston twins, she knew she had hit pay dirt. Good looking, American, and rich, but which one she wondered? The twins were not identical and it was easy to tell them apart. I think I will let them show me which one is the most interested in me, she decided. As a matter of fact, both boys were drawn to Mariella. Although Mona was just as pretty as Mariella, she was quiet and didn't have the outgoing personality of her sister. Soon Matt and Mark were bickering over which one of them would sit next to Mariella at dinner. Rosalyn noticed what they were doing and had the butler change the name plates around. As a punishment for arriving late to her party she placed Matt next to Mr. Mitchell and Mark next to Mrs. Mitchell. When they noticed the switch, they laughed and remembered never to cross their mother. She was the gentlest of ladies, but ruled with an iron first. All through dinner Mariella acted coy and would lower her eyes shyly when she noticed one or the other twin staring at her. *This is going to be easy,* she thought.

After the feast Rosalyn had a number of games set up for the children to play. She had a few for the adults also. Charades was a favorite of the family and Madam Sasha was going to entertain with her spiritual skills too. Matt was excellent at charades and tried to impress Mariella with his skills. The sisters found it hard to play because their English wasn't very good. Everyone tried to help them out and it made the game more enjoyable.

Matt pulled Mark aside in the middle of the game playing.

"Brother, what are you trying to do?" he said. "Can't you see that Mariella is interested in me? Stop trying to get her attention".

"What are you talking about? She has been flirting with me all night.

"I don't think so." argued Matt, "She clearly has eyes for me."
Mariella was shamelessly pitting one brother against the other, although she wasn't sure if it was working. Evangeline noticed her ploy and reprimanded her. "Don't let your father see what you are doing to those two men," she insisted.

"I'm sure I don't know what you are talking about Zia Evangeline," she pleaded; but was very happy to know that it was working.

Evangeline had her own problems that evening. Mr. Joe Cross was very attentive to her and she was sure everyone in the room could see it. If she moved to one side of the room, he happened to be on that side. If she moved to another area, he showed up there. He was ready with a cup of punch for her when hers was empty. He was getting on her nerves. Chance was busy talking to John Lee and never gave her a thought. She wondered, in a sort of day dream moment, why Joe Cross never smiled., It was sort of a grin, a self assured grin at that. Why did that seem to bother her so much? The music started to play when Mike approached her.

"Mother, may I have this dance?" he asked her
"Of course darling," she said.
The waltz was her favorite and they spun around the room until she was almost dizzy. Mike felt a tap on his shoulder and Joe asked if he could cut in. Mike bowed and stepped aside. The next thing she knew, she was in Joe's arms. The intimacy of the moment was intoxicating. She was a married woman and it was perfectly proper to dance with one of the guests. So why was this so different? She had danced with Mr. Mitchell on other occasions with no problem. Maybe it was the dreaded 'evil eye' Lorenzo gave her as she and Joe passed him on the dance floor. It was getting crowded now with all the couples dancing. Chance was spinning Alicianna in circles, and letting her step on his shoes so he could show her the dance steps. He loved that child so much. .

Larissa had been sitting next to her mother and pouting.

"What is the matter child? Aren't you having a good time?
"Yes." she sighed. But she wasn't. Not really. She got all dressed up

for Mike's benefit tonight and he barely nodded his head at her.   It took hours to get her hair just right she thought, he probably didn't even notice. Larissa felt that Mike had been ignoring her all night. He played with the children and asked his mother to dance; she barely got a hello from him. Was he mad at her because she won the race with him yesterday? Mike found Larissa sitting with her mother and asked her for a dance. She looked so grown up tonight he thought, yet just yesterday they were riding Edward's horses and she beat him in a race. Her blond hair was flying like a mad woman's as she passed him up. Tonight it was all twisted in braids and curls that fell on her shoulders. As Mike approached her, a wide smile appeared on her face. *Wow,* he thought, she is beautiful He took her hand and she felt as if she were dancing on a cloud. Rosalyn leaned over to Edward and said,

"My darling husband, your baby daughter is growing up."
He put his arm around her and sighed,

"I supposed it would happen someday, I just wish it were not today."

When the music stopped, Joe Cross thanked Evangeline for the dance and walked her back to where some of the women were sitting. Now that Lorenzo and Elsie were married and expecting a baby, Elsie didn't feel so threatened by Evangeline. She had sympathy for her knowing how Chance was disrespecting her with that woman in the city. She couldn't talk to her about it for fear of Lorenzo's temper. Elsie came over and sat next to Evangeline. Leaning over, she quietly whispered to her that she was blushing.   Evangeline was mortified. *Did the other ladies notice?* she wondered.   The butler announced that Madam Sasha had arrived and Rosalyn and Mrs. Mitchell greeted her with great excitement. The women had a large figure and wore very colorful clothing and a large hat. She seemed to be bathed in strings of multi-colored pearls, with bracelets to match.

"Oh darlings, thank you for inviting me to your home," she said in a thick Romanian accent. She looked around the room and pointed to Elsie.

" I think I have something to tell you, my dear," she announced. Elsie couldn't believe the woman could just walk in and pick her out of the crowd. *I bet she is going to tell her she is having a baby,* thought Evangeline.

"Your baby, my dear, will be a girl," she whispered when she got closer to her.

"I hope not," replied Elsie. "I'm looking forward to giving my husband a son."

"We shall see," said Madam Sasha.

"Well I didn't expect that!" Evangeline said surprised. Then Madam pointed to Mike. Evangeline froze dead in her tracks.

"This young man is going to be very important some day. Many people will look up to him, and he will have a lot of responsibilities on his shoulders. " *Thank God she didn't say something bad to scare him,* Evangeline thought.

"I don't think this is such a good idea." she complained to Rosalyn.

"Don't worry, my dear, this is all in fun, remember?" The next person Madam picked out was Joe Cross.

"This handsome man has a lot of secrets, very interesting secrets," she predicted. "He has been troubled in his past, but he has new interests. Watch out for big brown eyes." she told him, with a wink.

"Thank you for the advice," he said sarcastically.   "What is more attractive than a handsome man with secrets?" she laughed. When she came to Chance, she was very puzzled.

"I don't understand what the spirits are telling me. Stay away from bread and cakes? I don't know what that means," she said quietly.

"Maybe I should go on a diet." Chance laughed and everyone else laughed too. She went around the room and said insignificant things about everyone. She told Mr. Mitchell's son Ron, that his trip back to Savannah would be delayed for a few extra days. No one knew what that meant either. They took it all in stride and had fun with it. She then pointed to Evangeline and said, "Your heart is hardened." as she took both Evangeline's hands in hers, "Let it heal." She told Mona to start thinking about wedding gowns, Mona blushed and Mariella pouted like a child. Madam Sasha thanked everyone for their cooperation and said she had a marvelous time. She took the envelope Rosalyn offered her and put it in her purse.

"Merry Christmas everyone." she said, and left the house humming

Christmas carols.   Evangeline was a little rattled, and she was glad to see her go. She planned to talk to Rosalyn and Mrs. Mitchell very soon, about their association with such a woman.

Later in the evening the candles were lit on the Christmas tree and the gifts were handed out to everyone. The excitement of the day was more than some children could stand and they fell asleep in their mother's arms. Those who lived nearby went home and the others retired to their rooms. The men remained with their brandy and cigars to discuss the war in Europe and express their own opinions. The Americans took bets as to when the United States would join the effort. The Italians were worried about friends and family in Italy. It really put a pall on the party that year.

The next morning, the families gathered in the entry hall at Lenox Hill to ride in tandem to St. Patrick's Cathedral. Mike, Larissa, Alicianna, Andrew Lee, and the Mitchell grandchildren joined the children's choir as they had every year. Mike protested that he was getting too old for the children's choir, but he saw the disappointment in his mother's eyes and went along with the others. They sang the usual Christmas carols before mass and the worshipers were impressed as they always were. No one had breakfast yet so that they could receive the sacrament of Communion which was a must on Christmas. After church everyone dispersed to their own homes for brunch and a leisurely day.

Matt and Mark said their goodbyes to the Como girls with hopes that they would see each other soon. Antonino was glad to return to the bakery and be rid of the Americans for a while.   He appreciated the Winston's hospitality, but he was glad to be with people who spoke his language. He was happy that Roberto was going to be at his brother-in-law's Christmas party that night;he thought that Mona might take a likening to him. He was sure Roberto was interested in her; in fact Vincenzo mentioned it to Luna. Antonino was impressed that the young man had his own bakery and delivery truck in Bensonhurst. He probably didn't realize the Winston's had millions.

Evangeline and Chance drove to Long Island with Mike, Alicianna, and Joe Cross. The trip took an exceptionally long time, she thought. Chance had invited Lorenzo, Elsie, Nicolo, and Maria to stay for brunch.

When they arrived home the servants had a large spread of food ready for them. Lorenzo and Elsie, Nicolo and Maria arrived just ahead of them. Lorenzo as well as Elsie noticed the attention Joe paid Evangeline. *What is this guy trying to do he sputtered to himself. I bet he's hiding something*, he thought. *What kind of Englishman had such a thick Sicilian accent? Maybe like Franco, he had to leave Sicily in a hurry.*

At brunch Lorenzo asked Joe what his dealings with Winston Steel had to do for the war, or was it a secret?

"That Gypsy said you had secrets," he reminded him. The room got very quiet, it was a little uncomfortable.

"The world is a funny place, Mr. Rizzo," Joe replied, "it's full of lies and secrets, don't you agree?"

" Do you have any secrets, Mr. Cross?" asked Lorenzo.

"Don't all men?" he answered "She also warned me of big brown eyes," Joe said with a grin, as he glanced over at Evangeline. There was another second or two of silence when Chance broke in with a joke about President Wilson and it made everyone laugh.

The day after Christmas, most of the servants had the day off. Cook and the chauffer were the only staff at the house. Chance and Joe Cross went to the city or so Evangeline thought. She busied herself in her green house transplanting some amaryllis and other spring bulbs. The sun was shining so brightly in the glass windows that it was hard for her to see. The reflection off the white snow made it look like thousands of crystals were studding the ground. Suddenly she felt a presence in the room. She turned and saw Joe Cross standing in the door way staring at her.

"Oh, Mr. Cross, you should announce yourself. "

"I was enjoying the view Mrs. Winston."

"Didn't you go to the city with Chance this morning?" she asked.

"No, I begged off," he answered her. "Your home and properties are so peaceful I thought I could use the day off to relax. I took a walk by the pond until the snow was too high to walk through.

"You have a green thumb Mrs. Winston," he declared. She looked at her hands in disbelief. Joe laughed,

"It means you are a good gardener, that's all."

" Oh, I never heard that phrase before. After all these years I still don't know some of the funny words in the English language." She felt herself blushing again. She knew her cheeks must be red.

Evangeline had been sitting on a stool at the workbench. She got up to move to the other side of the room, but the heel of her shoe caught on the rung. She would have fallen if Joe hadn't been there to catch her. She found herself in his arms again. Their eyes met and not a word was said. He held her closer and the next thing she knew he was kissing her, or was she kissing him she couldn't tell. She didn't dare open her eyes. His lips covered hers; he couldn't believe how their lips seem to fit perfectly. Never had she been kissed like that before.

"What's happening?" she whispered.

"Don't worry Mrs. Winston, let this happen naturally," he said. It seemed funny to her that he could call her Mrs. Winston in this situation. Her head was spinning. She couldn't stop, she didn't want to stop. He was taking her blouse off as she was tugging at his shirt. The buttons were popping off and his lips moved from hers to her neck then to her breasts. *Dear God*, she prayed, *I've made love to Chance and bore him a child, but I never felt like this before.* She dropped her hands from his back to the back pockets of his trousers. She slipped her hands in his pockets and pulled him to her. That seemed to excite him and he lifted her up to him. She wrapped her legs around him,. *What kind of dream was this?* she thought, *Why can't I stop?*

He laid her down on the day sofa she used to take naps on. He ripped her stockings off and found his way to make her feel like she never had before. When they were both spent, she didn't know if she should laugh or cry.

"Who are you?" she asked when she finally found her voice.

"Your lover," he said.

"This is wrong Joe."

"Did it feel wrong my darling?" The sexual tension had been building from the first time he saw her. She knew it too.

"We better get out of here before we're found out," he said.

"Don't worry most of the servants are gone for the day and the children won't be home for hours."

She put herself together the best she could, took his hand and led him to her suite of rooms where they made love again in her comfortable bed. *I'm going to hell* she thought when Joe left her. She wished she had those same feelings for Chance. She knew her marriage was a sham. Lorenzo made Chance marry her because of a lie Elsie told. Evangeline went along with it because Mike would have security. Chance was good to her. He was good looking and smart, but she never saw sparks with Chance like she had just experienced. *What was she going to do now? This must never happen again*, she thought defiantly, but she couldn't wipe the smile off her face.

Later that evening Elsie stopped by to return some trays they borrowed for the holidays. Elsie kept looking at Evangeline.

"What do you want Elsie? Evangeline asked annoyingly, "Do I have a fly on my nose?"

"You slept with him didn't you?" she questioned.
Evangeline was horrified. "Why would you say such a thing Elsie,? You're crazy."

"No I'm not, you are positively glowing." she assured her.

"Oh my god Elsie, do you think anyone else will notice?"

"I knew it! You could cut the air with a knife around you and Joe the other night. Evangeline, I'm so happy for you," squealed Elsie.

"Don't tell Lorenzo, Elsie you know how crazy he gets. I would like for one time in my life to make my own decisions, right or wrong," Evangeline demanded.

"Where is Joe now?" Elsie asked.

"I don't know, I think he went back to New York. Chance came home a short time ago, but we didn't say much to each other." What *else was new*, thought Evangeline.

"Excuse me, Mrs. Winston," Cook interrupted. She was carrying a man's shirt in her hand.

"Yes Cook?" questioned Evangeline.

"Mr. Cross asked me to sew a few buttons on his shirt, do you know if he will be back tonight?" she asked.

"Just leave it in his room, Cook." said Evangeline with a straight face. When the cook left them, both women looked at each other and broke into a roaring laughter. It was a bonding moment for Elsie and Evangeline and it was good.

Joe hitched a ride back to New York from Chance's chauffer. He should feel terribly guilty being with Evangeline, seeing that Chance and he were friends. Somehow he wasn't, but then Joe knew about Rebecca Clay and the years of infidelity. When he first met Evangeline, he thought Chance was insane to risk his marriage for Rebecca. She couldn't meet Evangeline's qualities if she lived one hundred years. Now he couldn't imagine how Chance could leave her to go to work let alone go to another woman's bed. Evangeline was incredible: she was half innocence, half tigress. His head was hot just thinking of her.

When he arrived back at his hotel, a telegram was waiting for him. He was summoned to the steel plant in Pittsburgh to do some quality control work for a few weeks. He wanted to go to Hunters Point for Evangeline's New Year's party, but the telegram read *urgent*. The owners of the steel plant were good to him in his time of need. Through them he had gotten his new identity and he would be forever grateful. Running ammunitions for the resistance was a hanging offense and he was lucky to be alive.

Chance stayed home for the last few days between Christmas and New Year. Evangeline tried to stay out of his way most of the time. She and Aliciana did a lot of volunteer work during the day. They brought food to St. Mary's convent where the sisters dispersed it to needy families. While she was at the church, she thought about confessing her sins to the priest, but she didn't think she was ready for that yet. Evangeline brought Aliciana to the Bridge Market to buy the last minute fixings for the New Year's Eve party at Hunters Point. Then she made one last stop at Elsie's house to make sure her secret was still safe. Elsie and Evangeline had to speak in code because Aliciana was with her.

"Will your gentlemen friend be at the party," asked Elsie

"No, Chance said he had to go to Pennsylvania on business, I think," she said in a carefree way.

"Oh too bad," giggled Elsie. Evangeline spoke to her with her eyes to tell her to stop. Elsie couldn't resist. "Will he be back before spring?" she said teasingly?

"How would I know?" Evangeline answered and swatted her with the news paper. At that moment the paper unfolded to the front page "*Italy Enters War*" was the headline.

"Oh my Lord," said Evangeline. "I'm so glad Mike is here in America. I pray our families will be safe. I hope Mike doesn't get a notion to join in the fighting."

The only notion Mike had lately was Larissa. Since the Christmas Eve Party, he couldn't think of anything else. She had been with him all his life. They went to school together, they rode Edward's horses together, they played children's games together, my God, they'd skinny dipped in the pond together! When did she turn into a girl he wondered? He hadn't been to Lenox Hill all week and, unusual for her, she hadn't been to Hunters Point. *I wonder if she was cross with me, I don't think I did anything wrong,* he thought. *Maybe she was upset because of the Children's Choir before Mass; I did put up a fuss. I am going to talk to my mother about singing with the children next year. I'll nearly be seventeen! Oh well, I'm sure she will be here for New Years Eve like always. Maybe the adults will let us sip champagne instead of grape juice this year.*

Mrs. Mitchell found out what Madam Sasha meant when she predicted Ronnie's trip home would be delayed. The children were ice skating on the pond and Ron's little boy skated too far where the ice was thin and fell right through. The nanny ran to his aid and with the help of the other children pulled him to safety. It scared the life out of everyone, the children were forbidden to skate any more this winter. The Mitchell's took the boy to the hospital for a check-up; he was fine, but developed a nasty cold. Ron's wife was terribly upset.

"These northern customs of skating on frozen water are barbaric," she told her husband. "This would never happen in Georgia!" she insisted. Their trip back to Savannah was delayed for several days until he got better. When Rosalyn heard of the accident and remembered what Madam Sasha predicted she was amazed.

"Do you believe me now Evangeline,?"she asked her daughter-in-law, "I told you she has the gift."

Larissa who at the age of eight, had decided she was going to marry Mike when they grew up, had asked Evangeline if they were really related and Evangeline had told her they were not blood relatives. That was enough for her eight year old mind to take in. Mike was the love of her life and that was that. *Boys are so silly,* she thought. *Why would I always tag along with him if I didn't love him? I never liked catching frogs or baseballs.* If there was a chance to be near him she would take it. Larissa hoped Mike noticed her at Christmas Eve. Her heart sank to think Mike would be going to a boy's prep school next year. They would be done with their studies at St. Mary's and Rosalyn wanted her to go to a finishing School in Boston.

"Why so far away ?"she pleaded to her mother.

"I wouldn't send you somewhere you wouldn't be happy," Rosalyn argued. Lady Farnsworth's school for young ladies was rated at the top of the list and it wasn't easy to be accepted. The ladies had to have high scores in their studies and come from the best families in New England.

"You will be exposed to the cream of the crop, my dear. Don't you want to marry into a good family and hopefully a rich man?" *My poor mother*, thought Larissa, *she doesn't know my husband is right at her finger tips.*

Evangeline was suffering the same pangs as Larissa. Her Mike would be living at school next year. How would she separate herself from him? How lucky they were, he always made them proud. She and Chance never had to sit in Mother Superior's office listening to something he had done wrong.

Mike was a good boy, but he had Lorenzo's blood running through his veins. The boyish pranks he and his school friends played were never found out. He had a fondness for stealing fruit from the vendors at the Bridge Market. He had the money in his pocket to buy it, but he got such a kick out of stealing it. It was something he couldn't understand. Some of his school chums would go down to the East River shore near the steel plant and smoke cigars that his friend Sam stole from his father's humidor. Sometimes another boy, Dean, would bring liquor if he could sneak it out of the house. Once they went to the Little Italy neighborhood and met some fast girls who let them kiss them and touch their breasts. That's as far as it went, but Mike and his friends thought they were now real men. He knew his mother would die of embarrassment of she found out, so he had to be careful. Mike was getting excited about prep school. He would go to university the following year anyway and be away from home. He was glad to be away from Larissa and her childlike ways, at least he had felt that way until Christmas Eve.

Now he was rethinking this whole issue. He would discuss it with her at the party. Maybe he would go to university in Boston instead of New York, to be near her. This was getting complicated and he worried about the strange thoughts about Larissa that he was having; it felt strange to him.

Matt and Mark were still fussing over Mariella.
        "Why can't you see she is interested in me?" Matt exclaimed!
        "Your head is as big as a melon," said Mark.
        "Yours *looks* like a melon," retorted Matt. "I'm going to sit next to her at the party, Mark and you can't stop me."
        "Not if she pushes you off the chair to get to me," joked Mark.
        "I will get the New Year kiss from her." said Matt.
        "Not if her father has anything to say about it, brother." Markwas right. Her father's eyes would be right on the twins.
        "Why don't you ask for her hand, Mark?"
        "Hand,?"he questioned.
        "As in marriage"
        "Who said anything about marriage? Do you want to get married Matt?" Mark asked.
        "Not me," he denied, "I just want to be her boyfriend."
        "Me too," said Mark, "we are only twenty seven, too young to get married."
        "Although I bet she will have me if I asked her," said Matt.
        "You're nuts! I told you it was me she has eyes for." The argument lasted for days up to the party at Hunters Point.
        The weather was cold and windy Ice and snow mixed together made the roads dangerous, but fortunately everyone arrived at the house safe and sound. Evangeline had a spread on the table fit for a king, with treats of every kind. Many Italian deserts courtesy of Antonino and Luna

found their way to the table.

Roberto, the baker from Benson hurst, accompanied the Como family to the party. He had fallen in love with Mona and she fit perfectly in his plans for the future. He asked Antonino if he could see Mona, under the supervision of her family, of course. Antonino approached Mona with the news and she happily agreed. It was a done deal and the wheels began turning for Mona's wedding. Mariella was not only shocked, but disgusted. How could she jump at the first guy to ask her?

"What's your hurry, Mona?" asked Mariella. "You are so pretty and sweet. Lots of men will ask for you I am sure," Mariella tried to argue.

"I don't know, Mama told me he is a good catch; he has his own bakery and a delivery truck. Papa probably won't have that much for years. He seems to like me and I think he is very nice. I want a home and a family, Mariella," she cried.

"Roberto said he wants that too. Between the two of us we can make the bakery grow and have what they call the *American Dream*.".

"Sounds more like a nightmare, "Mona would be a slave to the bakery and a baby machine for Roberto. "What about the education our father gave us? Shouldn't we do more with it?"

"You are the smart one," Mona exclaimed, "you do something special with it. I am going to marry Roberto." Mariella wanted a rich husband it was true, but her sister's words were ringing in her ears. She was right. I amgoing to make something special with the gift of my education, I'll think about it after the New Year; and start the year like an American. Mona is Papa's favorite anyway, let him walk her down the aisle first.

The Comos and Winstons arrived at Hunters point about the same time. Elsie and Lorenzo arrived early to help Evangeline with the last minute preparations. Maria and Nicolo had food baskets to deliver to the needy. The Ladies society at St. Mary's Church made them from donations that local merchants and the congregation collected for the month of December. Nicolo, who now had a little truck that he used at the repair shop, filled it to the brim with the baskets. Maria told Evangeline to start the party without them because they had a big job to do. Evangeline worried about the weather, but Nicolo was an excellent driver and all the deliveries were local.

"Good evening Miss Como." Mark greeted Mariella, "You look lovely tonight".

"Thank you, Mr. Winston," she said coyly.

Mona introduced Roberto to Mark and they seemed to get along right away. Roberto had a pleasing way about him and people were naturally drawn to him. Matt was a little put out when his brother spoke to Mariella first. He was calculating his next move. He decided to keep Antonino close to him, make him his friend and then Mariella would fall in line.

"Mr. Como," he said, "how is the bakery business these days?" Matt had some training in economics and he felt he knew the right questions to ask.

"Oh, so much work," complained Antonino, "we are working six days a week. In Sicily we took a couple of hours to rest in the afternoon, here we work straight through. Sometimes ten or twelve hours a day, it's very much uncivilized here in America."

"Yes. I know what you mean." sympathized Matt, "The steel business is booming too. I also work many hours," he lied, "for my brother Chance. Well, that's the American way, Mr. Como. If we work hard, we will reap the benefits my dad always said."

"Yes, I agree, Matteo, have you seen my daughter Mariella?"

"No, I haven't spoken to her yet sir," Matt said with a smile.

"Mariella," her father called, "Matteo wants to say hello." Mark just stood there with his mouth open. *He got me again, but the night isn't over yet,* Mark said to himself.

The party goers were having a wonderful time. Maria and Nicolo finally arrived, feeling very good about the help they gave the poor. They had been very fortunate to have a good life in America and it was the least they could do to help those who needed it.

The stories about Sicily and Georgio and Alicianna Como made Evangeline very homesick. She was glad to have her only sibling in America with her. Mike was listening to the stories about the old country and he became very interested.

"Mother why haven't you told me anything about Sicily?" he asked.

"Some things were very painful for me to remember," she answered.

"Payou don't talk about it either," he commented to Lorenzo.

"I remember the first time I asked your mother for a dance," he smiled. "It was at the festa for the Blessed Mother. Neither one of us knew how to dance. We must have looked very funny because my friends were laughing themselves silly" Lorenzo remembered.

Evangeline defended herself by saying, "I don't remember any of those clowns asking a girl to dance. You were very brave Lorenzo, and I was very shy." The memory of that night made Evangeline melancholy. She couldn't believe she was defending Lorenzo and neither could he.

"There really isn't anyone left in Santa Fata for me to remember," she told Mike. "Nino and Paolo, Ziu Antonino's sons, are in Palermo, so I guess they would be the only other family we have."

"I have two sisters in Palermo also, Angelina and Caterina, they are older than Zia Maria and I. Zia Maria keeps in touch with them," Lorenzo told him. "My parents died several years ago, do you remember, Mike?"

"Yes Pa I do," he said.

"You know what I remember?" Lorenzo said, "The lemon trees. Franco and I used to steal the lemons from Ziu Emanuele's tree, boy, would he get mad at us. He never told our fathers though; he was a very good man." Mike got the biggest smile when he heard his father liked to steal lemons. *That must be where I get it from*, he chuckled to himself.

"Someday, I am going to go back to Sicily, I think I would like to put flowers on my mother Felicia's grave and my nonnu's and nonna's too,

"he said. Evangeline and Lorenzo had tears in their eyes thinking what a wonderful son they had. La Bedda Sicilia was just a dream to them now, but maybe someday Mike would get to experience the beauty of it.

Chance asked his brothers to join him in the study. He wanted to know if they were happy with their jobs. He said 1915 was going to be a great year for Winston Steel. Matt spoke up,

"Chance you know Mark and I have our hearts in the military. We can enlist with any allied navy and have officer status.

Mark then said, "We know Dad is getting older and he doesn't have much to do at the office any more. His health is less than good and Mother is very worried about him," he added.

"I wish both of you would stay on with the company," said Chance.

"I have a lot of business coming from the governments of Europe. I would like to put the two of you on that task."

"Would it mean that we would do business overseas?" asked Mark

"Yes, with the war going on I would like to do as much business there before the U.S. gets into the fray. The ports are still open to us and I would like to take advantage of that. Joe Cross will be my partner here in the states especially in Pittsburgh."

"Chance, you have always watched out for our best interest. You have been the best big brother two guys could ever have," said Matt. "If you think we should go to Europe for the company then I'm in."

"I feel the same way," echoed Mark.

"Keep this under wraps for a while," he suggested, "Mother is not going to be happy about this."

"Excuse me gentlemen," Evangeline interrupted, "we have a party going on out here. Would you like to join us?" she asked.

"I'm sorry, my dear, we will be right in," said Chance.

SIX

The idea of working in Europe intrigued the twins. They knew a war was in progress and it wasn't going to be a holiday. They were bursting to tell someone, but they promised Chance to keep it quiet. The party went on into the night. At the stroke of midnight, they all wished each other a Happy New Year. Mariella got kissed on the cheek by both brothers without her dad catching them. Elsie and Lorenzo toasted the coming year to their new baby. Larissa and Mike promised to stay close even though they would be far away in different schools next year. Rosalyn and Edward hoped for the best for their children and renewed their love for each other. Chance and Evangeline toasted to 1915 while holding a sleeping Alicianna in their arms.

The first Monday of the New Year, Mariella Como, boarded a bus that took her downtown to see what kind of job she would be skilled at. The tall buildings were terrifying to her. The directions she had gotten from one of the girls at the bakery made it easy to find. Her determination was all she needed; she would run through a jungle to get away from that bakery. When she arrived at the employment office a nice lady gave her a test to take to see what she was capable of doing.

As it turned out, she was skilled to be an interpreter. She was, of course, fluent in Italian and she just made the scale for her English. The department of defense was looking for people to interpret documents from foreign countries and Italy was one of them.
"Take this letter to the fifth floor and give it to the receptionist at the desk. She will call your name when they are ready to see you. Good luck Mariella," the lady said to her as she handed her the folder with her test and

her application in it. She also brought along her diploma from the University of Palermo and her papers to enter the United States. "Thank you, very much," she replied and headed for the elevator.

Mariella handed her folder to the pretty blond girl who was sitting at the desk on the fifth floor. She waited for what seemed like hours for her interview. There were several newspapers and some magazines on a table and she flipped through without really paying attention to the articles. She was so nervous that she really didn't know what she was looking at. Soon she heard her name called, and was escorted into the most beautiful office she had ever seen. It had fine wood paneling and a desk big enough for six workers. Beautiful draperies her mother would envy and portraits of older men on the walls.

"Hello, Miss Como," the man behind the desk said.

"Hello," she replied. There was another man and a lady sitting on two wing chairs alongside the desk, they both nodded in unison and smiled.

"Please sit down and let's talk about the job we would like you to take," the man at the desk said. *They want me to take the job*, she thought, the excitement was growing in her chest. *Look smart Mariella*, she said to herself, *these people don't know you are ready to kiss them.* She got the job after she concluded the interview with the people at the defense department. They were very impressed with her and her credentials. *See*, she thought, *my education was worth something. No hot bakery for me, what a relief!*

Her employment was to start on the following Monday and she had a lot of shopping to do. She asked her Zia Evangeline to help her pick out clothes suitable for such a position. Rosalyn, of course, went along, her taste was always impeccable.

"What did your father say when you told him you got a job in the city?" asked Evangeline

"Smoke was coming out of his ears," she told her aunt.

"I thought so," said Evangeline.

"You know Sicilian men and their daughters; they don't think you have a brain in your head. They have to do all your thinking for you. It makes me so angry," Evangeline cried.

"Why bother to send you to school? You should stay home and make lace hankies! Or get married to a baker and make babies," chimed in Mariella.

"That was cruel, Mariella, but I understand what you mean. I had to learn about life the hard way, after being sheltered , my father died and I had to fend for myself and Mike," Evangeline told her. "How did he calm down and allow you to take the job?"Evangeline asked.

"My mother, bless her heart, convinced him. Then I have to give my future brother-in-law credit too, he talked to Papa and told him in America it was good for a young girl to get a job and a job with the government meant a lot of benefits. I don't care about the benefits; I just don't want to be stuck in that bakery. Do you believe I overheard him talking to my Ziu Vincenzo, he was bragging that his daughter had a "government job". "

"That's funny Mariella, *now* he's an American, "Evangeline laughed.

The ladies went from shop to shop buying the perfect outfits for Mariella. Evangeline picked up the bill for everything.

"Zia, how can I ever thank you for your generosity?", cried Mariella.

"Thank you my darling, for allowing me to be part of this. Next time it will be Mona who will go shopping with us for her trousseau. "

"Mariella," she asked, "how do you feel about the woman's right to vote?"

"I don't know Zia, I never thought about it," Mariella confessed. Evangeline spent the next hour telling her all about her heroes.

Evangeline decided that since Mike and Larissa were graduating from St. Mary's, they needed to have their portraits taken. She went one step further and got the entire family in one room for a portrait. She heard at one of her suffragette meetings that a new photographer had just opened his studio on East 11th Street. Actually it was a photography school and his style of photography was new and exciting. His subjects were not just sitting in rows with no expression on their faces, they were almost animated. His name was Clearance H. Winter and his assistant was Maxim West. Mr. Winter agreed to come to the mansion to do his work. His assistant, a nervous little man, was running around the house to find the right room with the exact lighting. The portrait was to hold nine subjects so a sizeable room was necessary. The twins were being their mischievous selves and messing up the shot.

"Mark," his mother pleaded "stop fidgeting."
"I can't help it, Mother, this shirt is too tight."
"Just put up with it for a few more minutes," she begged.
"I think I should stand on the other side.," Matt decided. "Just stay where Mr. West placed you," Evangeline reprimanded. Larissa and Mike got in the action by crossing their eyes or sticking out their tongues. They were giving Mr. West a fit of anxiety. Aliciann whispered something in her mother's ear and they had to be excused for a few minutes.

"I can't do this Mrs. Winston," complained Mr. West. "These children are horrible!"

Finally Chance had to put a stop to the nonsense and the most beautiful portrait was taken. Edward and Rosalyn were, of course, the centerpiece of the picture. Rosalyn held his hand in hers as they were seated in her favorite baroque chairs. Evangeline and Chance were on their left with Aliciann in front of them holding a porcelain doll. Chance had his arm around Evangeline and she was holding her daughter's hand. The twins were on their right reading out of the same book. Larissa was next to them with her arms slightly extended looking at a long steamed rose. Mike was on the other end holding a football. Mr. Winter was so proud of his work that he asked Evangeline if he could display it in the 11th street studio. He wanted his students to study the lighting and the position of the subjects. She was delighted and agreed. Mr. West on the other hand, decided never to return to Lenox Hill without a whip and a chair.

Mike was happy to be in long pants and not the knickers his mother preferred. Larissa felt the same way about her shoes; she wore high heels with a little strap across the top. Her mother wanted her to wear the lace up kind that proper young ladies wore. She was going to wear the high heels at her coming out party in May anyway so she might as well break them in now. When the portrait was returned to them a beautiful gold frame surrounded it and it was hung in the drawing room at Lenox Hill. The people who saw it were very impressed and Mr. Winter got a lot of business because of it. The graduation pictures of Larissa and Mike were just as nice. Evangeline hired him to take Mona and Roberto's wedding pictures. It would be her special gift to them.

One day while walking down 11th Street looking at the store front windows Rebecca Clay came upon the Winter studio. There in the window she saw Chance with his arm around a woman and an entire family around two older people in the center of the portrait. *So that's what the happy little Winston family looks like. I haven't seen them in years,* she thought. How fake the smile on Chance's face looked to her. She couldn't stand to look at it and walked across the street so she could avoid it on her way home. A deep, burning jealousy stirred inside her and she didn't like the feeling.

Joe Cross returned to New York the second week of January. He was dying to see Evangeline again. He didn't want to sound too anxious to Chance, but he wanted an invitation to Hunters Point. Joe called Chance and told him he had the papers from Pittsburgh ready to sign.

"My father isn't feeling very well and he doesn't come into the office very often," Chance told him. I would like him to look the papers over before signing them," he said. "Do you mind driving over to Hunters Point this evening? My parents will be there for dinner, you are welcome to join us." Joe couldn't believe his luck.

"Do you think Evangeline will mind?"

"You of all people should know an Italian woman isn't happy unless she is feeding the multitudes," he laughed.

"Okay, I accept," said Joe.

"Good," Chance said, "we will see you around seven."

Joe hung up the phone he had not seen Chance since the affair with his wife. *Will it show on my face he feared?* All he could think about was Evangeline. It was a miracle that any work got done in Pittsburgh at all. If he closed his eyes, he could see the shape of her neck. *Oh, how he loved to kiss that neck. He could still feel his hands on her waist and hips.* Joe dreamed of the way he pulled her close on top of him. *I'm going to go crazy if I don't see her again,* he thought. Joe stopped at the Italian bakery in the Bridge Market. He bought five pounds of mixed Italian cookies so he wouldn't arrive there empty handed. He wasn't sure how much to buy, but five pounds sounded like an acceptable number. Aliciana had her dinner early and was sent to bed to nurse a cold. Mike was helping Lorenzo at the repair shop on Long Island and would be spending the night with them. Rosalyn and Edward were the only other guests that evening.

Chance announced as he was washing up for dinner, "I forgot to tell you Evangeline, Joe Cross will be joining us this evening. We have some papers to go over with my father, is that all right with you?" Evangeline felt a heat flush over her.

"Well my dear, it's a little late, even if I did object."

"I'm sorry I was busy all day and didn't get a chance to call you," he answered her.

He was busy all right, busy with Rebecca. He went to the brownstone at lunch time and spent the rest of the day with her. Rebecca seemed a little distracted, he thought.

"Are you feeling all right, Rebecca?" he asked her.

"Yes, I'm fine, Chance. I just have a lot on my mind these days." She didn't want to tell him she saw the picture of his family in the photographer's window. "You know I have been entertaining that Austrian delegation all week for my parents."

Rebecca's parents had been ambassadors to Austria for the last ten years and had lived in that country since then. They asked Rebecca to show the delegates the sights of New York as a good will gesture. They seem to have a good time where ever I take them, she would brag to her friends. Count Richard was showing a lot of attention to Rebecca. He was buying her lavish gifts and jewelry. He paid the bill at all the restaurants for the entire group all week. He was throwing money around like crazy to impress Rebecca. He thought she was wonderful and let her know it. She felt like she was out in the sunlight with Richard and not back streeted like she had lived all those years with Chance.

Evangeline was getting excited. She knew she would see Joe again, but hadn't expected it to be this soon. She took some extra time with her hair and picked out her prettiest dress.

"You look exceptionally beautiful tonight, is that a new dress?" asked Chance.

"Yes, your mother picked it out, I thought I would wear it for her pleasure," she lied.

"My mother has such good taste," he winked at her. She followed him out of the room and met up with Rosalyn and Edward in the drawing room. Chance had the housekeeper prepare a room for Joe, thinking their work would last into the night. Finally, Joe was announced by the butler. He walked in with his portfolio of papers under one arm and the cookies under the other.

"Good evening," Joe said, he kissed Rosalyn's hand and handed the cookies to Evangeline. He couldn't look her in the eyes. All the cool finesse he always appeared to possess disappeared just by looking at her.

"Mr. Cross did you rob the bakery?" she teased. "You are most generous.". All he could do was grin. He extended his hand to Edward and Chance,

"I hope you are feeling better this evening Mr. Winston."

"My family makes too much of my infirmity, Joe," he answered.

"I think you are looking well," Joe remarked.

The butler announced dinner was ready. They had their meal in the breakfast room which was a more intimate setting since there were only five of them. After dinner, the men went into the study to look over the papers. The ladies had their coffee and some of the cookies Joe brought.

"I'm glad I talked you into buying that dress, Evangeline," Rosalyn said," it looks lovely on you."

"I'm happy with it too," replied Evangeline. She thought it was extremely expensive, but she didn't feel guilty about buying things for herself anymore. The allowance she sent the nuns in Santa Fara to help the poor made her feel better about luxuries.

Chance broke their conversation. " Mother, Father is tired and would like to go home. I'll take you both now if that's all right? Evangeline, I talked Joe into staying the night, we have business to discuss when I return. Keep him company would you? I'll be back within the hour." The look on her face was of surprise and she didn't answer Chance right away.

"You don't mind, do you Evangeline? he asked again?

"Yes, yes, Chance, I'm sorry. I'll be happy to keep him company."

After Rosalyn, Chance, and Edward left, Joe boyishly walked in to the breakfast room.

"I hope I'm not disturbing you, Mrs. Winston," he said. He was grinning from ear to ear.

"Stop the Mrs. Winston business, Joe," she retorted. She was as happy to see him as he was to see her. She picked up the tray of cookies and took it to the kitchen. Cook had cleaned the kitchen and retired for the night. Evangeline was busying herself by putting the cookies in a box. Joe walked up behind her and put his hands around her small waist. He started to nibble at her neck and it was driving her insane. Suddenly she turned around and kissed him with all the force she had. He wanted to devour her.

"Evangeline, I am so in love with you," he said when they finally parted, "what are we going to do?"

"A sensible head would say we never see each other like this again," she cried.

"You know that can't happen," he said. He kissed her again and unbuttoned her dress. His lips started at hers and worked his way to her ears and neck, he knew that drove her crazy.

"No Joe, It's not fair," she insisted. "We can't do this here, Chance will be home soon and I don't want to make a scene." She buttoned her dress and kissed him one last time.

"I'm going to my room now Joe, please help yourself to some brandy or whatever you like to drink."

"Evangeline, tell me the truth, are you in love with Chance?" Joe asked.

"He's my husband, and the father of my daughter, but he has never been the love of my life." Joe breathed a sigh of relief. What would he have done if she said yes? "I'm not supposed to know, but he has had a mistress ever since we were married," she said with her eyes looking down at the floor. "I'm not a very good lover and he had to look elsewhere."

"You may be many things Evangeline, but a bad lover is not one of them. You are patient, kind, giving and even somewhat of a tigress," he laughed at her. "Don't demean yourself like that again. What Chance does is because of his own shortcomings." Evangeline left the kitchen, walked up the gilded staircase to her room. She undressed and got into her night clothes. How unnerving it was to undress knowing Joe was in the house. She crawled under the covers but didn't sleep; she had a lot to think about.

When Chance returned, he found Joe in the billiards room shooting pool. "Evangeline had a head ache," Joe told Chance. "She went to her room. She apologized but I told her I would be alright here." The two men went into the study and continued on with their business. Chance had no idea what was going on under his nose.

Chance didn't sleep well that night either. He was too excited about the fortune he and Joe were going to make with the new deal in Pittsburgh. Chance slipped a note under Joe's door telling him to meet him at the office later that afternoon.

Joe shared in their insomnia. Knowing that Evangeline was several rooms down the hall made him toss and turn throughout the night. That morning, Joe saw Chance drive down the long driveway headed to New York. Joe knocked ever so lightly on Evangeline's door. He opened it and stood by her bed. He slipped under the covers and he heard her say "Why did you make me wait so long my love"?

When Chance returned to his office that day, he found an envelope on his desk. It was addressed to him in Rebecca's handwriting. *How odd*, he thought, if she had something to tell him why didn't she just call on the phone? He opened the envelope and found a letter.

My dearest Chance,

I am writing this letter with tears in my eyes, but I must be realistic with my life. We have been seeing each other for many years now and it must end. I suppose I always knew it was impossible for you to leave Evangeline, but I always hoped you would.

As you know, I have been seeing Count Richard of Austria. He has asked me to marry him and I have accepted. We will be returning to Austria to live as soon as the war is over. This came as much of a surprise to me as I am sure this is to you.

Chance we have known each other since we were children. Now that we are adults we have to behave that way. You have had your family Chance, but I have had you. My love, I need more. I wish you all the luck in the world I hope you wish the same for me.

With a mountain of memories,

Rebecca

P.S. Please don't try to
   Contact me.

He couldn't believe his eyes, Count Richard of Austria? I knew she was entertaining those foreigners to help her father, but I really thought it was more of a babysitting situation, he mused. How *could I have been so ignorant*? he wondered.

Chance called his friend John Lee. "I need to see you right away, do you have time for me sometime today?" Chance begged.

"Come by at noon, I'll send for some lunch and we can talk" John agreed. Chance was there at twelve o'clock on the button.

"What on earth has you so upset, my friend?" said John.

"It's Rebecca, John, she is getting married." John tried not to laugh at Chance because he could see how troubled he was. John had been a popular New York lawyer, for the past ten years or so, his reputation was widely respected.

"Is this a legal matter, Chance?" John inquired.

"How could it possibly be, John, I never gave her anything but me. I just need you to hear me out, my friend." Then he gave John the letter.

"Chance, you know I never agreed with your affair. Evangeline is a wonderful woman, I never understood why you bothered with Rebecca."

"You really don't know how our marriage exists, John, she doesn't like to make love. Rebecca does," Chance explained.

"Excuse me, Sir, that's more information than I need to know!"John exclaimed. "Listen Chance, go home to your wife, be thankful she hasn't called you out on your infidelity. Let Rebecca go on with her life, she deserves a husband who loves her. She gave up her youth for you, Chance," John tried to reason with him. "Go home my friend, go home." John patted Chance on the back and walked him to the door. Chance wandered around Central Park for several hours trying to make his head ache go away. *I have been lucky enough to have my cake and eat it too*, he thought. I guess my luck just ran out. With that in mind, he went directly to the men's club and got drunk.

Spring 1915 was a happy time for Larissa Winston. She had just turned sweet 16 and her coming out party at the Waldorf Astoria Hotel was going to be fabulous. New England's wealthy brought their 16 year old daughters into the social scene at this time. The all white affair was a sight to see. The young beauties wore white ball gowns and the girls chose a partner to dance the waltz around the room. Larissa had taken dance lessons for the past year as had all the girls coming out that evening. Larissa, of course, wanted Mike to be her partner. He thought it was a silly time wasting thing to do. He couldn't understand why Rosalyn would want to put her daughter on display as if she were for sale. He didn't like the idea of people sizing her up for future daughter-in-law possibilities. Mike told his mother how he felt about it.

"Mother, I've decided not to dance with Larissa at the coming out ball."

"Mike," she warned, "you are going to disappoint her so much." Evangeline was looking forward to seeing Mike in White Tie and Tails herself. How beautiful they would look dancing with her ball gown swirling around them.

"It's ridiculous," he insisted, as he brought her out of the little dream she was having. "I'm not getting involved in that nonsense," he exclaimed. "Besides I have no interest in that monkey suit either." Evangeline looked at Mike with a pensive expression on her face. *Oh my, he does have Sicilian blood in his veins after all. Sicilian men don't want their women put on display for anyone to see.* When Mike told Larissa he was having no part in that folly, they had their first serious fight. Mike fully expected Larissa to be disappointed and then forget about the whole thing. To his surprise, Larissa told him to stay home or go smoke cigars with his creepy friends, she didn't care. He wasn't going to ruin her 16th party. She would simply ask someone else. He couldn't believe his ears.

"Come on Larissa, I'll race you with your dad's white mare, forget about this darn dance!"

"No Mike, this is my life and I'm going to do what I want," she declared.

"I think you have been listening to my mother too much and those crazy suffragettes," he argued. Mike went home in bewilderment., *Let them dress her up like some kind of china doll, and put her on the auction block,* he ranted all the way home. Boy she's mad, he thought.

Yes, she was mad at him, so much so, she asked Alan Mason to dance and he gladly accepted. He'd had his eye on Larissa for a long time, but Mike Winston was always in the way. Christmas Eve had faded in Mike's mind. He no longer remembered the beautiful young lady she had become. He wasn't going to school in Boston either. Mike had a selfish streak in him and it was strengthened by the women who loved him, he always got his way with them. He was too charming for his own good. He was now thinking about his future in politics and there wasn't any room there for Larissa. He and his buddies had big plans and that was going to be his objective.

When the day of the ball came, Rosalyn and the twins had a hard time getting Edward to the hotel. He was having trouble breathing and walking. Edward refused to stay home and a wheel chair was ordered to transport him easier. Edward was so proud of his little girl. She was so beautiful in her white gown. Rosalyn had it imported from France and she felt lucky to get it while the chance of getting items from Europe was still available. Edward told her to spare no expense, he wanted Larissa to look her best. He wished he would be able to see her in her wedding gown one day, but he doubted it.

There were a dozen young ladies coming out this year. The master of ceremonies called them and their dance partners out on to the floor by name. When they called Larissa Winston and Alan Mason, the twins were in shock. Where's Mike, they wondered? Evangeline told them he'd stayed home as he was suffering from Sicilian maleness. They didn't understand, but shrugged their shoulders in unison. Mike and Larissa were inseparable, they thought. It seemed natural for Mike to dance at the ball with Larissa.

Chance had the first dance with his sister after the initial waltz with Alan Mason. He told her how proud he was of her and that she was his first love.

"Larissa, when you were born," he told her, "I thought you were the most perfect child I had ever seen. I love you dearly," he confessed with tears in his eyes. Chance had been a little melancholy lately. No one knew why, but every one noticed it. The twins each had their chance with Larissa on the dance floor.

"Hey, punkin'," Matt always called her that, "what have you done with my sister? You are gorgeous," he said. "I'm going to have to have a talk with that Alan Mason and set him straight," he said.

"Don't be silly," Larissa laughed. Mark didn't have much to say, he, too, was very emotional about his baby sister growing into a woman so soon. After the music stopped, he gave her the biggest hug he had ever given her.

"I love you, sissy," he told her.

"Are you crying, Mark?" she asked.

"No I have something in my eye," he insisted. Edward was next. Chance set Larissa on his lap and pushed the wheel chair around the floor, her dress was so large it covered the wheels. Larissa wrapped her arms around Edward's neck and thanked him for the wonderful opportunity of this night. You are the best daddy in the world, she told him. The Mason's were sitting at another table with Mr. and Mrs. Brown and the Norton's. Mr. Brown was president of the People's Bank of New England. Their son Bradley was dancing with Abigail Norton that year. Mrs. Mason was beaming at the beautiful couple Larissa and Alan made. She told the ladies at the table that Alan had eyes for Larissa and she wished something permanent would come of it. Mrs. Norton knew Larissa had a mad crush on Mike Winston, but didn't want to burst the lady's bubble.

"I'm so happy Edward Winston felt well enough to be here this evening," she said, "the child adores her father so much." Evangeline and Rosalyn were standing on the sidelines with their hankies in their hand. They both knew this would be the last time Larissa would dance with her daddy.

They were right. Edward passed away later that month in his bed. The diagnosis was Congestive Heart Failure. The family was devastated, Rosalyn and Larissa were inconsolable. Chance knew his father had been very ill, but he wasn't ready to part with him yet. Edward wasn't his biological father, but he never made a distinction between him and the twins.

Rosalyn took to her bed and stayed there for days after the funeral. To add insult to injury, her twin sons were leaving for England soon. They tried to postpone the trip, but the day soon came when they had to leave. Chance had to make sure his brothers were still willing to go to Europe. Sailing had become a liability and one taken at great risk.

"I hate to send you on the voyage especially at mother's time of need," Chance told his brothers. Rosalyn was convinced that Germany was provoking the U.S. and wanted them to stop their aggression. She thought if the boys could help the effort by working in London for the company instead of actual combat she could go along with it. Chance explained that many more secret shipments would be made. The brothers had to be in London when the ships arrived to retrieve the contraband.

Lorenzo took Edward's death very hard. He spent more time with Edward than anyone. He was his driver, took care of his horses, and fixed everything that broke down. He respected Edward more than any other man, he was his friend and he loved him.

"Renzo," -he was the only one who called him Renzo-, "you have good hands for handyman work," he would say. "Your fingers are long and easily able to work in small places. Where would we be in this country without a handyman?"

When Rosalyn had forbidden him to drink his beloved brandy, Lorenzo always had a stash for him in the stable. What could a little drink hurt once in a while? Edward encouraged Lorenzo to get started in the repair shops. He thought of him as a visionary, and he was proud of his friend.

Evangeline had seen death in the worst of circumstances. The epidemic in Sicily was a nightmare. Edward's death was somewhat quiet and serene. He had been sick for such a long time, but neither complained nor caused anyone to be put out of their way. He was a gentleman to the very last day and he loved his family more than all the riches he acquired. His wife and children were gathered at his bed side and they each had a turn expressing their love to him. He passed quietly in his sleep and it gave Rosalyn peace to know he wasn't in pain. Evangeline felt lucky to have a man such as Edward in her life. She wanted to do something to keep his memory alive so she set up the Edward P. Winston scholarship for gifted children who couldn't afford to go to university. She met with her lawyers and had all the paper work done before the funeral. Evangeline was also glad she had the family portrait commissioned when she did, as it was Edward's last.

The funeral was one of the largest in New York City in a long time. He was entombed in the family crypt in a cemetery on the Upper East Side. The weather was the only thing that didn't cooperate that day. It rained buckets that morning and black umbrellas were everywhere.

"Look Mama," Aliciana cried, "the angels are crying along with us today for my Grandpa."

"No darling," Evangeline corrected her, "the angels are celebrating today. "

"Why Mama?" Aliciana didn't understand.

"The angels have Grandpa with them now and they are so happy."

"Yes, he is with the angels," she agreed strangely feeling better about her loss,

The reading of the will went as expected. Rosalyn inherited all his holdings and properties. The children who had been already collecting their monthly allowance continued to do so. The boys were employed by the company and Larissa had her funds invested in a trust to secure her future. The family lawyer continued reading the will: to *my loyal friend, Lorenzo Rizzo, I bequest my gold watch and fifty thousand dollars. Renzo,* he said, as if he were still alive, *you have been a joy for me to have in my employ. We had some good times together. I thank you for them and the stash of brandy.*
Lorenzo looked at Rosalyn out of the corner of his eye. She just sat there rocking in her chair, with a slight smile on her face. *We had some great road trips too* he continued, *with our Tin Lizzie, remember when we got her past 40 miles an hour?*

"Lorenzo!" Rosalyn scolded! He just shrugged his shoulders, looking at the weave in the rug. Maria and Nicolo also inherited fifty thousand dollars and cried like babies.
Then:
To my good friend Nicolo Romano you have been a God send to our family during my years of illness. You took over for me many times when I couldn't do for myself. Maria Romano you are like a sister to my beloved wife Rosalyn, I want you to know how much I appreciate it. The cook and butler also received a lump sum amount and a pension since they were getting up in years. Everyone had tears in their eyes hearing Edward's words through the lawyer. They all knew what a truly special man he was.

SEVEN

Now with Edward gone and the boys off to England the house seemed like a mausoleum to Rosalyn. Larissa would be attending finishing school in Boston this fall, despite her protests.

"Mother, please don't make me go," Larissa cried. "You will be here alone and that's just not right."

"Don't worry dear, I plan to stay with Chance and Evangeline several times during the week, they will keep me busy. I also plan to take up my watercolor painting again. I was quite good at it you know. Your father was the love of my life, Larissa. He was incredibly generous with everything he had. He married me and took Chance as his own. I have my memories and they were all good. I'll be fine," she insisted. *"Pensa La Salute,* as Evangeline always says, think of your blessings, it's good advice."

The Como's paid a visit to Chance and Evangeline a few days after the funeral. It was protocol for Sicilians to make a visit or visita to the grieving family to show their love and support. It was also a sign of respect. Sicilians held fast to the idea of respect. Respect to your parents was of the utmost, respect to your family name, respect to your church and of course respect to yourself. The Como's brought along boxes of cookies and other Italian pastries on their visita.

Evangeline had almost forgotten the ritual: living among the Americans she had not used the custom here. In fact she didn't know many people who had died that were that close to the family. Elsie told her that when people died it was usually the women from their church and neighbors who brought food to the grieving family. People like the Mitchells and the

Winston's had a staff of cooks and maids to take care of their needs, so it usually wasn't done. Evangeline was grateful for the show of respect her family paid her and Chance. She was especially grateful that she had them nearby.

Shortly after Edward passed away, Aliciana made her First Holy Communion. It was the first event without him. All the families came to the church in support of her receiving the sacrament. The sun was shining that May morning at St. Mary's on Long Island. There were twenty children receiving communion for the first time that day; ten girls and ten boys. Each girl wore a white dress and veil. They carried a rosary and a small prayer book. Their little hands were covered with white gloves and they held their hands together with their fingers pointed to heaven. The boys had white suits with a ribbon attached to the pocket. Their white shirts and neck ties were perfectly pressed. The nuns saw to it that each and every child looked angelic and ready to receive the Host. They made sure no one ate one morsel of food after midnight the night before. The children had to recite several prayers to them before they were even allowed to participate in the rite. When the organ began to play, the twenty little ones walked proudly down the center aisle until they arrived at their assigned seats.

Evangeline always cried at this time, it reminded her of the procession of the Blessed Mother in Santa Fara when the children wore their First Communion clothes and walked in front of the statue. She remembered when she was one of the little children who took part in that procession. Her thoughts were with her mother, father and Felicia; her thoughts were also with Joe.

She wrestled with the fact that she should not receive communion that day. If she didn't, everyone would want to know why, especially Chance. She hadn't confessed her sin of adultery to the priest yet, but then she would have to promise not to sin again. That was one promise she couldn't keep. She decided to pray the Act of Contrition and hope God would forgive her one mortal sin. She was glad she had the black veil to cover her face. Rosalyn and Evangeline were both dressed in their black mourning dresses with veils. Rosalyn hated black, it reminded her too much of Lord

Hennessey, and she wasn't sure she was going to keep it on for the entire year. She already told Evangeline not to wear black, but she wanted to honor Edward and said she would wear it until Mona and Roberto's wedding that summer. They only wore all black in public anyway. Edward wouldn't want us looking like this as he always said it reminded him of witches. I know it's not going to bring him back Rosalyn would say, so what's the use.

The sharp contrast between Alicianna's beautiful white lace dress and the mourning dresses were stunning to Mike. His sisters white dress reminded him of the way he disappointed Larissa on her coming out ball.

"I'm sorry," he said to her at the church. "I should have been your dance partner at the ball."

"You know Mike, when my father died I realized how unimportant that ball really was. It's the people in your life that are important. My brothers are going to Europe soon and I am going to Boston. I am afraid I'm going to miss everyone so much, it makes me very emotional to think about it."

"Does that mean that you forgive me? he asked.

"Yes, of course, I forgive you, "as she kissed him on the cheek. "Besides, Alan Mason is a great dancer," she teased.

"What?"he said, as he pulled on her blond curls? They were acting like the children they used to be, each knowing that this might be the last time.

The excitement for the upcoming wedding of Evangeline's niece was all Alicianna could think about. She was going to be the flower girl and sprinkle rose petals on the white runner before the bride walked down the aisle.

"Mama," she asked Evangeline, "what color dress am I going to wear to Mona's wedding?"

"You are going to be in pink dotted Swiss like the other bridesmaids," her mother said. "Just like the big girls?" she asked with surprise.

"Yes dear," Evangeline smiled, as she watched her daughter dance around the room with joy.

"I'm a big girl now too," she squealed.

"Do you want to go shopping with Zia Luna, Mona and Mariella today?" she asked Alicianna.

"Yes please, I would love to go too," she said happily.

That afternoon the ladies met at the corner of Times Square and Fifth Avenue. Evangeline took Mona to Macy's Bridal Salon and she found the perfect dress for her special day. The bridesmaid's dresses had already been ordered a few days earlier and Luna picked her gown out that day too. She decided on a silver blue chiffon, while Roberto's mother Mamie, chose sea foam green.

The cake was up to Roberto to dazzle the crowd and he promised it would be a winner. The church was in Bensonhurst at The Holy Name, with father Pirelli performing the ceremony. Roberto's family had been parishioners there since they came to America ten years earlier. The church had a fine social hall attached to the school and that's where the reception was going to be held. A whole crowd of sister's, sister-in-laws and *comari* of the mother's started cooking days before to feed the one hundred or so friends and families of the bride and groom. Larissa was honored to be a bridesmaid and Mike was a groomsmen. Mona had twelve bridesmaids in all. . For being in America less than a year, she had accumulated a lot of friends and cousins. Mariella was Maid of Honor, of course. Her biggest regret was that Matt was in London and not able to come to the wedding. They had been corresponding pretty regularly since he left. Mark backed down when he realized his brother was falling for this girl. He was only playing the game that they played over girls for years. This time it was different.

Mona and Roberto were busy fixing the apartment over the bakery into their first home together. It had two small bedrooms and a large kitchen. The bathroom had a washing machine in it and Mona thought that was a fine luxury to have. Roberto fixed a clothes line that strung across the room over the bathtub and the Mona thought he was a genius. Evangeline gave them a fine set of china and some beautiful linen. Rosalyn's gift was a nice set of flatware and some lovely drinking glasses. She had Mona pick out the pattern she liked the day she went shopping with Evangeline. Roberto's parents gave them their bedroom set which didn't fit in the room so a few pieces had to serve as side tables in the spare bedroom. Luna and Antonino were so proud that they purchased the ice box for the kitchen. Being in America for such a short time and working so hard in the bakery, they could afford such a fine gift for their daughter. Mariella was a New York working girl now and had a steady paycheck. She bought her sister and brother-in-law their living room sofa.

On the day of the wedding, the small apartment the Como's occupied was bursting with people. The bridesmaids helped Mona get dressed and fixed her hair in the latest fashion to compliment her veil. Antonino was nervous as a cat. He had never worn a tuxedo before. Luna told him to calm down and that he looked more handsome than the groom. She was disappointed that her sons and their families were stuck in Palermo and pictures were all they could enjoy of the wedding. Chance rented five white limousines to transport the bride and her attendants to the church.

People were starting to arrive for the ceremony. Some were carrying beautifully wrapped gifts, but most of the invited guests put money in an envelope and presented it at the reception. Roberto stood outside in the courtyard of the church with his best man waiting for his cue to enter. He was cool as a cucumber, but then he knew he had picked the right girl to spend the rest of his life with. They were so compatible in their thinking about what was expected of each other. The altar boy rang the chimes and the organist began the wedding march. Mona and her father followed the twelve bridesmaids in their pink dotted Swiss gowns. Alicianna was in front of them dropping the rose petals like she had been practicing for weeks. Right after the vows were said, a bouquet of roses was taken to the statue of the Blessed Virgin Mary. Mona asked the Virgin to look after them and bless them with many children. The organist played the recessional march and everyone left the church. The photographer Mr. Winter and his assistant Maxim West took many pictures in the courtyard of the couple with their bridal party. When the bride and groom entered the hall, the band started to play their music. The bridesmaids and ushers followed the couple and the guests fell in line for the grand march. They paraded around the room in a snake like fashion and came to a stop at the buffet table. The guests then congratulated the bride and groom, gave them their gift, and proceeded to the buffet. The best man was in charge of the bridal purse and guarded it with his life.

As promised the wedding cake was spectacular. It was a delicious fruit cake replica of Saint Peter's Basilica in Rome. The oo's and ah's were heard by the crowd and Roberto knew he did a good job. After dinner, the band played some lively music and the people danced and danced.

"What a great party," Chance said to Evangeline.

"It sure is different than ours was," Evangeline remembered. The elite of New York were at their wedding and it was very elegant.

"I remember," said Chance," this is much more fun. Do you want some wine Evangeline?",

"Yes, that would be nice," she answered. Off he went to get the refreshments for the two of them when she spotted Joe Cross walking toward her.

"Good evening Mrs. Winston," he teased.

"Good evening Mr. Cross," she teased back.

"Where is your husband?" he asked

"He went to get us something to drink, he will be right back," she warned.

"I don't think it would be a good idea if I took you in my arms and kissed you in the middle of the dance floor, do you Mrs. Winston?"

"No, Joe I don't think so," she said as she pouted with her lower lip. He looked at her with a seriousness she wasn't accustomed to. She felt a chill up her spine and she didn't like the way this conversation was going.

"Evangeline, this is getting a little tedious, I don't know how long I can put up with this sham," he admitted.

"You're right Joe, after all. I am a married woman." she remarked with chagrin. "This is my niece's wedding and I don't want to ruin it for her, maybe you should leave if you are so sensitive." Evangeline didn't understand why she was so defensive toward him. He gave her his famous grin as Chance approached them.

"Here you go, darling," as he handed her a glass of homemade wine.

"Hello Joe, what took you so long to get here? I'll have the cooks fix you some dinner. "

"No, please don't, I've had dinner a while ago with some people from Pittsburgh," he told him. "I can't stay," as he looked at Evangeline. "I just wanted to give my regards to Roberto and Mona and bring them an envelope," he explained.

"Come on Joe, they are playing a waltz it's Evangeline's favorite, I've had too much to drink and I'll make a fool of myself. Do me a favor and dance with my wife, please. " Evangeline didn't say a word, but her eyes spoke a thousand words.

"Sure, Chance," he said as he held her hand and took her to the dance floor. "Nothing like getting permission from the husband," he joked.

"We have to talk about this Joe, I can't think about anything, but you," she confessed. Joe never said a word to her. His face was expressionless. Joe knew deep in his heart that he could never have Evangeline for his own. She was a good woman who took her responsibilities for her family seriously. *I guess that's what I love most about her* he thought to himself. He whirled her around the dance floor several times and returned her to her husband. He kissed her hand and said goodnight to Chance.

"What happened?" Elsie asked, when she sat in a huddle of chairs with the rest of the married ladies. "Evangeline, you have a strange look on your face." Elsie could read Evangeline like a book.

"I'll tell you later," she told her. Evangeline didn't see Joe again for several weeks.

On April 30, 1915 the British ship Lusitania left a New York port carrying food, American made products, passengers, crew, and secretly loaded with munitions to support Britain in the war. On May 7th, the same day as Edward's funeral, the Lusitania entered the Irish channel. It was attacked by missiles from a German U 20 submarine. The German captain had no idea of the contents of the ship and sent out the missiles randomly. 761 people were saved, 1198 perished. Americans were enraged by the

Lusitanian's disaster. Germany defended itself by saying the ship was caring guns to kill German soldiers. In fact it was true, but the Germans couldn't have known about the deception. Generally the Americans believed the Germans were violating the rights of humanity with its torpedoing without warning. Many Germans believed the British exposed the Lusitania and tried to get it sunk to embroil the Americans and get them to join the war on the British side. Because of the sinking of the Lusitania, people in the U. S. were upset with Germany in a way no one expected. Lorenzo and Elsie became the subject of this discrimination when they went to a New York restaurant for dinner in early July, before the baby was born. When the owner of the restaurant heard Elsie's German accent, he refused to serve them.

"What do you mean? Why won't you serve us?" questioned Lorenzo.

"We don't serve dirty Germans in this restaurant," said the proprietor defiantly.

"We have been here many times before and who are you calling dirty?" Lorenzo yelled.

"Well that was then, and this is now," the man said pointing his finger to the ground. Lorenzo lunged at the man and wrapped his long fingers around his neck.

"This is my wife," he told him. "Can't you see she is with child? How dare you upset her like this!" he screamed. The man tried to release himself from Lorenzo's grip, his face was getting redder by the second. Elsie stood up, crying,

"Lorenzo, let go of him. Please let's go before someone gets hurt," she begged. Lorenzo let the man loose. He was so upset he could hear his heart beating through his chest.

"I don't want to be here if they don't want me, please, let's go." She was thoroughly up set and suddenly bent over with a flash of pain. Some of the patrons jumped up to help her and sat her in a chair.

"Are you alright, my dear?" an older woman asked her. "You should be ashamed of yourself!" she scolded the owner. "Do you think this girl sank that ship single handed?"

"Yes, please get me a glass of water if you can, "asked Elsie. The owner's wife got Elsie the water.

"Please mister, take your wife home we don't want any trouble," she asked. Lorenzo pushed past the proprietor and gave him an extra jab. He took Elsie by the arm and walked her out of the building.

"Have people gone crazy?" he asked Elsie.

"It's a bad time and it will only get worse," she said. "I got a letter from my sister Greta and she said people in Germany were afraid. In my home town, up in the mountains, they are only working people and they know nothing about this war. Lorenzo, I'm afraid for our baby all of a sudden," she shivered.

"Don't worry Elsie I'll keep our baby safe," he assured her. They got into their car and drove home to their little house,

"No one will bother us here he assured her." The harassment didn't stop there. A rock was thrown through the window of his New York shop. The note attached to it said "Krout Lover". That day Lorenzo bought a hand gun and kept it locked in his office safe. "You never know," he told Nicolo, "this thing could get out of hand."

Later that summer, Maria stayed close to Elsie as she got closer to her due date. It was extremely hot, the only relief they got was when a cool breeze came from the river.. Elsie was a small girl and the baby was going to be big. Eight pounds at least, Maria predicted. She was a good midwife and had delivered at least 20 babies. None were still-born she was happy to report. This time she wasn't sure it would be easy for Elsie. Maria spoke to Dr. Miller, the local M.D., about her fears. He had examined Elsie early in her second trimester and agreed the baby would be a big one. He told Maria if she had trouble with the delivery to call him and he could be there in a matter of minutes as his office was on the next block.

On July 23, Elsie's waters broke. Several hours passed before she had any contractions at all. Maria called Mrs. Mitchell, she was the closest thing to a mother that Elsie had. She also called Rosalyn and Evangeline. Rosalyn thought this was a good time for Larissa to learn a little about life and brought her along. The women took turns walking Elsie around the room. Maria was sure the baby would come faster that way. Evangeline was on the phone every half hour to keep Lorenzo informed. Morning went into afternoon, afternoon into night. Maria still didn't think Elsie was dilated enough. Since Elsie's waters broke such a long time ago, Maria was afraid of a dry birth.. Maria called Dr. Miller and he was there within the hour. Lorenzo was beside himself. Nicolo took him out for a walk to kill some time as he was driving the ladies crazy and they had enough to deal with. Dr. Miller gave her an injection to calm her down, but not enough to knock her out. He would do that after the birth if he had to. The heat in the room was stifling. Lorenzo brought in a table fan, but it didn't do much good. Cold water cloths were placed on her forehead to try to keep the perspiration off her face.

"Lorenzo?" Elsie called.

"Yes, I'm here Elsie," he said.

"Take care of our baby, Lorenzo, I'm going to die."

"No, don't say that, my darling. We are going to have a wonderful family, you know that," he tried to reassure her. Elsie was passing in and out with the pain. When she came to, between contractions, Maria gave her the birthing straps she used to deliver babies so many times before. Evangeline remembered Alicianna's birth. It had been so uneventful . It took only one or two pushes and she was able to be delivered. Why was Elsie having so much trouble? The doctor decided to do a vaginal exam and discovered the baby was face side up. No wonder she was having so much pain. The baby wanted to be born but its chin was caught on her pelvic bone. He dreaded this more than anything, but he had to go in with his hands and turn the baby around. Elsie's screams were deafening. The moment he flipped the baby, she shot out like a bullet.

"It's a girl!" he announced as he pulled the rest of her from her mother. The baby was screaming like a banshee so Dr. Miller could rest assured that her lungs were working fine.

"She was nosy," Dr. Miller said, "she wanted to see what was going on." Elsie had so many stitches the doctor lost count. The baby tore her pretty badly. Dr. Miller gave her pain medication and put her to sleep. Maria was instructed to give it to her every four hours and apply cold compress to her stitches to bring down the swelling. Rosalyn found a wet nurse to feed the baby; Elsie was in no condition to do that, yet. Mrs. Mitchell's friend, Mrs. Wallace, had an upstairs maid who had a daughter that was nursing a baby and had plenty of milk. She paid her generously and it worked out nicely for both women. Lorenzo was so happy his daughter was healthy and had all her fingers and toes.

"Look Evangeline," Lorenzo said in amazement, "she looks exactly like Mike did when he was born."

"Your wives don't seem have any choice in the matter do they?" Evangeline teased. "She is absolutely beautiful. What is her name?"she asked.

"Elena Maria," he said, "after my mother and sister." Maria started to cry and so did Evangeline. They both hugged him and the baby started to wail. He looked down at the new born.

"She is going to be just like me. What am I going to do? he asked desperately. "What goes around, comes around," Maria informed him, and they all laughed.

Elsie developed a fever, her incision had become infected and she was delirious. The women stayed with her day and night. Dr. Miller was very concerned.

"Make sure her dressings are clean and bleached," he recommended. "Bleach out the bathtub after she uses it so it will be sterile for the next time," he ordered. The poor girl was miserable, but worst of all; she wanted nothing to do with the baby.

"Take her away," she would scream, "I don't want her. I wanted to give Lorenzo a son."

"Elsie," Lorenzo begged, "please, I don't want any other baby, but ours. She is all I want. I already have a son, now I have a daughter, our family is complete. Look at her Elsie, she is so beautiful.

"You did such a great job while you were carrying her. Remember how careful you were to eat the right things so it will be good for the baby? It worked, Elsie, look at her."

"No, she tried to kill me. I don't want her," Elsie sobbed.

Her fever was so high; Lorenzo knew she was talking out of her head. Days passed, the doctor and the women used every kind of remedy known to them. Finally, more than a week later, the fever broke and Elsie was resting comfortably. Lorenzo was scared to death.

"Evangeline, what if she really doesn't want the baby?"

"Don't be silly. She has been so sick, give her time," she tried to comfort him. Larissa was the baby's nurse. She rocked her, cleaned her, and sang to her. She was falling madly in love with her. When the wet nurse came several times a day to feed her, that was the only time Larissa gave her up. Elena was eight pounds, eight ounces when she was born; they weighed her at the Bridge Market that evening. Corn syrup and canned milk were boiled and supplemented the feedings. The baby was always hungry Larissa, complained to Maria.

"It's because she was such a big baby when she was born. Look how beautifully she is doing. You're going to be a great mother someday, my dear. You are getting a first- hand education." Evangeline recognized the bond between Larissa and Elena. It happened the same way for her and Mike. I hope Elsie gets over her depression before Larissa looses herself in that baby like she did with Mike. Elena has a mother and a father and no epidemic to deal with. She prayed to God that a resolution to this situation would happen soon. Evangeline remembered her mother's words," When a problem goes beyond your ability to solve it, give it to God, he will take over for you."

Elsie's pain reliever wasn't working. Dr. Miller changed the dosage. That still wasn't enough. He decided to give it to her every two hours. Elsie was out of her mind most of the time. When she was awake all she wanted was more medicine. Watching her very closely Dr. Miller gave her a small amount of morphine. Soon she seemed better, her fever was gone and she could walk short distances, but the pain couldn't be controlled. The doctor knew at this point that Elsie was addicted. It wasn't her fault. The birth was horrible and it tore her so badly. The infection set in and caused more pain. Dr. Miller stopped giving the morphine and switched back to the lesser pain killer.

"Why can't I have the morphine anymore?" she cried. "I must have it for the pain! Lorenzo, get it for me, now! "

"No, Elsie it's bad for you," he tried to tell her. He couldn't get through to her; he threatened to take all her medication away if she didn't calm down. That only made things worse.

Elsie panicked. "Please Lorenzo, don't do that. I will die if you do." she sobbed, "Don't let me die. " Scenes like that happened every day until Elsie started to snap out of it. She still couldn't be trusted with the baby, but she didn't care. She took short trips to the Bridge Market and to church. *Please God help me get rid of this pain,* she prayed. She said novenas to St. Jude, but nothing worked. She took the baby for a walk in the park near her house one day, with Larissa, of course, at her side.

"If something doesn't happen to relieve me soon, I don't know what I'll do," she confessed to her.

"Don't worry, Elsie" Larissa tried to console her, "Mother said it will take time. "

"It's easy for Rosalyn to feel that way; she's not the one in pain," Elsie complained. On one of her trips to the Bridge Market she had a conversation with an old Chinese woman she had befriended years earlier. Elsie told her of her problem with pain from the baby's birth. The old woman sold some Chinese remedies along with her fresh vegetables. She told Elsie that she needed more help than she could give her. Wishing she'd been able to help more, the Chinese woman gave her the address of Mr. Cong in China Town telling her to be careful as his remedies were very powerful.

The next day Elsie told Larissa that she had to go out on some business and would be back later. The address on the paper matched the address on the door, but it wasn't a store front like Elsie imagined it would be. It was a steel door and had no other markings on it. She knocked on the door and after what seemed like an eternity a little Chinese man answered. She told him the lady from the Bridge Market suggested she see a Mr. Cong.

"What is your business," the man asked her? I

" have pain," she answered shyly.

"Come this way please," he said as he escorted her to another room. She passed a dozen or so bunk style beds with people smoking some funny smelling potion. She was getting scared, she had never seen such things in her life.

"Where are we going?" she asked the man.

"Mr. Cong will see you now." She entered a room that was like an office with brightly colored upholstery on the sofa and chairs. The windows were covered with silk drapes and it was a stark contrast to the room she had just walked out of.

"Hello Misses," Mr. Cong greeted her. "What can I do for you today?"

"The lady from the Bridge Market told me to come to you with my problem," she explained.

"Oh yes, my friend SoLi," he said.

"Mr. Cong, I have much pain and I can't get any relief. It is taking over my life and I am afraid," she cried.

"Don't worry Misses, I won't let you down. Do you have money,?"he asked.

"Yes, I have some," she told him.

"Give it to me and I will determine how much medicine to give you." Elsie gave him fifty dollars which was a fortune in her mind, but money wasn't the question here. He gave her some ground up powder and put it in a glass of water. He told her to lie down on the day bed in the office and drink the potion.
Mr. Cong recognized her to be a distinguished lady and didn't want her in the room with the others. People would be surprised at some of his clients; they ranged from rabble off the street to politicians. He gave her several packets of the powder and said she might leave when she felt better.

"When you get home, take the potion once a day-- but no more," he instructed her. Elsie drank the mixture and felt very sleepy; she slept for several hours. When she awoke, she left the office, walked down the smoke filled aisle of sleeping bodies and out the door.. When Lorenzo came home from the repair shop she still wasn't home. Elsie got home after dark and the whole family was worried about her.

"You are so kind to worry about me, but I hadn't been shopping in forever and I lost track of time," she tried to deceive them. It sounded logical to Larissa, even though she didn't have a single package with her. Her excuse was that she had too much baby fat on her and she wanted to buy her normal size. She didn't have to worry about feeding the baby so she was free as a bird. A few days later she did the same thing. When she arrived at Mr. Cong's office, he was surprised to see her.

"Mr. Cong, could you sell me more of the powder please?" she asked.

"Misses," he scolded her, "I told you to take it once a day, this potion is very powerful. I will give you a few more packets, but you must promise me to be careful with it," he reminded her.

Elsie went home, took her concoction and drifted off to a safe place in her dreams. Lorenzo knew something was up with her and asked Evangeline what to do.

"All she does is sleep again, like when she was on morphine," he complained.

"Do you think she is getting drugs somewhere/" Evangeline asked him. "I don't know from where", he answered.

"Don't worry, I'll find out what's going on," she reassured him.

Evangeline called upon Patrick Ryan again, the private detective she used to follow Chance several years earlier. He put a tail on Elsie and found that she was going to China town to buy opiates to feed her addiction. Lorenzo was furious with Elsie.

"What are you thinking about?" he screamed, "You will kill yourself with that dope! Where did you get this idea to go to China Town?" he grilled her.

"Don't underestimate an addict," she said sarcastically. "I asked around at the Bridge Market, you can get a lot of information there."

"I swear to you, that if you don't stop now I will leave you. I will take the baby and go to Hunters Point," he threatened. He knew that would at least get her attention, she would never allow that to happen.

"Will you get some help?" he begged.
Elsie had a faraway look in her eyes. "Don't fight with me, Lorenzo," she said. "I have to lie down now. "

Mrs. Mitchell, through her suffragette friends, found a doctor who could help women in Elsie's situation. Dr. Stein was located in the Jewish area of Bensonhurst and had a PHD in psychology. He called on Elsie and began a therapy program. It wasn't an easy thing to do; Elsie's withdrawal was more painful than the delivery of the baby. Her screams were horrible for everyone to hear. Lorenzo took it the hardest. He cried to Nicolo one night.

"All the women in my life suffer because of me," he said. "Felicia, Elsie, even Evangeline."

"No, Lorenzo, people suffer because of life; they are alive and have to travel the route God gives them, not you. Don't give yourself so much credit," Nicolo explained.

Larissa took the baby to Lenox Hill during this time. Elsie would go from chills to fever as her body was detoxified. To everyone's relief the treatments helped. Elsie eventually wanted to see the baby and started to bathe her and change her under the watchful eye of all her godmothers, of course. Her milk had long since dried up, but she could feed her with a bottle.

Elsie was getting well, she could feel it. She and Lorenzo had so much to be thankful for. Dr. Stein was a God send for them and the family. When she was completely cured, Elsie went once a week with Dr. Stein to help other people who were addicted to medications. Dr. Stein was happy with her recovery and grateful for her help.

"I don't know how else to show you our gratitude," Elsie told Dr. Stein.

"Helping other people so they can see how well you are doing is gratitude enough," he answered her. Maria said, "Behind every cloud there is a silver lining. "And it was true.

Lorenzo's plan for the baby to be baptized finally came to be. All the family and extended family met at St. Mary's Church the last week in September after twelve o'clock mass. Evangeline, Chance, and Alicianna bought the Infant the most beautiful christening gown in Little Italy. She had her jeweler make up a gold cross and chain with a substantial diamond in the center of it. Maria and Nicolo gave her a gold bracelet with a gold heart that dangled from it. The baby's name was on one side and the date of the christening on the other. Rosalyn and Larissa had a crochet jacket and bonnet made from fine wool with a blanket to match. Mike gave his sister a gold charm with a guardian angel on it to keep her safe when he wasn't around to protect her. Mike and Larissa were her godparents and this child couldn't have been loved any better. The priest did his duty with the oil and holy water to a crying baby. Finally, she fell asleep in Larissa's arms and a new Christian was offered to the congregation.

Larissa had a hard time giving up her duties as nanny for Elena.

"Oh my little sweetheart, are you going to forget me when I'm away at school? The next time I see you, I bet you will be crawling." School was starting soon and she would be off to Boston before she knew it. She learned more about life in those few months than she ever would in any educational institution. Mike and Larissa hadn't seen each other much that summer. Chance took him to the office every day to get the feel of the business. He did a lot of clerical work and ran errands. Mike liked the feeling of responsibility he was getting. He was envious that his uncles were in London working for the company. He was always hungry for news about the war. He wanted to enlist, but he was too young. He figured the U.S. wouldn't get involved for another year, unless some tragedy occurred that forced America into it. He talked to Joe Cross about it.

"Joe" Mike asked, "do you think America will get in soon?"

"No doubt about it," he said. "I believe we can't stand by any longer. It shouldn't take more than a year," he predicted.

"What do you think about my joining up?" he said determinedly.

"You are too young to think about that now. If I were you I would concentrate on my education and then you can enlist as an officer," Joe suggested.

"I have prep school to start in the fall and then four years of college," Mike reminded him. "The war will be over by then, and I will have missed it," he said with disappointment. *That's the idea*, Joe thought. Who will be able to live with Evangeline if he enlisted. There *is no way Evangeline will allow him to go, but when he turns 18 she won't have any say in the matter.* Mike brought up the subject to both Chance and Lorenzo. They gave him the same answer : to finish school. I'll ask them again after prep school in the spring, he thought.

"I talked to my friend, Sam's brother. He enlisted and is going overseas next week to fight for Italy. His family is all for it. They threw him a party and everything," he told Lorenzo.

"Maybe Evangeline should talk to his mother to find out what magic she uses to keep sane," Lorenzo told him. "Do you know what that would do to her, Mike?" he insisted.

"You know Pa, I need her to stop concentrating on me and spend more time on herself." "That's not going to happen, son, so forget about it," Lorenzo assured him.

EIGHT

The New York Preparatory School for Young Men was a fine establishment located in the center of the city. Although it was only several miles from Hunters Point, the young men were required to live in the dormitories there. Evangeline dreaded the day Mike would eventually leave. She thought back on his birth and how perfect she thought he was. She was his aunt, but his mother by circumstance. Never could a mother love a child more. She couldn't tell the difference between Alicianna and Mike.

The check-in time at the school wasn't going to work for Chance or Lorenzo. Mike didn't want Evangeline to take him to the registration, none of the other guys had their mothers there. Chance was in Pittsburgh and Lorenzo had an important meeting with people from Detroit that afternoon and would stop by to see him settled in that evening.

Mike called Joe Cross at the office "If you can Joe, do you think you may be able to take me to school today? Both my dad's are busy and I don't want my mother there; she might make a scene," he said. Joe started to laugh, knowing with Evangeline that might be a possibility. Joe was happy to comply; he thought a lot of Mike and in some ways reminded him of his son Giuseppe, they would be about the same age. He worried about the war and the safety of his family he left behind in Italy. The latest report was that Margarita had two more children with her present husband. They lived in the Calabria region of Italy. His parents were still alive and very much involved with Giuseppe. His marriage to Margarita was annulled secretly and she was remarried as a widow. His leaving them was something he couldn't control. They were in grave danger just being involved with him. He was better off dead to his loved one's; that was the price he paid for a job he felt he had to do.

Joe picked up Mike at Hunters Point around two o'clock and drove him and his belongings to the NYC Prep School. Evangeline was disappointed Mike wouldn't let her take him with the chauffer, but he insisted Joe was going to do it. When Joe arrived Mike was ready.

"Where is your mother?" Joe asked, as he looked around..

"She has a headache and I kissed her good bye in her room," Mike told him. Joe had been sure he would see her today and maybe he could have apologized for his behavior at the wedding.

"Okay, Michele," calling him his childhood name, "let's go to school." They scooped up his gear and put it in the trunk of the car and off they went. Evangeline watched as they pulled down the long driveway and turned toward the city. Tears were in her eyes, but not for Mike. She could see him anytime she wanted. No, her tears were for Joe. She thought he might ask to speak to her, but then what could he say in front of Mike? She must put him out of her mind. That was how they left it at the wedding, she was sure of it.

Later that evening, Lorenzo walked into Mike's small dormitory room. His roommate was a boy from Albany, his named Nick Jackson. Mike and Nick seemed to hit it off right away especially since Nick had an interest in going to war too. Mike introduced Nick to Lorenzo.

"Nice to meet you," Lorenzo said to Nick. "How do you boys like your room?" Lorenzo held his hat in his hands and was fidgeting with the brim.

"Mike, can I talk to you for a minute?" Lorenzo asked.

"Sure Pa, let's go down the hall to a sitting room and we can talk privately." I'll be back shortly, he motioned to Nick.

"What's up Pa?" he asked concerned. "Is it Elsie or Elena?" he asked him.

"No, no, nothing like that," Lorenzo reassured him. "As you know, I had an appointment with the associates of Mr. Henry Ford from Detroit today."
Mike nodded.

"They wanted me to put a showroom in my shop to sell the cars they build."

"That's great Pa, what did you tell them?" Mike asked.

"Well, I have to talk it over with your mother first. She is my partner, you know.".

"Do you have enough room at the city building?"Mike asked.

"It might be tight, but we have the empty lot next door to build on to."

"That's great! You can call it R&W autos for Rizzo and Winston," he added.

"Sounds good to me," Lorenzo agreed. He felt much better now that he told Mike. "Well, I'll be going home I have to tell Elsie before I tell Evangeline, you know how women get" he smiled. "You better do well in school, Mike; I might need your good head to help me along on this adventure."

"Don't worry Pa, you have done a great job so far, I'm proud of you." Lorenzo hugged his son and Mike hugged him back. Those were the best words he had ever heard, he had a lump in his throat when he left the school that night. He felt like he was ten feet tall.

Mike heard from Chance that night also. The Dean of the school called him into his office. "You have a phone call, my boy, long distance."

"Hey, Mike, It's Dad," he heard. The connection was bad but he could make out the voice.

"Hi, Dad, how's Pittsburgh?"

"Fine, son, I just wanted to tell you I was sorry I couldn't take you to school today, but I thought I would call."

"That's fine Dad, Joe took me.".

"That's good son, well do the best you can we will always support you in whatever it is you want. Have a good day tomorrow and I'll see you as soon as I can."

"Ok, Dad, I love you.".

"I love you too," Chance declared, and hung up.

"Is everything alright Winston?" the dean asked.

"Yes sir, it is. I was just thinking what a lucky guy I am," Mike told him. He left the office and went to his room and spent the evening talking to Nick about the war and when they could get in it.

Rosalyn was still insistent that Larissa attend Mrs. Farnsworth's finishing school. Abigail Norton would be going to school there with her as well.

"This is the last time I will speak of this. Larissa, you and Abigail go to your room and start packing your bags. I will send a maid to give you a hand. You will have uniforms to wear during classes, but you may wear street clothes at any other time. I have spoken to Mrs. Norton and we agree that ten outfits should be sufficient at least until Christmas break. You can write home for more things, should you need them. Evangeline, I and Mrs. Norton will be taking turns on the weekends to come to visit you girls. We have made accommodations at the Plaza Hotel in Boston already," recited Rosalyn.

"When your mother makes up her mind she crosses every tee, doesn't she?" Abigail remarked.

"That's a very true statement, Abigail, I guess she is only trying to keep me safe and as happy as she can," Larissa admitted.

"The only way you are going to be happy is if she packed Mike Winston in one of the trunks," giggled Abigail.

"What am I going to do?" Larissa cried, "I know I'm going to miss him so much. Mike is going away to school, but at least he will be in New York and he can go home any time he wants to."

"Maybe Evangeline will bring him with her on one of her weekends in Boston," Abigail suggested. Larissa hung her hat on that thought and happily finished her packing.

"Did you know Alan Mason will be going to school in Boston this year?" questioned Abigail.

"No, he never said a word about it the other day when I saw him in the park," Larissa said surprised.

"He has a crush on you, you know," Abigail insisted as she danced around the room with a silk scarf.

"Don' be silly, he does not."

"Why do you think he didn't tell you about school or anything else?" Abigail said. "He gets tongue tied whenever he sees you, are you blind girl? Or is Mike all you can see?" she asked her.

Larissa, looking pensive, tried to remember any conversation she had with Alan at the ball. He danced like a dream at the debutant ball, Larissa remembered. "You are right, I don't think we spoke ten words all night long."

"See I told you so," teased Abigail. They both fell on the bed and laughed like the best friends they were.   The next day the girls and their mothers boarded the train to Boston. Rosalyn and Mrs. Norton took the girls to school and proceeded to settle them   in their dormitory room. It was the smallest room Larissa ever saw.   It had two small beds, two dressers, a closet and that was it.

"We can make due," Larissa announced to Mrs. Norton and Rosalyn, with a defeated tone.   Abigail laughed. *The ever suffering Larissa,* she thought to herself. *I hope I can change her mind and make her want to stay.*

On the train back home Mrs. Norton asked Rosalyn a personal question.

"My Abigail is an only child, Rosalyn, and Larissa might as well be, have you had a talk with her about boys yet? Forgive me if you think I'm over stepping my bounds," said Mrs. Norton a little embarrassed. "I was hoping Mrs. Farnsworth's curriculum would cover that issue," she said.

Rosalyn smiled at her remembering her beautiful page, Chance. *Someone should have talked to me about boys and falling in love, she thought. Life is such a mystery, what would have happened to me if she never had her virginity taken by that boy,* she wondered?

"Rosalyn," Mrs. Norton asked, "did you hear me?"

"Oh forgive me, my dear," as she came out of her memory dream.

"No I haven't spoken to her about that yet, I don't think Evangeline has either," Rosalyn answered. "Our girls are good girls. I don't think we have too much to worry about. Mike Winston has been her companion since they were toddlers. He has always been her protector. I suppose I never gave it much thought."   *Although things have changed between them lately, maybe it's time for them to go their separate ways,* she thought. *They'll be in different schools this year I'm sure their eyes will wander to other people.* She was day dreaming again. "When Evangeline takes her turn to visit the girls, I'll have her speak to Mrs. Farnsworth about the subject."   That seemed to satisfy Abigail's mother and they continued on the trip with other pleasantries to discuss.

Two weeks later it was Evangeline's turn to take the train to Boston. She packed enough clothes for an overnight stay. When she arrived she got the grand tour of the school and a short trip to some of Boston's shops to buy Larissa and Abigail a few personal items. The question that eluded Mrs. Norton was asked of the principal by Evangeline. She was assured that the subject of keeping company would certainly be addressed in class. I don't know how I got elected to ask that questioned, she wondered? What would she say to Alicianna, when the time came? She didn't think leaving it up to the school at the age of seventeen was the right thing to do either. Evangeline suspected Larissa had thoughts of keeping company a long time ago. The three of them had dinner together and Evangeline returned to the hotel for a hot bath and a quiet evening alone.

She planned to take the early train back to New York in the morning. She put the 'Do Not Disturb' sign on the outside door knob and began to undress. Suddenly there was a knock at the door.

"Don't people read signs?", she grumbled to herself "Who's there?"

"It's me, Joe, Evangeline, don't be afraid." he said. She put on her robe and unlocked the door with shaking fingers. He walked in the room and just stared at her. She started to cry.

"I'm sorry, Evangeline, we didn't leave each other on very good terms," he confessed.

"I thought you were tired of our relationship or maybe had someone else by now," she cried.

"No, never anyone else," he insisted, as he held out his arms and she ran into them like a key fits into a lock.

"Who told you I was here?"she asked.

"Chance told me this morning, that it was your turn to come to Boston and visit Larissa. I couldn't resist," he said.

"Joe, you were right to say what you did at the wedding. We are not children, playing silly games. We are adults and it's time we started to behave like adults," she said as if it were a speech.

"Evangeline, I want you to ask Chance for a divorce," he demanded.

"How can I do that, Joe?" she cried. "I have Mike and Alicianna and Rosalyn is depending on me. Did you know Chance stopped seeing that woman in New York?" she questioned.

"Yes, he told me."

"It seems she left him for an Austrian Count. I almost feel sorry for him, isn't that strange?" she wondered.

"Evangeline, you are too good for words," he said, "Come wipe your tears." She tipped her head up to look at him and that was all it took for him to bend down and kiss her tears away.

"When two people love each other, there's no way they can be apart," he said, "no matter how hard they try." He scooped her up like she was a feather and carried her to bed.

"Where did you get those blue eyes?" she asked.

"Just lucky I guess," he laughed. He untied her robe and made love to her into the night.

Back in April 13, 1912 Franco's excitement was mounting. He was getting anxious about his trip the next day. He had about fifteen hours before the Titanic was ready to sail. *What should he do with all these hours?* He hung around the docks and decided to visit a pub for a pint or two. A pretty young girl with a low cut blouse and a very buxom figure caught his eye. She wandered over to him and asked if he would buy her a drink. He couldn't keep his eyes off her breasts and after several pints of ale, he couldn't keep his hands off them either. He bought another pint and they took it to her room upstairs. She undressed him and he watched as she undressed herself. She offered him the ale which he drank willingly. Suddenly the room started to spin, he couldn't keep his eyes open and he wanted to so badly. She was now lying on top of him, but he couldn't feel a thing. Then the lights went out.

When he awoke up all that was left in the room were his clothes and he had the most horrible headache. Every penny he had was gone and worst of all, his ticket was gone too.

"That tramp," he swore, "she drugged me! I've been with a hundred whores but nothing like this has ever happened to me." He got dressed and ran down to the docks just in time to watch the grandest of ships sail off in the distance. He returned to the pub and asked the barkeep about the girl.

"Do you know anything about that girl I was with last night?" he asked.

"Oh yeah," he answered, "she's a corker that one. She said she was going to America and we won't be seeing the likes of her around here anymore." When Franco explained to the man what had happened, the man laughed and said,

"Well my boy everything happens for a reason. Don't mess with destiny son, you will never win. Who knows what might be around the corner for you?" He took pity on Franco and gave him a job until he could save enough to buy another ticket on another ship.

A few days later the barkeeper's prophecy came true. The news of the Titanic's date with an iceberg was the talk all over the world.

"My God, that girl stole my ticket and is probably dead now." His ticket was in steerage even though Lorenzo sent him enough for first class. He'd pocketed the extra money, which was why he had enough money to buy beer for that tramp. The people in steerage, it was said, were the last ones to go above board. The ship's personal were instructed to lock the gates to insure the first class passengers were the first to leave on the life boats. By the time the gates were opened or broken down, the life boats were filled and the people perished.   Who would believe this story, he thought. *Could this be an advantage to me?* He wondered as he stroked his chin, *if I am dead no one will look for me.* Franco felt dead inside anyway. He was tired of always having to fend for himself and scratch and claw his way through life. His family life was nonexistent and he had no one to answer to.

When he finally arrived in New York, he was directed to an area on Mulberry Street called Little Italy so he could converse with people who spoke his own language. When he got there, he was mugged by two thugs who tried to steal his wallet. He was shocked at first. This was America, he thought, people were supposed to have money in their pockets all the time; why did they have to steal it? Franco fought like crazy, there were only two of them,

"I can take them easy," he was sure. The thugs were lying on the ground like road kill in no time. Franco was laughing at them.

"Hey Paesano," he said, "what are you looking for? I'm flat broke, I've got no money," he said in his native Sicilian. "I just got off the ship from the old country, give me a chance to make some dollars before you try to take them from me," he joked.

"You fight pretty good," one of the men told him, "you need a job?"

"If I want to eat, I do," Franco said.

"What's your name?" the other guy asked.

"Franco Valio," he answered.

"Siciliano?" questioned the bigger guy.

"Si, Santa Fara," Franco answered.

"How is it that you came to New York?" they asked. Franco told them of the girl who stole his ticket on the Titanic and the trouble he got into in Palermo. The two men whispered something to each other that Franco couldn't hear.

"Come with us," they told him, "we want you to meet our boss." They took him to a little restaurant which looked like a hole in the wall from the street.

" This looks just like Palermo," Franco said, amazed.

The store fronts selling their wares all had holy pictures situated between their products. The restaurant wasn't any different, A small statue of the Blessed Virgin adorned the entry way with flowers and greenery, a picture of the Sacred Heart was hung over the door of the kitchen. Along the walls were other pictures of various scenes of Sicily and other big towns such as Rome, Naples, and Venice. Seated at a table near the kitchen door was a rather large man. A dubious looking character was standing guard nearby.

"Stay here," the one thug told Franco, as he sat him in a chair by the door. The two thugs went to talk to their boss, they told him of Franco's capable fighting and the Titanic story and how he had to leave Sicily.

The boss said, "Give me a minute." He made a phone call and then gestured for the guys to come over.

"I hear you fight good, what's your name Paesano?"

"Franco," he answered.

"Not anymore," he laughed, "from now on you are known as Lucky

Frankie. Anyone who got a whore to take your place on the Titanic is one Lucky son of a bitch!" The thugs, whose names were Enzo and Tutti, filled Frankie in on what was expected of him in his job. Basically it was an organized crime run business. They reminded him that no one crossed the mob, and everything he did was being watched.

"You know this upfront," said Tutti, "Do you still want the job?"

"Sure," said Frankie, "a job is a job."

He was sent to Bensonhurst, in Brooklyn and after a few years became a feared member of the association. He was the front man who collected protection money from the small business owners and professionals in the area. The irony was that no one ever was protected and it was Frankie that everyone needed protection from. The few dollars he took from store owners added up to a good take for the mob. He was respected by the higher ups and had found his niche in life. By this time he had forgotten about Lorenzo and anything to do with Santa Fara. He was Lucky Frankie and that suited him fine. People in Bensonhurst resented giving their hard earned dollars to Frankie, but they were afraid to do anything about it.

Frankie and his thugs approached Roberto at his 16th Street Bakery near closing time one day.

"Signore Roberto, with your permission," Frankie said sarcastically, "I would like to talk some business with you."

"I have no business with you sir," Roberto, replied.

"It would be to your benefit if you did, you know a lot of bad things happen to people in this neighborhood when they don't take advantage of our, what you call insurance. Maybe ten dollars a week, just enough to call us friends, would be suitable," Frankie suggested.

"You and your cretini will get nothing from me, now get out of my store and off my street, you disgrace to Italy. Don't ever come back!" screamed Roberto

With that remark, Enzo and Tutti jumped Roberto and held him down while Frankie punched him in the stomach. They kicked him and broke a couple of ribs. When Roberto couldn't help himself anymore, Frankie opened the cash register and took all the cash that was in it. He threw a five dollar bill at Roberto and said, "I don't want to leave you penniless,

Signore." Then they fled out of the store. Roberto lay there helpless until Mona came downstairs to see what was keeping Roberto from his dinner.

Mona found him and the opened cash register when she came into the bakery from the back stairs. She screamed and tried to lift him. "No my darling, please call Doctor Palazzolo. " The doctor wrapped the broken ribs, but couldn't help Roberto's spirit. He told him this time it was only his ribs, next time it might be his life. The doctor also confessed that he too paid for the protection. His office had a mysterious fire one night, fortunately it wasn't too bad and he saved the building, but it did a lot of damage to his medical supplies.

Once a week, like clockwork, Lucky Frankie collected ten dollars from his receptionist. "I have her give him the money because I can't stand to look him in the face. This is not how one Sicilian treats a fellow country man. I pray the Bedda Madre di Trappini saves his soul," he said sorrowfully. Roberto knew he would have to pay them off every week.. He wanted to kill them, but he had Mona to think about, and they had already made mention of how beautiful his wife was. It made him furious to think they would do anything to Mona and he wanted to be sick every time they left. Mona knew she needed bigger guns than the neighborhood had to offer. She went directly to Hunters Point to see Evangeline.

"Zia, do you know anything about this protection money that these monsters steal from the hard working people?"

"No, I don't, I never heard of such a thing," Evangeline answered. They came to the bakery yesterday and when Roberto tried to throw them out they beat him up and took the money out of the cash register. He is hurt Zia, they broke his ribs and now he is afraid they will do something to me. Doctor Palazzolo said we have to pay to stay in business, he pays too, he told us."

"Oh my God Mona, that's terrible," she said as she started to shake. She realized how safe and sheltered Chance kept her. Her life was sort of a fantasy compared to the outside world. When Chance gets home tonight I'll ask him what he knows about it. Maybe Lorenzo can help too," she said.

When Chance came home for dinner, Evangeline was very agitated.

"What's the matter?" he asked, "you look like something's wrong."

"Oh Chance, Mona came to me today to ask if I knew anything about this shake down some shady characters are inflicting on the shop owners of Bensonhurst. I don't know anything about that sort of thing, do you?" she wondered.

"Well, I've heard of organized crime, if that's what you mean?"he said. "I don't deal with anyone like that in my business, they are thugs and mobsters. My associates are all gentlemen I'm sure," Chance assured her.

"Chance, Roberto is hurt, they broke two ribs and he is bruised all over," she cried.

"My God, Evangeline, you didn't say anything about that," Chance said.

"Please let's do something to help them," Evangeline begged.

"I'll make some phone calls in the morning, I don't know what I can do but I'll try. I know the police commissioner, and some other officials, maybe they can give me some information." Chance called Lorenzo that night. "I know the mob has hit all the shop owners in and around New York. I also know they are frustrated and some can't afford their so called protection money," Lorenzo said. "They haven't approached me yet, thankfully," he replied. The reason for that was Frankie. Although he wanted nothing to do with Lorenzo and that part of his life, Frankie told his partners that Lorenzo's Auto Repair Shop was off limits. He passed it once and noticed the plaque of honor for Franco Valio on the wall. He almost started to cry, but then he remembered he didn't know any Franco Valio, so what was it to him.

Lorenzo said he would go to the sons of Italy hall and find out if they knew of anything to help. The next day Lorenzo approached the committee on American-Italian relations. They were happy to hear someone was interested in looking into the matter, but they knew of no one who wanted risk their life to do it.

"That was a waste of time," Lorenzo told Chance, when he called him as soon as he got back to his shop.

"I know," said Chance, "I called on the Police Commissioner today and he didn't know what I was talking about. Something fishy is going on there," he said. "I had lunch today with some of my associates and they said they were interested in doing something before it seeped into the corporate world," Chance reported.

"I have an idea," said Lorenzo, "let's do a sting operation on these guys." He felt like he was 18 again and back in Santa Fara doing petty crimes.

"I'm sure if I had a civilized conversation with these men we could work something out," Chance said. It took a few weeks to work the plan out, it wasn't perfect, but the players all knew their parts. Frankie liked to collect on a Tuesday afternoon when the shop was busy with customers, that way Roberto was less likely to give him trouble about the money.

Roberto sent Mona to Little Italy to visit her mother. When she arrived she asked, "Where is Papa?"

"Oh, he said he had some business to attend to. You know a wife doesn't ask her husband about his business my dear," Luna responded. Mona was glad *she* was living in a time when the wife wasn't a puppet for her husband. Her Zia Evangeline had been telling her about a group of ladies she associated with. She got so excited when she talks about the suffrage. She shrugged off the question and they went on about the gossip of the day.

"Roberto is going to meet me here later for dinner," Mona told her mother, "let's make him spidini, it's his favorite."

"That's a good idea. Mariella, will be starving when she gets home tonight, "Luna told her.

"Good, I don't get to see her much since she got that job at the Defense Department" she remarked.

Antonino's business had to do with Chance and Lorenzo confronting Lucky Frankie. His brother-in-law Vincenzo came along to see if he could help. He, too, was tired of the protection money he spent every week. Chance had two associates to accompany him and Mr. Mitchell thought it was an outrage, so he tagged along also. Vincenzo knew of a police officer from

Bensonhurst that tried to clean up the activity around the neighborhood, but he was getting nowhere either. The officer requested he remain anonymous for the protection of his family.

"Please Vincenzo," he asked, "Don't tell anyone my name. I have a wife and two kids. I don't want any of this to fall on their heads."

"Don't worry, we all have families, we know the risk," Vincenzo assured him. The officer was going to stand outside the bakery in case there was trouble. He had half a dozen officers on his side, on the force, who wanted to help him with his quest. They were on standby anytime they were needed. The sting consisted of eight men ready to clean up Bensonhurst. To their credit, they were very brave, but also very naive. The men came into the bakery about fifteen minutes before Frankie and his thugs arrived.

Chance wanted to talk some sense into Frankie. He wanted him to leave these poor people in peace. Chance thought of it as an intervention, Lorenzo liked the word sting. Lorenzo wasn't convinced Chance had the right approach toward Frankie, in fact he thought he was crazy. Dump them in the East River was his approach. The men Frankie would recognize tried to hide their appearance by wearing a hat or turning their coat collars up, they lingered toward the back of the building.

Soon Frankie, Enzo and Tutti entered the store. Frankie looked like a big shot with his camel cashmere coat and suit to match. He wore it slung over his shoulders like a king wears a robe. The two sidekicks wore pinstripe suits.

They swaggered right up to the counter, "Hey Roberto, how's your ribs?" they giggled. "Put the money in the envelope, and don't give me any of your back talk," demanded Frankie. Chance approached them.

"Is your name Lucky Frankie?" he asked. When Frankie turned around to look at who was talking to him he spotted Lorenzo. He couldn't believe his eyes. Lorenzo was in denial, *it can't be him* he said to himself.

"What do you want?" Frankie asked in a smart guy tone.

"I want you to leave these people alone," Chance insisted.

"And who are you?" Frankie questioned.

"My name is Chance Winston and these are my friends." Frankie noticed Antonino and the others.

"Go away, you don't tell me what to do," he said calmly. Frankie brushed him away like he was swatting a fly. Then he stared at the bakers,

"You are going to pay for this," he informed them. He pointed a finger at them and shook it. A cold shiver ran down Antonino's spine, *what did we get ourselves into,* he wondered? At that moment Chance reached in to his jacket pocket to give Frankie a business card. Frankie thought he was going for a gun and pulled out his little berretta revolver and shot Chance right in the chest. Enzo and Tutti started shooting randomly. Lorenzo took the gun out of his pocket and shot Frankie right between the eyes. He then methodically shot the two sidekicks. Lorenzo was so distraught he passed out and was taken to the hospital with Chance. Since it was a gunshot wound that Chance suffered the authorities were told it was a botched robbery. If Lorenzo hadn't had his gun with him it could have been a slaughter. Lorenzo had bought the gun after the rock came crashing through his window at the repair shop. He never dreamed this would be the occasion to use it.

"I better take the gun with me today, you never know," he had told his brother-in-law Nicolo. "I don't like the idea of you caring that thing, but maybe it is a good idea," Nicolo had admitted. Like the barkeep told Franco, "things happen for a reason."

Apollinia   ------   Evangeline's Destiny

NINE

Chance lay bleeding on the floor of the bakery, Roberto had a flesh wound on his upper arm and one of his workers was hit by flying glass. Thankfully none of the customers were hurt, they were so grateful to get the scum off the street. The policeman heard the shots and ran into the bakery. He locked the door and called an ambulance for Chance. He sent Lorenzo along for the ride. Chance was alive, but barely. The ambulance doctor said he was near death and they had only minutes to get him to the hospital. Doctor Palazzolo was called to patch up Roberto and his worker. The customers were given instructions not to talk to anyone. Their names were taken as witnesses, but that was only a formality. No one would dare talk: Chance and Lorenzo were their new heroes. The policeman sent for a paddy wagon and the three bodies were loaded in it. He then picked up the gun and put it in his pocket. The officers who were in the paddy wagon and the officer on desk duty that day were his friends and happy to oblige. The dead men and the gun were disposed of in a fashion Lorenzo would approve of.

Not a soul spoke of the incident to anyone. it didn't even make the papers. The 16th Street Bakery opened for business the next day as if nothing happened. The glass was cleaned up by some of the customers and Doctor Palazzolo cleaned Chance's blood off the floor with peroxide and it came up quickly.

"Let me help you with that," Roberto asked the doctor.

"No, it is my pleasure," he said defiantly, "this is the blood of a very brave man. I am proud to be of service to him."

Lucky Frankie's luck had just run out to the delight of the Bensonhurst businessmen. When Frankie and his goons didn't show up at the restaurant for a few days, the boss didn't bother to look for him.

"Ah, that Frankie was small potatoes," he told his body guard, "I was going to get rid of that gang anyway. I have bigger fish to fry in the corporate world these days." Rosalyn, Evangeline and Elsie were wondering if their men were coming home for dinner. It was getting late and Cook was not happy about her cold meal. Unexpectedly, Joe Cross came into the room where the ladies were sitting. Elsie had been telling them about her one day a week with Dr. Stein and how fulfilling it was to her. Rosalyn was knitting a pair of gloves for Larissa, that girl is always losing her gloves, she complained. Evangeline was just going to tell them about the suffragette meeting she went to that week.

"Hello, Joe," she said with surprise, "I didn't know you would be joining us tonight, the men are terribly late I'm afraid" Evangeline could read Joe pretty well and didn't like the look on his face. Rosalyn and Elsie breathed a sigh of relief, they were bored to death about the suffragettes, they were glad Joe came in to save them from the speech.

"Sit down, ladies," Joe said, "I have something to tell you." He took a deep breath and while holding Rosalyn's hand, he said, "Evangeline, Rosalyn, I'm sorry to tell you Chance is in the hospital. He has been shot."

"Where is Lorenzo?" Elsie jumped up, screaming.

"He's fine Elsie," as he tried to comfort her.

"What happened?" Rosalyn asked. She felt like someone had just dumped a bucket of ice water over her. Evangeline couldn't speak. He relayed the story as it was explained to him by Roberto.

"Where did you say Chance is?" his mother asked.

"He's in the hospital, he's alive, come with me now I'll take you to him. " The three ladies walked out of the house as if they were in slow motion. The nanny was instructed to care for the children until further notice. When they arrived at Chance's room, Lorenzo was holding his hand and tears were streaming down his face. Elsie ran into his arms and wouldn't let go.

"I was so afraid," she said. Rosalyn and Evangeline rushed to

Chance's side.

"He hasn't opened his eyes since Franco shot him," Lorenzo said.

"What are you talking about?" Evangeline asked him. "Franco? I don't understand."

"I don't understand either," cried Lorenzo, "I thought he drowned on the Titanic, but believe me I'm going to find out."

Roberto and Antonino arrived at the apartment together. When the ladies saw the bandages on Roberto's arm they were horrified. When the story was repeated to them, Mona began crying.

"This is my fault," she wept, "I asked Zia Evangeline for help and now she has to suffer because her husband is in the hospital."

"No," Roberto tried to comfort her, "Chance is a brave, good, man who tried to help people who couldn't help themselves. We just came from the hospital and Chance will be fine, they think. He had a chest wound, but miraculously, the bullet didn't hit his heart. Evangeline wants you to know that if it weren't for you, those thieves would still be on the street hurting innocent people."

When Chance woke up, the first thing he saw was Evangeline's face. "Why are you crying?" he asked her. "What happened to me? The last thing I remember, I was reaching for my business card."

"You were shot in the chest, but you are going to be alright," Evangeline explained, "Lucky Frankie shot you. Fortunately, he and his companions are dead." Evangeline told him. "Lorenzo shot them."

"How? He doesn't have a gun," he questioned.

"I got one the day after the incident with the rock through my shop window. The cop that was outside the bakery disposed of the bodies and no one was the wiser," Lorenzo explained.

"That's incredible!" Chance said excitedly. "Did anyone else get hurt? How about Roberto?"

"Roberto had a flesh wound on his upper arm, but he's opening the bakery tomorrow morning like nothing happened."

"So our sting operation worked?" he asked.

"All except for you, my friend," Lorenzo made clear.

"How do you feel?" Rosalyn asked him concerned.

"I'm a little dizzy, I suppose. I would like to get up and stretch my legs," he answered. Evangeline reached over to help him, she tried to move his legs and he looked at her in shock.

"Evangeline!" he screamed, "I can't feel my legs! I can't feel my legs! "

Lorenzo tried to help, he felt like a bat had just hit him in the stomach.

"This can't be happening," he said. "Please God, let him be able to walk," he prayed. The doctor, hearing the commotion, came rushing in. He examined Chance and said he needed more tests. When the results were confirmed, it seemed that the bullet that fortunately missed his heart, nicked his spine and his legs were rendered useless. Chance would be in a wheel chair for the rest of his life.

"Oh my God!" Rosalyn cried, "Madam Sasha told Chance to stay away from bread and cakes."

"What are you talking about?" Evangeline asked sounding very annoyed.

"Chance was shot in a bakery!" Rosalyn exclaimed.

"Please don't mention that woman to me again, I feel very uncomfortable around her," Evangeline demanded.

"Feel anyway you like, my dear, but she hit the nail right on the head, "Rosalyn insisted.

Mike came to the hospital every night after school. He did his studies in the hospital room and kept an eye on Chance.

"Go back to school," Chance begged Mike."You can't get your studies done here. It would be so much easier for you to work in your dorm room."

"I don't want to leave you, dad," he insisted.

"Your mother and grandmother are here all day long, and I think I could use the rest. Please go back to school."

"Okay Dad, I won't come tomorrow, but I'm here now, so I might as well stay."

"The doctor said I can go home in a few days. The bullet wound is healing well and I don't have any complications with that. I'm going to prove to them that I will walk someday. My mother has hired a private therapist to help me move my legs and keep my muscles strong," Chance told Mike.

"That's great, Dad, if anyone can do it you can," Mike assured him.

"Your Mother has a notion that she is going to work at Winston Steel while I'm in this wheel chair.   Once she has put her mind to something, no one can change it," Chance joked.

"Lorenzo must be relieved, this way she won't want to sell cars in his new showroom," Mike laughed.

"She won't need the vote with her lady friends, she would rule the world if she could," Chance declared.

"No, she just wants what's best for her family, don't you agree?" Mike answered.

"I can't wait to get home and start my therapy so I can get out of this damn chair. " Evangeline was completely devoted to his every need. She went through a gamut of emotions after the shooting. Lately he had developed a cough.   The doctor realized Chance's lung had been injured and it was going to take some time to heal. She was sure God was punishing her for her affair with Joe. I should have confessed my sin to the priest, she felt with deep guilt. She told Joe they were never to be together again.

"What do you mean? Joe demanded. "You can't blame yourself for what happened to Chance."

"Yes I can, Joe, if I confessed my sin to the priest this might have never have happened!"

"That's ridiculous," he tried to console her. "Look at your life, Evangeline, your husband makes every decision for you. You have a brain, use it. He has been unfaithful from the beginning and you put up with it."

"No, Joe, he has been wonderful to me and Mike in every other capacity. Chance went to the bakery to help my family and came out on a stretcher. He kept the lies and secrets to protect Lorenzo. Most of all, Joe, he did it for me, to make me happy."

"Alright Evangeline I know when I'm beat, I won't be far away, you know where to find me," he said, and walked away from her.

Evangeline with all the strength she could muster went to see Father O'Reilly at St. Mary's. She told him she needed to make a good confession to clear her conscience.

"Bless me Father for I have sinned," she started her confession. "It has been many months since my last confession," she recited.

"What are your sins my child?" asked the priest.

Evangeline took a deep breath and said, "I have been unfaithful to my husband." She heard the words coming out of her mouth, but it seemed as if someone else was talking.

"That is a grievous offence against the Commandments," he scolded her.

"Yes Father, I know, "she cried. "I can't live with myself any more with this on my soul." "You have to promise never to do it again, you know, or I can't give you absolution," the priest reminded her.

"Yes, Father, I have already made that promise," she assured him.

"Very well, I absolve you in the name of the Father, and of the Son and of the Holy Ghost, Amen."

Evangeline mimicked the priest and crossed herself along with him.

"Go my child, in peace," as he finished the confession.

"Thank you, Father," she humbly said, and got up from her knees to leave.

"Evangeline," he called.

"Yes?" she said.

"You are a brave woman," and blessed her again. Evangeline felt like the weight of the world had been lifted from her shoulders. Now she could concentrate on the business. Although Father O'Reilly hadn't given her any; she knew her penance was to work alongside Joe and not feel anything for him. Their relationship must now be business only.

Joe Cross was pretty much in charge of Winston Steel. Evangeline decided that she was going to be Chance's legs in the business.

"This is very inappropriate, Evangeline," Chance complained, "women just don't become head of a large corporation."

"I have to look out for you and the family," she retorted. "It will just be until you get back to work," she promised.

"Don't you trust Joe?" he questioned.

"Yes, of course I do, but the name on the sign reads Winston Steel and a Winston should be in charge," she reasoned. Mike came to the office on Saturdays to help out. He finished his school work on Friday night so he could be free on the weekends.

Evangeline was proud of the way he took the responsibility on his own.

"Make sure your work at school isn't suffering," Evangeline demanded. "That comes first, you know," she told him.

"Don't worry, mother, I was on the Dean's list the first marking period."

"That's great, Mike," she said proudly. Joe walked in on the conversation.

"That's a smart boy you got here, Evangeline," he said. "He also knows the in's and out's of the office, he is a great help to me."

"I got the memo on the order for the Jones building this morning," she announced, It seems there is a discrepancy on the amount of steel needed to erect the first floor. Could you call on that information Mike?" she asked.

"Sure, I can," he answered excitedly. That was a tall order for him to take on. Not that he couldn't do it, but that he was asked to do it, made him happy. Mike rushed off to the other office to make the phone call.

"You're good with him, Evangeline," Joe told her. "It's good for him to know what's going on around here."

"Sometimes I wonder," she said, "just where his loyalties lie. When Lorenzo needs him, he rushes to help him, too. I hope he comes into his own someday and be happy with his choice. I hope the same for Alicianna too. Right now Winston Steel needs him and he is eager to help."

Joe stepped closer to Evangeline. He could smell the jasmine cologne in her hair. "This is driving me crazy, being this close to you," he confessed to her.

"I'm sorry Joe, you know my heart is breaking, but I made my decision. I received absolution for our love making and I can't go back on that promise." He took her hand, "I can't promise anything," he said, and let her go. Joe walked back to look for Mike to see how he managed with the task, he didn't want the other office staff to notice he was alone with Evangeline and start tongues wagging.

1915 was disappointing for Rosalyn as she was still in mourning and couldn't have the fabulous Christmas party at Lenox Hill. She prayed

1916 would be a happy one for the Winston family. Hopefully the twins would be home from London and Chance would start to walk again. His cough was getting worse and the doctors brought in an oxygen tent to help him breath. He was on the verge of pneumonia and he was really sick. Rosalyn spent most of her time at Hunters Point. It was a job she gladly would have given up. She couldn't believe Chance's good will gesture was so grievously misinterpreted.

Mark and Matt wanted to come home the minute they got the telegram telling of the shooting. They were just about to go to dinner with Mary Churchill when the telegram arrived.

"Oh my God, Matt!" Mark exclaimed when he read the words,

"Chance has been shot! He's alive but he can't walk. Don't come home yet," the telegram said, "more to come later, your Mother."

"What should we do?" Matt asked.

"Wait for further instructions," his brother told him. They were both shaken by the news, but they knew Chance would send for them if he needed them. When they arrived at the restaurant they met up with Mary. They told her the unbelievable news. She was very sorry to hear about the trouble and offered to help if she could. Her family was in the government and maybe she could get messages across the ocean in a timelier manner.

"That would be great," Mark told her, as he took her hand in his. He really liked this girl and hoped she felt the same way towards him. Matt was totally involved with Mariella. Their letters were crossing the ocean as often as they could. They were getting very lonesome for each other and Matt wanted to go home badly. Several days later they were relieved to receive a telegram from Chance. He wanted them to stay in London for a while yet. At least two more ships were to arrive and the cargo was for their inspection. The U.S. will be in this war soon, he told them, and then one of you can come home. The twins got a lot of information from Mary whose family had a lot of influence with the government. Mary didn't know the contraband from the ships were from Winston Steel, no one knew it. Joe Cross was in charge of loading and the twins were in charge of unloading and getting it to the right people to support Britain. Because of the secrecy of the shooting, all the brothers knew was that it was a robbery. It wouldn't make a difference to them how it happened anyway. They were relieved that their brother was alive and able to communicate with them.

Evangeline and Rosalyn took turns watching over Chance while he was in the oxygen tent in his bed. It was an evil looking contraption that fit over his bed and circulated the air. Medicine was injected into a water bottle and the steam shot out of it to help Chance breathe. Aliciana was horrified and wouldn't come into the room when the oxygen was administered.

"Please Daddy, get well soon so I can come to see you," she would tell him through the crack in the door.

"I will darling," he would answer, "soon." Chance did get better and the tent was gone. He could breathe easier and so could his loved ones. His therapy was taking much longer though. His legs were exercised daily and the muscle tone was fine, but he couldn't stand alone. He wanted to return to the office and get his brain back in working condition.

"I want to go to work," he told Evangeline that spring. It had been over six months since the shooting.

"Are you sure Chance, you are doing fine here at home. I bring you papers to sign and you are able to make decisions from your room," she told him.

"No, I want to go out and get some fresh spring air. I've been cooped up here all winter and I've had enough. My nurse can drive me to and from the office and administer my medication there. Please, Evangeline don't stand in my way. I want to show everyone I can still maintain my position at Winston Steel. You have done an excellent job and so have Joe and Mike, but I want to get back to the job I love."

"Alright, I won't stand in your way, but I will accompany you for the first day to see for myself how you react."

"It's a deal, my hovering wife. I bet you really want to get back to your suffragettes, don't you?" he laughed. She hadn't thought about the movement in a long time. Taking over for Chance was far from what most of the ladies ever dreamed of achieving. Maybe she would have a few things to tell them at the next meeting. Mrs. Mitchell will be happy to have a companion again, she thought. The temptation of being near Joe would be easier on her now. She wouldn't see him every day and he wouldn't be around her. Suddenly sadness crept over her; she wouldn't see Joe every day. *It's God's will,* she thought. *Chance is better, Pensare la salute,* she said to herself.

Spring was here and the young people would be home from school. How wonderful to have Mike under foot again she thought. Despite his extra work at Winston Steel, Mike did very well at school. Mike and Nick Jackson finished their final exams in June of 1916. They both finished in the top ten of their class and were accepted at several universities. The boys decided on New York University. They had until late July to make a decision about their dorms and fraternity.. Mike didn't want to think about any of it. The war was going to start and he wanted to join, but he would only be 17. His mother would never sign for him to go, he had to wait. Mike and his roommate, Nick had a pact that if the war started before they were 18, they would wait until their birthdays, which were only one week apart, to sign up. February 14, 1917 was the day for their enlistment, no matter what.

TEN

Mike and his friends were looking forward to a great summer of fun before N. Y. U. opened their doors to them in September. Nick was spending a month at Hunters Point in July. Evangeline was happy to have a house full of her son's friends around again. Mike had divided his time those first few weeks between Winston Steel and the repair shop. He was most interested in the people who worked there and their customers. He wanted to know how they lived their lives and what they needed to make them more prosperous. He was going to major in Political Science in college and was hungry for the information.

Larissa was home from Boston too. It was all she could do to catch up with Mike. She would bribe him with Edward's horses and challenge him with a race. He never could refuse a race with Larissa.

Larissa's first year at Mrs. Farnsworth's was surprisingly pleasant for her. Her weekly visits by Rosalyn, Evangeline and Mrs. Norton had diminished to once a month. Abigail loved living on her own, but Larissa still missed her family too much. Every time she went home, she expected to see her father there and it made her homecoming very sad. Mark and Matt were in London and Mike was in school. She loved her mother and Evangeline and Alicianna hung on her every word, but it just wasn't the same.

Alan Mason was very attentive to her. He took her out to dinner at least once a week and she noticed she had started to depend on him. Alan was in his first year at Boston University. He told Larissa he wanted to be a corporate lawyer.

One night at dinner a strange thing happened. Alan asked Larissa to wait for him. "What do you mean, wait for you?" she smiled.

"I have three more years of university studies and then law school," he explained. "I know it's a long time, but if you will have me I would like to ask your brothers for your hand in marriage."

"Marriage?" she asked she didn't know if she'd heard him correctly.

"Yes," he said, with a surprised tone. *What did she think he was doing all year, courting her every chance he could,* he thought.

All she could think of was Mike, Mike, Mike, Mike. His name was circling around in her head like the ticker tape in Chance's office.

"I'm sorry," Alan said, "if I mistook your friendship for affection. I truly respect you and would be proud to have you as my wife and mother of my children."

Larissa knew her face was now beet red. Because she was so fair skinned she blushed easily. "No, Alan, please don't misunderstand, you took me totally by surprise. I think of you as a dear friend. Marriage for now or even an engagement wasn't in my future plans. When the war is over my mother wants to take the Grand Tour of Europe, even though I told her it really wasn't done any more. People can travel anywhere they want, she told her, any time they want to. I think it's an excuse to see the twins in London. Did you know Mark has a nice girl he is seeing there? Am I talking too fast?" Larissa was babbling on, not even thinking of what she was saying.

"Larissa," Alan took her hand, "you don't have to make excuses. I have fallen in love with you. When I close my eyes all I see is you," Alan confessed.

"You are so dear," Larissa cried, "please give me more time. I will miss you very much if you decide not to see me again," she told him.

"Larissa, please, I will give you all the time you need," he assured her. "Just answer one question," he begged. "Where does Mike Winston fit in this picture?"

She was really taken aback with that remark. "Mike?" she questioned.

"Mike is my brother's stepson. I don't remember living without him," she told Alan quietly.

"Okay," said Alan patiently, "I think I understand."

You don't understand at all, thought Larissa, *no one understands*. "Thank you Alan for being such a wonderful guy," she told him.

"Come along now," he said, "Mrs. Farnsworth will have a fit if I bring you home late. How about next Friday for dinner?" he asked, "is it a date?"

"It's a date," Larissa said with a smile.

Now that the big question was out in the open their relationship wasn't so formal. They could kid around with each other freely. Letting your hair down is how Alan explained it. She knew how he felt about her and he felt better that she knew. Larissa thought it was best if she kept this information to herself. Somehow Abigail knew something was up when Alan brought her home from the dinner. She bombarded her with a million questions until she guessed Alan proposed.

"Darn you Abigail, you know me too well," she complained.

"I know Alan," she said, "he has been in love with you for years, I told you that before. What was your answer?" Abigail pleaded.

"I told him I needed more time," she answered. "We will remain friends and see where it leads."

"You have all the luck Larissa, I'm so jealous! I've had a crush on Mike's friend Sam for the longest time and he doesn't know I'm alive," she cried. "Oh my, Larissa, what about Mike?" she said with her eyes opened wide.

"I'm mad at him right now!" she answered. "He never answered any of my letters and he has never come to Boston to see me. I see him at home and he treats me the same way he did in grade school. So why do I love him so much Abigail?" she wondered. The thought triggered a reaction in her and she started to cry. "Alan is so much more of a man than Mike. Tonight Mike seems like a child." She continued sobbing all night and poor Abigail couldn't console her.

The next day was Evangeline's turn to visit the girls. She was only going to be there for the day, she couldn't risk the chance of Joe showing up again. When she got to the school, she thought Larissa looked terrible.

"Larissa do you have a cold my dear?" she asked, "Your eyes are so swollen" Larissa couldn't tell her the truth, so she said she was getting over the sniffles, as she and Abigail exchanged glances.

"Listen, I have a wonderful idea that will make us all feel better, we need a good time for a change," Evangeline said excitedly.

"What is it?" Larissa wondered.

"It's a birthday party, Mikes 18th," she said. "What do you think?" she asked the girls. "Sounds like fun," Abigail agreed. She wondered if Sam would be invited. "But Evangeline, Mike's birthday isn't for several months," she reminded her.

"I know, but this way we have time to make it a great party," Evangeline insisted. "I will give you a list of jobs to do to help," she told them. "Alicianna wants to take care of the decorations. She has first, what do you young people call it, dibs?"

"That will be fine," Larissa assured her. She also knew Mike would have a fit when he hears about it.

Mike had only seen Larissa a few times during the school year. She came to see Chance and they went to visit baby Elena together once. The baby was getting bigger and was starting to roll over and crawl. She couldn't be trusted on the bed alone any more. Elsie turned her back on her once and she rolled herself off the bed. Elsie was more hurt than Elena, but all babies do that, he was told. It seemed Larissa didn't have much to say at those meetings. Small talk was the conversation and it made him feel weird. The last time he saw Larissa at Lenox Hill, she asked him the question that was foremost on her mind.

"Why don't you answer, my letters?" Larissa asked.

"I answered a few of them," he reminded her. "I was busy all the time. I had my studies and my dad was sick, remember?" he said.

"He's my brother, yes I remember," she said sarcastically. "Oh Mike, let's don't fight, we only have a few hours together."

"I heard you spend a lot of time with that Alan Mason," he told her.

"I've seen Alan a few times. Why do you ask?" she wondered.

"I don't like to hear that kind of stuff, that's all."

"Are you jealous, Mike?" she laughed.

"Don't be silly, Larissa. I just don't like other guys talking about you that's all," he insisted.

There goes that Sicilian blood, Larissa thought to herself. "Come on Mike, let's saddle the horses and go for a ride."

"Now you're talking," he said and they ran to the stables like they had done all their lives.

Chance returned to work and except for the wheel chair, his day wasn't much different than it had always been. He missed going to Rebecca's in the afternoon, but he wasn't sure he missed Rebecca. *It doesn't say much about me*, he thought to himself shamefully. When he got tired, his nurse made him rest a few hours a day on the sofa in his office. He was getting a little stronger too, the sunlight was a plus and Evangeline made him sit on the patio outside the drawing room on Sunday afternoons.

Joe Cross picked him up one afternoon and they drove to Belmont Park for the horse races. The last time they went, Edward was with them, it made them a little melancholy, but they laughed at the way Edward would swear at the houses to make them run faster. Once again Joe lost his money and Chance came away with a pocket full.

Lorenzo was at Chance's side whenever he could get away from the repair shop. The Ford Motor Company put a showroom in Lorenzo's New York shop. He was selling several cars a week in the beginning and he doubled his volume in a few months. Sometimes he couldn't keep enough models in the showroom. Lorenzo hadn't told Evangeline yet, but the Company wanted him to go to Detroit and open a showroom there.

"We have a lot of Italian immigrants in Detroit and you could be of service to us there," they told him. Elsie was happy about the move because her sister Gretta had come to America a few years back and settled with her family in Detroit. It was an area near the Detroit River called Germantown. He told the people from Detroit that he had to think about it and talk to his partner.

The thing Lorenzo couldn't get out of his mind was Franco. *Where had he been the past few years and how did he become Lucky Frankie?* He hired Evangeline's private detective, Mr. Patrick Ryan to help him find the answers. He also sent letters to Santa Fara to find out what Masi and Carlo new about Franco's departure from Sicily. To his surprise, Masi and Carlo had immigrated to Detroit and worked for the railroad there. When he contacted them, they were happy to hear from him. They told him Franco had gotten involved with some bad guys in Sicily and stole some money from a bank in Palermo. That's why he had to leave town in such a hurry. They wanted to know if Lorenzo had gotten in touch with him and maybe they could all get together some time.

Lorenzo told them he didn't think so, but maybe he would be in Detroit on business and they could see each other then. The detective, Mr. Ryan, stopped by Lorenzo's office one afternoon. Mr. Ryan found out that Franco Valio missed the launching of the Titanic because he lost his ticket to a prostitute. He then took another ship out of London and arrived a few months later in New York. He was taken in by some mobsters and given the name Lucky Frankie. He harassed the people of Little Italy and Bensonhurst and the rest was history.

"How did you find out this story?" he questioned Mr. Ryan.

"It's my job to find things out, Mr. Rizzo; it's your job to pay me," he laughed.

Lorenzo gladly paid the bill he gave him and shook his hand.

"Thank You so much, I have spent many nights awake thinking how this could happen" Lorenzo told him.

"Oh, by the way, no one is looking for Lucky Frankie. They wrote him off as small potatoes and a pain in the ass. Just so you know, Mr. Rizzo. " With that information given Mr. Ryan left Lorenzo's office.

Lorenzo went to see Chance and Evangeline with the story he just heard.

"I can't believe it," said Evangeline. "He didn't have the decency to let you know he was in America and he was alive?"

"I guess he wanted everyone to think he was dead," figured Lorenzo.

"He sounds like someone you didn't need to be around anyway," said Chance.

"Oh, they got into plenty of trouble as children in Santa Fara," Evangeline told Chance. "What one didn't think of, the other one did," she remembered. "Good riddance to both of them," she said, "Franco and Lucky Frankie". "He almost killed my husband and tormented the honest people who just tried to make a living. He has to answer to God now," she declared. "Why did he ask you for money?", Evangeline asked, "What happened to the bank money?" "Knowing Franco, he spent it faster than he could steal it, that miserable, "Lorenzo explained. "Well, it's over now and I can rest easier. Elsie will be happy to know no one is looking for the three of them and we can go on with our lives. Chance you must work harder to get those legs working," Lorenzo encouraged him.

"I didn't want to tell you until I was sure, but look at this." He pushed himself up from his chair and stood alone without help from anyone.

Evangeline started to scream, "Chance, don't fall."

"Leave him alone," Lorenzo shouted!

"I can't take any steps yet, but with more therapy I bet I will soon." Everyone started to cry and they all hugged each other.

"Thank God," Lorenzo shouted, "Thank God."

Mike was working with Chance one day soon after he returned from school. "Dad," he said," have you noticed all the construction around Lenox Hill these days? Yesterday, Larissa and I were riding the trails there and the noise was so loud it spooked the horses. I don't know if it is safe to ride there anymore.

"I've been thinking about Lenox Hill for a long time now, that place is much too big for my mother and Larissa to be in. I have written to my brothers about it and they would be in favor of selling the place, Chance informed him. "Mark will probably stay in London when he and Mary get married and Matt and Mariella would like to build a home on Long Island someday soon."

"Wow," said Mike, "they both are thinking of getting married?"

"Yes, it happens to the best of us, son," Chance laughed. "As soon as the war is over things are going to change around here, hopefully in a good way," he wished. "I think I'll expand our stables and bring Edward's horses to Hunters Point. You young ones can ride to your heart's content then," he told him.

"What do you think Grandmother will say about all this?" Mike asked.

"She is a very wise women, my mother," Chance pondered. "I think she will say, there is no one in that house that I want to see when Larissa and I leave, it's people who count not buildings."

"That sounds like something she would say," replied Mike. "When was the house built?"

"I'm not sure, but I think it was over a hundred years ago," he answered. "That old house was built for Edward's grandparents when they got married. It was so well equipped, the new bride could barely believe she was living the high life. At least that was the story my dad liked to tell the family. He said his grandmother was a local girl from the farm lands and his grandfather was an aristocrat whose family arrived at Plymouth Rock. They helped build New York City when it was purchased from the Indians. Great Grandfather met her in the market place one day and fell head over heels in love with her. He went back every day until she agreed to marry him."

"I never knew that," said Mike," there are a lot of things I should know about my Pa's and Mother's families too," he figured.

"I will approach John Lee, my lawyer, and see what he can do to give me advice on the house," Chance said. "But first I should talk to my mother. "

When Chance arrived home, Rosalyn and Larissa were there also.

"I'm glad to see you Mother, as usual. I have a proposition to discuss with you, if you don't mind."

"What is it darling?" she asked

"I have been going over this with my brothers and we want you to sell Lenox Hill," he answered. "The twins don't want to live there and it's too big for the two of you," he informed her.

"Oh, what a relief!" she said. "I have wanted to leave for the longest time, but I was afraid you children wouldn't want me to."

"That's wonderful," he said, "I will contact my lawyer as soon as I can. What do you think about it, Larissa?" asked Chance.

"I would like to stay here with you and Evangeline if you wouldn't mind? she asked. "That is the plan Evangeline and I have talked about for a while now. You and Mother can have the west wing of the house as the east wing is plenty for the four of us."

Truth be known, Larissa didn't care about that big old house. It was drafty and empty, her brothers were gone and she missed them. If she lived at Hunters Point, she could be near Mike when he came home from school and she could help Chance with his therapy. Chance was getting better all the time. Rosalyn and Evangeline were willing him to walk and were relentless on his achievement.

Chance still had problems with his lungs, but he went to work every day. Evangeline was able to stay at home and continue her daily routine. As far as she was concerned, her business career was just getting started. She loved being at the office and had her fingers in all aspects of the business. Joe had been under foot all the time and she missed not being able to see him. It hurt like the devil, the way he looked at her.

It was driving him crazy to have her there all day where he could see her but couldn't touch her. Memories of their making love, was foremost on his mind and it was killing him. He was so sure she was in love with him, but she had broken her wedding vows and now she would not break her promise to God to not sin again. He thought about moving to Pittsburgh or even back to London, but he just couldn't be away from her. So he went on with the mundane chore of working at Winston Steel and being Chance's friend.

On the first of July 1916 Nick Jackson arrived from Albany to spend a month at Hunters Point. The young men were happy to see each other and Mike couldn't wait to introduce him to Sam and Dean, his two oldest friends. Sam's brother was on the western front and Mike wanted Sam to tell Nick all about it. Nick and Mike still had a pact that after the first of February, if the U.S. was in the war, they would join up together. They were so war crazy that's all they talked about. Sam decided he was in on it too, but Dean wasn't so sure. He wasn't ready to enlist and he was needed at home to bring in a few dollars to help his dad with the bills. So his intention was to get a job and then see what came of the war later.

The boys were making plans to go to the New Jersey shore for a few days of swimming at the beach. The Bellflower Inn and Resort was a favorite of the Winston's. Edward would bring the family down from New York on hot summer days to take advantage of the cool ocean breezes. Mike wanted Nick to see what the beautiful New Jersey shores had to offer. Albany was the state capitol, but it didn't have beaches.

"No talk of war," Dean insisted, "I just want to swim and see if there are any pretty girls at the beach." Lorenzo offered Mike his Model T Ford Torpedo for their trip and the foursome gladly accepted. Cook prepared a basket of food for the boys to take along with them in case they got hungry. Evangeline gave them a couple of blankets to use on the beach and warned them of the pain of sunburn.

"Put on a shirt if you feel you have had too much sun," she implored, "You don't want to ruin your trip with sunburn."

"Mother, don't worry," Mike told her, "we will be fine, we have been to the beach dozens of times."

"As a mother, it's my job to say things like that, remember," she said. "Keep the shirts handy, so you don't have to go back to the Inn to look for them," she instructed.

They left Hunters Point at the crack of dawn so they would have the best time of the day for swimming. As the sun arose, they could tell there wouldn't be a cloud in the sky. The temperature in New York was in the 90's and the humidity matched it. Larissa and Abigail were upset that the boys left without them. How selfish they were to go off and leave us to this sweltering heat, Abigail complained. The boys traveled light with only a towel, swim trunks and a small bag of clothes each. They were only going to be gone three days, what else did they need? If they took the girls, they would have to travel by train with several trunks for their belongings. 'No Girls Allowed' was their motto for this trip.

Sam and Mike took turns driving the three hour or so ride down the coast.

They stopped at a road side picnic area and ate the sandwiches and cake that Cook provided. Nick was amazed by the beauty of the shoreline.   It seemed you could look out and see nothing, except for an occasional ship in the distance.

"Thanks, Mike, for bringing me out here," Nick said, "this is wonderful."

"I love the smell of the ocean," Mike replied. "My Pa said the Mediterranean Sea is like this, he told me he played and swam in it as a kid. Some day I'm going to see it too," he confessed.

"Hey you guys let's get going," Sam yelled out to them, "we're wasting time."

"Okay," Mike yelled back, "let's go, Beach Haven here we come!"

On the last hour of the trip, Mike was explaining the Winston tradition of Beach Haven and the Bellflower Inn. "The Winston's spent many summers here as a family before my dad married my mother. They stayed at the Inn in those days. When my mom and I came along, Grandfather rented the large cottage so we could all stay together more comfortably.

"My grandfather Edward loved it here, I wish he was with us today; he was always so much fun," Mike reminisced. "My uncles taught Larissa and I to swim here. I have such great memories of the Inn, at night they lit up this huge gazebo and the band would play music and everybody got up and danced. My mother taught me the waltz there, that's her favorite dance," he bragged.

"Your mother is very young, isn't she?" asked Dean.

"Yes, you see, my birth mother was her sister and Evangeline was only 15 when I was born. There was an epidemic in Sicily and she and I were the only survivors in our family. She has taken care of me since and I can't think of her as anything but my mother."

"Then Chance isn't your real father?" asked Nick.

"He is as real as I want him to be, he is a great guy. Lorenzo is my real father and I love him too, very much," Mike explained.

"I'm glad Lorenzo gave us the car to use", Dean said, "otherwise we would have to take the train like in the old days."

They all laughed and soon the Bellflower Inn appeared straight ahead. Mr. and Mrs. Handley who owned the Inn were glad to see Mike again. They asked about the family and were saddened to hear of Edward's passing. They set the boys up in a two bedroom suite and asked if there was anything else they could get for them. Dean wanted to know if there were many girls registered here this week because he heard about the dancing at night and he loved to dance. I'm sure you will have a wonderful time tonight Mrs. Handley assured him. As soon as she left the room the boys got into their swimwear and ran to the beach. Mike laid out the blankets and brought along extra shirts to appease his mother and dove into the ocean with the others. The temperature was well over 90 now and the cool water of the ocean was refreshing.

"This is so much fun!" Nick exclaimed.

"I know," said Dean. Nick turned around to say something else to Dean, but he wasn't there. They were only in waist high-- water where did he go, he wondered? Suddenly the water turned a deep red from the beautiful blue it had been moments before.

"Hey, Dean!" Nick yelled! "Mike, where's Dean, he was just here, Oh my God, blood, blood, blood!" Nick screamed The others saw the fin and the black shadowy figure in the water behind them. Dean finally bobbed up from under the water screaming,

"My legs!" Sam dove under the bloody waters and started punching the shark. Nick was on the other side and tried to poke his fingers in the monsters eyes. That was his first reaction and didn't know if it was right or wrong. Mike started punching the shark with his fists until it let go of Dean's legs. They thought the shark was through with them until they saw it swimming around them in a circle. Then it attacked Dean again. It pulled him under and Nick went under to try to pry the beast's mouth open. Sam, who was a big strapping boy, started punching again when it surfaced with Dean in its mouth. Mike helped Nick and Sam punching until it let loose and swam away. Sam carried Dean to shore and put him on the blanket. Mike tore the shirt his mother told him to take for an emergency and wrapped it around Dean's legs to help stop the bleeding. Dean was bleeding profusely.

Someone on shore had already called the police and an ambulance. Dean's legs were cut badly by the shark. Dean passed out from the pain; the flesh was gone from one of his calves.

"Hail Mary, full of grace," Mike kept repeating over and over again. Finally the ambulance arrived and took Dean to the hospital. Thankfully the Monmouth Hospital was nearby and the team of doctors went right to work on their patient. Mr. and Mrs. Handley, from the Bellflower, put in a call to Chance. They were in shock also as they had never seen a shark in those waters before. The Handleys gave the boys a shot of whiskey to help bring them around, but all they wanted to do was go to the hospital to be with Dean. Chance called Dean's parents and they along with Lorenzo drove to the beach that afternoon. Joe Cross was delegated to stay with the women until further notice. Nick's parents were notified of what had happened and that their son was safe. None of them knew what safe meant. The trauma they all suffered would show up later.

It had been reported that the hot days lured the bull shark toward land. The boys were only in a few feet of water when the shark attacked. The local people tried to catch the shark, but it swam back to the colder waters of the Atlantic. It was a terrible tragedy for all the people who make their living by the ocean. The beaches were under the watchful eye of the lifeguards, but most resort goers were shy of the water.

Chance and Lorenzo arrived at the hospital with Dean's parents. The news was bad, but he was alive. His right leg was amputated below the knee. The other leg was bitten and had over a hundred stitches in it. Fortunately Mike was the same blood type and donated all the blood he could to save Dean's life. Dean's parents were terrified when they saw the ashen, lifeless body of their son. The doctor reassured them he would live if the infection didn't get any worse. Mike, Nick, and Sam kept vigil at his side for the rest of the night.

Joe Cross had his hands full with the Winston women. Rosalyn and Evangeline were crazy with worry. Larissa only had Mike on her mind and Abigail was afraid for Sam. Alicianna cried and cried, that she would never swim in the ocean again. Evangeline tried to calm her fears, but whom, she thought would calm hers? All the years the Winston's went to Beach Haven nothing like this had ever happened.

Joe couldn't calm Evangeline either. He was ashamed of himself for taking her in his arms and holding her tightly after he told her the news. Evangeline asked Joe to stay at Hunters Point until Mike and Chance returned.

"Of course I will stay, my dear," he said. "I will stay as long as you want me."

"Thank you, Joe, you are always so good to me," Evangeline said.

"I love you, Evangeline," Joe told her for what seemed to be the hundredth time. Evangeline lowered her eyes and pulled away from him.

"I love you too Joe, but don't take advantage of me."

He apologized and gave her his famous grin. "I can't help myself," he told her as he shrugged his shoulders.

Chance talked Mike into coming home after Dean woke up. He was pretty sedated so he couldn't talk too much.

"Thank you for saving my life like you did," Dean whispered. "You guys are the best friends a guy could have," he said with tears coming down his face.

"It could have been any of us," Mike assured him.

"That shark didn't have a chance with the three of you in the water," he tried to laugh. "Don't waste your strength," Sam coaxed him.

"We are going back home now, Dean. They say there are too many people here now. Your mom and dad will stay until you can be transported to a New York hospital. Mr. Winston is going to make sure the best doctors will be there to look after you.". Sam's dad drove Sam and Nick back to Hunters Point. He was so thankful that Sam was in one piece that he offered to pay the hospital bills. He knew Dean's father wasn't a rich man and he knew the bills would be a hardship on the family. Chance thanked him and told him the bill was taken care of and perhaps he could take care of the family in a different capacity. He said he would see to it and returned Nick to Hunters Point. Sam and Nick retold the story to the ladies and they became afraid all over again.

"Why are you crying, Abigail?" Sam asked her.

"I'm not crying," she said shyly.

"Yes, you are, you can't fool me. Are you sad for Dean?" he asked.

"Yes," she said, "but I'm happy you are safe." She started crying louder.

"You were worried about me?" he asked again. He was surprised to find out she even knew he existed. "Wow, I can't believe a girl like you would care about a big slug like me."

"Don't you talk like that, Sam Genoa, I won't have it. You are the sweetest guy I know!" she said..

"Thank you, Abigail, I think you are pretty sweet yourself," he said with a grin. They had been out on the terrace and when they walked back in the house they were hand in hand.

Elsie and Elena were waiting for Lorenzo's return at Hunters Point.

"What next?" Elsie complained. "Hasn't this family been through enough?"
Rosalyn put her hand on Elsie's shoulder. "My dear," she said, "this is God's way of reminding us that we are family." She recited a little prayer in German about guardian angels. She loved to speak to Elsie in German whenever she had the chance. "We are so strong that we can't do anything else, but pull through together." I" guess so," agreed Elsie, "I guess so."

Mike had a few weeks of nightmares. His screams were so loud that it woke up the household. Evangeline ran to his bed to calm his fears every night. He felt so foolish, he told her.

"Mother, it's Dean who should be having these dreams, not me," he cried, "he's the one who suffered. Yet he says he sleeps like a baby. How can that be?

"It's the same dream every night-- I can't find Dean in the dark. He lost his leg, but I dream that I lose him. I try to put my arms around all the guys, but I can't protect them," he sobbed.

"Mike, what do you think life is?" Evangeline said to him.

"Everyone has a responsibility for themselves, you can't protect them all." His night shirt was soaked with perspiration and Evangeline helped him into a clean one.

"Your friends are safe and you all are going to have a beautiful full life. Now go to sleep and try to get some rest," she coaxed him. "You will probably see them again soon," she reminded him. She was right Nick came down from Albany for the weekend and Sam and Dean spent the day at Hunters Point. Dean was learning to walk with his crutches and prosthetic. The boys would tease him by using the crutches as swords and pretending to impale each other.

"Oh, it's good to see the four of them playing around like kids again. Youth has its advantages," Evangeline thought.

Evangeline started to put the gears in motion for the first recipient of The Edward P. Winston Scholarship Fund. Dean McCall was eligible for the full ride scholarship to the school of his choice. He chose to be close with his friends at NYU. Dean and Mike were both looking at political science degrees. They had their futures all planed out. When the war was over Mike would finish his schooling and Dean should be way ahead of him, plotting how to get Mike elected to the New York House of Representatives.

Nick's forte was journalism and he would be his press agent. Sam never thought of himself as a college boy. He was groomed to work in his father's pasta factory. He loved the business and was looking forward to building it up. His grandfather started with five employees when he came from Italy twenty years ago. Genoa Pasta now had seventy five employees and was growing. Sam had most of the large restaurants and hotel kitchens as clients and now he was working on places like the Bridge Market to buy their wares. He thought if Mike was in office he could help the working man and small business owners get a better break on their investment. They had big plans, these young men, and didn't think anything would get in the way. Rosalyn told Mike, "You can achieve anything you want as long as your reputation is impeccable. If you want to get into politics, your nose has to be clean as a whistle"

"That sounds like something Grandfather would have said," he answered her.

"Where do you think I heard it from?" she laughed. "You're a good boy, Mike, you have made us very proud to be your grandparents, I wish you all the luck in the world," she said as she held out her arms for one of his big hugs.

After Dean was fitted with and gotten used to the prosthesis, if you didn't know him you would never guess he was an amputee. He limped slightly, and when the artificial leg was off, he was a champ on the crutches.

He adapted very well to his situation. He was so grateful to Evangeline and Chance for all the help they gave him and his family.

The McCall's were a proud Irish Catholic family whose faith was unshakeable. They looked on the accident as a cross they had to bear and the help from the Winston's as a blessing. Dean's father worked for the port authority of New York and his mother helped cook for the priests at St. Mary's. Genoa Pasta delivered a year's worth of pasta to the McCall household. The note said in honor of Dean McCall and his strength and bravery in the eye of danger. Mrs. McCall, being the fine woman she was, took several cases to the rectory to feed the priests and several cases to feed the poor of the parish. She felt it her duty to help others especially since she still had her son alive and well and coping with his injury. Dean was very proud of his Mother and showered her with kisses. "God is good," she said.

Rosalyn wasn't taking any chances with the mentality of these young men. The terror they endured was immense. She and Elsie called on Dr. Stein to see if he could be of any help to them.

He had heard of the attack from the newspaper reports and was glad to be of assistance. First he took the four of them in a joint session to see if they had different views of the event. He was sure they would as it was a personal attack on each individual. He was, however, surprised to see how close these boys were to each other and how important their welfare was to one another and especially to Dean. Sometimes in an accident, the people shy away from each other so as not to relive the tragedy.

Mike seemed to be the head of the group. He was the one they wanted to groom to become politically advanced for the welfare of the people. Dr. Stein thought that was quite interesting. Sam was the strong arm. He showed his strength by pounding on the shark, he would pound on anything that got in Mike's way; he had that much respect for him. Nick was the second in command of the group, he was as smart as Mike, but didn't have the charisma Mike had with people. Dean had followed Mike since he was a child, and Mike was very protective of his friend. They were an odd group in a way, but even Dr. Stein was envious of them. His report to Rosalyn and Elsie was favorable. Mike's nightmares were normal, they should subside as soon as he got back to school and his mind had something else to keep it busy.

Larissa got a surprise visit at Hunters Point from Alan Mason in early August. He said he missed her and couldn't wait for them to be back in Boston. Larissa decided to take an advanced curriculum at Mrs. Farnsworth's so she could be a teacher when she finished.

Abigail was seeing Sam regularly now and decided to stay at home and pursue their relationship. He was teaching her how to handle the bookkeeping at Genoa Pasta. While this wasn't what her parents had envisioned for her when they sent her to Mrs. Farnsworth's, they saw how happy she was and were sure Sam was a good catch. Evangeline had a long talk with Abigail's mother and expressed to her the views she had about woman advancing themselves and not depending solely on a husband. Mrs. Nolan, who was becoming a modern woman in her own right, agreed.

"My husband thinks Sam has an opportunity to make a good living with Genoa, but I think Abigail has an opportunity to make her own way there too."

"I'm glad you agree," said Evangeline, "I think these two are made for each other," she added.

Larissa invited Alan to stay for dinner with the rest of the family.

"Good to see you my boy," Chance said, as he held out his hand.

"Thank you, Mr. Winston," Alan replied.

Mike gave Alan an icy hello.

"I hear you are home from school on a semester break?" Chance asked.

"Yes sir, I decided to take summer classes this year so I could speed up the process," Alan replied.

"Larissa tells us you are doing a fine job there in Boston," Chance continued to grill him. "Well, Sir, I have made the president's list after each semester, if that's what she meant," and he gave Larissa a wink. Mike wanted to push in his face when he saw the wink. He never had any bad dealings with Alan, but now he knew he didn't like him.

Evangeline was a little surprised to see Alan at the table. She and Rosalyn were a few minutes late for dinner. They ran into some lady friends while they were shopping and the conversation got long winded.

"Sorry we're late," they begged their pardon. "How nice to see you again Alan," Rosalyn said with a welcoming smile. *What's she so happy about*? Mike thought with a grimace.

"What's the matter darling?" Evangeline asked Mike, "Aren't you feeling well?"

"I'm fine, Mother." he said without taking his eyes off Alan. Larissa was enjoying the show; *this is going to be interesting.* she thought. *Mike looks exactly like Lorenzo when things aren't going his way.*

"Mike," Alan said, "I was amazed to hear of your shark encounter. You and your friends are incredibly brave. I should have been scared to death if I were in that situation." *Oh why did he have to say something nice?* "We were just lucky I guess," Mike replied.
"Larissa didn't seem to think so," he said, "brave and gallant were the words she used." "Larissa talks too much," Mike replied, as he glared at her.

"Mike, that wasn't very nice," all the women said in unison.

"May I be excused?" Mike asked. "I had a late lunch and I have to help Dean with some things tonight," he lied.

"Run along son, if you have things to do, don't let us get in your way," Chance said sarcastically. He was a little disappointed at his behavior.

"Alan don't pay any attention to him, he hasn't been the same since he came home from the Ocean. Did you hear, Alan, that Abigail and Sam are seeing each other pretty steady now?" Larissa asked him.

"That's great." he answered, "Since when?"

"After the shark attacked, Abigail was crazy with worry. We thought it was for Dean, but it was for Sam," she told him.

"Sam was always so shy around girls, I'm surprised he got her to notice him."

Love conquers all, they say, Chance remarked.
Evangeline had been quietly sitting with a bemused smile on her face, Like

the Mona Lisa.*Does it* she thought?

With Chance's comment, everyone laughed and left the table.

ELEVEN

Larissa and Alan sat out on the terrace to enjoy the evening breeze.

"Larissa," Alan asked, "have you given any thought to my proposal yet?"

"I think about it every day, Alan," she said. "If I were to tell my sister-in-law and my mother, they would start thinking of how they are going to decorate the ball room." "You're, probably right, I was just wondering, that's all."

"You are the sweetest man I know, Alan Mason, I may not have an answer, but I love the question just the same,: Larissa told him.

The next day Alan went back to Boston and Larissa started packing again for her second year at Mrs. Farnsworth's. This time, she would room alone. She was a little nervous about that, but the rooms all around her were brimming with girls ready to start their first year. Mike ran into her in the garden as she and Evangeline were picking the colorful asters that grew in the late summer.

"Look, Larissa, I'm sorry for my behavior last night," he apologized.

"I'm sorry too," Larissa replied with a cool response. "You made a perfect fool of yourself. I was embarrassed for you," she scolded. Evangeline walked around the flower bed pretending not to notice the conversation. Larissa was holding her own and didn't need her help. After all Mike *was* acting like a child, she thought.

"I don't know what got into me," he said. "I will apologize to Alan when I see him," he promised.

"Thank you Mike, that will be acceptable," Larissa agreed.

"Are we friends again?" he asked.

"Sure," she answered. *Was friendship all he required of her*, she wondered, *if that were true, then why did he behave so badly last night?* Larissa decided she need a clearer head than hers for an answer, she was going to talk to her Mother about it.

A few hours later, Larissa knocked on her mother's door.

"Mother, may I come in?"she asked. The room Rosalyn occupied at Hunters Point was beautiful. It was done in a cool blue damask fabric that she had ordered years before, but never used on Lenox Hill. Rosalyn was fussing with the ruffle on a bed pillow when Larissa entered the room.

"I would like to ask you a few questions if you don't mind?" her daughter asked.

"I have always been available to my children, what is it darling, Alan?" she guessed. "Yes that's it partly, Mother," she answered surprised.

"Then the other part is Mike, am I correct?" she guessed again.

"How do you do that?" said Larissa amazed.

"I think each mother is tuned into her child's needs," answered Rosalyn.

"I haven't told you this, but Alan asked me to marry him a few months ago. He has several years of college and then law school to finish before he wants to get married, but has asked me to wait for him." Rosalyn was trying to keep her emotions in check until her daughter finished.

"I told him I needed more time to think about it, but he is so wonderful to me."

"What's the problem, then?" her mother asked.

"Mike," she said and started to cry again.

"Now, now, my precious daughter tears aren't the answer. Let's take a look at this picture. Has Mike given you any reason to believe he wants to marry you?"Rosalyn asked.

"No, all he can think of is school and war and maybe a race with father's horses. But did you notice how he behaved last night at dinner?" she said between sobs. "What was that all about?"

"Immaturity," she answered. "Mike is a handsome guy, and I love him dearly, but he hasn't grown up yet. He has Lorenzo written all over him. It wasn't until Elena was born that Lorenzo finally grew into the fine man he is today. Do you have feelings of love toward Alan?" she asked.

"I think so, but not the way I feel about Mike," she confessed. "I have loved Mike since I was old enough to know the difference between loving someone and liking them. He hurts me every chance he gets and he doesn't even know it. He wouldn't take me to the debutant dance. He ignores me when his friends are around. Worst of all, he treats me like one of the boys most of the time."

At this point Larissa was pacing up and down the room twisting her handkerchief.

"What should I do, Mama?" She sank to the floor and rested her head on her mother's lap.

"That is for you to figure out, Larissa," Rosalyn suggested. "I wish I had the magic answer for you, but each woman has to make that decision. I had that decision made for me with my first marriage and it was a terrible thing to endure. I never told you this, but my first love was a young man who was just a little older than I. He also wanted to marry me, but he had to work his way up the ladder in order to support a wife and that was going to take some time. I was willing to wait for him, but my father and uncles had other ideas. They arranged a marriage to an older man who had millions already and much land. I had no say in the matter, so I married him. I left my beautiful love and became the wife of a Lord. My husband couldn't consummate the marriage and arranged for my lover to sire an heir, Chance."

"Mother, I never heard anything about that!" she cried

"I never told anyone, but your father. You are my daughter and of an age where you can appreciate my situation."

"So Chance isn't really a Hennessey?" she asked.

"No, he wouldn't have inherited anything if I told the truth."

"What happened to your lover?" she wanted to know.

"I never heard from him again, after I became pregnant. I was told he thought it was foolery and never came to see me again. After Chance was born, I came to America with my mother and that's when I met Edward. Larissa, he was the true love of my life. The past was the past and nothing mattered after I met your father. He loved me and Chance without question. He was the finest man I ever met. No one can come close to his goodness, not even his own sons. He was one in a million, Larissa." "We had a wonderful life and I have no regrets. I miss him every day more and more, but I have no regrets."

"Oh, Mother, I had no idea you suffered so much. My little story seems so petty next to yours," she said compassionately.

"Everyone has a story my darling, and each story is important because it belongs to the owner.

"Thank you for sharing with me and trusting me with your past."

"I trust you with my life, Larissa, why wouldn't I trust you with something that doesn't matter anymore?

"Would you feel comfortable confiding in Evangeline, since she knew Lorenzo when they were children and Mike is so much like him? Maybe she can give you some information that might help you with your decision."

"I don't know. How do I fall out of love with Mike by listening to stories about his father?" she questioned.

"Maybe falling in love with Alan is the key, not falling out of love with Mike," she answered. Larissa felt better after talking to her mother, what a strong woman she was, Larissa was proud to be her daughter.

Just for the sake of asking, Larissa approached Evangeline with some questions about her life. "Evangeline," she asked, "did you leave a boyfriend in Sicily when you came to America with Mike?"

"Why would you ask such a question?" Evangeline asked her.

"Just curious," she said. "A lot of my friends are getting engaged and I was wondering about you. You are so beautiful I can't believe you didn't have a boyfriend."

"Well I think you are old enough to know a few things about me, my dear," she announced. "No, I didn't leave a boyfriend: I came to an old boyfriend," she said. Larissa was very confused by that statement, Evangeline could tell by the look on her face.

"You see I was in love with Lorenzo when we were in Sicily."

"You mean, you were in love with your sister's husband?" she said in shock

"No, but it's a long story. Do you have the time?" she asked her.

"I will make the time for this one," she said excitedly, as she pulled a chair up next to her.

"Well, you see I was only fifteen at the time. I knew nothing about life or love. I was raised under the watchful eyes of my parents and the nuns at school. Every day walking from Mass to the class room I would see Lorenzo sitting under a tree waiting for me to walk by. He would tip his hat to me and give me one of his gorgeous smiles and it would make my head spin around. I couldn't give him a gesture back for fear my father would find out about it, so I simply would smile and hope he got the message. Sometimes in the market place, he would walk past me and get a little too close and brush my arm against his. It was all I could do to walk in a straight line after that. My sister Felicia would tell me what a fool I was to moon over a boy I couldn't have. Our father would have no part of him," she explained.

"Then why did he marry your sister?" Larissa asked.

"You know how hot headed he is, and he jumps into something before he has the time to think about it. Well, he decided if he kidnapped me, my father would have to let us get married. So he made a plan with three of his friends to do just that. They broke into our home and put a flour sack over my head and took me to the mountain. He took my virginity, or so he thought. When he took the sack off, he discovered it was my sister Felicia, not me."

"Oh my goodness!" screamed Larissa.

"Yes, he had to marry her. Nine months later Michele was born. He abandoned them and came to New York to work for your father. There was an influenza epidemic in Sicily a few years later and we lost our family. Just Mike and I survived. My brother Antonino made Lorenzo call for us and the rest is history."

"Oh poor Lorenzo," said Larissa, half laughing half crying.

"What do you mean *poor Lorenzo*?" said Evangeline.

"What made you fall out of love with him?" she asked.

"Oh, I didn't at first, but when he left them and came here, he never wrote to Felicia or sent money to support Mike. That's when I realized he wasn't the man for me. I think I hated him the most on Ellis Island," she remembered. "There has been a lot of water under the bridge since then, Larissa.. I love Lorenzo dearly, we have been through a lot together, but it's not the all consuming love that I was looking for. "

"Did you find it with my brother?" she asked.

"Chance has been the best husband I could ask for," she answered.

"Evangeline, what about the rumors he had a mistress?" Larissa asked.

"I don't listen to rumors, Larissa, I know he loves me and he has provided for Mike as if he was his own. Life is very funny, you take the good with the bad and make the best of what's left," she instructed her. "I know one thing, we work well together, last week we closed a million dollar deal together. Lorenzo, on the other hand, would have kept me home washing the floor, like a good Sicilian wife.

"Elsie doesn't have a problem with him, does she?" Larissa wondered.

"Not now,."

"But then why did it take fifteen years for him to marry her?"

"His first priority has always been me then Mike then Elsie."

"That's just not right. A man's priority should be his wife and the same for the wife, her husband should come first. What a mess," Larissa thought. "I don't think I should ask anyone else about their past."

"Do me a favor, Larissa, please don't tell anyone about this. I'm afraid Mike will be hurt by it and I don't want anyone to think less of Lorenzo. He has turned out to be a wonderful upstanding man. I still think he is the best looking guy I have ever seen, next to Mike of course. "

"Your secret is safe with me Evangeline, I love you all so much, I wouldn't want any of you to be hurt by all this," promised Larissa.

"It seems so long ago, and we were so young," Evangeline reminisced. "Now you tell me the reason for all these questions, young lady.. Does it have something to do with how badly Mike acted last night?"

"You and my mother can read me so well," Larissa told her. "Alan proposed to me a few months ago, but I can't get Mike out of my heart. I don't know what to do," she started to cry again.

"Larissa, I know people make fun of me when I say this, but if Mike is your destiny then that's the end of it. If Alan is your destiny then that is where you must go. I can't tell you what to do. Either way I know I will have you always."

"I love you, Evangeline," Larissa told her.

"I love you too, baby," Evangeline responded. "Have you given any more thought to Mike's birthday party?" she changed the subject.

"I guess I'm in charge of the guest list, that's what Alicianna told me. "

"Okay, I have the invitations on order, so just tell me how many I need," Evangeline asked. When Larissa left the room, Evangeline felt so bad for her. She knew Larissa had been crazy about Mike for years, she also knew her son wasn't ready to marry anyone yet. He might miss the boat when it comes to Larissa, but she hoped not.

School started in the middle of September at NYU. Dr. Stein was right about the nightmares, they stopped as fast as they started and Mike was grateful for that. Dean, Mike and Nick decided to stay in the same dormitory room so they could have more time to coordinate their future. Nick and Mike were going to enlist as soon as they could, hopefully the first semester would be over and they would have that much credit under their belts. The news now was that President Wilson couldn't hold off much longer and the first of the year was inevitable. Sam kept up with the news with the boys on the weekends. Abigail wasn't happy about the time he spent with them, she always felt like a fifth wheel when they were around. So she took it in stride and went shopping with her mother to pick out china patterns and silverware. Sam hadn't set a date with her yet, but she didn't know he was going to enlist either. He felt badly about not telling her, but he didn't want her to worry. He thought he would give her a ring at Christmas and have a big party-- that should appease her. Abigail was so crazy about Sam that she let him make all the decisions. *For an American girl*, he thought she was going to make a great Italian wife.

In early November, Chance received a call from his lawyer and friend, John Lee. "It's good to hear from you," Chance said.
"I have some good news for you, Chance. A real estate conglomerate contacted me about Lenox Hill. They are willing to offer you your asking price, but they want a few acres to go along with it. What do you think?", John asked,
"I think it's a good deal. I was hoping to just sell the mansion and the attached grounds, but I could part with a few acres. What do they want to

do with it?" Chance inquired.

"They want to open a private school and they need the property for tennis courts and possibly an addition for more green houses," John told him.

"Oh," said Chance," that's going to be right up Evangeline's alley. Let me talk to her and I will call you in the morning. Thanks John, let's get together soon, good bye," he said.

When he approached Rosalyn and Evangeline on the subject, they couldn't be happier. "I'm so glad they didn't want to just tear it down," said Rosalyn.

"How wonderful, what a perfect school it will make!" Evangeline interjected.

"I have more good news for you, Mother," Chance teased.

"What is it darling? I'm still reeling over the house," she said.

"Mother, Matt is coming home," he said with a big smile on his face.

"Oh, what a glorious day," said Rosalyn. She missed her twins terribly. Does Mariella know?" she asked.

"I'm sure the news has reached Little Italy by now," he laughed.

"I better start planning another wedding," said Evangeline.

"This time, the sky's the limit," said Chance. Two weeks later, Matthew Winston arrived on the dock of the New York Port Authority. He arrived on a ship that was slated for troop transport when it was needed. Joe Cross was amazed that Matt managed to jump on a ship at all, it was almost impossible these days.

"Oh Mother," he said as he held her in his arms, "it's so good to see you. I am so glad to be home." He didn't know if he imagined it, but it seemed she was much frailer than when he left. Mariella, Mona and Roberto picked him up at the ship and brought him to Lenox Hill. The whole family was there to greet him.

"Chance, are you alright?" he asked with concern. Chance was still in a wheel chair and looked a little pale to him.

"Evangeline, you are as beautiful as ever and my Sissy you are a woman full grown," he said in amazement. He approached each and every one with a hug and a hand shake. "I hear this old house is going to be a school, can you imagine that?" he said.

"I think it's a crime," Mariella said, "it's too beautiful for a school."

"Who cares?" said Rosalyn, "I will be free of it and its expenses. It wasn't built for me anyway. I didn't care where I lived as long as it was with Edward. Now he is gone, so I simply don't care," she said adamantly.

"Mother," he said, as he held Mariella's hand in his. "Mariella and I want to get married as soon as possible. We have been apart for so long, we don't want to wait any longer. We thought a Christmas Wedding would be nice, what do you think?" he asked.

"Well, the house is sold and we have to be out by the first week in February but I suppose we can still have it here. You'll be the last Winston to be married at Lenox Hill, that's something to tell your grandchildren," she laughed.

"Instead of a Christmas party we will have a wedding." A big cheer was sent out and everyone agreed. What a wonderful Christmas it would be.

Evangeline and her sister-in-law had to scurry to put a wedding together in six weeks. Larissa was back in Boston and felt out of the loop.

"I wish I could contribute more," she told her mother.

"Don't worry dear, there are plenty of people to take charge of things. This wedding won't be as extravagant as Chance and Evangeline's because, honestly, there just isn't the time. Matt gave me a limit of one hundred people to invite. He said he didn't want a circus, just a wedding."

"How do you do that with all the Italians in Little Italy and Bensonhurst?" Larissa laughed.

"I don't care, I'm just so happy for Matt and Mariella that all of Mulberry Street can attend," Rosalyn joked. "Larissa, my dear, you just have to show up and look pretty as a picture, like always," her mother complimented her.

"Oh sure," she complained, "always the bridesmaid, never the bride."

"I believe that is your decision, my darling," Rosalyn teased.

Mariella decided on a silver and white wedding theme. Rosalyn had the tree farm in Albany spray the huge tree in white flocking. She packed her Spanish ornaments and used only silver balls and crystal tear drops for the entire tree. She had the garland decorated with silver and white satin bows and the crystal tear drops to bring it all together.

The wedding was at Saint Patrick's, of course. Mariella looked like a vision in her wedding gown and veil. Mariella's bridesmaids were in white satin with silver bows. Mona was her sister's matron of honor and Larissa was her maid of honor. Several cousins and friends were bridesmaids, and of course Alicianna was now old enough to be the junior bridesmaid.

Antonino had a hard time giving the bride away.

"She is still my little girl," he complained to Luna.

"She is a grown woman, she makes her own money and has an important job. You should think of that, you silly man, not your old fashioned ideas from the old country. Forget about those days, Antonino, you brought us to America, now act like an American."

"Why don't you ask me to stop breathing?" he complained to her.

"I think you will live, my husband," she scolded him fondly.

The tables overflowed the ballroom at Lenox Hill and spilled into the grand hall. They put the children that were old enough to fend for themselves out there. The string quartet played all through dinner and afterward some of the tables were taken away for dancing. That's when the fun began according to Chance. He loved an Italian wedding. The Five Sorrento's played music from Sicily, all the favorites. Antonino got on stage and sang some funny songs from his home town along with his brother-in-law Vincenzo. Matt banged a spoon against a glass and asked everyone for their attention.

"I want to make a short speech," he said. "I just want to thank everyone for coming tonight during this busy holiday season, and celebrating with Mariella and I. I am so proud of my wife and what she has accomplished in the short time she has been in this country. She has advanced in her job and her bosses are very happy with her work," he said. A rousing cheer went up from the crowd and Mariella blushed.

"My brother Mark couldn't be with us today. But in true Mark Winston form, I received a telegram from him early this afternoon. He said he wasn't going to let me get one up on him and marry a beautiful girl, so he married Mary Churchill this morning in London." Matt could hear gasps and cheers from the people he was addressing. "Wait a minute," he said, "this is a good thing. Mary is a great gal, she loves Mark dearly and she is a good friend to me. I can't wait for everyone to meet her. I'm sorry Mother, I hope you aren't disappointed, but now, not only do we have the same birthday, but the same anniversary!"

Rosalyn threw up her hands and said, "You two have done worse things to me in your lifetime, this is wonderful. Now I don't have to worry about him being alone, he has a wife to take care of him," she laughed.

"What do you think of the news?" Joe Cross said, as he approached Evangeline.

"I think it's great," she said, "I gained two sisters-in-law in one day."

"It's nice to hear of people in love getting to be together," he said sarcastically. She shot him a look of annoyance, then one of pity.

"I know Joe, I know," she cried. "Can I at least ask you for this dance," he pleaded? It was a slow dance and he could hold her to his body without anyone's scrutiny. He held his arms up waiting for her to fill them.

"It would be my pleasure, my darling," she whispered. How could she deny him a dance at her niece's wedding, she thought? She was thinking of her conversation with Larissa about the all consuming love she had been looking for. *She knew she had found it with Joe, but she couldn't act on it. Was it worse to find it and not be able to act on it or never find it at all? That was the war going on in her head.* Her perfume was intoxicating to him. He had stolen her hankie one afternoon at the office and kept it on his pillow. He felt closer to her somehow, he also felt like a foolish school boy all at the same time. He knew it couldn't be easy for her either. Right now he had her in his arms and that's all he cared about. Too soon the music stopped and he had to let her go. Chance wheeled over to them, "Having a nice time Joe?" he asked.

"Yes, you can always count on your mother and wife to give a beautiful party."

"This isn't the last one," Chance replied, "Mike will be 18 on February 13 and Evangeline is planning another party for him. We can count on you I presume?" he said.

"Sure, Chance, I'll be there," Joe assured him. Joe excused himself and went off to talk to Mariella's boss from the Defense Department.

"Evangeline, I have a wonderful idea for Mark and Mary's wedding gift," Chance said excitedly, after the wedding.

"Really?" she asked, "What is it?"

"You know how I have told you about the Hennessey Manor House, and how huge it is?"

"Yes, " she remembered. "Well, since I'm the only living heir, I have access to all the grounds. When we got married, the outlying property was sold and the money was invested. I have since, reinvested it in other properties all over the world. But what I'm getting at is the Manor House and the out buildings are still intact. There is a beautiful gardener's cottage on the property. I would like to have it refurbished and give it to my brother and his wife, what do you think?" he asked.

"I think it's a very generous offer," she said. "But what if they would rather live in town?" she questioned.

"You're right, they might, but I bet they will be glad to have it, even for a weekend retreat," Chance said. "There are a few smaller places on the site that perhaps I can sell off, too. The idea of a school at Lenox Hill has spiked my interest to turn Hennessey Mansion into some sort of learning facility also," he told her.

"Do you think you would ever want to live there?" Evangeline asked.

"Absolutely not," he insisted, "I am American, through and through. I live here!" he said as he pointed his finger to the ground. Evangeline was relieved to hear that, she didn't want to go to London either.

"I think a school is a perfect idea, Chance. The Winston's are educating the world." she laughed.

"Maybe." he smiled at her, "Really, I just want to be rid of all my holdings in the Hennessey name," he said. "I don't want Alicianna strapped with any of it. A nice trust fund will be the best legacy I could give her," Chance confessed.

"You're a good father, Chance," Evangeline told him.

The plans were still in the works for Mike's 18th birthday party. Friends and family were invited to share all of Mike's favorite foods. Evangeline planned a huge spread for the table. Cook prepared various pasta's, including lasagna, ravioli and salads. For desert, canoli, Italian cream cake, and chocolate cookies, would be a gift from Zia Luna. Larissa had the guest list finished and sent to Evangeline. Alicianna made paper hats and had crape paper strung across the room in a draped fashion.

"I hope Mike likes what I've done," she told, her mother.

"If you made it then he will love it," she reassured her daughter.

When Mike walked in that evening, he wanted to turn right around. *I'm 18, not eight*, he thought to himself.

"Mike, Mike!" Alicianna called, "How do you like how I decorated the room?"

"It's beautiful honey," he told her. He would never hurt her feelings, especially since she was so excited. Mike thought it was silly to make such a fuss. He was thinking he was now a man and a children's party was embarrassing. He gave his mother one last chance to baby him, for tomorrow, she will know the truth.

Evangeline had the invitations engraved rather than printed. She wanted it to be more of a keepsake rather than a plain invitation. Evangeline remembered her own eighteenth birthday. Her family had just died and she was left to raise Mike on his own. She was remembering what a joy he had been to her then as he was now. If her brother Antonino hadn't insisted that she bring Mike to his father, none of this would have been possible. Fortunately, Lorenzo accepted him as his son and brought her to the Winston's. *God knows where they would have ended up*, she thought. Evangeline wanted to acknowledge Rosalyn and Chance and the others that their kindness made this all possible. She was beginning to think this party was more for her than Mike.

Mike was doing well in his classes. He discovered he could carry on a conversation with the janitor of the school as well as a few politicians he met, he felt comfortable with both ends of the spectrum. With his gift of gab, good looks and personality, he was a natural to become the perfect politician. When his friends arrived he took a lot of teasing from them.

"Hey Mike, can I have a pink paper hat?" asked Sam.

"I don't think pink is your color," Mike teased back.

"Go get something to eat," Abigail scolded him, "You will hurt Alicianna's feelings." So they went off to the buffet table together. She wanted to show off her beautiful engagement ring to the others who had gathered around the table.

This was the first time Larissa saw Mike since the Christmas break. They both stood up in Mark's wedding, but with different partners. Larissa didn't know it, but Rosalyn had a hand in that decision and Evangeline agreed. Mike didn't pay any attention to the girl he stood up with and it made Larissa feel a little better.

"Hey stranger," Larissa said as she approached Mike, "Happy Birthday!" and she kissed his cheek.

"Thank you, how have you been?" he asked politely? "Was Alan invited?"

"Yes, he will be by later," she answered. *How does he do it?*, she wondered? He can annoy me at the drop of a name, she thought to herself. He thinks of Alan and me as a couple, I bet, she thought.

"You know, I promised to apologize to him for that remark I made last summer," he said. "Oh, don't worry yourself about it. I'm sure he has forgotten all about it by now."

"I hope so," said Mike, "I don't want to leave things like that."

"What do you mean?" Larissa questioned him.

"Oh, nothing," he said and excused himself to greet more guests. *What's he up to?* Larissa wondered, *I know he has something up his sleeve.*

"Happy Birthday Mike," Lorenzo greeted him holding Elena in his arms. Mike kissed his father and the baby.

"You look more like your dad every day," Elsie said as she reached out to kiss him.

"He might look like me, but he is smarter than me," Lorenzo said and softly slugged him on the arm.

"Don't say that Pa, I think you're great," he replied to his father. Elena reached out to Mike and he held on to her most of the night. That child adored her big brother and the feeling was mutual.

"I have two of the most beautiful sisters in the world," Mike said to Evangeline. "They look nothing alike, one is dark and one is light, I'm going to miss them," he said aloud.

"What do you mean?" Evangeline questioned, "You see them all the time."

"Oh, I mean when I'm at school," he covered his words.

Maria and Nicolo walked in with a handful of wrapped presents in their hands. "My favorite aunt and uncle," he said, "you always did spoil me.".

"That's because I love you so much," his doting Aunt Maria said.

"You were three years old when you came to me. I put you and Evangeline in the room next to ours so when you woke up in the middle of the night, I could run in to rock you back to sleep. Now look at you, you are a man," she said with tears in her eyes.

"Don't cry, Zia, I will always remember you and Ziu Nicolo on winter nights when I was cold, and I would crawl in bed between you and fall fast asleep."

"You won't try that now will you? Nicolo asked grinning.

"No," he said.

"Good said Nicolo. And it made them all laugh.

Apollinia   ------   Evangeline's Destiny

TWELVE

The Como's arrived with Mona and Roberto they had an announcement to make to the family. Roberto asked for everyone's attention.

"I have wonderful news," he said, "Mona is going to have a baby next summer!" Oh, how happy everyone was for them. "Luna will finally have a grandchild in New York. The others in Palermo couldn't get out of the country and the borders were closed."

"If it's a boy will you call it Michele?" Mike asked, "after all it's my birthday."

"Maybe we will get you another gift," Roberto said. He was beaming from ear to ear, at this point he would call it President Wilson, he was so happy.

President Wilson was a big part of the conversations that went on that night. The war was on everyone's mind. None of the boys made mention of the fact that they all went down to the army recruiters that day and enlisted. They knew it would upset Evangeline and ruin the party. Joe was the only one who knew what the boys had done. He took them in the office that day and talked to them about their decision. He wanted to make sure they were going for the right reason.

"Sit down, men," he directed them to the chairs. He wouldn't, out of pure respect, address them as boys. Each one, one at a time, gave him the reasons they wanted to enlist. Joe knew he wasn't going to talk them out of it, any more than the people who tried to talk Joe out of joining the Resistance. The boys had high hopes for a better America if Europe was safe, and of course they were invincible.

"Wilson hasn't declared war yet," Joe said.

"We know that," Sam answered. "President Wilson believes in the League of Nations, but I don't think that will keep us out of this war," he added.

"Nick," Joe asked, "what is your take on this?"

"The slaughter that's going on in Europe in a disgrace to the human race, I feel America has a responsibility to help clean up the mess," he told him. "Our semester is over and we have a few credits to our name, but when we get back we can finish with nothing but school on our mind and, of course Mike's election."

"Mike, you are eighteen now, we can't tell you what to do but do you know what this will do to your mother?"

"With all due respect, Joe, what makes my mother any different than every other mother of a soldier?" he answered. "If we enlist now, we will have our training over by the time the first troop ships leave New York," Mike told him.

"Well, thank you very much for talking to me," Joe said. "I'm terrified and proud all at the same time."

"Thank you, Joe for talking to us," Sam answered, "everyone else has tried to talk us out of it. My brother is over there now, and he said it's a living hell. My parents were all so proud to let him join the Italian army, but now they are sorry he went. I know I have to leave my parents and Abigail and believe me, that's not easy, but I made up my mind. I want my children to live in a safe America and this is what I have to do to insure that." Joe smiled at him; he's just like me he thought.

"Those were my sentiments exactly when I joined the Resistance. God bless all of you, you are all fine Americans," he said as he shook their hands and walked them out of the office. "If this is the generation of young people we are raising, America can do anything. " *Mike, didn't have to go to war, his father had enough money to buy his way out of it. He was sure though, that Evangeline had a lot of influence in his upbringing to make him such a fine person. It just made him love her more.*

The morning after the party Evangeline was awaken by voices coming from the drawing room. The morning was cold and the snow was blowing drifts across the lawn. She put on a warm robe and went downstairs. She saw a fire had been lit in the drawing room fireplace. When she entered, she saw a man in uniform warming his hands by the fire. His back was to her, how handsome he looked, she thought. When he turned around she almost fainted.

"Good morning Mother," he said and handed her a red rose. "Happy Valentine's Day," he said.

"Oh Mike, don't do this, you are too young," she cried.

"I'm old enough," he said determined to go through with his decision.

"Please Mike, I couldn't stand it if something happened to you," she moaned.

"Nothing will happen, Mama, I promise," he said.

"What about school?" she was reaching for every excuse she could find.

"I have to report to boot camp this morning. Sam and Nick are going with me," he told her.

"You already sound like a soldier," she sobbed. "Why are you going now? War hasn't been declared yet," she asked.

"It will be soon, then we will be ready," he said.

"Have you told your fathers?" she questioned as she dabbed the tears from her eyes. "I told them last night, after the party," he told her. "They both took it very well," he added.

She didn't believe for one minute that Lorenzo agreed with Mike. "Even Lorenzo?" she asked.

"Even Lorenzo," he laughed. "I was saying good bye to both of them before you came down. Joe Cross is going to drive me to the camp in a few minutes," he informed her.

"He knows about this too?" she said in disbelief.
Could no one talk him out of going to the Army? she thought.

"Mama, please don't let me leave like this. When Dean lost his leg, I realized that there are no guarantees, any minute things can change. I want you to be proud of me," he told her.

"I am so very proud of you," she declared. "I know you have talked about the Army for years, but I never thought you would act on it," she cried. "What about your grandmother, and your sister, and Larissa?" she said, grasping at straws?

"I've written each of them a letter, I gave them to Dad earlier. I think I have all the loose ends tied up," he said.

"Look Mother, as he took both her hands in his, "this is something I have to do. When I get back and finish school, I'm going into politics. I want to help people. I want them to know I stand behind them and have their best interests at heart."

" You are just like your Nonno Georgio, "she declared. "I guess the apple doesn't fall far from the tree," she exclaimed.

"It's time to go." She heard Joe's voice from the hall. The men had been having their coffee in the breakfast room, waiting for Mike and Evangeline to finish their goodbyes. He took her in his arms and hugged her one last time.

"Good bye, my precious son," as tears poured from her eyes again. He walked out of the room and hugged and kissed Lorenzo before Joe drove him away. Evangeline ran into Lorenzo's arms and they hung on to each other. They cried until they couldn't cry any more.

"He will be home soon, darling," Lorenzo tried to comfort her as he stroked her hair.

"He's a man now, Lorenzo, it will never be the same," she said, as she tried to gather her wits and let the fact that he left sink in. Chance with the three letters in his hands went to deliver them to their owners. Evangeline knew Joe had something to do with Mike's decision. She would deal with him latter.

Mike met up with Nick and Sam at the camp. Dean stayed home, not only because of the loss of his leg, but because he wanted to go to school and study politics so that when Mike got home, they would put on a campaign for state representative. He had to prove to himself that he wasn't only handicapped, but his mind was his gift to the community.

Chance knocked on Larissa's door.

"Come in," she said.

"Good morning, sweetheart," Chance said as he wheeled himself in.

"Is something wrong?" she asked.

"I have a letter for you, from Mike. He asked me to give it to you this morning."

"I don't understand," she said as she opened the letter.

"Do you want me to leave you alone?" Chance asked. "Stay," she said as she started to read.

Dear Larissa,

I don't think you will be surprised by my decision, but I'm leaving for the army today. To tell you the truth I didn't want to see your beautiful face when I said good bye. I'm afraid I have hurt you many times in the past because of my clumsiness and immaturity, please don't hold that against me. You are my dearest friend and someone I can always trust, I love you   very much. I'll send you my address when I get settled, please write.

Yours always,

Mike

"What do you make of that information?" she asked Chance, "what does he expect me to do? He tells me he loves me and that I'm his friend in the same sentence. Is he confused or am I,?" she asked. "I'm not going to shed one more tear for Mr. Mike Winston with Sicilian blood running through his veins. Do you hear me?" she screamed at her brother, "not one more tear!" With that, she collapsed on the floor and cried for the rest of the morning. Chance didn't say a word. He was sorry for his little sister, but he was disgusted with Mike. He wheeled himself out of the room and went to see his mother.

"Good morning, Mother," he said, as her door was opened a little. "How do you feel this morning?" He didn't care for her coloring the past few weeks and she seemed so thin.

"I'm sorry, I didn't hear you," she said, as she walked out of her dressing room.

"Mike left for the army this morning and left this letter for you," he said as he handed her the envelope.

"What has that boy gone and done now?"

Dear Grandmother,

I'm sorry to tell you in a letter that I've joined the army. I have sent one to Alicianna and Larissa too. I want you to know how much I appreciate the Love and Care you have given to me in my life. None of my friends knew that I wasn't a blood Winston and I liked it that way. Grandfather was the best a boy could ask for. I hope to make you proud of me in the future, as proud as I am, to be called Mike Winston.

With Love and Respect
Mike

"He certainly is a charmer," claimed Chance. "I just left Larissa in a pool of tears in her room. I don't know what to do," he said. "He is my son and I never thought of him as anything else, but damn it, she is my sister!"

"Don't be so hard on yourself," Rosalyn consoled him. "Larissa's wounds are self inflicted. He never made her any promises, yet she reads a promise in everything he says to her. "

"He has Aliciana completely mesmerized too," Chance said, "I hope she takes this better than the rest of his women."

"Wake up sleepyhead," Chance shook his daughter awake.

"Hi daddy," she said as she rubbed the sleep from her eyes. "What's the matter?" she asked.

"I have some news for you," he said softly.

"What is it?" she wondered.

"Your brother has joined the army," he said as he tried to soften the blow.

"Oh, I know," she said, "I heard him and Nick talking the other day. What does that mean,\?" she asked.

"Well, it means he has gone away to be a soldier," Chance said a little confused.

"Did he leave already?"

"Yes, darling, he left this letter for you," Chance handed the letter to his precious daughter. .

"Wow, I never get a letter from anyone," she said excitedly, as she opened it.

Dearest Alicianna,

I hope you aren't mad at me for not saying good bye in person. I just thought you might like to get a letter instead. You can save it and put it with the others I hope to send you. I want you to be a good girl while I'm away and please take care of Mother and Dad for me. I love you my angel and will think of you always.

Your loving

brother,

Mike

Chance just shook his head, *no wonder his women love him so much, he has them eating out of his hand,* he thought. Chance went to see Evangeline, she was back in her room sitting on the window seat and staring out at the falling snow.

"Did Lorenzo leave?" he asked her.

"Yes, just a few minutes ago," she said. "Chance, I feel like the wind has been knocked out of me. I haven't cried like this since Santa Fata and my family died. I was alone then, but I still have that feeling of dread."

"I know, I don't feel so well myself," he remarked.

"Did you deliver his letters?" she asked.

"Yes, you might want to look in on Larissa. She took it very hard."

"I will," she assured him.

"Alicianna seemed to know all about it, but she just doesn't know what it means."

My darling girl, she will keep our spirits up, just by her innocence, Evangeline imagined.

"Lie down Evangeline, at least for a while, you have had a couple of busy days and an emotional morning," he encouraged her.

"Chance, did Joe have a part in Mike's joining the army?" she asked. "Of course not, but he did speak to each of the boys yesterday and he felt satisfied with their decision," Chance told her. "Okay, I was just wondering," she said. Evangeline took the rose Mike gave her and pressed it in her prayer book next to the 'Prayer for a Soldier'. She went back to bed and fell asleep. She dreamt of the day Mike was born and the midwife handing him to her to care for. What a beautiful dream, she mused.

Two weeks after Mike left for the Army, Evangeline was still upset. She relented to a visit to Madam Sasha's. She didn't want Rosalyn or Mrs. Mitchell to know about it, since it was she who made such a fuss about her predictions at the Christmas party. She had to be sure Mike would be safe. After the shark attack, she wasn't sure about anything. Evangeline had Chance's chauffer drive her to the area of New York called Harlem. She swore him to secrecy and walked to the door that had the address on the paper she copied out of Rosalyn's address book.

The building was a shabby grey with the number 810 painted on it. Evangeline walked into a narrow hallway with a row of mail boxes on the wall. She searched for the name Comanink and rang the buzzard on the box.

"Hello?" said a raspy voice. "Who is there?"
Evangeline realized it wasn't Madam Sasha and she asked for the psychic.

"Come up," said the voice. Evangeline walked up the two flights of stairs. The walls were grimy and the smell of cabbage lingered in the hall way. 2B was the number on the mail box. When she found the apartment, she knocked on the door. The door opened slowly and an elderly woman, probably Madam Sasha's mother invited her in. Evangeline wondered what she had gotten herself into, and why was she here. Maybe she should have brought Rosalyn along with her after all. She was questioning all her personal decisions these days. Suddenly she felt afraid. The room was a mix of fringed shawls and pictures of saints in golden frames. The furniture was dark and a little sparse.

"Hello Evangeline," she heard a friendly voice call out to her. There was Madam Sasha standing in a doorway. "I've been expecting you."

"Why?" said Evangeline, "I didn't let you know I was coming."

"Don't ask me how I knew, I just knew. Come, sit down and we can talk. What is it you wish from me?" she said. *If she knew I was coming*, she thought, *then why doesn't she know what I want?*

"Would you like to use the tarot cards?" Madam Sasha asked.

"Oh, Madam Sasha, I'm so worried about my son Mike. He has joined the army and will soon be going overseas to the war and I am so afraid," Evangeline cried.

"Why do you question what I told you last year?" she wondered. "The cards haven't changed for him." she scolded, "Remember I said he was going to be a very important person and people are going to respect his ideals. Don't you remember?" the Madam asked her.

"Yes, I suppose I do," said Evangeline sheepishly.

"He has to come home to make all these things happen," she assured her.

"Yes," Evangeline smiled, " that's true." Suddenly she felt the weight of the world lifted off her shoulders.

"Mrs. Winston, cut the cards," Madam Sasha instructed her. Evangeline cut the cards and placed half the deck in front of her.

"Very good," Madam Sasha praised her. "You cut the cards toward you not away from you. That means it will be a matter of the heart for you personally. Mike will come home in one piece," she said, as she placed the cards strategically on the table. "He will be happier than he has ever been. His happiness will break the heart of another and his home life will be in jeopardy," the woman predicted. "I see a war, but it will be in the family, I'm sorry I don't know anything else about that.

"Evangeline I see you aren't fulfilling your destiny," she said.

"What do you mean?" Evangeline asked her.

"Your heart is heavy; you love one and care deeply for another. You have to make up your mind," she insisted.

"No, I can't do that, I promised," she cried.

"Who did you promise?"

"Why, God." Evangeline was shocked she was having this conversation with this woman. Elsie was the only other person who knew about Joe.

"You may not have to make that choice," she said. "Sometimes, life makes choices for you. This won't happen soon, but it will happen. The man you love has a lot of secrets about his past. It won't do you any good to ask him, because he won't tell you about them. Secrets have a way of sneaking out without your help." Madam Sasha flipped over a few more cards. "Oh, I see you will be moving west in the future."

"West?" she questioned. All she could think of was cowboys and Indians and it made her chuckle. "I can't imagine why," she answered,

"haven't I moved enough in my life?"

"Keep an eye on the young girl in your house, the one with the blonde curls," the woman told her.

"Is it my daughter?" Evangeline said with fear in her voice.

"I don't know," the Madam said, "I'm sorry."

"Evangeline you have so many people who truly love you. You are indeed a lucky woman. I'm sorry this is all I can see for this reading. I don't know what else to tell you, but I can say that you are never bored with life, am I right,?" she said.

"I suppose not," Evangeline said, with a smile. "Thank you for the imposition, Madam Sasha, I'm sorry I didn't call you first," Evangeline apologized.

"Don't think twice about it," she said as she put the envelope Evangeline handed to her in the sideboard drawer. "Call me any time you need me," she told her.

"Please don't tell my mother-in-law or Mrs. Mitchell about this reading," she implored her.

"Of course not," she said as she showed her to the door. "If you know me, you know I'm very discrete."

Evangeline didn't say a word while driving home with the chauffer. He didn't dare ask any questions, it wasn't proper, but he could tell she was agitated, not sad, but agitated. When she arrived at Hunters Point she went to her desk and wrote Mike a letter. She told him how much she loved him and looked forward to his return. *Be safe my son but then I know you will be. Love Mother.* She tucked a silver medal of Saint Michael the Arch Angel inside to help with his protection. Evangeline seemed more relaxed after her reading. She put the rest of the predictions in the back of her mind and concentrated on Mike coming home.

In April of 1917 President Woodrow Wilson declared war on Germany just as most of America expected he would. Mike Winston, Dean McCall, and Sam Genoa deployed on the first troop ship out of New York.

The families and friends said good bye to them from the docks waving American flags and throwing kisses. 'Return soon' was the battle cry from those docks.

Rosalyn, Evangeline, Elsie, and Mrs. Mitchell busied themselves at the American Red Cross, rolling bandages and any other duties that they could perform. Elsie had learned to drive the year before and drove the boxes of rolled bandages to the ships as they were being loaded with other goods for the American soldiers. The ladies were busy with gossip of the day and happy to be able to do their part for the sailors, soldiers and marines.

Mrs. Mitchell took Evangeline aside one day and expressed to her that Rosalyn was getting weaker and her color was an ashen grey. Evangeline who only had Mike on her mind and didn't pay much attention to anyone else was taken aback by her remark.

"Rosalyn spends most of the day in her room," Evangeline told her. "I guess I haven't noticed. She hasn't complained, but then she never complains. I know she has been very quiet lately. She misses Edward very much and all the children are gone except Chance. I'll mention it to him tonight. I see her every day, maybe I'm missing something."

That evening after dinner, Evangeline told Chance of Mrs. Mitchell's fears.

"I noticed her moody attitude lately, but I thought it was about the house," he said.

"When the movers had finished clearing everything out of Lenox Hill after Matt and Mariella's wedding, I thought she was having regrets about selling the house," said Evangeline.

"Mark mentioned to me that when he returned from London she seemed frail to him," Chance recalled. "I'm going to call Dr. Murphy from Our Lady of Consolation Hospital tomorrow and see if he can give her a checkup."

The next afternoon Evangeline took Rosalyn to see Doctor Murphy, despite her protests.

"Now Rosalyn, we love you and just want to make sure there isn't something that can perk up your spirits a bit," Evangeline insisted.

"I think I miss my family being under one roof, that's all, my dear."

"Maybe so," said Evangeline, "but let's find out for sure."

Dr. Murray gave Rosalyn a thorough check up and called Chance with the results the next day.

"Mr. Winston," Dr. Murphy informed him, "your mother has extremely high white cells in her blood.".

"What does that mean, Doctor?" Chance questioned.

"I'm afraid your mother has cancer," he told him sorrowfully. "We think it is in advanced stages by the amount of cells and her frail condition. The best we can do is to keep her comfortable and pain free. I'm terribly sorry to give you such grave news. She seems like a wonderful woman.

"You have no idea, Doctor, you have no idea," Chance assured him.

Chance called Matt in the office. The doctor just called, he told him.

"What did he say? It can't be good by the look on your face," Matt said fearfully.

"She has cancer, Matt."

"What can we do?" he asked Tears welled up in both of her son's eyes.

"Do we tell her?" Chance asked his brother, knowing he didn't know what to do either. "Evangeline is coming into the office in an hour. We will have a meeting when she gets here, how does that sound?" Chance said.

"Mariella is working late tonight, so I know she won't be able to get here in time, but she will go along with whatever we decide. " Matt said of his wife.

Evangeline had some figures about the new office building that was being built downtown. She was going to go over them with Joe. It always made her nervous to sit that close to him in the office. She felt that God was testing her daily. When she arrived she could see Chance and Matt were upset.

"Did you too have a disagreement?" she asked?

"No, darling, sit down," Chance said directing her to a chair. "

Mike! what's happened to Mike?" she yelled.

"No, Evangeline, it's not Mike. It's my mother. She has cancer," he told her and started to cry.

"Oh God, no!" she wailed. "It can't be, it can't be." The words kept whirling around in her head, but didn't make any sense.

"She is the strongest person I know. Mrs. Mitchell saw it, why couldn't I?" she cried.

"Get a hold of yourself, darling. We need your good head for the family to get us through this. Matt and I were wondering if we should tell her?" he asked.

"Well, she would be mad if we didn't, but then if we did she might just give up. Larissa is in no shape to help even if she wasn't in Boston. Her nerves are shot between Alan and Mike. Alicianna is just a baby, I don't want her to get involved in this."

"She is twelve, Evangeline," Matt spoke up, "twelve going on twenty. I think she is going to take care of all of us someday."

Evangeline shot him a look. "She is still my baby," she said with clarity.

"Okay, whatever we decide, we have to do it today. The doctor said she doesn't have much time," Chance said as he felt his throat tighten.

"I think we need to keep this between us and Mariella," Evangeline decided.

"What do we do about Mark?" Matt asked.

"He couldn't come home if he wanted to," said Chance. "So let's not worry him for awhile and see what happens."

"Maybe she will last past this war and then Mark and Mary will come back here, for a while anyway," said Evangeline. "I say we pray and offer a novena for mother and maybe we can keep her a little longer," added Evangeline.

"Good idea, sister" said Matt and gave her a hug.

Mrs. Mitchell came calling the next day, wondering about how Rosalyn's visit to the doctors went. Without saying the word, cancer, Evangeline told her that her Mother-in-law was very sick.

"I know of an herbalist that Mary Jane from the suffragettes uses and she swears she feels one hundred percent better. Maybe we should take Rosalyn there?" she wondered.

"I guess it wouldn't hurt, but let me speak to the boys about it first. The doctor said to give her plenty of sunshine and lots of vitamins to keep her strength up. Now that the flowers are coming up, I thought we could put her in Chance's old wheel chair and keep her in the garden on warm spring days," said Evangeline. "We told her the doctor prescribes fresh air and sunshine. If it didn't hold so many bad memories as of late, I would take her to the beach for the whole summer."

"Speaking of the beach, how is Dean doing these days?" Mrs. Mitchell asked She had a fond affection for Dean, he was always so kind and unspoiled.

"He is wonderful," she said, "he comes over once a week at least and helps Chance master the crutches. Now they have races to see who can walk the fastest. I think he lets Chance win," said Evangeline. "Chance was so glad to be out of that wheel chair, it's amazing how far he has come. You should see him climb the stairs, she told Mrs. Mitchell.

When Dean heard Rosalyn needed sunshine, he was the first to suggest they take her to the New Jersey shore.

"Please, Evangeline, don't keep her home because of me," he begged. "I have to face my demons every day and I'll be damned if a fish is going to keep me from the things I love to do. If you would do me a favor and let me go with you for a little while to the shore, I think it will do me a lot of good and Rosalyn too."

Chance called the Handleys at the Bellflower Inn and rented the old cottage they used years before. Evangeline thought Larissa could use this time to relax and take her mind off her troubles. Alan was putting a little pressure on Larissa again. He wanted her to spend time with his family to get to know them better. She was putting it off, but if she was going to the beach for the summer to help her mother get better, he couldn't fault her for saying no. Alicianna was apprehensive about the ocean, but Dean talked to her and convinced her by telling her that if he wasn't afraid, then neither should she be. Evangeline wasn't going to let her go out more than two feet from shore anyway.

The last week of June after Larissa came home from school and Dean finished his exams, the whole gang left for Beach Haven. Matt and Mariella were only staying one week, because Mona was going to have her baby in a few weeks and Mariella didn't want to be too far from home.

Chance was leaving with them and Joe was taking his place. Someone had to be in command at the office, Chance felt. Joe was glad he didn't have to be away from Evangeline all summer. He knew Chance wanted to be there if something happened to his mother. He didn't want all the responsibility to be on Dean.

Apollinia   ------   Evangeline's Destiny

THIRTEEN

The caravan of three cars, full of suitcases and people, left Hunters Point with hopes of a good vacation. The Winston's hadn't had a vacation for a very long time. The Handleys were thrilled to see the family arrive. Rosalyn was happy to be there, but Edward's spirit seemed to be all around them and it made her melancholy. When the family unpacked and settled in, the outdoors was the only place to be. Evangeline and Mariella were the sun worshipers, Matt, Chance and Dean took the row boat out for a ride and Larissa and Alicianna combed the beach for exotic shells and sea glass.

Rosalyn brought her water colors with her to see if she had the magic in her hands to paint like she did when she was much younger, and she did. She painted the beach in the morning and the beach at sunset. She painted a man walking on the beach who looked exactly like Edward. She painted one of Larissa and Alicianna that turned out so beautifully that Mrs. Handley asked if she could purchase it for the Inn's dining room.

"No, Mrs. Handley," Rosalyn insisted, "please take it as a gift from me and Edward for many years of joy at the Bellflower." Mrs. Handley was so excited, she took it and hung it that day for the guests to see at dinner time.

"The doctor was right." Rosalyn told Chance. "The sun and fresh air has done me good. I feel so much better than I did in New York," she said, as they walked the beach arm and arm. Chance was so glad to hear that his mother was feeling better. He was too, he was only using one crutch these days. Dean loved the beach as he always had, he couldn't go too far into the water mostly because of his crutches. Alicianna was at his side most of the time. She was determined to defend him from any old shark that decided to get near him. She was developing a school girl crush on Dean and Larissa was worried.

"I was younger than that when I fell in love with Mike," she told Mariella, "I hope Dean doesn't string her along like Mike did to me all these years," she said.

"Don't be silly," Mariella said, "little girls always get a crush on their brother's friends. I had a crush on one of my brother's school mates and I can't even remember his name now. Don't worry about it," she told Larissa.

Soon the week was over and Chance, Matt and Mariella said their sad goodbyes. They had a wonderful time and were sorry to see it end. They decided to make The Bellflower Inn an annual event.

"Maybe Mark and Mary will be home from London by then and we can have a real reunion," Evangeline hoped.

Joe showed up a few hours after the Winston's left the resort. He couldn't believe the Jersey shore was so beautiful. Dean was the first person he encountered.

"You are a brave man to come back here so soon," he told Dean.

"I'm not brave, I'm just practical," he said. "I can't hide from the world because I'm afraid. Besides, I'm having a great time. Joe, can you row a boat?"

Joe thought of the boat he had to row to smuggle guns from Sicily to Greece.

"It's like riding a bike," he asked Dean, "right?"

"That's right," Dean laughed. When Joe saw Evangeline, he couldn't believe how suntanned she had gotten. She was walking the beach with Aliaianna looking for sea glass with the front of her white skirt tucked into her belt to hold their treasures in the folds. Her blouse had fallen off one shoulder and her legs were exposed. She had a red bandana holding her long hair off her face, but a few curls had escaped the scarf and dangled in her eyes. She looked just like a Sicilian peasant girl. His heart skipped a beat; he couldn't breathe. *Get a hold of yourself, old man,* he thought. These people don't need you acting a fool with Rosalyn so sick.

Joe brought a supply of herbs the herbalist subscribed for Rosalyn. Mrs. Mitchell made sure he didn't forget them when he took his turn at the beach. The Rizzo's would be coming in a few weeks and they would bring a fresh batch. No one knew if Rosalyn was getting better from the herbs or from the fresh air and sunshine, but she seemed to have perked up a bit.

Evangeline didn't see Joe standing on the porch when she got back to the cottage. She almost ran into him.

"Oh, Joe," she said, "I didn't see you. The sun was in my eyes." She tried to pull her blouse up over her shoulder when he stopped her.

"Don't do that," he said, "I was enjoying the view. I haven't seen that shoulder in quite some time," he teased, as he tried to caress it.

"Oh, you are a devil," she said as she scurried into the house.

"Are you going to pull your skirt down too?" he asked, "I haven't seen those legs in a while either."

"Joe, stop it, someone might hear you," she cried.

"Who? Everyone is outside. Come here." He grabbed her by the arm, swung her around and kissed her full on the mouth. The temptation was more than she could handle, and she kissed him back.

"This is Chance's fault," he told her, putting us in this situation.

"Come on Joe, we have to be careful, my daughter is here and I don't want her to catch us doing something she wouldn't understand." Joe put the herbs in the ice box and went out to find Dean.

"Are you ready for that boat ride?" he asked. "I need to cool off a bit." Dean was ignorant of what Joe meant, but was happy for the offer to go on the boat.

When Chance returned to the office, his clerk announced that he had a visitor waiting inside. Chance opened the door to find a women standing, looking out the window.

"Hello, Chance," she said, as she turned around slowly.

"Rebecca!" he said totally surprised, "What are you doing here?"

"Oh, Chance," she said, as she rushed into his arms, "my Austrian Count turned into a perfect cad. Please don't turn me away it's taken me months to get the nerve to come to see you."

Chance was shocked that she was here, but to his surprise he was very glad to see her.

"Kiss me, Chance. I have been like a dry well since I saw you last." When he kissed her a flood of warm memories washed over him.

"Rebecca, what happened?" he asked, "Did you marry him?"

"I came real close," she told him, "but first, I had him investigated, thank God. All the money he had been throwing around didn't belong to him it was the Austrian Government's and he had to repay it or go to jail."

"Where is he now?" Chance asked.

"Where do you think ?In the city jail! Chance, please come to me tonight. I'm so alone in New York and the clerk said your family is in New Jersey."

"Rebecca, I haven't been well. A while ago, I was robbed and shot. I just got on my feet again. I'm only using one crutch now and soon I will walk alone. I don't even know if I can make love to you."

"Let's worry about that later, just being in your arms will be like medicine for both of us."
She kissed him good bye with the assurance that they would see each other at the end of the day.

"I'll have dinner sent in for us, I can't wait," she said, and rushed off to plan her romantic evening. Chance felt like he had been hit by a train. *What am I getting myself into again, She was right, being in her arms was like a tonic*, he thought. Evangeline and he hadn't even slept in the same room since the shooting. Now he was curious to see if he could perform like a man again.

Matt walked into Chance's office. "Was that Rebecca Clay that just left?" he asked him.

"Yes, that was she."

"Oh no, Chance, don't get involved with her again. Think about what you are doing to Evangeline," he scolded him.

"I'm a man, Matt, not a child; I don't appreciate your meddling in my affairs. You are a married man now. Does your wife satisfy your needs?"

"Why, of course."

"Then mind your own business, please," he told him. Matt realized he had stepped in muddy waters and walked out of the office. He couldn't believe a woman of Evangeline's charisma and stature couldn't keep his brother faithful.

Rebecca ordered a light dinner for them and several bottles of Champaign. She went shopping and bought a red silky night gown and robe to entice him even further.   When he arrived that evening, he took his time undressing her. He soon knew he could make her swoon like he always had. He was relieved to know their lovemaking was back on track and it would stay that way. Rebecca wanted him to divorce Evangeline; it was the only sensible thing to do. She decided she wouldn't bring it up while Rosalyn was so sick, she would see how things went with their relationship and then she would insist.

Evangeline mixed the potion of herbs and vitamins that Joe got from Mrs. Mitchell. She used a good portion of honey to sweeten the drink so Rosalyn could get it down easier. They all dined on fruits and cheeses, prosciutto and other salami's. No big dinners at the beach, the ladies insisted. Joe also brought several loafs of hard crusted bread from Roberto.

"Roberto sends his love, Rosalyn," Joe interjected. "He said, 'bread is the staff of life,' and get well soon." The evenings were cool at the beach. Evangeline wrapped in an old handmaid quilt was very comfortable on the porch swing. Dean went to sleep right after dinner, his medications kept him from doing too much. Rosalyn went to her room to read her prayer book. She prayed for the souls in purgatory, her family, and all the service men in the terrible war. Joe also brought letters from Mike for Evangeline and Rosalyn and she wanted to read hers in private.

Dear Grandmother,

My mother said you weren't feeling very well. I hope this letter finds you in better spirits now. Dean is at the beach with the family, I hear from Larissa. What a gutsy guy, don't you agree? I am fine, both Sam and Nick are stationed with me right now. The motor pool is where I'm working because of the training at my Pa's garages. Don't worry about me. I miss you very much. Get well soon.

Love Mike

She put the letter in her nightstand drawer and crawled under the blanket in her bed. The herbs Joe brought made her sleepy and the pain she didn't tell anyone about was getting worse.

Larissa and Alicianna were in the living room. They sat near the fire Joe had built for them and were happily playing a board game.

Joe walked out to the porch to sit with Evangeline. She just smiled at him and he sat on an Adirondack chair and relaxed his bones.

"This is what it would be like if we were married," he told her. "Only I would be under that quilt with you>"

"Such a lovely vision," she told him and giggled at the thought.

"Who needs a big mansion? We have all the stars to decorate our world.

"I know, Joe," she said, "this is a little bit of heaven."

"Our time is running out, Evangeline. Life is so short, ask Rosalyn she'll tell you."

"I can't divorce Chance, you know that."

"I know nothing of the sort," he said determined not to let her get the upper hand. "I know we love each other and we can't be together. You could get an annulment just on the fact of his infidelity," he told her.

"Please don't ruin the evening, Joe, this is so wonderful."

"I can never win with you, Evangeline, I'm going to bed," he said.

"No Joe, please stay let's change the subject and have a nice conversation."

"You're impossible," he said in disgust, and slumped back in his chair. She continued on with small talk until he fell asleep. She got up and covered him with the quilt. She kissed him on the forehead and said "good night, my love" and went to bed.

The sun was shining through the window in Evangeline's room. It was a beautiful way to wake up in the morning. She thought she heard a cat meowing, *how strange* she thought. There was a tap on her door and Alicianna peeked in. Immediately she saw the tears streaming down her face.

"My God, my darling, what's the matter?" she said as she jumped out of bed. She sat the girl down on the edge of the bed. "Tell me what is it?"

"Mother, I think I'm dying," she said between sobs.

"What gave you such a crazy idea?"

"I think I'm bleeding to death and I have pains in my tummy."

Oh, lord, she thought, *my baby is becoming a woman*! Her daughter was obviously upset, and she tried to hold back a smile.

"Well, you are old enough," she told her; "I was the same age when I had my time." Evangeline cursed herself for not warning her daughter of what was to happen to her. "I know for a fact that you are not going to die, my precious, you are just becoming a young woman."

"What do you mean, Mother? there is blood on my panties!"

"Alicianna, your body is changing and you are growing up. It probably won't be for many years, and we don't need to talk about it now, but when a woman gets her time, it means she is getting ready to be a mother."

"Do you mean I will have a baby like Mona?", she said horrified.

Alicianna had watched Mona's belly swell over the past few months. She knew a baby was in there, but didn't know how it got there. She was just happy to have another baby around to love.

I'm not doing a very good job with this. Felicia told me about my time and how to take care of myself. I don't think she knew very much about it then.

"Maybe I should call Larissa to talk to you," she said.

"No Mother, don't tell anyone about this, please?" she pleaded.

"Every woman has this Alicianna, it happens around your age. You will get this bleeding once a month," she told her, "it will last 4 to 5 days and you come sick again in 28 days. It's usually that regular so you can prepare yourself. In fact my mother wouldn't let me take a bath or wash my hair during my time. I'm not sure why," she wondered, " she said it had something to do with the moon. I think that was an old wife's tale though. We will wash you without you sitting in the tub and washing your hair will be fine. You will have to pad yourself so swimming isn't possible. It is all simply being old enough to be a woman."

"Mother, do boy's have their time?" she asked.

"No darling, just women. Remember, boys don't carry a child. Come with me honey, I'll show you how to care for yourself. then I'll make you some bay leaf tea with sugar to help with your cramps." her mother comforted Alicianna,

"It will make you feel better. I have a great idea," Evangeline announced. "We are going to celebrate this day of your stepping into womanhood. We won't tell anyone, but you and I will know it," she said.

"All we have to do is wink at each other and we will know what that means. It will be our little game," she said.

"Okay, mama, just you and me," and she winked at her. They went into the bathroom and Evangeline gave the girl her instructions. Then they went down to the kitchen to start breakfast. Soon Larissa joined them.

"What do you say we go for a morning swim, Alicianna?" Larissa asked her.

"I, I, don't think so, Auntie," she said quietly. Larissa didn't understand until she saw Alicianna sipping on the bay leaf tea. When she was sure Alicianna wasn't looking Evangeline mouthed, 'she came sick.' Larissa suddenly felt happy and sad all at the same time. Her baby niece was growing up.

"That's all right darling. Remember, I didn't feel like swimming last week," Larissa reminded her. Alicianna's eyes opened up wide, suddenly she understood. *I guess I'm not going to die after all, I'm just going to be a woman,* she thought and she gave her mother a wink.

"Evangeline, is my mother still sleeping? Should I wake her? Larissa asked,

",No, let her sleep she seems calm," Evangeline suggested.

"Yes, let her sleep," Joe agreed, as he came into the kitchen. He was wearing just his undershirt and his summer slacks, he had been drying his hair with a towel and it made him look very rugged. His muscular body was almost breaking through the shirt and it made Evangeline very uneasy. He and Dean slept in single beds in the room next to Rosalyn's on the first floor. "I fell asleep on the porch," he shot a look at Evangeline; she looked away as if she didn't understand what he meant.

"When I finally went to bed, I think it was around one a.m., I found her walking the floor and she seemed in pain," he said.

"Oh no," said Larissa, "I hope she isn't getting worse."

"I made her some of her herbal drink and I think it made her sleepy, so let her rest a bit longer," he suggested.   Evangeline was amazed at this man. Chance would have woken the whole household to help him, but Joe took it on himself to comfort her. *Oh how she loved him,* she thought.

"Joe," Evangeline said, "can you drive me to town to get some supplies "Just you?" he asked with surprise.

"Well, Dean asked if he could come along," she said.

"I thought it was too good to be true," he said.

"It wouldn't be proper now, would it?" she teased him.

"I'm ready any time you are, my lady," and he bowed like a cavalier.

Joe borrowed Mr. Handley's little blue pickup truck.   Evangeline sat between the two men. Dean was telling them how he planned to help Mike get elected when the time came. His political science classes were helping him understand the governmental mentality. Dean thought that Mike and he could bring a breath of fresh air into politics. He loved to read about the Constitution and its writers. He wanted to know about the problems of the time. He figured you had to start at the bottom and work your way up to the top. Taxation without representation was a big history lesson for him and he loved every minute of it.

"You keep up the good work, Dean," Evangeline said, "my son will need a smart man on his side if he is going to be a politician."

"Don't worry Evangeline, I've got his back," he said. Joe was very impressed with Dean, everything he did was always done with a lot of class. He could see him going far. He wondered how his own son Giuseppe was doing. He wasn't getting information like he had before the war. The agent who kept him informed had died and the replacement wasn't interested in the case especially since war had been declared. Giuseppe was probably in the Italian Army as he was over 18 now and Joe was worried. He decided to pull some strings when he got back to New York.   The little blue truck pulled up to the general store in the village. Dean ran off to the bait shop while Joe and Evangeline picked up some milk and fresh fruits and vegetables for the week.

"This is how it will be when we get married," he told Evangeline.

"We'll shop together and pick out our favorite foods, just simple things," he said.

"Joe, don't do this to yourself," Evangeline cried. "I don't see this happening for us."

"Then open your eyes, Evangeline, it will happen."

"You make me feel so bad Joe. I don't want to hurt you, I love you," she insisted.

He took her by the wrist, his blue eyes were fierce, Evangeline felt threatened, but also sorry for him. He lifted her arm and pulled her close to him.

"Listen to my words, my love, it will happen," he whispered. Tears were forming in her eyes; he let her go and left the store. He got back in the truck and waited for the others. Evangeline was relieved that no one saw Joe's tantrum. She tucked her blouse back in her skirt, paid for the groceries, and met the men at the truck. She asked Dean if she could sit by the window which he agreed to. The ride home was very quiet. Dean wondered what could have happened in that short time to make Evangeline so mad at Joe. Suddenly Joe started to sing an Old Italian folk song and it made Evangeline start to laugh. *Well, whatever it was it couldn't have been that bad*, Dean thought. They both started singing now and Dean sang the part of the instruments.

"I love you people!" Dean confessed, as they drove back to the cottage.

Chance and Rebecca spent the entire week together. He went to work for a few hours a day so Matt wouldn't get too suspicious. The rest of the time he said he was in therapy. Chance covered his tracks well, as he was now walking with a cane only. Chance called the Bellflower Inn every couple of days to get information on his mother's progress. He was saddened to hear she wasn't feeling too well lately. Larissa said she was sleeping past noon and her painting had slowed down a bit. Chance knew Lorenzo, Elsie and

Maria were going to the ocean for the last week of the vacation. Lorenzo stopped by the office to pick up Rosalyn's fresh batch of herbs and vitamins. Chance told him he spoke with Larissa and that she said Rosalyn wasn't feeling as well as when I left.

"I can't take Larissa's word on face value," he told Lorenzo. "My sister is such an alarmist since Mike left."

"Don't worry, if she is much worse I'll let you know," Lorenzo assured him. "Chance, are you sure you don't want to drive down with us? We could pick you up first thing in the morning," Lorenzo suggested.

"No thanks, there are plenty of people there, I have my therapy to finish this week anyway," Chance answered.

"Joe is staying at the cottage now isn't he?" Lorenzo asked.

"Yes, he got there after Matt and I left," Chance said.

"He would let you know if things were out of control," Lorenzo assured him. Because of Mike, Lorenzo and Joe were on good terms. Mike really respected Joe and he knew Mike had a good eye for the character of people, so Lorenzo trusted him too.

Soon the next batch of visitors arrived at the cottage. The Rizzo's and Maria arrived on the third week of the vacation.

"Mama, Mama, baby Elena is here!" said Aliciannna excitedly, as she saw the Ford Torpedo pull up at the cottage.

"Oh, Maria," Rosalyn said, "I've missed you so much. Did you have a good trip?" she asked, as she kissed the baby.

"I can never get enough of the ocean," she said, "it reminds me of my hometown in Sicily."

"Elsie, I'm glad you're here," Evangeline said as she gave her a hug. "Was it a good trip?"

"Oh yes," said Elsie, It's always a beautiful drive. Listen, everyone, I have wonderful news. Mona gave birth to a beautiful baby boy last night. His name is Robert Anthony, because he is an American born son. He was six pounds and seven ounces and bald as his grandfather.," she laughed. "I prayed hard for her and everything went well," Elsie exclaimed.

Lately she has been an advocate for prenatal health. She had a horrible delivery which no one could predict, but Elena was perfect in every way and she was sure it was because of her careful prenatal ritual of good food, vitamins and plenty of rest. She even went with Mrs. Mitchell to a suffragette meeting and gave a speech on it. Lorenzo thought they went shopping, he didn't go for that sort of thing. Everyone was glad for Roberto and Mona and hoped to see the baby soon.

"We are having the Christening party at Hunters Point," Evangeline told them. "The apartment is much too small for all the family and we have plenty of room."

"Just another excuse for you to throw a party, Evangeline," Joe spoke up.

"Looks like you have my number," she laughed and the women went into the house.

Joe helped Lorenzo with the luggage. "I thought traveling with the ladies was a lot of work, but the baby is double the work," Lorenzo said, as he unloaded the trunk of the car. "When I picked up Evangeline and Mike from Ellis Island, she only had one small bag between the two of them," he remembered. "Because that was all she had in the world.", he admitted.

"Times have changed for the better, thank God. Don't complain," Lorenzo, you have a beautiful family, a little luggage is nothing," said Joe.
"You're right," he said, "I'm a lucky man. Last year I thought everything was lost when Elsie had the baby and she became addicted to the medicine. That was probably the scariest time of my life," Lorenzo confessed to Joe.
"It always seems worst after the fact," Joe told him. "When you are in the middle of the crisis you are too scared or stupid to know the difference."

"How have you been getting along here?" Lorenzo asked.

"With all this beauty surrounding us, how could we not enjoy ourselves?" Joe answered.

"Even Rosalyn? Chance has been concerned about her."

"Listen Lorenzo, if he's been so concerned, why didn't he come out with you?" Joe questioned.

"That's what I wondered," he replied.

"Not to change the subject, Lorenzo, but I want to talk to you, I need your opinion on something," Joe said to him.

"Sure," Lorenzo said, with a question in his voice. He wondered what a guy like Joe could possibly ask his opinion on.

"Let's get these bags in and grab a Coke, we can sit under that tree and talk, ok?" said Joe.

"You have my curiosity going now," Lorenzo confessed. The men carried the bags into the house.

"Well," Evangeline said to him, with one hand on her hip and the other hand extended out palm side up.

"What do you want?" Lorenzo asked.

"Come on, Lorenzo, don't make me beg," she whined.

"Oh, do you mean this?" as he pulled Mike's letter from his jacket pocket, and waved it in her face.

"Give it to me!" as she happily grabbed it out of his hand. She held it to her chest and ran out to the porch to read it.

"Don't tease her like that," Elsie scolded him. Lorenzo was glad to see Evangeline, but he couldn't resist getting under her skin. She looked so beautiful with her new suntan. It reminded him of the young girl in Santa Fara he fell in love with.

Evangeline sat on the top step of the porch and opened the envelope. She started to read to herself. Joe rested his foot on the second step and leaned on his leg.

"May I ask how he is?" Joe inquired.

"He's says he's fine and working every day in the motor pool. Joe, what does that mean?" she asked him with a curious look on her face. He just wanted to kiss her that minute.

"That's just what they call the place where the trucks and autos are kept to be maintained," he explained.

"Yes, that's right, he says with his experience in Lorenzo's auto shop he was a natural for the motor pool. Sam is an ambulance driver he sees him every day. Nick is in a different platoon and he runs into him once in a while. He says he loves us all and hopes we are well. I wish he would write more, but I'm happy to get his letters even if they are short."

"I'm happy for you Evangeline, I hope it lightens your heart my darling," Joe said sincerely.

Lorenzo came out of the house carrying two Cokes in his hands.

"Excuse us Evangeline, I owe Joe a cold drink for helping me with the luggage," he said.

"By all means gentlemen," Evangeline said, and walked back in the cottage just as Larissa was walking out.

"Lorenzo, was there a letter for me?" Larissa asked.

"Not this time, darling, maybe there will be one waiting for you when we get back," he assured her. The pitiful look on her face disturbed him. *What's the matter with that boy, if he doesn't want her, then he should just tell her,* Lorenzo thought. Evangeline opened the door, took her by the hand and walked her back in the house.

"I care a lot about that boy," said Joe, "but what he is doing to that girl is criminal."

"I agree," said Lorenzo, "maybe you could give him some advice in your next letter." "Better yet," said Joe, "I'll ask Dean about it."

FOURTEEN

Joe and Lorenzo sat under the big weeping willow tree near the cottage. The shade it gave made the rooms feel cool even in the hot summer.

"I want you to know how impressed I am with the way you have developed your company."

"Thank you, I didn't know you were watching," Lorenzo laughed.

"Could you give me some advice on a change I want to make in the next year?"

"Tell me what change," Lorenzo's curiosity was peaked.

"I want to leave Winston Steel," he said.

"I don't believe it," Lorenzo said with shock. "Has Chance done something to offend you, Joe?" Lorenzo asked.

"No, nothing like that," Joe said, "although it is personal."

"Don't you do very well at Winston Steel?" Lorenzo asked.

"Yes, Chance has made me a very rich man and I appreciate all he has done for me. Matt is home now and Evangeline helps a lot at the office, so I don't feel like I'm leaving him stranded."

"What about the Pittsburgh plant?" Lorenzo asked.

"My work will be done there after the war anyway," Joe told him.

"It seems you have your mind made up, my friend, what can I tell you?"

"I heard you may be moving to Detroit," he said.

"Yes, I have a lot of loose ends to tie up. Nicolo can stay on as supervisor; the problem is Maria wants to move with us. She is too attached to Elsie and Elena."

"I think she likes you a little too," Joe told the truth.

"I have three sisters and Maria has always been closest to me."

"Do you think you have room for me in your new venture," Joe asked? "I don't need the money, I need something to keep my mind off, well, never mind."

"Keep your mind off what?" Lorenzo asked.

Joe couldn't believe he was saying this to him, but somehow he thought he would understand. "Off Evangeline," he said. "Lorenzo, I'm so crazy about her and I can't do anything about it. She won't leave Chance, she takes her vows seriously."

"Join the club," said Lorenzo. "I've loved her since I was 18 years old. It's funny how that love turned to protector, to brother figure, to respect. I couldn't do anything without her input. She is silent partner in my company, you know," he said.

"No, I guess she didn't feel the need to say anything," Joe admitted. I was afraid my clients wouldn't take me seriously if they knew my partner was a woman, so she became my silent partner. I still need her advice today; when I get in trouble, she has a way of turning things around for me," Lorenzo replied.

"Why didn't you marry her?" Joe questioned.

"That my friend, is a long story for another day," he laughed. "I've been with Elsie for a very long time. I didn't know how much I loved her until I almost lost her. Elsie knew how enchanted I was with Evangeline, but she stuck by me, she loves me that much. "Enchanted is a good word, it's like she put a spell on me the first time I laid eyes on her," Joe laughed.

"I knew Chance was having an affair with that Clay woman and I couldn't believe it when I saw his wife."

"Funny you mentioned her," Lorenzo said, "I saw her coming out of the Winston Steel building yesterday when I went to get Rosalyn's herb supply."

"Damn, him!" swore Joe,

"He's picked up with her again. How could I have missed that? Lorenzo said. Chance and I have been through a lot of ups and downs over the years, but he is going to hurt Evangeline and he has to go through me first. I mentioned it to Elsie, but I never put two and two together. I bet she didn't react, because she knows my temper and is afraid I'll do something stupid.

"I don't know if I should be happy or not about it," said Joe, "she can divorce him on his infidelity alone. I know she will marry me if the church says she can get an annulment."

"What about Alicianna?" Lorenzo asked, "I know she won't share her with Chance. Look, I know Evangeline and Chance care very much for each other, I think they can work something out."

"Now I know I have to leave Winston Steel," Joe insisted, "I can't allow him to embarrass her openly."

"How do you think Rosalyn will take it?" Lorenzo asked?

"Rosalyn won't make it that long, she has a lot of pain now. This trip helped her a little, but the cancer is well advanced. I had a good talk with her late one night and she is ready to go to Edward. She is worried about Larissa, but she hopes she opens her eyes and takes Alan up on his proposal. Personally, I'm very worried about Larissa, she cries all the time. Evangeline found her in her closet sitting on the floor crying like her heart was breaking; I think it's already broken," said Joe.

"Evangeline will feel responsible for Larissa because of my son," said Lorenzo.

"Maybe he will come home to her after all," said Joe, "Mike is a good kid."

"We better go inside," said Lorenzo, and stood up with his empty soda bottle in his hand. "Joe, you would be an asset to my company in any way you decide," said Lorenzo. They shook hands and Joe thanked him. The ladies will think we solved all the world's problems by now. The men walked into the house to find the ladies setting the table for lunch. Dean came in with a bucket of cleaned fish ready for the grill.

"I started the fire outside, these babies will be ready in ten minutes," he called out to the crowd.

"Dean, you are my hero," Lorenzo said, "I have been craving grilled fish all the way here. " The families sat at the table, said grace and asked God for Mike, Nick, and Sam's safety, they prayed for Rosalyn to get well and thanked him for their blessings.

Rosalyn picked at her lunch and drank her herbal tea. Maria tried to get her to eat more, but realized how frail she was and that her apatite was gone. When the others went out to the beach, the ladies were left alone to talk.

"My old friend," Rosalyn spoke softly, "I'm so glad you are here. I want you to know a few things about my funeral."

"What crazy thing are you telling me?" Maria said in her broken English. She had been in America for over 20 years but her English was still a little shaky.

"Please, Maria, be my friend I can't talk to my girls about this so you will have to handle the burden, I'm sorry," Rosalyn said as she held her hand. "First of all I want a private funeral. I want to be taken from Hunters Point to Mass, then directly to my Edward. Maria, I can't wait to be with him again," she said with a smile. "I absolutely do not want my girls dressed in black, white would be nice and no veils. Flowers in their hair I think. I want my sons in white suits. I have a beautiful pink beaded dress in my closet at Hunters Point. I hope it's not too big. I wore a pink dress the first time I went on a date with Edward. Chance was an infant and we met him in Central Park. I want to go to him in a pink dress again," she reminisced. "I want an old fashioned horse drawn hearse and I want my team of horses to pull me. I know they are old, but I want them to carry me one last time. My home has been divided up already," she said. "Larissa will receive my jewelry with exception of the ruby ring Edward gave me on our 25th anniversary-- that goes to Alicianna. All my money is to be divided among my children and Evangeline is considered one of my daughters. I hope Mary and Mariella understand, but she has been my daughter for the past 15 years. Will you see that these things happen for me, Maria?" By now, Maria was sobbing into her hankie.

"Rosalyn, I will miss you so much, she cried. I think you should write this down and I will take it to Mr. John Lee your attorney, to be sure there are no mistakes," she suggested.

"That's fine." Rosalyn agreed. "Oh yes, one more thing, I want all my children to wear red bloomers at the funeral."

"Red bloomers!" Maria said in horror.

"Yes, I used to tell them when they did something that made me crazy, that when I died I wanted them to wear red bloomers at my funeral. I have a feeling they will understand," she laughed.

"Oh Rosalyn, only you could make a solemn occasion funny. I love you very much," and with that she gave her a hug.

Elsie and Evangeline were in the kitchen chopping vegetables for the next meal. "Don't they smell fresh out here in the ocean air," Elsie said as she pushed a bunch of fresh basil to her face?

"Everything is better out here," Evangeline answered. "It's so sad Dean had such a bad experience in this place," she added.

"All the boys did," Elsie replied, "he seems to have to handled it quiet well."

"Look out the kitchen window, Elsie," Evangeline said, "see how cute Alicianna and Elena are playing in the sand, I can hear them laughing all the way in the house. Chance has decided we will come back here every summer," Evangeline told her.

Elsie suddenly became uneasy. "Evangeline, I have something to tell you, I think you should know," Elsie said as she was folding kitchen towels.

"What has you so troubled Elsie?" Evangeline said, "Are you going to have another baby?"

"No," she laughed, the doctors tell me I shouldn't. "But who knows what God has in store for us.

"Lorenzo told me about something he saw at Winston Steel the other day, she continued.

"Tell me what it was," Evangeline said and stopped what she was doing.

"When he was walking in the building to get Rosalyn's herbs, Miss Rebecca Clay was walking out," Elsie confessed. Evangeline froze in her tracks. "Elsie, do you think they have started seeing each other again?" she questioned.

"Unless she has decided to build a building or a bridge, what else could it be?" she replied sarcastically.

"You know we have never spoken of it," Evangeline said.

"Never?" asked Elsie.

"Never, I didn't want to rock the boat," she told her friend. "I thought she took off with her Austrian lover. How convenient of Mr. Winston to send his family off to the Bellflower Inn so he could resume his affair with that woman!" Evangeline said between clenched teeth. "I'm not going to do anything now, especially since I don't know the facts, but when Rosalyn can't be hurt from it, the hammer will come down," she said defiantly.

"Evangeline, you always put yourself last, why do you do that?" asked Elsie.

"Rosalyn has been my mother as long as my own mother was on this earth. She is so fragile, I think this news would kill her and I won't have that on my conscience. When we get home I'll figure something out," Evangeline guessed.

The women continued on with their work in silence. Finally Evangeline said, "Elsie, thank you, you are my only true friend."

Later that evening everyone was busy with games and reading or just relaxing. Lorenzo was outside on a hammock tied between two trees, the smell of the ocean reminded him of Santa Fara. The fresh caught fish they had for lunch were just like the dinners his mother served her family. When he fell asleep, the conversation he had with Joe, made him dream of the Festa of the Blessed Mother and his dance with Evangeline. In his dream the music never ended and they danced into infinity with Evangeline holding a baby Michele in her arms.

Suddenly Felicia appeared and stole the baby from Evangeline. Lorenzo tried in vain to stop her but they kept dancing. *If the dance never ended the horrible events of that night never happened, if it never happened there would be no Mike.* The reality of the fact woke him up and he nearly fell out of the hammock. He shook the sleep out of his head and when he stood up, he saw the headlights of a car pulling up next to the house. A man got out and walked up the steps of the cottage.

"Hello, is there room for one more?" Alan Mason asked.

"Yes!" was the consensus as they all got up to greet him.

"We are so happy to see you," Rosalyn said.

"Come," said Maria, "have you had something to eat?" Larissa smiled for the first time in weeks and Evangeline was so relieved.

"I couldn't stand it one more day without my girl," he said to Larissa.

"Don't make me blush," she told Alan.

"Hey Al," said Dean, "I found a great fishing spot; do you want to try it tomorrow?"

"I didn't come all the way out here to go fishing," Alan teased him and pulled his hat down over his face.

"I'll go with you, Dean," said Alicianna.

"That's my gal," he told her, "it's a date. Is there an objection to a walk on the beach with Larissa?" he asked.

"No one will object," she said as she grabbed a shawl and pushed him out the door.

When they had left, Elsie said, "he's like a shot in the arm," while she rocked her baby to sleep.

The fresh air was too much for Elena and walking in the sand made her tired. Her dark skin, proof that she was Lorenzo's child, was already tanning under the summer sun.

Alan and Larissa took off their shoes and let the water ebb back and forth over their toes.

"Have you had a good time?" Alan asked her.

"It's been hard watching my mother slip away. When we first got here, she was painting and now she has no interest. I'm glad Maria is here, they have so much in common."

"Two women from different parts of the world can have the same understandings. It's a sisterhood," said Alan.

"How have you been? "she asked.

"Missing you like crazy," he told her. "I couldn't stand it anymore so I took a couple of days off school, borrowed my dad's car, and here I am." as he held his arms out wide. He took Larissa by the arm and pulled her close to him; he kissed her tenderly and told her how much he loved her.

"Tell me how you feel, Larissa," he begged, "am I spinning my wheels?"

"No Alan, I do love you, but I can't trust myself or you with my feelings. My mother is dying. I don't want your sympathy to mask your intentions. Does that make sense to you?" she asked.

"No, not at all, but just kiss me again and I'll feel better," he laughed. The girl had never made it easy on him, but he had the time to keep on trying.

"Oh Alan, you have a way of making me feel better," she said. They walked all the way to the open air gazebo where the music was playing and people from the Inn as well as a few of the townsfolk were dancing.

"May I have this dance, my lady?" he asked jovially.

"Certainly," Larissa curtsied, and they danced as they had at the debutant ball. By the time they finished, they had drawn a crowd, and a round of applause made them blush. They stayed the rest of the evening and danced until the music stopped. Walking home, Alan again told her how he wanted to spend the rest of his life with her.

"Please, let's see how my mother makes it through the summer. I have my job at Saint Mary's to look forward to and you have school. We have a lot of time before we can get married any way," she told him.

"I can't wait until after law school, Larissa, we can get a small place and we can be happy, I want to make you happy," he insisted.

"I'm tired and so are you, tonight. Let's talk more about this tomorrow," she said. They reached the cottage and blankets and pillows were waiting for Alan on the sofa.

"I guess this is home," he teased her.

"I guess so," she said and kissed him good night and went to the room she was now sharing with her mother.

"Did you have a nice time, daughter?" Rosalyn asked.

"Oh yes," she said, "Alan always shows me a good time. We danced the waltz like we did at the ball. You should have seen us," she told her mother. "We actually drew a crowd around us, it was a little embarrassing, but you know Alan, he took it all in stride. It was so much fun," she admitted.

"I'm so happy, Larissa, you have been so sad lately," Rosalyn replied.

"Mother, if I accept Alan's proposal, what happens if Mike comes home and wants to marry me?" she asked.

"Mike has only sent you two letters in the past seven months, my darling, does that sound like a man in love?" her mother replied.

"That's harsh, don't you think?" Larissa cried. Her eyes started to well up and Rosalyn wished she could eat her words.

"Isn't it better to marry a man who makes you laugh rather than one that makes you cry?" Rosalyn asked her. "Believe me I know," her mother announced. Suddenly she went into a coughing jag and Larissa jumped to her aid.

"Mother, are you all right?"she cried.

"Yes, I'm just all talked out," she told her. "I think I will be able to sleep now.
Larissa gave her a drink of water from her bedside table, "I'm sorry if I upset you, I love you so much," Larissa said.

"I love you too baby," Rosalyn declared, and nodded off.

The next few days were happy and fun. It was the last week of the vacation at the Bellflower, when a severe summer storm came down on them. Water poured out of the sky and the waves were getting close to the cottage. Elsie was afraid they were going to get flooded out and convinced Lorenzo to leave.

"If it were just you and I," she said, "I wouldn't mind so much, but Elena has no defense against the water."

Alan had the same sentiments about Rosalyn and told Larissa he wanted to drive them back to Hunters Point. Evangeline asked Lorenzo to take Alicianna along with them and sent Dean, home with Alan. She feared with his leg, he might get trapped somewhere and not get out.

"Come on Evangeline, I can handle myself," he protested. "Haven't I proven myself this past month? I'm as good as any man with two legs," he complained.

"Of course you are, my dear, but what if Rosalyn gets real sick on the way home. Do you think Alan can handle both of those women by himself?" Dean knew Larissa wasn't much use in a crisis, so he begrudgingly went along.

"Thank you for this favor," Evangeline told him "Joe and I will be along right after I close up the cottage and settle the bill with Mrs. Handley. I'm sorry the weather decided when our vacation was over," she said with a sigh.

Rosalyn wasn't sure it was proper for Joe and Evangeline to be left alone to finish up the rest of the chores.

"Honestly Rosalyn, I don't think my virtue is at stake here. I'm responsible for ten people and they will get out of here safely," she said defiantly!

"I'm a silly old lady," she admitted, "of course you are right."

Evangeline was thinking to herself, *why didn't Chance come along with Lorenzo? Was he too busy keeping Rebecca's bed warm? He should be the one to settle all financial matters not me. Then he could drive back to Hunters Point with Joe.* I won't think about that now, she told herself. She was beginning to feel like a balloon that was going burst when it came to Chance.

The vacationers all rushed to pack up the cars and leave while there was a lull in the storm. Evangeline kissed them all and told them to drive safely. She kissed Aliciana four times before she let her go.

"Stay close to each other in case one of the cars has trouble."

"Yes boss," Lorenzo teased as he saluted her.

"Hey, listen to her" Dean suggested, "she insisted that Mike bring along extra shirts to the beach and it saved my life."

"She has a way of saving everyone from something," Lorenzo agreed and shook his head.

Joe shook Lorenzo's hand. "Drive safely. You have precious cargo," he told him.

"Your cargo is precious to all of us too," he said, and shook his finger at him. Joe laughed and closed the car door.

"Well, they're gone," Joe said as they drove down the road.
"I miss them already," Evangeline cried.

Evangeline climbed the stairs to the third floor where there was a small bedroom to make sure the windows were latched. When she looked out the east side window she saw the blackest, ugliest cloud she had ever seen heading towards them fast.

"Joe," she screamed, as she ran down the stairs to the second floor bedrooms. Joe was on the west side of the cottage latching windows and didn't see the cloud coming down on them. Just as he figured out what she was screaming, the front French doors flew open and smashing glass went everywhere. The rain was coming down like sheets of steel shattering everything it could. The wind was like a freight train blowing through the house. Joe dragged an unbelieving Evangeline into a closet that ran under the stairs. They hung on to each other for dear life.

" We're going to die!" Evangeline insisted.

"No," whispered Joe to calm her fears, "we will be alright, don't worry." He had no idea what they were going to find when they opened the closet door, but he didn't want her to know that.

"The family got away just in time," Evangeline quivered.

"I hope so," said Joe, "I'm not sure but the clouds seem to be blowing towards the west, not north toward New York." The whirling sound of the wind seemed to slow down and they thought the worst was over.

"Was it a hurricane?" Evangeline asked, as she cracked open the door of the closet?

"I don't think so," Joe answered her, "but it was a hell of a storm."

"I hope people had time to come into shore before the big cloud hit."

"Evangeline you are always looking for something to worry about. With the bad weather we have had, there shouldn't have been anyone out on a small boat today," Joe insisted. "Mr. Handley is pretty strict about letting any of his boats out during foul weather," he added. The rain was coming down very hard now. The wind that caused so much damage was now more like a breeze. The couple stepped aside the broken glass and walked out on the porch. It was unbelievable; water was past the third step of the porch. Joe's car was swimming in water half way up the door.

"Do you think it will start?" Evangeline asked him innocently.

Joe laughed, "My darling, do you even see the road?"

She never thought of that, she had never been in a flood before, and had no idea what to expect. "How are we ever going to get out of here?" she cried.

"When the water goes down, and it will, but I don't know when," Joe told her. "I say we make the best of it while we can," and he started to nibble on her neck.

"Stop, Joe!"she insisted, "I have to have a clear head right now. The family will expect us home in a few hours and when we don't show up they will worry," she told him.

"There is nothing else we can do about it, but wait." He held her close and stroked her long black hair, "Don't upset yourself, my love," he gently told her, "this will all work out."

"Listen!" Evangeline pulled away from him. "Someone is calling! Over here, Mr. Handley, we're on the porch!" she yelled.

"Is everyone alright?" he asked, as he rowed his little boat near the house.

"Yes, we're fine," she assured him. "We got the rest of the family on their way home before the last storm hit. It's just me and Mr. Cross here now," she said.

"The power is out and so are the phones," he shouted. When the phones are working again, I'll call Mr. Winston and let him know you and Joe are alright, is that ok?" he asked.

"Yes, thank you so much, that would be wonderful," Evangeline, answered.

"I'll help you with that car tomorrow, Joe. The waters usually go down in ten to twelve hours," he promised.

"When you get the time, I would appreciate it," yelled back Joe.

"Good bye, I have to check on some other people," he said and rowed off.

"You should have been stranded with Lorenzo," Joe told her.

"Why?" Evangeline asked as she looked at him with her head cocked to the side.

"I don't know anything about cars except to drive them," he confessed.   Evangeline laughed and it broke the ice, she wasn't worried anymore and finally relaxed. The rain hitting the metal roof of the little shed outside was mesmerizing. She and Joe were lying together on the porch swing wrapped in the familiar quilt.

"I couldn't have planned this more perfectly," Joe said.

"Elsie told me something that I still can't believe," she told him.

"What is it, *Cara Mia,*" he said in Italian.

"Well, it seems Chance has picked up with Miss Clay again," she announced. He knew about it from Lorenzo, but he let her tell the story. "I'm not jealous," she said, "I'm mad. Somehow, Joe, wrapped in your arms I feel silly being mad. Is it the pot calling the kettle black, as Edward used to say?"

"I told you before; Chance has broken every vow he has ever made to you. He has never taken your marriage seriously. Evangeline you are more my wife than his. You should have left him years ago, and then you would be my wife already. A priest could annul your marriage, and bless ours," he insisted.

"I have a lot to think about, Joe, I did everything for Mike's benefit. He is a man now and can't be under my thumb any longer, I realize that. Alicianna loves her daddy and I can't take her away from him, but I'll be damned if I let Rebecca Clay near my daughter," she said with a clenched fist.

"Calm down tiger," Joe said as he tried to calm her.

"You realize you will still be a very wealthy woman if you divorce him? But who cares about that? I have made millions at Winston Steel, you won't want for a thing," he assured her.

"Joe, money for me has never been an objective. I just wanted Mike to have the best of everything," she admitted.

"Evangeline, Lorenzo can take care of Mike, his business is so big now, and when he moves to Detroit, I'm going with him."

"Who's going to Detroit?" Evangeline sat straight up on the swing.

"Lorenzo is going to open a showroom for Mr. Ford in Detroit. "Didn't he tell you?" Joe questioned.

"No he did not!" she protested.

"I'm shocked. He tells you everything," Joe said.

"When is he going?" she asked.

"I really don't know, but sometime in the near future, after the war, I assume. I'm going to give Chance my resignation when we get back to the city," he said.

"Here we go again," she said. "My destiny, once again in the hands of the men who love me. What about Mike?" she asked suddenly.

"He has plans in New York, Mike will figure it out for himself," Joe assured her.

"I've never been to Detroit, she said."

"Neither have I, it will be an adventure for the both of us," he imagined. "Come with me Evangeline," he said softly, and walked her to her room in the cottage. "We have until daylight to worry about it. Tonight belongs to us. God sent us those clouds, don't you agree?"he asked.

"Yes," she said, and followed him to her bed. They made love with real passion, she never felt more wanted in her life. It was the first time they talked about their future together and not once did she feel guilty.

The next morning the sun was shining and the waters had receded a few feet. The road wasn't visible yet so they breakfasted on wine, cheese, and some bread left in the ice box. A few grapes and peaches were in the fruit bowl. Evangeline sliced the peaches and soaked them in the wine.

"My father used to give us wine soaked peaches when Felicia and I were children," she said. "It brings back many memories," she told him.

"You had a good childhood?" Joe asked her.

"My parents loved me, that's all a child needs to know; they protected me to a fault," she explained. "The sisters of the Sacred Heart had a hand in my upbringing also, I loved them very much. When I was left alone with Mike, they took me in and gave us shelter until Antonino put us on a ship for America.

"How brave you are Evangeline," Joe told her.

"Well, my mother always said 'when you can't make it through a crisis, give your problems to God,' he has always seen me through," she said

"Yes, my mother had the same idea only she prayed to the Blessed Mother," he said.

Suddenly she remembered Madam Sasha told her not to ask him about his past. She knew he wouldn't tell her anyway. Evangeline smiled, she didn't want to ask any questions that would make him uncomfortable. Maybe it will come out in small bits of information. She didn't care, she felt too happy today. The wine made her feel a little dizzy and carefree.

This time she made the advance to Joe. She unbuttoned her shirt while he watched with amusement. She saddled him in the chair and allowed him to take it off. They made love again on the sofa and she fell asleep on top of him.

When the water fully receded, the road became visible. Joe tried to start the car. *Ok Lord*, he prayed, *Evangeline said when I can't do anything about a crisis I should give the problem to you. Since I'm so bad at mechanics, I hope you can help me.* He put the key in the ignition, crossed himself, closed his eyes, and miraculously the engine turned over. Joe's arms flew up and he praised the Lord.

"I can't believe it!" he told Evangeline.

"You should listen to me more often," she teased.

"Are you ready to go?" he asked her.

"No," she said, "but she got in the car with the few packages they had left."

They drove to the Bellflower Inn to settle the bill with Mrs. Handley.

"I'm so glad you got out in one piece!" she exclaimed.

"Did you get a call in to Mr. Winston?" Evangeline asked, "I'm worried about the family."

"The phone line was repaired last night and we called him then. Chance said the others returned home with no problems," Mrs. Handley repeated, The storm didn't go that far north."

"Thank goodness," said Evangeline. "They will expect us then?" she asked.   "Yes, we told them the car was flooded and as soon as the road was visible you would leave."

"We cleaned the cottage the best we could, but some windows are broken, and the front doors were blown out," she explained.

"Well, Mr. Handley will have his work cut out for him," she said as she raised her hands in disgust. "The Inn didn't get hit as hard as the cottages," she added, "but everyone is present and accounted for, thank goodness." Evangeline settled the bill with her, Joe started the car again and the two of them drove home together. They went back to their lives of pretending to be just business associates.

Chance stayed at the office waiting for a call from Evangeline. This caused an argument with Rebecca.

"You left my bed and came to the office to await your families' return, " she hissed at him. "How fatherly of you," she said sarcastically.

"There has been a terrible storm and it's delaying Evangeline's homecoming," he told her. Alicianna and my mother and sister came home with Alan last night. I received a call from Mrs. Handley late last night to tell me they were safe."

"Who are *they*?" Rebecca asked.

"Evangeline and Joe I suppose, they stayed behind to close up the cottage and got stuck in a wicked storm. Dean might have been with them also, I don't know. " Rebecca was making it a habit of coming to the office while Evangeline was at the ocean. It was getting on Matt's nerves. He even made a snide remark to her one day.

"Oh, it's you Miss Clay, again," he said, as he ran into her in Chance's office. "You seem to be a regular customer. Are you building a bridge?" he asked her. "What kind of steel are you looking for?"he asked with a half smile. Chance gave him a dirty look.

"Chance," she whined, "you promised you would ask Evangeline for a divorce. Either you do it or I will."

"Don't you dare go near Evangeline, she doesn't know about us. Why would you hurt her like that?" he demanded.

"Hurt her? What about me? I've been waiting all these years for you."

" Evangeline is off limits to you, understand?" he said as he grasped her arm. "Rebecca," Chance reminded her, "I told you I would tell her when the time was right. My mother is dying, and I won't upset her now. I don't want her death on my conscience." He released her and she stormed out of the office. *Who does he think he is dealing with?* she said to herself, *enough is enough.*

When Larissa arrived at Hunters Point with the others she was overjoyed to find a letter from Mike.

Dear Larissa,

I hope this letter finds you and my family in good health. By now you might be home from the ocean and I wish I could have been there with all of you. I miss my family so much that when I get home, I hope I never have to leave them again.

Larissa, don't tell anyone, I'm intrusting this information to you alone. I'm writing this letter from my hospital bed. It seems I got in the way of a bomb and received some shrapnel for my efforts. I'm alright, but I needed stitches on my arms and face. Don't worry I'm still beautiful. Not as beautiful as you, I'm sure.

I was in a fox hole waiting for my orders to start shooting when a grenade was thrown several feet away from me. Some of my fellow soldiers didn't fare as well as I did. Larissa I never want to see a young man die like that again. We were all screaming to get out of that trench of fire, when a big guy pulled me out. Who do you think it was? Sam of course. God has a way of keeping us close enough to save each other. I see him all the time at camp. He's an ambulance driver and I work as a mechanic on the ambulances. This particular battle required all soldiers to participate so there I was. Sam pulled me out of that fox hole and carried me to the ambulance and to safety. He dropped me off at the make shift hospital and took off again. The doctors evaluated my wounds as non life threatening and I didn't get care for two days. I was a little shell shocked and slept most of the time.

I dreamt of my mother and dad. My pa kept telling me to go to Palermo to see his sisters. Your father was there also with that half smile of his. He just stood there saying go home Mike, go home. It was the weirdest dream ever.

Write and tell me what you think of it. I saw Sam today, he is such a good soldier, he finally got the day off. We lost a lot of men in this battle. He has been carrying the dead and wounded for three days. He sat next to my bed and fell fast asleep, in fact. he is still asleep. All he does is talk about Abigail and how much he loves her. I'm jealous of how lucky he is to have found his future with Abigail. Maybe someday I'll find someone like that. Tell Alan to stay in school, this war is more than we bargained for. Nick sent us a message to say he was fine. He is a news correspondent for the Army. He knows more about the intelligence of this army than the average soldier.

I hope grandmother is feeling better now that she got some fresh air. Tell her I love her and hope to be home soon.

Kiss my baby sister for me and take care of yourself.

Yours Always

Mike

Here we go again, another confusing letter from Mike. She couldn't keep her promise and went straight to show Abigail the letter.

"My poor Sam. He works so hard and his work is so sad," she cried.

"Abigail, what do you make of Mike's letter about me?" she asked.

"What about you? He didn't say anything about you," Abigail told her.

"He said he is still looking for his future mate."

"Larissa, Mike is so up in the air, he is not settled at all," she told her. "Alan loves you so much, that's where you should be putting all you attention," she advised her.

"What should I say about the dream?" she asked her.

"I don't know, tell him he was delirious, and funny dreams happen when you are in that condition," Abigail was getting impatient with Larissa. "How can we talk about dreams, when our men are in the line of fire?" she scolded her. "We need to get down on our hands and knees and pray that God will bless us with their return," she said. "You're right, Abigail, you're right about everything." She was tugging on the lace of her hankie, she got up from the chair she was sitting on, kissed Abigail good bye and went home with nothing more than when she came.

Evangeline was having trouble adjusting to life at Hunters Point. Rosalyn had taken to her bed and nurses were coming in several hours a day. Larissa and Evangeline took turns staying with her in the evening until she fell asleep. She didn't know if it was her imagination or not but Chance was acting strange. He didn't look her in the eye when he spoke to her and he always had someplace to go.

Larissa started her job at Saint Mary's school as a second grade teacher. The chauffer drove her and Alicianna back and forth to school every day. Evangeline was missing Joe, but knew she would probably see him soon. The day after her return from the ocean, she called on Mr. Ryan the private detective to put a tail, as they say, on Chance so she could get information about him and Miss Clay. This time she might need it as information for her lawyers. Evangeline and Rosalyn practically got Chance to walk by sheer will. She thought he would reward her by being faithful, but he didn't. Evangeline was in the drawing room writing Mike a letter when the butler announced a visitor. "A Miss Clay to see you," he said.

"Do you know who I am?" Rebecca asked Evangeline.

"I wish I didn't," Evangeline confessed.

"So you know about Chance and I?" she asked.

"Of course." she answered and stayed seated.

"Chance thinks you are ignorant of our situation," she told her.

"Ignorant is an interesting choice of words," Evangeline said. It was so cold in the room, ice sickles were forming on the chandelier.

"I'm here," she said, "to ask you to give Chance a divorce."

Now the fire was taking over, Evangeline's wrath came out. "Madam, to whom do you think you are talking to?" I am Evangeline Winston, current matriarch of this family. I have nurtured my husband through his illness and I am currently seeing to his mother's needs. I have been in charge of Winston Steel for the past year," as she stood up. "Who do you think you are? Evangeline said as she walked a little too close to Miss Clay.

Rebecca underestimated Evangeline. She was under the impression she would be dealing with a quiet little Italian immigrant with no education and plain looks. She was amazed to see how beautiful she actually was. Rebecca had been sure she would leave Evangeline in a pool of tears and ready to sign papers.

"If you think I have nothing to offer my husband, think again," she said. "I am a business woman in my own right.

"And another thing, you should think about is my daughter. She will never be left in your care and maybe never meet you at all, that I am sure of. If it's Chance's money you are after, don't hold your breath. I can ruin him with a stroke of a pen." Evangeline was breathing heavy now, her fists were clenched and her face was tight. *Don't cry. Don't cry!* She kept telling herself.

"Mrs. Winston," Rebecca retorted, "I have been sleeping with your husband since the day before your wedding," she smiled, "and if truth be told, years before that. He recently returned to me and we want to be married. You are not meeting his sexual needs. Have pity on him, Evangeline, give him up," she begged.

"My husband has never backstreeted me like he has you. You, I have pity for," she said. "For your information, Chance is a loving, generous, husband and father. You are standing in a home he built for me. What has he built for you?" she asked. "You live in a brownstone that belongs to your family, isn't that true?" she inquired   Rebecca   was shocked that Evangeline knew so much about her. Had Chance lied to her about this woman? She didn't seem to be the unlovable women that he had described.

"Miss Clay, I have a lot of support from the Winston family," as her voice got louder.

The butler walked in with a worried look on his face. "Mrs. Winston, is everything alright?" he asked.

"Yes it is. Please show this person out of my house. You are never to come here again, do you understand?" she told Rebecca.

"You haven't seen the last of me, Mrs. Winston," and she marched out of the house. Rebecca stood by the side of her car breathing heavily.

"Are you alright, Miss?" her chauffer asked.

"Yes, take me home please," she ordered him. Chance had a lot of questions to answer. Evangeline was right. Count Richard gave her more jewelry than Chance ever had. He didn't set me up in a nice home or New York apartment. The brownstone was old and starting to crumble around her. Chance was perfectly happy to just stay in her bed. *What has he done for me?* Rebecca asked herself. Evangeline used the word backstreet, that's exactly what he has done to me. We never went out in public. We never had friends over for dinner or drinks. It has only been him and I alone. He must have told her about me, how else did she know so much, she wondered? Evangeline gave her a lot to think about in a short visit. And Chance had a lot of questions to answer.

Evangeline was shaking like a leaf after Rebecca's visit. Cook brought her a cup of tea to calm her nerves. Lorenzo walked in the back door of the kitchen as he was accustomed to doing.

"What's the matter?" he asked Evangeline, as she looked up from her cup and gave him a fake smile.

"Oh, I just had a visitor, a Miss Rebecca Clay," and she rolled her eyes.

"That *putanna*, what did she want?" he asked.

"She wanted me to give Chance a divorce," she said. "as a matter of fact."   "Why can't Chance ask you himself?"

"Who knows, do you know she slept with him the day before our wedding?" she told him.

Lorenzo was running his fingers through his black hair and pacing around in circles. "How do you want me to take care of this?" he asked.

"Please don't deny me the pleasure of getting some revenge on them," she said coldly.

"That is so unlike you, Evangeline," Lorenzo said.

"You have no Idea what I'm like these days," she said. Lorenzo didn't understand, but was sure Rebecca's visit was going to make trouble for the Winston household.

Apollinia   ------   Evangeline's Destiny

FIFTEEN

Joe walked into Chance's office the first thing in the morning.

"I have to get here early if I want to talk to you anymore," he told him. "You're usually gone by noon these days. I hear Miss Clay is back in your life, that's the buzz around the office," he said as he shrugged his shoulders and gave him a stern look.

"I don't see that it's any of your business, or the office staff's for that matter," Chance said in defense. "You should put a buzz out that I'm looking for all new replacements for my employees," he said sarcastically.

"Did you think it's been a secret all these years, Chance?" he asked him. "Again, what's it to you Joe?" he asked.

Joe lost his temper and grabbed Chance around the neck. "What it is to me, my friend, is Evangeline. I don't want her hurt," Joe explained.

"She knows nothing of my affair with Rebecca," he said, as he pried Joe's fingers off of him.

"How stupid do you think she is?" Joe questioned. "I'll not have her hurt, or Alicianna or your mother for that matter, do you hear me?" he demanded. "And if you think I'm a problem, you don't want to know what Lorenzo will do to you!" he threatened. "He knows a lot of shady characters and remember what happened to Lucky Frankie?" he reminded him.

"Get out of my office, Joe," he said, "get out of my building, you are no longer employed at Winston Steel!" he yelled. By now his face was flushed and he was breathing heavy.

"I'll save you the trouble of firing me." Joe pulled his letter of resignation out of his pocket and threw it in Chance's face. He then walked out of the room. Joe bumped into Matt on the way out and apologized for the argument.

Matt went to Chance's aid as he was breathing heavily now. "He knows about Rebecca, doesn't he?" Matt asked his brother.

"Yes," Chance choked out, "he just resigned."

"Chance, I told you to let her go," Matt reminded him. "This is going to come down hard on your head," he added.

"Get me some brandy," Chance told his brother, "I need a drink."

Rebecca was back in the brownstone pacing back and forth like a lion. She felt as furious as one also, thinking how Chance lied to her about Evangeline. Where did she think he was all those nights that he didn't come home? Rebecca started drinking early that night and when Chance came in, she threw the glass at him. He ducked and it missed him.

"What was that for?

Rebecca came after him in a rage. "You have been lying to me about Evangeline all these years," she lunged at him scratching his face.

"What are you talking about?" he asked.

"Evangeline knows a lot about me and my business," she said.

"How do you know that?"

"She told me!" Rebecca yelled.

"She came here?

"No, I went to Hunters Point," she informed him.

"Are you insane? I warned you, Rebecca." With those words, he slapped her face.

"Get out, Chance, Get out. How dare you slap me? Is this something new for you?" she screamed. "I have more class in my little finger than you and the whole Winston family put together," she said with her voice shaking.

"You, my dear, are nothing more than a kept woman," he said to demean her. "Keeping me?" she said, "If anyone is being kept. it's you. "

"I thought you loved me," Chance questioned.

"I loved the man who would never lie to me," she cried. "Did you stay awake at night thinking of things to lie about?" she asked, and began weeping loudly.

"No, Rebecca, that's not true," he said honestly. He reached to cradle her in his arms and she spat in his eye.

"Get away from me," she said. "I'll never trust you again! Get out or I'll call the police!" she screamed.

Chance turned around and ran out of the brownstone. *What a surreal day he was having, a black cloud was chasing him,* he was sure.

Chance returned to Hunters Point in a state of disarray.

"What happened to your face?" Evangeline asked.

"I fell," he told her curtly. This waiting for the next blow to fall was unnerving.

"Are you staying for dinner,? she asked in her usual manner.

"Yes, I'll be home tonight," he said.

What an honor, Evangeline thought to herself.

"How is my mother today>" Chance asked her.

"She is slipping away, I can see it more and more," she answered. "She hasn't been out of bed for two days now. She sleeps hours on end with all the medicines she is prescribed. She told me she dreams of Edward and the day she met him in the park. She said you were in the pram and they walked and walked," Evangeline repeated.

"I'm glad she's happy," Chance said. He showered and hoped he washed the events of the day away. He went to his mother's room and sat at her bedside. Rosalyn was in a morphine induced sleep.

"Mother," Chance said, "I wish I could talk to you about the foolish mess I've made of my life. You've always been so wise, but I think I know what you would say. You would say, 'Chance, stop this foolishness immediately and show some respect to your wife.' I'm not going to promise something I might not be able to keep, but I'm going to try," he said, and rested his head on her folded hands.

Rosalyn moaned and opened her eyes, "Chance, my darling, have you been here long?" she asked.

"No, Mother, I just sat down," he answered.

"I was dreaming of Edward," she said, I "loved him so. He's waiting for me and I can't wait to see him again." She fell asleep again and her breathing was very raspy.

I better gather the family, he thought, and got up to call Matt. Maria had already informed Lorenzo and Elsie and they were on their way to

Hunters Point. The doctor's diagnosis was very unclear. He said she could last a long time in this state, or she could pass quietly in her sleep. Rosalyn was getting the best possible care at home. There was no reason to put her in the hospital away from her familiar surroundings, besides the hospital was totally unacceptable to Evangeline.

Lorenzo and Elsie went in to see her with Elena in their arms. "Put the baby on my bed," Rosalyn asked, "I want to play with her." Elena loved Rosalyn and immediately started to play patty cake with her. "My beautiful Elena," she said, "I saw you take your first breath, I saw you in your christening gown, I had hoped to see you in your Communion dress, but that is not to be. Elsie and Lorenzo, keep her close to you, she is your most precious possession."

"We will," Elsie cried, as she wiped her tears away.

"Lorenzo, keep an eye on Evangeline, I know you have always protected her; she will need you now more than ever."

"You know I will," Lorenzo assured her.

"Please, I need to speak to Matt, will you let him come in?" she asked.
"Of course," they both agreed. Matt and Mariella had been waiting their turn, and Matt went in to see his mother.

"My darling boy," she said. "Please tell Mark what I'm telling you. This war is keeping us apart only in miles, he is in my heart as if he were standing next to you."

"I know Mother," he said, "sometimes I feel his presence also. It must be a twin thing," he agreed.

"Your brother, Chance is in trouble. He has played a foolish game with his marriage. People think I don't know, but a mother can read her children more than they think. Winston Steel will be up to you and Matt to handle on your own. I just want to prepare you, my son."

"I know, Mother, I've taken care of it, Mark knows too."

"Good, now go and tell them all that I'm not going to die tonight. I just needed to get this off my mind. I want to sleep now, I love you, my darling son, tell Mariella I'll talk to her tomorrow."

"Good night Mother, we all love you too." Matt walked out of the room with a smile on his face.

"She says she isn't going to die tonight so we can rest easy," he laughed. "She is really something, our mother," he said.

Larissa asked Cook to make a pot of strong coffee. The families went into the dining room for the refreshment and conversation.

"What did she say?" Chance asked Matt.

"Only that she wished Mark was here and that she loved us all," he answered. Chance didn't know his brothers were planning a takeover of the business if Chance didn't come to his senses and give up Rebecca. His absenteeism at the office was putting the company in jeopardy. Edward would never have stood for this latest lapse in judgment on Chance's part.

"How did you get those scratches on your face?" Matt asked Chance, "Get in a cat fight?"

"I fell." It was the same answer he gave his wife.

Evangeline was fighting her own war with Chance; it was a war of silence and indifference. She felt she was losing.

Rosalyn perked up a little after her meeting with her loved ones, but she stayed in a weakened state during the holidays. Evangeline had a Christmas tree brought in to her room. All her favorite ornaments were placed where she could see them, especially the ones she imported from Spain.

"You are so thoughtful, Evangeline," she said. "It would have been such a disappointment if I had no tree this Christmas."

"To tell you the truth, I'm missing Mike so much I like to keep myself busy."

"I miss Mark too," the other mother confessed. "Has Mike written to Larissa yet?" Rosalyn asked.

"No, not since we got back from the ocean," she said. "I mentioned in my last letter, that Larissa would like to hear from him. I had a hard time putting it into words without sounding like I'm butting in," she explained.

"You did the right thing," Rosalyn said.

"How do you feel today, darling?" Evangeline asked her mother-in-law.

"I'm so tired, Evangeline," Rosalyn sighed.

"Let me fluff your pillows and you can take a nap," she suggested.

"Thank you, dear," she responded and quickly fell asleep.

Elsie was stirring the sugar in her tea when Evangeline left Rosalyn's bedroom.   "How much does she sleep these days?" she asked.

"Sometimes twenty hours a day," she told her, "she really has no life."

"What a shame," Elsie cried, "she was such a vibrant women."

"She is the best," Evangeline insisted.

"How are you handling Chance? "Elsie asked.

"I called Mr. Ryan and his latest report is ready. Chance had been seen coming and going to the brownstone, but for the past couple of months, he goes there and bangs on the door but never goes in."

"What a pitiful man he has turned into," Elsie sighed.

"Elsie, tell me the truth, have I been such a bad wife for him to behave like this? I don't dare cry for fear I'll become like Larissa and can't stop."

"Don't do this to yourself," Elsie told her, "you know better."

"That's what Joe tells me," she said.

"Is he coming for Christmas this year?" Elsie asked.

"I'm not sure, Chance and he had an argument when he left the company. Matt asked me if I knew what it was about, Chance wouldn't tell him. He told him it was personal," Evangeline explained. "Joe knows he is always invited, I just don't know how comfortable he will be around Chance."

"Men handle these things better than women," Elsie said.

"I think you're right," Evangeline agreed.

Alan Mason walked out of a Fifth Avenue jewelry shop like he was walking on air. He had just bought a beautiful engagement ring for Larissa. Maybe, if he gave her a ring, she would think more seriously about their future. He was thinking of a special way to give her the ring at Christmas. His parents were invited to Hunters Point for the festivities and he was starting to feel like family. He wanted her to get better acquainted with his parents, but she was still standoffish. He gave her the benefit of the doubt, that her mother was so ill, she didn't have time for teas or luncheons.

Larissa went through her days in a mundane fashion. She wasn't getting the satisfaction she thought she would as a teacher. The children loved her and she was pleasant, but something was missing, and she knew what it was. It was Mike.

She only heard from him through Evangeline. She sent letter after letter and all she got was a Christmas card from Italy in return. She never answered him about his dream, what could she say? So she told him to listen to her dad and come home. Her letters were as bland as she felt--what could she write about, her second grade spelling test? She was afraid to mention Alan in case he thought they were a couple.

While Larissa and Abigail were shopping one Saturday afternoon, the subject of Alan came up.

"What am I going to do about Alan?" Larissa asked her friend. "I do think the world of him and I'm pretty sure I love him, but Mike keeps looming over my head," she cried.

Abigail didn't have patience for Larissa when she took on the victim role. "Larissa, you do this to yourself," she told her. "Alan is a dream and you know it. You are a different person when you are with Alan. Like it or not, he makes you happy. Think about it, all you do is laugh and sing and dance when you are together. Your family adores Alan. He's smart and handsome. I could go on and on." Abigail debated.

"Ok, I get the idea," Larissa cut her off. "I know I have to grow up and let go of Mike. I know what I'm going to do!" she said as if a flash of light appeared on her face. "I have decided to put Mike away in a corner of my heart and get on with my life," she told Abigail.

"That's my girl," she said with approval.

"He doesn't have to go away forever, I'll just keep him safe in my heart and concentrate, instead, on a man who loves me," Larissa said. "Thank you, Abigail, for always making me see the right side of things. What would I do without you?"she said and embraced her friend.

"Did you get a letter from Sam today?" Larissa asked.

"Yes, he said he and the boys were fine and hoping the war will be over soon."   "How long was Mike in the hospital? Did he say? Evangeline still doesn't know anything about it

"Just a few days after he was attended to, he was back in the motor pool," she said.

"Well, I wish him well, but I'm not going to write him another letter," Larissa insisted.

"Smart girl," Abigail said, and they walked into Macys Department store to buy Christmas presents.

Elsie and Dr. Stein were visiting some patients one afternoon when she asked him a question. "Dr. Stein," she said, "I don't pretend to understand your profession, but I see a pattern in my family that is starting to make sense to me."

"Really?" he said, "That's interesting Elsie, it is not a hard thing to read people, but when you see past their everyday actions, they become something else. Who is it you are analyzing?" he asked.

"Well, my husband, my friend Larissa and her brother Chance."

"Three people, Elsie, you are quite astute," he teased her.

"Don't make fun of me." She turned away from him.

"Believe me, I'm proud of the person you have become. Because of your own addiction you can now help others, that's why I ask you to come along with me on these visits; you really are a wonder," he added. "Now appease an old man and tell me what you have discovered."

"This is confidential, right?" she asked.

"Absolutely," he said.

"Well, I call it 'obsessive dependency'. You see Lorenzo has been dependent on his sister-in-law Evangeline since he was a teenager. I don't feel threatened in the least by her as far as my marriage goes. I did early on, but she is my best friend now. Lorenzo can't make a decision without her. He can't be away from her for very long either. He has protected her since she brought his son to America. Evangeline isn't Mike's mother, but her sister was. Lorenzo did an unthinkable thing to Felicia which Mike was the product of. When Felicia died, Lorenzo had already settled in New York and the relatives sent Evangeline and Mike to him. Mike was attached to Evangeline and thought she was his mother when he was a little boy. Lorenzo has shared Mike with Evangeline and her husband Chance all these years.

"Evangeline became Lorenzo's partner in the auto business, because she had the funds to support it. It's not her money he cares about, he has done quite well on his own, but he can't separate himself from her and her problems," Elsie told him.

"It sounds like you have named it quite well, Elsie," he said "Are you sure you aren't jealous of her?" he asked.

"Dr. Stein, Evangeline is a wonderful woman, her loyalties go beyond the normal. I know she loves Lorenzo, which hasn't always been the case. I also know she loves me and Elena too. If you got to know her, you would understand."

"Who's next on your list?" the doctor asked.

"It's Larissa Winston. I've known her since I came from Germany and she was an infant. I think the world of her and hope Elena takes up some of her good qualities. But Doctor, she has an obsessive dependency on my step-son Mike. They were raised together since they were toddlers. When you saw one child, you saw the other. Mike takes her for granted and she loves him beyond reasoning. He was her protector also and I think she saw that as a romantic gesture. He has never actually mentioned a future with her, but she reads it in everything he says. He throws her off by saying how beautiful she is and comments on her goodness. He never tried anything sexual with her, she has been very sheltered in her life.

"Alan Mason, a young man she has known for a long time, is very much in love with her and tries everything he knows to win her over. I hope it happens soon, hopefully before Mike returns from the War," she said.

"Does she realize he loves her as a sister?" he asked.

"I think so, but how do you cut someone like that out of your heart? Mike is a dead ringer for Lorenzo, so I can sympathize with her in that department. He is so handsome and has a personality to match."

"I'd say Alan has his work cut out for him, but if he really loves her, I bet he breaks her down. Something tangible is always better than some fantasy, and I think her affection for Mike is a fantasy," he suggested. "Very good Elsie, you have named both your subjects correctly," Dr. Stein agreed.

"Let's see if you get the third one right," he said.

"This one is the hardest for me to understand. Chance Winston is Evangeline's husband. He loves her as much as any of us. It has been confided to me that they don't have a normal husband -wife relationship.

Apparently Evangeline doesn't respond to Chance and isn't interested in his advances. He had a girlfriend when I first came from Germany. I thought he was the most handsome, wonderful guy I ever saw and envied Rebecca for having captured him. I knew they were fooling around a lot back then. I caught them a couple of times in the stable, while I was walking between the two mansions on errands from my employer. It seems he has never stopped sleeping with her.

"She went to Europe for a year, against Chances wishes, and that was when Evangeline came to America with Mike and he fell in love with her. The day before their wedding, Chance went to see Rebecca and they continued their affair. It's been over fifteen years and he still keeps her under wraps," she told him.

"How do you know about this?" Dr. Stein, asked her.

"Evangeline was confronted recently by Rebecca and she wants her to give Chance a divorce. Evangeline told me and so did Lorenzo," she said. "Evangeline is so hurt although she always knew about the affair. She had a private detective follow him years ago. She never said anything because she didn't want to "'rock the boat' as she put it, for Mike. Chance afforded him all the best money could buy and she kept it that way. They also have a child between them and she loves her daddy completely. Evangeline is totally devoted to her mother-in-law who is currently dying of cancer."

"My goodness, Elsie, what a mess! Chance definitely has an obsession with Rebecca, an unhealthy one at that," he said. "Larissa could have a very bad reaction to Mike, if she isn't careful, especially if she finds out he doesn't want her. I certainly hope Alan gets through to her. Lorenzo is the lucky one. He has you, my dear. From what you say, he recognizes his obsession and doesn't try to hide it. I know he adores you and Elena. You gave him quite a scare, you know," he reminded her.

"I know I did," she said, "It drew us closer together,"

"You missed one other person: Evangeline. She has an obsession with Mike too."

"You are absolutely right, Doctor Stein," she said in amazement.

"To tell you the truth, Elsie, I would love to have a session or two with Mike, he sounds like a very special specimen," he said. Elsie laughed to think of Mike as a specimen.

"You talked to him after the shark attack along with the other boys, remember?"   "That's right Elsie, but the questions would be different this time." "Thank you for listening to me," Elsie told him.

"No, thank you, it sounds like a good paper to write for the Journal of Psychiatry." They both laughed and went in to see their patient.

Christmas Eve at Hunters Point was quite typical: the guest list included the Rizzo's, the Mitchells, the Lee's, the Como's, Joe Cross and Alan Mason's parents. Rosalyn wanted to be wheeled into the ball room where the festivities were taking place. She could only stay up a few minutes and all the children gathered around her and sang Christmas Carols. She was thin as a rail, but her smile was infectious. It made everyone a little happier, but the hosts were miserable. Chance and Evangeline ignored each others as much as possible and it was noticeable. Everyone knew about their problems, but no one dared mention it.

John Lee approached Chance when they had a minute alone. "It pains me to say this Chance, but if you proceed with a divorce, I'm asking you to use another lawyer. I'm too close to the family and I adore Evangeline. I can't put her on the stand and ask her embarrassing questions. I'm just giving you a heads up, my friend," John told him.

"I'm not ready for that, John I don't know how this is going to shake out. I don't think Evangeline will forgive me, if I ask, so I won't ask," Chance said.

"You are walking a tight rope, Chance, I wish you luck," John said, and rejoined the party.

"Larissa," Alan said, "I have something to show you."

"What is it?" she said. She was feeling very good after singing carols with Alan and the children. He played the piano and knew all of her mother's favorite songs.   "Come here by the tree," he said. "Can you reach under the tree and get that pretty pink box with the mistletoe on the top?"

"You can't fool me, Alan Mason, I know what you are going to do with that mistletoe," she said jokingly.

"I can't reach it," Alan told her, "without knocking the whole tree over, then Evangeline will throw me out on my back side in the cold."

"Don't be silly," she said, and reached under the tree and retrieved the box.

"Oh look!" Alan said, "The tag says Larissa."

"Can I open it?" she begged.

"By all means," he urged her.

She hurriedly tore the paper off the box and opened it. When she looked inside, she let out a scream that made everyone look at her. Alan got down on one knee and said, "Will you marry me Larissa?"

She was holding her hands to her mouth in case the wrong words slipped out. She took a deep breath and said, "Yes I will."

Alan jumped to his feet and kissed her in front of the entire crowd. He slipped the ring on her finger and noticed how perfect it looked. A loud roar of approval was heard and the families descended on them with their best wishes.

"Come Alan, let's show mother," Larissa said, and they crept into her room. She was still awake and her attendant motioned for them to come closer.

"Mrs. Winston," Alan said, "I'm sorry I didn't ask you first, but I couldn't wait." Larissa held her hand out to show her mother her wonderful gift.

"You know very well what my answer would have been," she said, "The entire family loves you dearly." They kissed her and stayed until she fell asleep.

Larissa was busy all night showing off her engagement ring. Mr. Mitchell who was self -imposed patriarch of the family gave the Christmas speech that Edward always gave. He wished all the children a Merry Christmas and hoped they were good children this year so that Santa Clause would bring them what they wanted. Then he wished good cheer and prosperity for the fathers in the room. He wished the mothers the strength to raise good children and be good wives to their husbands for he believed they are the glue that holds the household together. Then he wished a safe return to all the brave military men who are in the war, especially Nick Jackson, Sam Genoa and Mike Winston. He raised his glass and everyone said cheers!

"Mike Winston," Larissa said, she stopped in her tracks. She held her ring hand close to her heart. "I haven't given Mike a thought all night." *What did she do*, she panicked. Alan came to her that moment and took her by the hand and held her in his arms. They started dancing to the music; the musicians were playing a beautiful slow melody. The others were dancing around them and suddenly her fears were calmed.   Alan whispered in her ear, "I love you Larissa," and she knew all was well.

Joe and Chance avoided each other all night ,in fact almost every one avoided Chance. When the guest started to leave the party, Chance excused himself and went to bed. Lorenzo, Elsie, Evangeline and Joe sat by the fire with a glass of brandy.

"Joe, the people from Detroit are calling quite often with plans for a showroom," Lorenzo said. "They probably won't start until the war is over, but they want to be prepared. I'm going to send you out to look at the designs and find some land for me and Elsie to build a house. I hear there is a place called Grosse Point that has some beautiful estates, maybe you could look there," Lorenzo said.

"Oh yes," said Elsie, "on Lake St. Clair."

"Sometime in April, when the snow is mostly gone," he added. "Does that sound alright with you?"

"Sure, I'd love to," he said. "I understand Lake St. Clair is very beautiful and the ships travel that route to the ocean," he told them.

"I have my investment in Detroit, so I may need a house there, too," joked Evangeline.

"Oh, how wonderful! I can't stand the idea of Lorenzo and I in Detroit and you in New York," Elsie said gleefully. Evangeline looked into the fire. "A lot of changes have to happen before I go to Detroit," she sighed.

In the middle of January, Evangeline hosted another party. This time it was for the Christening of Mona and Roberto's little boy Robert. He was six months old and the priest was putting pressure on the parents to get the boy baptized. As it turned out, Roberto's best friend, Sergio Donatutti, was wounded in the war and came home on an honorable discharge. He had been in a hospital, in Washington, for many months and Roberto wanted him to be godfather for his son. As soon as he returned to New York, the Christening was able to take place. Luna had the same sentiments as the priest and sprinkled holy water on the boy every chance she got. Mariella and Matt together were godparents also. Evangeline was happy to help her niece with the festivities and the party was in usual Evangeline fashion.

"You should rent yourself out as a party organizer," Joe told Evangeline, as he teased her about her extravagance.

"Why shouldn't I give my family the best?" she replied. "Let Chance Winston pay for this little party, at least Rebecca won't reap the benefit," she insisted. "That was a vindictive statement, Joe," she said, "I'm sorry, Chance never said no to anything I wanted to give my family. I feel ashamed I said it," Evangeline cried.

"Evangeline, I'm afraid you are becoming vindictive; I don't like to see you this way. I hope this doesn't last much longer," he told her. He wanted to hold her in his arms and soothe her anger away, but he couldn't with a room full of people.

Joe had an idea that he couldn't get off his mind.

"Matt," he asked, "how did Sergio get back in the states, do you know?"

"I think it was a hospital ship," he said. "Why do you ask?" he wondered.   "Could Mark come home on one of those ships?" he asked. "I've been trying every way I could to get him home before something happens to my mother," Matt said, "you just might have the answer." The men approached Sergio and asked a few questions about his return.

"Mary has family in high places; if I get a letter off to them with this information, it just might work. I don't think they torpedo ships with a red cross on them, do they? he added.

"I'll get to work on it right away," Matt said.

Joe had some interests himself in Italy. He was worried about his son and what had become of him. The last he had heard, his son was still living at home with his mother and her new family in Calabria. The people who were involved with his new identity in Italy had given his case to the U.S. intelligence. The war had damaged the resistance in Italy and the people who were looking for him were either disbanded or dead. Joe asked a favor of Mariella who worked for the War Department.

"Mariella," he asked, "I have a story to tell you. I hope you will use your discretion upon hearing it. I haven't told a soul about it for fear of my family in Italy being hurt or worse."

"My God, Joe, why trust me with this information?" she asked.

"I trust you because of your job and your education, and mostly your love of your Aunt Evangeline."

"What does she have to do with this?" she asked.

"Nothing yet, but when she is free of Chance, I want to marry her."

"You both have been very discrete about your love for each other, but the way you look at each other, breaks my heart. I can tell because I love Matt so much," she admitted.

"It's to the point now that I don't care who sees it, but Evangeline cares. Mariella," he said, "I was in the Italian Resistance years before the war started. Our idea was to stop the insurgents from coming into Italy and killing the innocent," he told her. "We were a group of very strong minded young men who thought we were doing the right thing. Our message was right, but we were outnumbered. I was captured during a run of ammunitions from Sicily to Greece. They should have hung or shot me on the spot, but they were going to make a hostage of me. Fortunately they were overrun by the Italian Army and I was released and sent to London with a new identity. "From London they sent me to New York and Pittsburgh to work with the steel manufacturers. That's when I met Chance," he said.

"Why steel manufacturers?" she asked.

"We have been smuggling steel and ammunitions to London all these years," he said. "That is where the confidential part of my story is. Can you deal with that?" he asked.

"Yes, I suppose so, who would I tell?"

"Your husband could be in very dangerous trouble if it got in the wrong hands," he said.

"I see, "she understood. "What do you want me to do? , You are scaring me a little, Joe."

"If it is in your power, I'm looking for my son. Can you help me find him? I was married and had a little boy when I was arrested. The government had my marriage annulled and my wife remarried several years ago. She has other children from her new husband which is very legal. I had information on them about every six months, but since the war I have heard nothing. I'm very worried and I had hoped you could help me," Joe implored.

"My aunt knows nothing about this? she questioned.

"I think she knows something mysterious is going on with me, but she never asked," he told her. "She trusts me that much Mariella, that's one of the things I love about her." He had tears in his eyes and Mariella had a lump in her throat. Joe seemed to have a million reasons to love Evangeline, he couldn't help it.

"I'll do everything in my power to find him," she promised. "I'll take a lesson from my dear aunt and not say a word to Matt about the steel business. Maybe he will love me more for it, do you think so Joe?"

"Believe me, she makes my life easier, I love her, that's just how it is," he said.   "What is his name and how old is he?"she asked.

"Giuseppe Croce and he is 22 years old, he was born August 14. 1895.   "Giuseppe Croce translates to Joseph Cross in English," she said with a smile. "I'll do everything I can to help you, I promise," she said and kissed his forehead.

The winter of 1918 was mild compared to the past few years. Before they knew it, spring was upon them. Mike and Sam were still working their jobs for the army. The camp site changed several times, but Mike was still working in the motor pool. Sometimes he had to transport supplies to other areas of combat and that always scared him to death. The bombs would go off all around them and he had to drive through the road to get his supplies delivered. Although most of the time he stayed at camp and changed oil and fixed tires.

Sam gave up his ambulance job when his sergeant found out his family had a pasta factory in the states. He was now head cook and pasta maker for the camp. He was a shoo-in for the job with all his credentials. He was relieved he didn't have to see boys die in combat anymore; that would stay with him for the rest of his life. Abigail was relieved also, she was busying herself with wedding plans with Larissa. Although Larissa knew her wedding was a few years off,it was fun to look through magazines for ideas.   Alan was doing so well at school and she was very proud of him ,time was flying by it seemed.

April was a sad month in the Winston household as it was the anniversary of Edward's death. Rosalyn spent a lot of time talking to him in her hallucinative state. It was heartbreaking to watch as she constantly asked him to open the widow or she asked for her pretty dress. She didn't react to any of the family members very often, she would get a name right on occasion, but she slept most of the time. The family gathered around her bedside one Saturday afternoon. Evangeline sat on one side of the bed and Larissa sat on the other.

"Where is Matt?" everyone asked Mariella.

"He should be here soon, he had an errand to run," she explained.

"He better get here soon," Chance said, "it doesn't look good. "

The weather that day was warm and breezy. The windows were opened to let the fresh air in along with the sunshine.

"This was the kind of day Mother loved best," Larissa said and gave out a long sigh. She was picking at the lace on Rosalyn's collar. Evangeline mentioned that she wanted to plant more tulips next fall so the east garden was as spectacular as the west garden.

"Rosalyn always looked ahead in life, not back, Father was the only person she looked back on, and that was her joy, for he was the love of her life, "she said as she held Rosalyn's frail hand.

"Look what I found," Matt said, and stepped aside to let his brother and Mary through to see his mother.

"Mark!" everyone cried, and they rushed to embrace him.

"I'm so glad to be home," he said. "Mother can you hear me?" he asked her.   Evangeline gave up her place on the bed to her brother-in-law so he could be closer to her and maybe she could see him.

"Mother," he asked again," this is my wife, Mary."

She opened her eyes and said, "I've been waiting for you my darling. What took you so long? I'm very tired."

"I'm sorry mother, this is the best I could do," he said.

"I always told you boys to do your best," she whispered. "She is lovely Mark, see that she gets some tea," she said. "I love you Mark, I told the others already, now I'm telling you." The tears were dripping off his face and he used his shirtsleeve to dry them.

"Get a hankie, dear," she said, "don't go to school without one."

"I won't forget," Mark told her.

"You're a good boy," she said. "Matt, watch over your brother, he always leaves one of his books behind," she said as she was becoming delirious. "Larissa is getting her Italian lesson from Evangeline today, I must remember to tell Chance. Where is Edward," she said, "Oh, there you are my love, is the window open?" she asked.

Rosalyn took one more breath and died peacefully with all her loved ones around her. A few minutes after she died, a breeze blew the curtains around Rosalyn's bed. It was a surreal moment as the winds weren't blowing that hard outside. Suddenly the window shade from across the room made a sucking sound and the shade stuck to the screen. Everyone saw it but no one mentioned it. The grief they were feeling was taking over all their senses. Mark laid his head on her folded hands and cried uncontrollably. Matt tried to comfort him, but Chance stopped him.

"He has some time to make up for," he said; "let him grieve in his own way." Larissa had to be taken out of the room after she fainted. Cook got her some smelling salts and they put her on the drawing room sofa.

Mariella and Matt sat with Rosalyn and Mark until the undertaker came to take care of the body. The friends had accumulated at the house to give their support to the family.

"Did mother have a will?" Matt asked Chance.

"Yes, John Lee wrote one for her from a scrap of paper she had given Maria, at the ocean last summer."

"Do we have to wear red bloomers?" Mark asked, his brother.

"Yes, I'm afraid so," and they both started to laugh out loud.

"What's so funny?" Matt asked less than amused.

"Red bloomers," Mark answered.

"Oh no," he said, and the three of them laughed until they cried.

"Did anyone notice the curtains and how they blew around her?" Matt asked. "What about the window shade on the other side of the room?" Mark added. "That was just Dad coming to get her," Chance was convinced.

SIXTEEN

Evangeline needed to be alone for a while and walked out to the garden. Her head was hurting her and the tears were stinging her eyes. Somehow she felt alone in the world without Rosalyn. She knew she wasn't, she had a very large family and circle of friends.

She was looking at the flowers when two yellow butterflies flew around her face and landed on a rose bush. She wanted to touch them because they were so beautiful but they flew away. "Good bye my darlings," she said, "good bye." She walked back into the house with a feeling that the world had been taken off her shoulders. She could breathe easier and she felt as free as those butterflies.

The morning of Rosalyn's funeral, John Lee took Evangeline aside and handed her a letter.

"Rosalyn wanted you to have this on the occasion of her death," he said. The envelope read 'For Evangeline's Eyes Only'. She took the envelope with a questioning look. "I have no idea what's in there," John said.

"What have we here?" Mark asked as he walked by just as John handed her the envelope in question.

"I don't know," Evangeline said truly surprised. She tore open the letter and it read 'Chance Morgan for Alicianna's sake – Please destroy.' Immediately Evangeline knew what she meant. She was privileged to know the story of how Chance came to be born. Rosalyn confided the story to her after she recounted it to Larissa. The look on her face was sort of a smirk.

"Is it funny Evangeline?" he asked.

"You know your mother," she told him. "You children have to wear red bloomers. I got the recipe to her secret wrinkle cream. Now I have to destroy it as she has directed me." Evangeline walked over to the fireplace and tore the letter in a hundred pieces and threw them on the coals a few pieces at a time.

"My mother was one of a kind," Mark said and walked away with a tear in his eye.

Chance Morgan was the name of the Page in the Queen's Court that fathered Chance. Chance Morgan-Hennessey-Winston-- who was the real Chance she wondered?

The funeral was exactly as Rosalyn dictated; Maria orchestrated it just as she wanted. Her girls all wore white dresses and fresh flowers in their hair. Her sons donned white suits and, of course, they all wore red bloomers. Rosalyn lay in state at Hunters Point for one day and then was taken by hearse and her team of horses to St. Mary's Church for the funeral mass. Maria had no control over the crowds that gathered at the church, Rosalyn was a beloved member of the community and she had many friends. The so-called *royalty of New York* were also in attendance in respect of Edward. Rosalyn's private funeral turned into a grand spectacle as a tribute to her. After mass the horse drawn hearse took her straight to Edward and her final resting place.

The Winston family held their heads high for their mother and no crying and carrying on was accepted. They knew she was happy now and her faith that Edward was there to lead her to their heaven made the occasion easier.

Among the crowd was a women who stood out from the rest of the mourners. She had on a red dress and large red feathered hat. *How odd* thought Chance that someone would wear red to a funeral, but then the family was dressed in white. When he got closer, he recognized her as Rebecca. He didn't want to say anything to bring her to anyone's attention, but Evangeline noticed her too. She let out a small whimper and then froze in her seat when she realized who she was. Chance tried to ignore the incident, but Rebecca's plan was to be seen and her plan worked. Matt and Mark saw her and so did Joe and Lorenzo.

"That woman has a lot of nerve," Matt told Mark.

"I haven't seen her in years," said Mark; "I think she has aged quite a bit."

"That's just the evil in her," Matt said, "to do that at our mother's funeral has to say a lot about a person don't you think?"

"That has to be on Chance's conscience," Mark answered; he knew what he was doing when he started seeing her again.

A couple cars behind the family were Elsie, Lorenzo, Maria, Nicolo and Joe. When Lorenzo spotted Rebecca, he tried to jump out of the car. Joe and Elsie had to hold him down to stop him from making a scene.

"Lorenzo," Maria scolded, "stop and think before you and your temper get us all in trouble. Have some respect for Rosalyn, leave that tramp alone."

"I have all the respect for her that I can, that's why I want to wipe that witch off the face of the earth. Look at how she is dressed, like she is a burlesque queen," he cried.

"Chance has covered her up for so many years; she now feels the need for everyone to notice her. That's what Dr. Stein would say," said Elsie.

"You are probably right," said Joe; "Chance has done a lot of damage to that woman, and to everyone who cares about him."

Finally they reached the cemetery and Rosalyn's casket was placed where she longed to be, next to Edward. The family returned to Hunters Point for a small meal and the reality that the glue that held them all together was gone. Evangeline made a promise to each and every one of them that her home was their home also and a safe place to land in a storm. Rosalyn always told her children that saying and it was true today as it was when she was alive.

The evening edition of the newspapers in New York covered the funeral for the social pages. *The funeral in white* was the byline. It was irregular to see the family dressed in white to honor a loved one, but somehow the story got out that Rosalyn insisted that her children wore white like the angels and the fresh flowers the women wore were a tribute to her flower gardens at Lenox Hill. As usual the newspaper got the story a little twisted, but it made for good press. Some people tossed it up to eccentric rich people who didn't have respect for the dead. Some people thought it was a beautiful gesture, others didn't care.

One paper that was always good for the gossip factor caught the lady in red. "Who is the Lady in Red" was the headline? Why did she show up at the funeral of a beloved benefactor of New York? Tongues were wagging all over town. Was she her long lost love child, one paper asked? Did Rosalyn Winston belong to a secret society, another paper asked? The beautiful memory of Rosalyn was being smeared by these news seekers. Needless to say the family was in an uproar.

Lorenzo was on fire, he told Elsie, "I should have gotten rid of her a long time ago."

"How were you going to do it, my darling?" she asked?.

"I don't know. Don't ask me silly questions while I'm enraged." Elsie went with him to Hunters Point to have a word with Chance. She didn't trust him to be civilized. When they got there, the twins and John Lee were in discussion on how they were going to handle law suits against the papers for slander of their dead mother. Chance was being beaten down by Evangeline for the first time in their marriage.

" I don't care what you do to embarrass me," she yelled, "but look what she has done to your mother!" She had a copy of the paper and threw it in his face. "You have gone too far Chance, this time you have gone too far. I know you never gave a thought to me but what about Aliciana? She has to go to school and listen to the gossip from the other girls," she raged. "What about Larissa? She is a teacher at that school. How is she going to defend you when you are guilty as sin?" she yelled. "Stop this now," she insisted, "or you will be sorry."

Alan took Larissa into the garden so as not to hear any more talk of the scandal.   "The irony," Alan said, "was Rosalyn didn't do anything wrong, the papers made up a bunch of lies and printed it."

"How stupid could my brother be?" Larissa cried, "Matt told me he was warned to stay away from her."

"Do you think Chance invited her to come and, by the way, wear that red dress I like so much?" he joked.

"Of course not," Larissa said, "but he is to blame for this anyway."

"He probably is honey, but give him a little slack, he has to be hurting too."

Mariella went to Evangeline to see if she could help her after Chance left the room. She was sobbing like her heart was breaking.

"Zia, please don't cry or I will start too. Rosalyn was a wonderful mother-in-law. You are so lucky to have known her so long, I wish I had the fortune to be her daughter like you," she told her.

"I never thought I could hate Chance like I do now," Evangeline insisted. "For this wonderful woman to be smeared in the papers like this, is unthinkable. All she wanted was a private funeral, the way she wanted it conducted. It wasn't that much to ask for, was it?" and she started crying again.

"Maria is beside herself, she feels like she failed her somehow. She is in bed and can't get up," Nicolo told Cook.

There was a tapping on the door. "Come in," Evangeline said. Elsie opened the door and embraced her friend.

"How is Maria?" Evangeline asked,

"She is so upset that she won't get out of bed. Somehow she blames herself for this fiasco. Lorenzo is confronting Chance now, I had to leave before I took a swing at him too," she said.

Chance went to the study   and looked for a bottle of brandy. He needed a drink to calm his nerves. Lorenzo walked in and threw the paper on the desk.

"Have you read this one?" he said, "They accused Rosalyn of having a secret love child. I came here to rip your throat out, but somehow you look so pitiful I don't have the heart," Lorenzo said with surprise.

"Do you really think I sent Rebecca to the funeral dressed like that, do you think I sent her at all?" he asked Lorenzo.

"No, I suppose not," he said, as he thought about it. "I haven't seen her in months," he added.

"She shut me out of her life again, Lorenzo. How can everyone blame me for this?" he wondered.

"Because you were stupid enough to get involved with her in the first place," he said.

"No one knows what goes on in my house, but me," he hollered. "Everyone thinks Evangeline is the perfect person, the perfect wife and mother, the perfect lover, she isn't!" he insisted.

"I could rip your throat out for that comment alone." Lorenzo lunged for him.

"Go ahead, kill me, you have blinders on when it comes to her,"

Chance screamed. "I've had to share her with everyone, she never saw me as her husband, just a purse to support your son!" he insisted.

"Leave Mike out of this. He has nothing to do with you and Rebecca, he loves you as much as he loves me," he yelled "You know Chance, I don't think I will kill you today, but watch your back, "he decided. "You may not think much of Evangeline, but you, sir, are not the gentlemen your mother raised you to be," Lorenzo said, and walked out of the office.

The women were having tea in the drawing room when Lorenzo walked in. I'm sorry Evangeline, I don't know what to say to you," Lorenzo said.

"Did you kill him?" Elsie asked.

"Not this time," he told her, "Let's go home. I have a headache," he said.

"Good bye, my darling," he said to Evangeline. "It was nice to meet you, Mary, I am sorry it was under these circumstances," Lorenzo said and kissed her hand.

"Call me if you need me," Elsie added, and they left the house.

"So that is the famous Lorenzo?" Mary asked, "I don't think I have ever seen a more handsome man in my life. In all the commotion Matt never introduced us yesterday."

Evangeline rolled her eyes. "You don't know the half of it, my dear," she said.

Chance got the cold shoulder from everyone he encountered at the house, including his lawyer. He limped out of the house and got into his car. He drove to the brownstone and banged on the door. Surprisingly Rebecca opened it and let him in. He went in and sat in her drawing room by the fire. He had a chill he couldn't shake and the fire was warming.

"What possessed you, Rebecca?" he asked.

"I'm not sure, but it was something Evangeline said," she answered.

"I don't understand," he said.

"She told me you backstreeted me, you kept me in the shadows, like an ugly dog. We were never seen in public and now the public has seen me."

"Do you know what you have done to my mother?" he said.

"Do you know what you have done to my mother?" she asked him in return.   "What are you talking about Rebecca? You are saying things I don't understand," he questioned.

"You are such a man," she said, "ignorant of your surroundings. When I went to Europe all those years ago for my grand tour, do you remember that?" she said.

"Yes of course, I didn't want you to go," he remembered.

"Well, when I arrived I thought I had a bad trip across the ocean. I was sick in my cabin a lot of the time. Well, it was morning sickness, I was caring your child, a little girl I gave birth to six months after I arrived. To avoid any scandal my mother pretended the child was hers and my fathers. We went to the country where no one knew us and I had the baby. So you see it isn't only your mother that has been touched by all this."   "Rebecca, why didn't you tell me about this I would have married you," he insisted!

"Chance, I was going to, but a friend of mine sent me a newspaper clipping about you and Evangeline on your engagement. How could you have forgotten about me so soon?" she cried.

"Where is the child now?" he asked.

"Don't change the subject, how could you have forgotten about me?" she insisted.

"We had a fight, remember, I didn't want you to go. You said you had to, because your mother expected you to go. I thought you didn't care about my feelings and went anyway. When I met Evangeline, she took over my life. She became the sweetheart of the family. I thought I fell in love with her and Mike. Mike was the child I could take care of like my dad took care of me when my mother and I came from England. You know how much I wanted to be like him," he said. "Where is the child now?" he repeated himself.

"You will never know," she told him. "She thinks I am her sister and you will never hurt her with the truth."

"She is my child, I want to take care of her, I have money," he said.

"Yes, like you took care of me all these years? You took care of another man's child while yours was out of your reach and it is going to stay that way. My parents have raised her to know the difference between what is right and what is wrong; which is something I never learned. You are a pitiful man Chance; I wish I never knew you. Except for Molly, you have never given me anything," she said. "Get out Chance and never come back here again." She pushed him out the door and locked it.

The spring rain was coming down on him as he banged on the door. "Rebecca," he called over and over, "Let me in, I want to know more about my daughter. Rebecca," he called as he banged over and over. He stayed there for at least an hour.   Rebecca went upstairs to her bedroom so she couldn't hear the sound of his cries anymore. She felt like stone, her life was a disaster and she decided she would return to Europe after the war and be with her family.

Chance was soaked through his clothes. He lay on the stoop of the brownstone. Around midnight, a cop walking his beat found him there passed out. He rang the bell and Rebecca finally opened the door.

"Sorry Miss, do you know who this man is? I just found him lying on your stoop."   "No, I'm sorry, I don't know who he is, would you remove him from my property please?" she said, and closed the door.

He called for an ambulance and took Chance to the hospital. With the information the orderly took from his wallet, he notified the family and Mark and Matt rushed to the hospital. The doctors said he had a severe case of pneumonia and his chance of living was slim.

"We buried our mother yesterday," Mark told the doctor, "please do everything you can to help him." The doctor sympathized with the twins, but couldn't give them much hope. Evangeline waited for news from the twins.

The policeman told them where he found him. "I didn't think he was homeless because of the quality of his clothes and shoes," he said. "I'm just glad he was found before anything worse happened to him. The lady at the brownstone said she didn't know him, do you think he got lost?" the cop asked the brothers.

"I'm sure he did," they agreed and thanked him for his good work.

"She left him to die," they said to each other in disbelief. "I hope we have seen the last of Miss Rebecca Clay," Matt added.

When they reported the happenings of the evening to Evangeline, she insisted she come to the hospital. Lorenzo drove her to the city so she wouldn't be alone.

"Look at him Lorenzo," she said, "he looks like a beaten dog," she said with disgust. The doctor came in and gave them the results of his most recent tests.

"I'm sorry, Mrs. Winston, he is in bad shape. He wasn't very strong any way and the passing of his mother couldn't have helped," he said. "We don't know how long he was lying in that rain, but he was soaked through when he came in. He has a one hundred and four degree fever right now and we are going to pack him in ice to try to bring it down, so if you don't mind, please step out," he said.

"Certainly," Lorenzo said, and escorted Evangeline out into the hall. When Matt and Mark arrived they all stepped into the waiting room.

"What's going to happen now?" asked Mark.

"They are going to put ice around him to lower his body temperature," Lorenzo explained.

"I'm sure he will be better after they lower his temperature," said Evangeline. "Chance is like a cat with nine lives," she said assuredly.

"What are you going to do, Evangeline? How can you keep up this game he is playing with Rebecca? She was just going to let him die at her front door," said Matt.

"I know I sound like a fool," she said, "but he is still my husband, in good times and in bad. When he wakes up, I'll ask him what he wants to do and if I like his answer I'll go along with him, if I don't, then you don't want to know the person I will become," she announced.

"Evangeline," Lorenzo said, "you are making me afraid. I don't want you to change," he begged.

"We don't either," the twins chimed in.

"Don't worry my loved ones. I'll be fine," she said like ice was in her mouth.

The doctors and nurses worked for hours to get Chance's fever down. Finally, he opened his eyes.

"Where am I?" he asked the nurse.

"You're in the hospital, Mr. Winston. You have a fever, but I think you are going to be better soon." She left the room and called the doctor. The family noticed the doctors and nurses running in and out of the room.

"What's happening?" Matt asked one of the nurses.

"He woke up," she told him. Evangeline was the only one allowed in to see him. She walked in, her back as stiff as a board.

"You're alive?" she asked him.

"I'm not sure," he answered her. "Evangeline, I have the most incredible news." he informed her through gasps of air. "Rebecca told me I have a daughter in Austria."

"What am I to do with this information?" she asked coldly.

"It seems," he said, "when she left on her Grand Tour, she was already pregnant, and had the baby there. Her parents have passed her off as their child, but she is really mine. I have to find out more about her and make up for lost time, don't you see? Alicianna has a sister," he said, "she will be so surprised!"

"What are you talking about?" she asked him. "You will never tell my daughter about this scandal," she insisted. "If you want to make up for lost time, I suggest you get on one of the troop ships and go find her, but leave us out of it. This happened before I was your wife, so it doesn't pertain to me, but your legal daughter will never find out of your promiscuity this way," she demanded.

Evangeline couldn't believe his enthusiasm about this young woman. He could hardly breathe, yet he was making plans to find her. *He should be keeping her a secret especially to me, it just goes to show how little he thinks of me as a wife*, she thought. I've always been another sister to him and Rebecca is his true wife. Chance was talking out of his head and fell asleep again.

"Joe was right all the time," she told herself. *I have wasted all these years on a man who doesn't love me.* Evangeline stood up and walked back to the waiting room where the other men were sitting.

"How is he?" the twins asked in unison.

"I have to sit for a minute and process this in my head," she said.

"Is he alright?" they asked.

"I'm not sure," she said, "he is still pretty sick, he fell asleep again."

"What did he say to make you so upset?" Lorenzo asked.

"It seems Rebecca has his love child in Austria. She was expecting when she left on her Tour and had the baby there, her parents have raised her as their own all these years," she repeated the story to them. "She must have told him in an argument tonight, I don't know the whole story," she said. "I think I am ready to move on now, I want a divorce," she said, with all the strength she could muster.

Evangeline contacted John Lee the next morning. "I think you better go see Chance at the hospital," she told him. "He has an incredible story to tell and I think you should hear it," she explained.

When John got to the hospital he found Chance in an oxygen tent. The nurse told him he had double pneumonia. Chance was awake and recounted the story to him.   "John, I want to help her as much as I can. Her name is Molly and I want to set up a trust fund of two million dollars in her name. After the war. she can collect it when she is twenty one. I told Evangeline about the girl and I was surprised she wasn't more enthusiastic about her," he said.

"Chance, have you lost your mind completely?" he asked him, "You want your wife to get excited about your mistress' child, especially the way she behaved at your mother's funeral?"

"I don't know John, Evangeline is so good all the time and accepts everyone. I thought she would accept Molly too," he said.

"Chance have you ever thought this girl may not even want to know you as a father. Does she know about you at all? Has Rebecca kept you from her as well?" he wondered? "I have to look into a few things before I make up a trust for her," John said. "You have been talking too much, I can tell you are getting winded, I'll come by here tomorrow and let you know what I find," he said.

John went straight to Evangeline after his visit with Chance. "You are right about his story being incredible, but what I find more incredible is that he wanted you to be just as happy about the girl as he was," he told her.

"Thank you John, I didn't think I was the only one who could see that," she said, a little relieved.

"He isn't in his right mind, Evangeline, I'm sure of it," he said.

"John, I want a divorce. I can't live like this anymore and Rosalyn isn't here to get hurt by it," she said.

"The problem is, my dear, I don't think a judge will grant you one if Chance isn't found competent, and then it could take years," he said. "Chance wants me to put two million dollars in a trust for her to be taken after the war; or when she turns twenty one." "What?" she cried. "That's some payoff, Rebecca will benefit by his money in the long run after all," she said.

"I have to look into this matter a little deeper. What if Molly doesn't know about Chance at all, she might think her grandfather is her real father," he said.

"Her name is Molly?" Evangeline said, "I wondered about that."

"The child is innocent, Evangeline, I don't want to cause her pain," John insisted. "You're right," she agreed, "but Alicianna is innocent too and I don't want to cause her pain either," she told him.

"I understand," he said. "My family loves you Evangeline and if this divorce happens, I'm afraid I can't consul you, I hope you understand," he said. He kissed her on the cheek and gave her a brotherly hug. "I'll talk to you soon," he said as he left the room.

Evangeline was sick to her stomach. *How did this get so messy? What did Chance see in Rebecca anyway? She seems so cold and impersonal. I can't understand why she kept the girl away from him in the first place, I'm sure if Chance knew about her, he would have married Rebecca right away.*

All these questions were swirling around in her head when Joe was announced by the butler. Evangeline ran into his arms and cried her eyes out. She told him the story and he was astounded.

"I told John Lee I wanted a divorce, Joe," she said.

"This was the last straw, Evangeline, your vast amount of friends will give up on you if you take him back", Joe reminded her.

"He has double Pneumonia, as soon as they say he can leave, I'm bringing him home," she said, "but the divorce papers will be already in the works," she insisted.

John Lee paid a visit to Rebecca Clay.

"Hello, Rebecca," he said when she walked into the room. "It's been a long time since we've seen each other," he said.

"What can I do for you? John," she said coolly.

"Did you know Chance is in the hospital?" he asked her?

"He can go to hell," she retorted.

"He asked me to set up a trust fund for a certain Molly Clay," he told her. Rebecca was shocked. "I thought you said he was in the hospital? When did he hire you for this assignment?"

"It seems it's all he can think about," he said. "He wants to set up a trust in the amount of two million dollars for his daughter, but I have a lot of questions to ask first. Do you mind telling me what I need to know?" he asked.

"We have gotten along very well without the Winston money so far. My father is the only father she knows," she said.

"That's what I thought," John said, "but Chance is not going to let this go. Rebecca. Chance has destroyed the trust of a lot of people," he informed her. "I don't want Molly to be hurt by his selfishness to get to know her."

"Absolutely not," Rebecca jumped up from her chair, "she is a happy girl who has parents who adore her and a sister who feels the same way."

"It's not my business, but the two million is a drop in the bucket compared to his total worth," he informed her. "I think I can write the trust as a silent benefactor, who wishes to remain nameless. How do you think that would work for you?" he asked.

"I don't want a thing from Mr. Chance Winston, but I suppose I must think of the child. I want absolutely no physical contact by Chance or any Winston who wants to get involved. She wants to be an architect, and she is having trouble getting into good schools that believe she is serious about her studies. Maybe if we paid up front, it wouldn't be so hard for them to see her as an academic student, "she said.

Rebecca pondered the offer for a few minutes before she came to a conclusion. "Well, if she could get tuition and housing for a couple of years in the school of her choice, then I would consider the trust. No strings attached," she reminded him. "She believes my parents are her parents and it would break their hearts if it were to get out that they have been betrayed. My family wants nothing to do with the Winston's and their fortune. My father has worked for the government for almost twenty years in Austria and supported my mother, Molly and I all these years on his own. After the war he wants to retire and live in the country in a cottage he owns there. Molly can do whatever she wants with the money, but I'm sure she will take care of my parents for the rest of their lives. Thank you John for making me stop and think about someone else besides me and Chance, for a change," she said.

"I'm afraid Chance is on his last legs," he said, "I want to get these papers signed before something happens to him. He is talking out of his head lately and not making much sense.

"I'm sorry, Rebecca, that you felt the need to demonstrate your dismay for Chance at Rosalyn's funeral. She didn't deserve to be disgraced in that fashion and the newspapers made a mockery of her life. It sickens me to think of it," he said with disgust. "Chance may have hurt you and your family, but he hurt Evangeline too and she was a good wife to him. She would appreciate it if you don't speak of Molly to anyone for fear of it getting back to Alicianna," he urged her.

"I already told you that no one knows about her. If I hadn't been so angry with Chance, he wouldn't have ever known about her either," she confessed.

"Well then, my work is done here, I will call you when the papers are ready to sign, good day," he said, and left the house. The woman sickened him; he could hardly wait until he left her. Two million was a small price to pay to get rid of her; the idea that she didn't want anything from the Winston's was a joke. *Who did she think she was talking to, a first year intern? The* papers will stipulate that the Winston's never contact her or her family, but they will also stipulate that she never darken their door either. *What's done will be done,* he thought, that's the kind of lawyer I am.

Speaking of interns, he reminded himself, he wanted Alan Mason to work for his firm while he was on hiatus from school this summer. He felt Alan would make a fine lawyer someday. His cool head under stress impressed John and of course his grades were impeccable. Larissa was a lucky girl to have snagged such a fine young man, he thought.

John's next visit was back to the hospital to talk to Chance about the trust fund. I'm going to tell you this one time, Chance," he said. "You are never to attempt to see this girl or contact her in any way, do you understand?" he asked.

"Why not?" he questioned, "She is my own flesh and blood and I need to get to know her."

"No, you don't," John replied. "She has a father and a mother and an older sister. She is a perfectly happy young woman who is looking to become an architect, that's all I know about her and that's all you need to know. When the papers are prepared, you will sign them and that will be the end of it. You will have taken care of your desire to support her financially and that will be taken care of as a benefactor who will remain nameless. I swear to God, Chance if you don't do this my way, I will beat you to a pulp myself." John could feel the heat rising to his forehead as he talked to him. "You have been very generous in all your past dealings with your family and you are not going to stop now," he insisted.

"But Alicianna has a sister," he said, "they should get to know each other."

"If it is her destiny to know her, then it will happen, but now she is too young to find out how this sister came to be. Have some respect, Chance! You have behaved indecently with Rebecca all these years; do not disgrace Alicianna now. You will ruin any chance she has with a decent family in her future. Do you want her to end up an old maid because of you? Evangeline is not taking this sitting down either; she is having divorce papers written as we speak with one of my colleagues. I'm too close to the family to take sides," he said.

"I didn't know," Chance said almost in a whisper.

"Alicianna is being guarded against you by the entire family so she won't be by to see you either. I suggest you try to heal yourself first, then you might be able to reconcile with Evangeline, but I doubt it," he told him. "Because of your sexual appetite, or whatever you call it, you have ruined a multitude of lives. I'll have an intern from my office stop by to give you the papers to sign and I suggest you sign them on the spot. I'll not be coming to see you again, my old friend, you leave a bad taste in my mouth," and with that said he turned and walked out of the hospital room. John had tears in his eyes thinking he just cut out a big part of his life. Times had changed with the death of Edward and Rosalyn and it would never be the same again.

Chance tried to sit up in his bed, but he didn't have the strength. He tried to understand how all this trouble started. *Why was everyone against him?* Many men had mistresses and they never came to the surface. Rebecca was more than just a mistress, he knew, she was a true love to him. If she didn't like the way she was living why didn't she just leave, he thought? *She loved him, that's why*, he came to the conclusion.

He fell asleep and dreamed of what could have been. He dreamt of how happy they would have been just Rebecca and Molly and he.

"Wake up." the nurse aroused him, "Mr. Winston, it's time for your injection," she said. Then reality came back and he felt the loss of everything. His beloved parents were gone, his wife was divorcing him, his daughters were being kept from him. His friends had betrayed him. *What did he have to live for*, he wondered?

"I'm so tired, nurse," he said, "could you see to it that no one comes to see me for the rest of the day, I want to sleep."

"Certainly, Mr. Winston."

But no one came.

After Chance had been in the hospital for eight weeks, the doctors decided he should go home as there was nothing more they could do for him. He wasn't worse, but he wasn't getting better, either. They couldn't understand the reason why he had so few visitors. His wife and mother had been by his side constantly the last time he was a patient there. He would get an occasional visit by one of his brothers to get an update on his condition, but that was it. They concluded if he went home to where his family was, he might get out of the depression he was experiencing.   It was June now, and the days were warm. He needed the sunshine Hunters Point had to offer. He was taken there by ambulance and set up in his own quarters by the orderlies. One stayed with him until another aide came to spell him off. This went on around the clock.

Evangeline had a hard time keeping Aliciana out of his room. She didn't want him to tell her anything about Molly. The trust fund was put in place and hopefully that was the last they heard from the Clays. Larissa was always in the room when Aliciana went to see Chance, so his secret would be kept safe. Larissa's disappointment in her brother was hard to take. She still loved him very much, but what happened at the funeral couldn't be explained away.

"Good morning, Daddy," Aliciana called out to him, "How are you feeling today?"

"I'm fine, my darling," he lied to her. He was getting weaker every day. "How are you today, Larissa?" he asked.

A short, fine, was all he heard from her. "Come, Aliciana, we will be late for school, say goodbye to your father," and she rushed her out of the room.

Chance felt badly about Larissa's coolness towards him, but he couldn't have known the ridicule she endured when she returned to school after the funeral. Stories about Rosalyn were swirling around the teacher's preparation room and she had to set a few of the teachers straight about her mother and brother. She always felt up against the wall when she heard a conversation stop when she got close enough to hear. She hated Chance for the situation he put her in. She wasn't as strong as her mother or Evangeline for that matter. She knew she had come a long way due to Alan being her protector. He had a way of calming her fears and showing love in the smallest things he did for her. Her love for him was growing stronger every day.

"Miss Winston," the butler said one day when she returned from school, "you have a letter on the entry table, it arrived this afternoon," he said.

"Thank you," she said and ran to retrieve it, she knew it had to be from Mike. Her heart was beating like a drum while she tore it open.

My dearest Larissa,

I'm writing to give you my sincerest sympathy on the passing of Grandmother, I am sorry I haven't written sooner, but there was a huge battle north of Rome and our unit was involved in it. I was wounded again, in my leg this time, and I was in the hospital for several weeks as there were complications and I have a slight limp now. Sam didn't tell Abigail, because I didn't want my mother to worry. She doesn't know about it like last time. I haven't heard from my dad lately. Is there something wrong at home? My mother's letters are very short. I think she is mourning Grandmother very much and I can understand that. The house must seem very unhappy now that she is gone; it makes me want to cry. My sweet Larissa, please look after them; until I can get home and take over for you. I can't believe you are teaching now. Is Alicianna one of your students or are you teaching little ones? I know you will be a wonderful teacher, you got me through grade school, remember? Write to me as soon as you can, if you can. I miss everyone so much.

With love as always,

Mike

Larissa was in conflict the minute she unfolded the letter. She took Mike out of his safe place in her heart long enough to read the letter. She needed to wallow in his memory for a while before she had to put him back.

Of course no one told him about the mess going on at home. Evangeline had been walking around in a fog since the funeral. She seemed strong one minute and fell apart the next. The only one who could make her laugh was Joe Cross. He seemed to be around a lot of late. She was grateful for his help. He didn't go in to see Chance, he just sat in the drawing room or took walks with Evangeline in the garden. Lorenzo and Elsie are here often and the four of them have a lot to talk about. Larissa heard the word *Detroit* in their conversations and knows enough to realize Detroit was where the cars were made. All of this was more than she could take in. She folded the letter and put it back in the envelope. She then put Mike back in his special place in her heart and waited for the phone to ring. Alan will be calling soon, she said to herself. She was right, the phone rang and it was Alan.

"Larissa, John Lee asked me to intern in his office this summer. You remember I told you that several weeks ago" Well, I start on Monday and I can live at home and save more money for our own place," he told her.

"That's wonderful, Alan," she answered. "You will be home this weekend?", she asked.

"Yes, I'll see you then, I love you, Larissa," he said. I

" love you too, Alan." She hung up the phone and went to tell Evangeline. She searched the house for her until she found her sitting at Chance's bedside watching him sleep.

"There you are, I've been looking all over the house for you," she said.

"I come in here just to see how he is breathing once in a while. I sent the aide on an errand so I could be alone with him," she said. "I try to think back on happy times when all the children were little and the house was noisy and busy," Evangeline confessed.

"Be like my mother, Evangeline, look forward, not back," Larissa reminded her. "I got a letter from Mike today," she informed her. "He wants to know if everything is alright here at home. He hasn't heard from his father lately, and said your letters have been short. He thinks you are mourning Mother, but has no clue about Chance. What do you want me to say to him?" she asked.

"Nothing, darling, the war can't last too much longer according to today's paper. He will be home soon, safe and sound. Then he can hear all the sad news for himself. Do write, though, tell him how much we all love him and can't wait to see him in person, "she encouraged her.

"I will do that much." she said. "Oh by the way, Alan just called and said he is taking the job offer to intern in John Lee's office for the summer. He has only one more year and then he is off to Law School," she said excitedly.

"Do you think he will give you an idea about the wedding date then?" she asked.   "Probably, he said he wants to be married while he is in Law School. We will get a little apartment in Boston and just be happy."

"Sounds wonderful Larissa," Evangeline said and gave her a hug. "I don't know if your brother will be there or not," she said, "look how shallow he is breathing."

"I know," Larissa agreed, "he doesn't seem right. Evangeline you are so wonderful to take him in like this, I know how hard it is for you."

"This is his home, Larissa, remember the port in the storm your mother always called it. I can't throw him out like the cat, he would die if he were on his own," she said assuredly. "How are the gossips at school these days?" she asked her sister-in-law.

"Everyone is so busy with the end of the year grades and awards that they have forgotten about the Winston scandal for now," she told her. "Alicianna is a little distant these days, I'm worried about her," Larissa said.

"Dean will be here for the weekend, I'm sure she will perk up a bit then," Evangeline added. "He has some new exercises he wants to put Chance through, although he is very cautious," she assured her. Evangeline knew that all the therapy in the world wouldn't help Chance, the demons he was fighting were imbedded deep in his heart and she was afraid only Rebecca could help him, but that wasn't going to happen.

At the age of 12, Aliciannan Winston was head over heels in love with Dean McCall. She admired him so much for coming through his awful ordeal with the shark. Last summer was wonderful to be able to spend so much time with him. It wasn't looking good for a month at the Bellflower Inn this summer.

"I wish daddy were better." she told Larissa. "Then maybe we could go to the ocean again, like last year," she said.

"Oh, honey, I don't think so, he would have to get much better for all of us to go and enjoy each other," she told her. "Larissa, he looks so old to me, don't you think so too,?"she asked.

"Yes, he looks bad and so thin, he has to eat more and take the herbs Evangeline ordered for him, but he refuses," she said. "Dean is going to come this weekend to try some new exercises on him, maybe he will get him to eat too," she told her niece.

"Yes, I'm looking forward to his visit," Aliciannan confessed.

"I bet you are," Larissa said and grinned at her.

"Don't tease me, Auntie, I can't help it, I have a terrible crush on him," she admitted.

"I know, my darling, and I feel sorry for you," she added.

"Why sorry? I think it's grand," she said.

"I had a crush on Mike for years," she said, "it hurt me very much because he didn't feel the same way toward me."

"He loves you, Auntie, I know he does," said Alicianna.

"Yes, he does, I know that, but not the way Alan loves me," she answered.

"Oh, I see," said the younger girl. "I'm glad you have Alan now," she said.

"Me too," Larissa answered her, "me too."

SEVENTEEN

The summer dragged on like it was in slow motion. Everyone went through the routine of living, but sometimes the sadness in the house was unbearable. Chance stayed in his room day in and day out. He utilized the balcony off his dressing room to get some sun. His old wheelchair was commissioned to get him from his bed to the bathroom to the balcony by the men who served as his aides. Dean met with him several days a week to give him therapy, but he was getting weaker every day. Some days he didn't get out of bed. He wasn't making sense when he talked anymore either. "Dean," he said at one of his sessions, "did you know I have two daughters? No sir, I didn't know that, I only know Alicianna."

"I have Molly too," he said, "I don't really know her, but I hear she is real smart. What a lucky man I am," he told him. Dean agreed with him, but didn't take much stock in what he was talking about. He had said a lot of foolish things lately so this revelation didn't mean much to him.

"I promised my wife we will go to the ocean this year again, are you ready to go too?" he asked Dean.

"Any time you say, I'll get my fishing poles ready, it won't take me long," he answered.

"Maybe we can go after lunch, but I have to take my nap now, I'm so tired. Is that ok with you?" Chance asked him.

"You relax, Mr. Winston, we can work on your therapy later." Dean and the aide helped him back in his bed and he slept for the rest of the day and night. Dean went into the dining room where Evangeline, Larissa, Alicianna and Joe Cross were having lunch..

"Sit down and eat with us," Evangeline invited him. "How did you find Chance today?" she asked.

"I'm sad to say I don't think my therapy is doing any good. He is too weak to do any of the stretching he needs to do to keep his legs limber."

"You are good for him, Dean," Evangeline said, "he needs to know someone is trying to help him."

"He talks out of his head, also. Did you know that?" he asked.

"Yes, he says all kinds of strange things lately," Evangeline assured him.

"If you aren't busy this afternoon," Alicianna asked Dean, "would you like to go riding with me?"

"I might need a little help to get on the horse, but I would, love to go, "he said. "Larissa, what about you? Will you join us too? You promised to show me some techniques you and Mike learned awhile back."

"Sounds like fun, I can be ready after lunch."

"Great," Alicianna said, "it's a date." The young people finished their lunch and rushed out to the stables for an afternoon of riding the trails of Hunters Point.

"Well that just leaves you and me alone at last," Joe teased Evangeline.

"I don't know how much more of this I can take," she told him. The divorce papers are almost finished, but John's firm is having trouble finding all of Chance's assets from England," she told him.

"Do you have to have them all? Who cares if a few million slip through the cracks," he laughed.

"I would think my daughter will care some day," she said.

"Is the Rebecca Clay business finished?" Joe wondered.

"Yes, John said we are through with that, thank God."

"What have you heard from Mike?" he asked.

"Not much. He doesn't say anything about the war, just that he can't wait to get home to all of us," she told him.

"There have been some terrible battles in Italy, but it doesn't sound like they are anywhere near Mike and Sam. I don't know where Nick is now; he travels around a lot as a correspondent," Joe told her.

"Larissa got a letter a while back asking about Chance. I don't know if she wrote back yet, but she wasn't going to tell him about the funeral or the Rebecca scandal. Chance is so ill, I don't know what to do, I can't divorce a man who can't think for himself," she said. "I can't ask you to wait forever either, Joe," she cried.

"Don't worry about me, my darling, I can wait, but it's killing me. I want you so badly right now," he pulled her to him and kissed her hard on the mouth.

"Joe, the children left ,but not the servants," she laughed.

"I told you many times that this house is much too big with too many people around. I dream of the ocean and the cottage at the Bellflower and how we made love with not a soul around," he reminisced.

"I dream of that too," she said. "Joe, spend the night. I'll have the maid get your room ready and when everyone is asleep you can come to me."

"Are you sure? Evangeline, I don't want you to feel badly later,"

"I'm sure, Joe, you have been patient long enough. We love each other, God knows that," she said.

Evangeline had the maid ready two rooms for Joe and Dean, so it wouldn't look like Joe would be staying over alone. When asked, Dean was grateful for the invitation, his plan was to stay, but with Chance not responding, he didn't think he would be needed. The girls wanted to go riding again in the morning and Dean was able to go along then too. It was the first time in a long time that there was a little laughter in the house. After dinner they all had a grand game of charades.

Alicianna announced she was changing her name to Ali. "Dean called me that as a nick name and I liked it," she said. Evangeline rolled her eyes, she knew of the crush her daughter had on Dean.

"I guess it's all right if you like it," she told her. "I don't know what your father will have to say about it so maybe we will call you Alicianna in front of him," she decided.   "Ok, but don't you think it sounds more grown up?" she asked.

"Yes darling," her mother replied, "more grown up." She didn't have the heart to argue with her, she has had so much taken from her in her young life, a name sounded trivial at this point.

Larissa, Dean and Ali were exhausted from riding all afternoon and went to bed early. Evangeline excused Cook and the butler from their duties earlier than usual and they were glad to go home.

"You have thought of everything, Mrs. Winston," Joe whispered in her ear.

She blushed and said," it's about time I took control of my life, don't you agree sir?"

"Absolutely, madam," he gave her one of his famous grins and said good night.

Evangeline readied herself for her lover and bathed with the jasmine oil that drove Joe crazy. She found one of her prettiest night gowns, brushed her long hair fifty times so it would be soft and he could run his fingers through it all he wanted. She left a small light on in the room so it wasn't totally dark and curled up on her bed waiting for Joe. She heard the door to his room open. The anxiety was driving her crazy. Then she heard another door open, *oh my god* she thought what if it was Alicianna.? She heard some voices and they were definitely male. What happened, she wondered? She didn't dare get up so all she could do was wait.

When Joe stepped out of his room, a door from Chance's suite opened too. It was the aide that stayed with him all night; Evangeline must have forgotten about him, Joe cursed.

"Can I help you sir?" the aide asked Joe Joe was so taken aback by this man he told him he was going to the kitchen for some milk.

"So was I," the man explained, "I'll go down with you." Joe wanted to scream at that minute, but then the whole household would wake up.

"That's fine," Joe answered him and they walked to the kitchen together. Joe poured a glass of milk for him and one for the man.

"Thank you sir," the man said to him. "This is a beautiful house, don't you think so?" he said making small talk.

"Yes, but I think you better get back to Mr. Winston and I need to get some sleep," Joe said.   "Yes, you are right," he said and followed Joe back to their rooms. Joe couldn't stop at Evangeline's door so he had to take his milk and return to his room.

"Good night, sir," the man said.

"Yes, yes, good night," Joe said with disgust. Joe waited a few minutes longer and opened his door, he peaked out and ran to Evangeline's door and opened it without knocking.

"What happened" she asked him.

"It seems you forgot about Chance's night man," he said, "We shared a glass of milk together."

"Oh my," she held her hands to her face, and laughed into them.

"What's so funny?" he asked, as he locked the door, took off his robe and climbed into bed with her. "He almost gave me a heart attack when he opened that door," Joe told her. They were both laughing now. "So much for my sexy entrance," he said.

He rolled on top of her and they made up for lost time. They had become so comfortable with each other it was second nature to them to make love.

"This is how it is going to be when we get married," he told her for the hundredth time.

"I hope so," she said. At sunrise Joe tiptoed back to his room, in case the night man needed more milk. *This woman is going to kill me,* he thought, *but it will be worth it.*

Joe got a call from Mariella the following week.

"I have some information on your son," she told him.

"Wonderful," Joe replied.

"Can you meet me at the defense building downtown today for lunch and I can give you the papers I have received?"

"That's fine, Mariella. I'll meet you in the lobby at 12:30.

Joe was happy to hear from her He hoped the information was good. Joe met Mariella and took her to a little café around the corner for a bite to eat.

Mariella handed him a packet of papers she collected on Giuseppe Croce telling him, "It seems he attended the University in Rome, studying Italian Affairs. He got a job with the Italian government and was drafted into the army in 1916. His status with the government afforded him an office job in Rome and he hasn't seen much action except for liaison between Rome and Venice. He married Rosalia Cardinali in 1915 and they have a son Giuseppe, the third. His wife and child are safe in Rome sheltered with other army families by the government. " J

Joe was crying now, to know his son was safe and to think he had a grandson. Mariella was wiping the tears from her eyes and offered Joe her hankie.

"How can I ever repay you, Mariella?" he asked.

"It's going to cost you a pretty penny, Joe," she joked, "I have a special request to ask of you."   "Anything," he told her.

"I want you to marry my Zia Evangeline the minute she if free from Chance," she demanded. "Matt and I have talked about it and we know you are both in love with each other and all these years have looked after each other's welfare."

"I'll see what I can do for you, my dear," and gave her a wink. "It's good to know Matt has given me permission too," he said humbly.

"The whole family does, I hope you know that," she replied and reached up and gave him a hug.

Joe drove straight to Hunters Point to confess the whole business to Evangeline. He was sure she would understand, his son wasn't at all like the business with Chance. He was sure, but his heart was pounding just the same.

"Joe," Evangeline said, as she cut flowers from her garden for the dining room table, "I didn't know you were coming today."

"Evangeline, I have something to tell you," he said. By the look on his face she could see he was troubled.

"Have you been crying, my love?" she asked with confusion.

"Yes, but tears of joy," he said.

What a relief, she thought he had brought bad news of Mike. "Tell me then, I want to be happy too," she asked.

"You know I never told you anything about my past life in Italy," he said.

"Yes, I've been waiting for you to find the right time," she admitted. "If you never tell me, I don't care, as long as you don't leave me," she told him.

"When are you going to understand, I will never leave you; It would be like taking the breath out of my body," he told her.

"Tell me your news, Joe, what made you cry?" she asked.

Joe told her the whole story of his life as a gun runner before the war, and how he got to London and why the government changed his name.

"Joe," she said, "I'm afraid for you, are they still looking for you?"

"No, that business was over many years ago. The people who were looking for me have long since died and the Resistance disbanded."

"So that means you are free, am I right?" she asked

"Yes, my love, I'm free. I'm free to be Giuseppe, Joe or President Lincoln if I wish," he said, with a smile.

"What do you mean? I don't understand?"

"My given name is Giuseppe Croce," he told her.

"Oh, my, Giuseppe Croce means Joe Cross. Of course they just translated it," she said with wonder.

"I have something else to tell you," he said. "When I was arrested I left my parents, a wife and a son," he confessed.

"Joe, you are married!" she cried.

"Not any more, my darling, don't be upset. The government faked my death for the safety of my family, they could have faced torture or death themselves if I was still alive. My wife, Margarita was given an annulment in secret by the Vatican. As far as she knew, she was a widow and free to remarry," he told her.

"Did she?" Evangeline asked.

"Yes, to a good man who accepted my son and they have two more children. I was given updates on their lives up to the start of the War in Europe, then my contact died and no one took over the job. I have been worried ever since. I asked Mariella if she could find them for me and through her friends at the defense department, she gave me some information today."

"Mariella knows this story?" she said in shock.

"Yes I asked her not tell anyone until I was sure of what she found out. Evangeline, I'm so happy I have a family too," he started to cry again. "I have been so envious of the Winston's and I have been so lonely for such a long time, until I met you," he cried and kissed her hands.

"I have a grandson, Giuseppe the third," he told her. "Can you believe that? I just want to burst, I'm so happy!" he exclaimed.

"What are you going to do about this?" she asked

"I don't know yet, help me to decide, I need you, my love now more than ever," he assured her.   "Where is your son now?" she asked.

"The papers say that he is in the Italian Army stationed in Rome. He has an office position and doesn't see combat except when he travels to dispatch papers. He went to the University in Rome and has a degree in Italian Affairs, that's how he didn't get drafted into combat."

Tears were running down her face now, to see Joe so vulnerable was a little unnerving. Strange thoughts were running around in her mind, she never had to share him with anyone before and she wasn't sure she wanted to now.

"Joe, listen to me, you have a lot to think about," she said. "If your family finds out you are alive will they turn against you for not telling them sooner?" she asked.

"I don't know," he said.

"You can't do anything until the war is over anyway. What about your parents?" she asked.

"I don't know. The last time I talked to my contact, they were alive and living with Margarita in Calabria. The report Mariella gave me was mainly about my son," he said.

"I'm so happy for you, my darling, I pray everything turns out the way you want it. Whatever you want, I want," she assured him, and cradled him in her arms. So these were the secrets Madam Sasha was talking about, she thought. *I don't have any answers for him, maybe he should leave well enough alone.*

The weeks were flying by, Chance was totally bed bound and still had around the clock aides. It was early September and everyone was planning back to school activities. Evangeline and Mariella went shopping in the city for Alicianna's new school clothes. She had grown so tall this past summer that her dresses didn't fit anymore. Evangeline boxed her outgrown wardrobe to send to Santa Fara for the poor.   Styles   were changing and the new fashions took Evangeline by surprise.

"Don't these fashions look too grown up for Alicianna?" she asked Mariella.

"Don't forget, she is going into the 8th grade," Mariella reminded her. "If she were in Santa Fara she would be under the eye of future suitors by now," she laughed.

"Well thank heaven we are in New York City," Evangeline prayed with her fingers pointing toward the sky.

"Mariella, Joe told me about his son in Italy. I have always known he had a secret, but didn't care to find out if he wasn't ready to tell me."

"Oh, Zia, he was so excited when I gave him the papers, it made me cry to see him that way," Mariella said.

"I know, I felt the same way," she said. "He has decided to wait until the war is over to make a decision about confronting him. He is afraid his son will reject him for waiting so long," Evangeline said.   "That's true, what if he is perfectly happy about the way his life is now?" Mariella exclaimed. "Joe would be a fantastic father, look how he has taken to Mike and Alicianna," she said.

"Mariella, I have a confession to make, I'm not sure I want to share him with another family. I've had him all to myself for so many years now, I think I'm jealous and I feel really bad about that."

"Zia, you are the most giving person I know, Uncle Chance too. I'm sorry he has changed and is so sick, but I can't forget the incredible way he welcomed us to his home and shared it all with us. I'm sure his son will feel the same warmth that we did, if he comes to America."

"Thank you Mariella, you've made me feel better about myself," she said, and they continued shopping.

"We better hurry if we are going to meet Mary for lunch," Mariella reminded her aunt. They finished their shopping and walked to the Waldorf Astoria to meet Mary in the garden café. Mary had fallen in love with New York. When they first arrived, they stayed at Matt and Mariella's apartment on Fifth Avenue. Not knowing how long the war would last, they rented a place near Central Park where they had more room and were very comfortable. Evangeline wanted them to stay at Hunters Point, but the brothers wanted to be closer to each other and they drove into work together every day.

"Are you finding your way around the city all right Mary?" Evangeline asked.

"Yes, Mark shows me little short cuts and tricks to get around. I have a few relatives here, you know, and I spend some time with those ladies too. Everyone has been wonderful to me since I arrived, but I'm a little homesick too," she confessed.

"I suppose I was lucky, when Mike and I arrived; I had Rosalyn and Maria to hold my hand and they made me feel at home," she added.

"Yes, I feel very unfortunate, not to have known Rosalyn," she said in her British accent.

"Don't worry Mary, we have Evangeline as our rock. She has been the best aunt and sister-in-law rolled into one."

"Thank you, darling, but I'm afraid I've been very distracted these last few months. Mark and Mary should have had a proper welcoming home party, but because we are in mourning, it wasn't possible," Evangeline made the excuse.

"Mary, you should see the parties Evangeline throws, they are fit for a Queen," Mariella, said. Then she realized the relationship her English sister-in-law had with royalty and the three to them laughed until they were red in the face.

"What do you hear from Mike? Does he write regularly?" Mariella asked Evangeline.

"Not much. He writes once a month or so and his letters are short and sweet. He doesn't know about Chance, I don't know how to tell him. He has such a close relationship with him, I wonder if he knew about Rebecca too?" she questioned.

"Don't you think he would have told Lorenzo at least, if he knew?" Mariella asked.

"He knows what a hot head Lorenzo is, so who knows?" said Evangeline. "Let's talk about pleasant things. Joe says the war won't last more than a year," she added.

"The Queen and the Kaiser are cousins and I think they are acting like children over land and mountains, but don't tell anyone I think that," Mary whispered.

"Mary, this is America, you have a right to express your opinion," reminded Mariella.

"One would only hope so," Mary sighed.

Fall turned to winter and winter into spring. In 1919 the battles of the war were fierce and many lives were lost. Boys in uniform were more prevalent in the street with arms or legs missing. It was upsetting to Evangeline knowing that Mike was still in combat zones and that anything could happen to him. She relied on Madam Sasha's predictions to get her through and of course her faith in God. Elsie, Evangeline and Mrs. Mitchell still spent their days volunteering at the Red Cross rolling bandages.

At least she kept her mind off Chance, who she believed was truly dying. A lot of her suffragettes were volunteers also and she kept up on the gossip of the day. The ladies seemed to be making great strides in their fight for voting rights and equality in their own standing. It made her feel good that she had a hand in this glorious transition. Mrs. Mitchell was a force to be reckoned with when the subject came up around the men folk. Mr. Mitchell gave up trying to quiet her on the subject and most men thought of her as a silly old woman. Evangeline knew differently, and always gave her much encouragement. Her southern daughter-in-laws thought of her as an embarrassment, and had no trouble informing their husbands of it. Mrs. Mitchell secretly wished Evangeline was her daughter, and always envied Rosalyn for her luck. "I miss Rosalyn so much," she announced, one day while rolling bandages. "She was my only true friend," she said.

"We are your friends," Elsie told her as she wrapped her arm around her shoulder.

"I know dear, but Rosalyn and I were of the same age and sometimes the conversations would go toward our aches and pains and we felt better knowing we shared the common ground."

"Oh my goodness," laughed Elsie, "shall we talk about the Change of Life?"

"Oh dear me," Mrs. Mitchell blushed, "oh, dear me, Elsie you are such a tart," as she pulled her apron over her face. The ladies roared with laughter and it made the sadness of their task a little lighter.

Alan was invited to dinner on his first week home from summer break. He was going to work for John Lee again this summer and he wanted to make an announcement to the family. The twins and their wives were at Hunters Point that night and it almost seemed like the old days when the Winston's would have a table full for dinner.

"Larissa and I have set a date," he announced proudly.

"It's about time," Matt teased.

"June of 1920, a year from now."

"How does that sound to everyone? Larissa asked the family. "Alan will have finished his studies in Boston and start Law school there in the fall. I hope to get a teaching job while he gets his degree. A little apartment for just the two of us will do just fine," she added.

Evangeline was surprised to hear she still was talking about the apartment. "Larissa, my darling, you have your allowance to get you through very comfortably, why not take advantage of it?" she asked.

"It's nice to know the money is available, but we want to see how far we can get on our own," she said.   "I don't want to live off my wife," Alan chimed in, "and we realize she has an enormous trust, but I'm not marring her for her money. I truly love her. Let us play house for a while and someday when we need it, we will take advantage of the money," Alan explained.

"It seems you both have it figured out," Matt said.

"I wish you all the best, because you are the best," Evangeline said with tears in her eyes. With that the family surrounded the happy couple and had a toast to many years of happiness.

"You will have to come to London for your honeymoon," Mary added, "the home we have there that Chance gave us is just beautiful. We have plenty of room and the country side is gorgeous."

"Thank you," they both said, excitedly.

Ali, as she was now being referred to, wanted to know if she could be a bridesmaid this time like the older girls.

"Absolutely," Larissa said, "you and Abigail have a lot of planning to do. We'll talk about that later with her," she suggested.

"June will be the best month," Mariella said, "Mona's wedding in the summer was much too hot, remember everyone?" she said.

"Sounds great," Alan said."I'll let the ladies plan the event, the only thing I want to remember is 'I do'," he said.

"I hope Mike will be home by then," Evangeline exclaimed.

Larissa caught her breath, "Mike," she said, as she felt her face flush, "yes I hope he will be home by then."

Joe had been to Detroit to look for property for the families to build their new homes on. The properties he looked at were adjacent to each other on Lake St. Clair. He knew Lorenzo would love it because he loved the water so much. Joe had a photographer take pictures of the property to take back to Evangeline and Lorenzo to help them decide if it was right for them. The dealership they were building for Lorenzo was no more than a few miles away. Joe had hoped to live in the new house with Evangeline, but if that wasn't possible, then he would have a guest house built on the lot for himself. The house plans he acquired from an architect had two different plans for the manor house and two small cottages each for guests and staff. Joe still dreamed of a little house for he and Evangeline, but knew it was just a dream. Evangeline would always have her door open to friends and family to stay with her. Joe stopped in at Lorenzo's New York showroom with plans and pictures in hand.

"This is beautiful!" Lorenzo exclaimed. "Has Evangeline seen these yet?" he asked.

"No, I wanted to bring them to you first. Isn't the water amazing?" he asked his friend.

"It's not the ocean, but it certainly is amazing, "Lorenzo repeated. "I'll pick up Elsie and we can meet you at Hunters Point tonight," he suggested.

"Sounds good to me," Joe said.

Later that evening, the four of them got together to look over the plans for the new houses. Elsie was awestruck over the size of the homes. "It's almost a small Lenox Hill," she said. "What are we going to do with all that room?"

"These are the kind of homes the executives are building in that neighborhood, Elsie," Joe explained to her. It also reminded her of the Barron's Mansion her mother cleaned in Germany. My mother would be proud her daughter lived in a house like this, if she was alive, she was sure.

Evangeline liked the one that showed a sketch of a baby grand piano in the window of the second floor.

"Yes, "Joe said, "you see," as he pointed to the plans, "there is a gathering room where receptions can be held and young impresarios can have their music heard. Any way that's what the architect told me," he confessed.

" I was thinking more of Ali, giving her family small recitals," she said, "now I have to go looking for impresarios."

Lorenzo was confused, "Please tell me what that means," he begged. And they got a good laugh out of it. "Elsie, look how big that bedroom is," Lorenzo said. "I think we will have to live a different life in Detroit, my dear."

"No we won't," she explained, "we will just have to follow the Rosalyn Winston rules and regulations on how to behave around rich people and we will be just fine."

"I agree," said Evangeline, "she didn't have any patience for people of class with no class themselves. I think we were around her enough to handle ourselves properly."

"Look!" Elsie said, "A small cottage for Maria and Nicolo to live in."

"It only looks small, because the mansion is so big," Joe told her.

"I don't know why they just can't live in our house?" Elsie wondered.

"Everyone needs their own privacy," Evangeline insisted, "don't you think so?"

"I suppose," she agreed.

"When do you think we should get started?" Lorenzo asked Evangeline.

"Larissa is getting married in June and I would like to have the wedding here, I want to make sure she and Alan are settled in Boston before I leave Hunters Point." Suddenly she broke into tears, "I'm sorry," she said, "I guess I don't take to change very well. I miss Rosalyn so very much I seem to second guess my decisions lately."

"That's not like you, Evangeline," Lorenzo said. "Don't let me down, you know how much I depend on your input."

"It's alright," Joe said and put his arms around her, "we are all looking forward to a new beginning."

"Mrs. Winston," the butler called out to her, "the aide's in Mr. Winston's room want you to come as soon as you can."

Evangeline ran out of the room and the other three followed right behind her. She ran into Chance's quarters to find him in a very bad way.

"Call the twins, get Larissa and Ali, they are in the garden," she told Joe.

"Chance, Its Evangeline, can you hear me?" she asked.

"Yes," he whispered.

"Can I get you something to make you feel better?" she asked him.

"Just listen to me," he said between gasps of air. "I'm so sorry for being such a bad husband to you. I wish I had been faithful." He stopped and took a deep breath. "I should have listened to everyone when I had the chance to. You were the best wife and mother a man could ask for and that was how I repaid you."   "Chance," she said, with tears running down her cheeks.

"Don't say anything, listen to me, I know Joe loves you, any fool could see that. He loves Mike and Alicianna too. He will make a good husband for you." Joe turned around and walked into the hall, it was too much for him to hear.

"Oh Chance," she cried. "You have supported me in everything I wanted to do especially for Mike and my family I forgive you," she said sobbing into her hankie.

"Those are the words I wanted to hear, Evangeline. I fell in love with you the day you came to Lenox Hill with that beautiful little boy. I wanted to be the father Edward was to me." He took another deep breath. "I wasn't strong, I failed you, I'm sorry."

Ali ran into the room with Larissa behind her, "Daddy, it's Alicianna I love you Daddy," she cried.

"I know darling, I love you more than I can tell you."

"Chance," Larissa said, "don't leave us, I can't bear it".

"I'm sorry for all the trouble I caused you, my little one. I didn't know how out of control my actions had become," he confessed.

"No, Chance, I love you always, don't think I don't," she cried, knowing her brother was taking his last breaths.

"That makes me happy, Larissa, I love you too..

"Evangeline, hold my hand!" he cried out. The three women, held on to him, trying to will death to go elsewhere. They lost their battle and so did Chance. He closed his eyes, with the three women left in his life holding on to him.

"He's gone," the aide announced. The silence in the room was defining. The aides left the room to give the women some time alone with the body.

Lorenzo, Elsie and Joe walked out and met the twins as they ran through the front door.

"Is he gone?" they asked. Lorenzo nodded his head and they went to his room.

"Did this happen suddenly?" Matt asked the aide.

"You know yourself, he was failing the last few days," he said to him. "This afternoon he started to lose his breath more often. He asked for the family a little while ago and he slipped away," he explained.

Mark didn't handle it any better than when his mother died. "I sailed across the ocean and got here before Mother died, and I couldn't get here in time across town," he cried.

Again the family stayed with Chance like they did when Rosalyn passed away until the funeral director came. He took the body to be prepared for burial, as was the custom, and then return it to lie in state for the funeral.

The family gathered around the dining room table and discussed the next few days. Shortly John Lee and Alan arrived as well as Mariella and Mary. Joe, Lorenzo and Elsie sat quietly in the drawing room almost in shock.

"He's dead," Elsie said quietly," I can't believe it."

"How am I going to tell Mike?" Lorenzo worried. "Should I send a letter or a telegram?" he wondered.

"Isn't it funny how you think of things at a time like this," Joe said. "How do you get a telegram to the front lines? I'm sure Mariella will know what to do," he said. When the people from the funeral parlor took the body out of the house, they made sure the dining room door was closed so it wasn't so gruesome for the family to observe.

Larissa was crying softly in Alan's arms. "You are always there for me in my time of need," she told him.

"Where else would I be?" he asked her.

"Did he have a will, John?" Mark asked.

"Yes, it was fairly cut and dry," he said. "Everything he had went to Evangeline, Ali, and Mike. The shares of Winston Steel were divided among the four of you when Rosalyn died, and he willed his stock shares to his wife. The business with Miss Clay was taken care of months ago so that won't be addressed. Hunter's Point was a gift to Evangeline when he built it and the Hennessey account was closed before he got sick this last time. Ali has the Hennessey account in a trust for her future. Chance was a smart man, most of the time, and he took care of his business in a timely manner. I will have to have a reading of the will at a later date, but I'm telling you what I know now because of our friendship. I have always felt more like family than just a friend," he told Mark.

"My parents always thought of you that way, John, believe me," he said.

Joe didn't have the nerve to look at Evangeline at this time. He sat on the sofa in the drawing room with an uncomfortable feeling. Chance practically gave Evangeline to him on a silver platter. He was glad the rest of the family wasn't in the room to hear it though. *Should he stay or should he go?* he wondered. He couldn't bear to leave Evangeline, *what if she needed him?* So he sat quietly on the sofa and waited for instructions.

Elsie brought the men some strong coffee. Cook was crying so hard she wasn't able function at her job. Elsie gave her a cool towel for her head and sent her to her quarters to lie down. Ali was snuggled in her mother's lap. As big as she was, she always loved to sit on her mother's lap with her arms around her neck. "What are we going to do now Mother?" she asked.

"I don't know, baby, I don't know," Evangeline tried to think.

John took over as if he had done that job a million times. He advised Evangeline to have a private funeral, with the priest coming to the house for Mass. Then the hearse will take Chance and the family will follow in separate cars so as not to draw attention.

"We don't want a circus like the last time," he said, "those reporters are vicious. Chance will be buried next to Edward, I'm sure he would have wanted that, do you agree?" he said.

"Of course," Evangeline nodded her head in approval.

"Then that will be that," he said, "a person's life all rolled up in a little ball and no one really cares."

"We all care," she said, "and I know you do too, but he made it difficult for us in the end. I suppose the divorce plans are canceled," she said, calmly.

"I suppose so," he agreed. He hadn't felt right about the last time he saw Chance, he wanted to make it right with him, but just never found the time.

EIGHTEEN

By the end of July 1919 the Red Cross found Mike fighting with his unit in the northern hills of Italy. He was informed of the death of his father Chance Winston. The letter said his lungs had failed him and he died peacefully at home among his family. They sent their condolences and to let them know if there was anything they could do for him. Mike couldn't let go of the letter the man from the Red Cross gave him. His hands were shaking. To think his dad was gone, was impossible.

"Shall I call a Chaplin, sir,?" the man asked.

"Yes, that would be fine," Mike answered, still unable to understand what just happened. They sat him in a pup tent to wait for the priest.

"Mike Winston?" he asked.

"Yes, Father that's me." He could barely talk.

"I'm known around here as Father Clement," he told him, "I'm sorry for your loss."

"Thank you, I haven't gotten it through my head yet," he explained.

"I understand, do you want to pray?" the priest asked.

"Yes, maybe that will make me feel better. When I was sad, my grandmother told me to pray and I would feel better," Mike confessed. "She passed away last year. Now I have two people I'll never see again," and he started to cry.

"If you have the faith you know you will see each other again in paradise, isn't that true, my son?" "That's what I was brought up to believe," Mike told him.

"Keep your faith, Mike, it will hold you through the hard times," he promised him.

"In a place like this, it's all I can do, Father, I see young men blown apart and lose their limbs, and I can't even remember what brought me here in the first place. I had a wonderful home and parents who did everything they could to keep me happy. I'm very disillusioned right now. I just want to go home."

"Where are you from, Mike?", the priest asked.

"New York City," he told him. "I was born in Santa Fara, Sicily and came to America when I was three years old," he added.

"Have you ever been back to your birthplace? It's a beautiful place to be born."

"No, my Pa wants me to visit his sisters in Palermo after the war, but I want to go home, I miss my mother so much."

"Winston doesn't sound Italian to me, were you adopted?"

"Not really, my birth mother died in an epidemic when I was three and my aunt who I believe is my mother, took me to America to be with my Pa. When my mother married Chance Winston, my Pa allowed them to raise me, but he has always been in my life. I took the name of Winston because I admired him and my grandfather so much. My name is Michele Rizzo on my birth certificate, but had it changed to Mike Winston when I went to school," Mike explained. "I know it sounds strange, but a guy couldn't have had a better life. I have a wonderful stepmother, Elsie and two beautiful sisters. I just want to hold them right now," he started crying again.

"I think your grandmother was right, it's time to pray." The priest blessed Mike and started to pray the Hail Mary, finishing the prayer with him. When they completed their litany, Father Clement said, "Your Pa was right, you should go to Palermo and see his family. You know Italians can never have enough family. I hope the war hasn't destroyed too much of that beautiful place," he added. "Go in peace my son," and he blessed him again.

"Thank you Father," Mike said, "and after the war, I will."

November 11, 1919: the headline in all the newspapers read "Armistice." The war was over. People were dancing in the streets of the world. This horrible war was over and the promise of never fighting again was the on everyone's lips.

Evangeline was so happy: Mike would be coming home soon. *She would throw the biggest party for him, maybe he will be home for his birthday this year,* she thought.

"Joe, "she said, as he entered the house, "Mike will be home any time now, isn't that wonderful?"

"Yes, darling, it is," he hugged her and swung her around. He was happy for her, but all he could think of was now he could look for his son too.

"When are you going to marry me?" he asked her.

"New Years Eve," she said, "that will be my six months of mourning."

"My God, Evangeline do you have to do everything by the book? Six months, six days. what's the difference," he asked? "Ask anyone, they think you are crazy to wait one minute more, come let's celebrate this armistice day and elope," he begged her.

"Oh Joe, do you think we really should?" She put her hand to her mouth and giggled.

"That's it, I'm going to make an executive decision in this relationship," he demanded! "Get your hat, woman, we're getting married."

He took her by the hand and walked her out the door grabbing her hat and coat on the way out. They drove to City Hall and got married. The witnesses were the clerks in the office. Joe bought a bunch of flowers from a peddler outside the building and promised a big fat ring whenever she wanted one. He took a signet ring off his finger and put it on hers and it was done.

:"Mr. Cross, you may kiss your bride." the judge said, "May I introduce Mr. and Mrs. Joseph Cross."

"This was the best wedding I've ever been to," she told her husband. She couldn't stop smiling. Evangeline knew Joe must have paid a lot of money to have all the paper work waived so they could get married so quickly, but she didn't care. Now they could go home together and he didn't have to tip toe into her room any more.

"You know, my darling, I have been such a hypocrite," she said.

"Why do you say that, Evangeline?" he asked.

"Well I wanted to wait the proper six months, but I didn't think a thing was wrong with you stealing into my bed at night," she said thoughtfully. Joe almost ran off the road on their way home, he was laughing so hard.

"You're not a hypocrite darling, you are just human," he told her, "and I love you all the more for that."   "Let's stop at Elsie's and Lorenzo's and tell them," she said.

"Absolutely not. The only people who will know are Cook and the butler. Tonight you are mine alone, no sneaking around, we are legal," he said. "We will tell the girls in the morning, after their armistice parties. Then all the family will be invited for a grand party," he decided.

"Yes sir, after all you are the man of the house now, " she said and snuggled up next to him. "Joe, I'm so happy," she said, honestly. They received congratulations and best wishes from the staff and went directly to her room.

"Who did they think they were kidding?" the cook said to the butler.

"Not me." he told her. They gave each other a hug and went into the drawing room for a celebratory glass of brandy. Good luck and God bless them, was the toast they offered the newlyweds.

"Hello, Mrs. Cross," Joe said, and spun her around to face him.

"Hello Mr. Cross," she replied. He slowly undressed her being careful not to miss a second of their wedding night. "Good things come to those who wait," she teased him.

"I'm sure of it," he answered her, and they made love and fell asleep in each other's arms.

It was noon before they even opened their eyes. "Are we married?" he asked her.

"Yes sir, we are," putting out her hand to show him his ring.

"Oh good, I thought I was dreaming," he said.

"You can't get rid of me now, I'm yours forever, my dearest," she announced.

"Evangeline, I know you want this union blessed by a priest and so do I. What do you say we go to Italy and get married in a church in Rome and have our honeymoon there?" he asked her.

"Whatever you say, Joe, I'm tired of making decisions, I know you have my best interest at heart," she told him. Secretly he felt ashamed of himself, he wanted to go to Rome to look up Giuseppe, so why not kill two birds with one stone, he figured. "Joe, while we are there we could try to find Giuseppe!" she said excitedly.

"Thank you, Evangeline, that's a wonderful idea, I love you so much," he said. Now he really felt like a bum, he thought. "I think we should wait until Mike gets home first, before we go traveling around the world," he added.

"Yes, of course, that would be best," she agreed.

Cook spilled the beans to Larissa when she came home from the armistice parties she and Ali had attended. Larissa called her brothers and the grapevine took over. When the bride and groom came down stairs, a huge crowd had gathered to wish them well.

"Mother, I'm so happy," Ali said, and ran into their arms. All their family and friends were there and Lorenzo offered a toast to the happy couple.

"I'm not very good at these things, but I want my friend Joe and my darling Evangeline to know we wish them all the best a life has to offer. *Salute*," he said. A big round of Salute was heard from all and the Champaign was flowing into their glasses.

"See, Evangeline, we didn't have to wait until New Year's Eve," Joe teased her. "Salute."

"*Salute*, my darling," she said as she raised her glass up to his.

"*Che bedda Sicilia!* That's what my Pa always says," Mike told his friend Mario while they were driving from Naples to Sicily. They rented a car so they could travel anywhere they wanted to and then return it when they got ready to leave for home.

"Thank God this war is over. I want to go home so badly it's killing me," he said.

"Me too," Mario told him, "the trouble is I don't have much to go home to."

"I appreciate your company on this adventure I'm taking," Mike said, "when my dad died, I told a priest I would visit the town where I was born."

Mario was a Sicilian boy from the Bronx whose parents died when he was young and he was sent to live with his oldest sister and her family. When the war broke out, he thought it was time to go out on his own and he joined the Army. After a few months, he too, realized he could have made a better choice.

"I wrote my sister," he said, "and told her I will be home in a month or so, I don't think she will miss me too much, she has ten kids," he said.

"Wow, I only have two sisters," Mike told him, "but I can't wait to see them. Where did you say your father was born?" Mike asked.

"Isola Dele Femmine, near Palermo, I've heard a million stories about that place over the years," Mario said, "my parents never got over the fact that they left all their family back there to come to America."

"It's hard to leave your loved ones," Mike added, "my family is from Santa Fara, south of Palermo."   "Well, I guess we're free to come and go as we please, no sergeant to give us orders, hey Mike?"he said.

"That's for sure, *Paesano*, we're free," he answered.

"I would like to go to Palermo first, if you don't mind?" Mario asked, "I want to pick up some things for my family."

"That's a great idea! My mother would never visit anyone empty handed," Mike said.

As they drove along the country side, they couldn't get over the beautiful views of the Mediterranean, and the lemon groves and olives trees that seemed to be hundreds of years old.

"My Pa talked about the lemon trees and how he and his friend would steal the lemons from his uncle," Mike told him. "I loved to steal lemons from the Bridge Market, I don't know why, I had the money to buy them," he said with a grin, and they both laughed.

"I never stole anything," Mario confessed, "if I got caught, my brother-in-law Petrino would crack me with his strap, I was afraid of him when I was a kid."

Suddenly the city loomed before them. There were a lot of people in the street, coming and going about their business. When you looked closer you could see the ravages of war in their faces. Hunger seemed to be the enemy and a lot of children were without supervision, it was evident.

"This isn't as pretty as I pictured it. What do you think?" Mario asked.

"Not so far," he answered. "Let's stop here on this street. It looks like there are some shops we can go into." Mike pulled over and they got out of the car. They went into a few places and bought some trinkets for the ladies, candy for the children and cigarettes for the men. Everywhere they went they were greeted with," hey Americano" and the children saluted like soldiers. They took it all in stride and were rather used to it by now.

"I think I would like to get some of those pretty shoes for my Mother," Mike said, and pointed to a shoe shop across the street. They walked across the street to a shop that was more like a tent with racks of shoes on the sides. Mike realized the small room on the inside was the cobblers shop and the tent was the showroom of sorts.

He heard a sweet voice ask, "I can help you, please?" He turned around and saw an angel. The sun was in his eyes and it formed a halo around the most beautiful girl he had ever seen. He couldn't speak, he just looked at her. Mario recognized the signs and pulled Mike out of the store.

"Hey, Mike, let's get out of here before you get in trouble," he insisted.

"Wait, I need to know her name!" he said.

"No you don't, these girls can mess you up, or their father's will," he said and dragged Mike across the street and back to the car. "We have everything we need, let's go find your father's sister, do you have the map?" he asked.

"Did you see that girl?" he asked Mario.

"Why do you think I dragged you out of that place? I thought you were in a trance or something," he answered. "Sicilian girls are bad news, the guys at camp always warned me. Watch yourself!" he begged him.

Mike drove a few blocks when Mario announced, "there it is Via Fellini, number 715."

"Where am I going to park?" Mike said, "there isn't even a sidewalk."

"Just stop anywhere, we can figure it out later. How long do you plan to stay anyway?" Mario asked.

"I have no idea, I can barely speak the language," Mike answered, "We can play it by ear." Mike and Mario got out of the car and a small crowd of people gathered around them.

"*Unni sta a casa di Angelina Noto?*" he asked anyone who would answer.

"*Sta ca,*" an old woman pointed to the door.

"Angelina, veni, surdati Americano! Che dici?" a woman answered. A pretty lady who looked like his Zia Maria came to the door drying her hands on her apron. She stopped dead in her tracks when she saw Mike.

"Lorenzo?" she said almost in a whisper.

"No, Zia, *suno* Michele," he said.

She ran to him and embraced him and announced to the neighbors who he was. "Michele fighu de me frati Lorenzo di America."

Mike introduced Mario to his aunt and she embraced him as family too.

"Come, come," she showed them into the house. "My daughter teach little English to me," she said proudly.

"Oh good, Zia, I know little Italian." He had picked up a lot of slang and cuss words at the camp, but a few phrases slipped in too. Mario was better versed in the language because it was spoken at home, but he understood more than he spoke.

"I think we will get along fine," he said.

"*Veni ai a mangare?*" she insisted, and motioned with her hand like she was eating.

"Sure," he said, "*a vemo pitittu,*we're hungry," and rubbed his stomach. In a flash she produced pasta with tomato sauce and hard crust bread that must have just come out of the oven. She poured them each a glass of dry wine and sat down to converse the best she could.

She told them, "they would have starved to death if it wasn't for Lorenzo sending them money every month. He had to be clever in the way he sent it, because the mail was censored and any cash was stolen before it reached them. He would send the money to Mark Winston in London and he had channels to get it to Angelina and her husband. When Mark returned to America because his mother was sick, his wife Mary's family helped them. It would be in small amounts, but every little bit helped.

They must be wonderful people," she added. Her sister Caterina was a nun
and lived at the convent in Palermo so she at least had food and shelter
when things really got tough. "I'll take you to see her tomorrow," she told
Mike.

"Angelina!" A man's voice resounded through the house, "Where
did that car come from?" he said in his native language.

"Filippo," she said, *"supresa pi tia"*, meaning I have a surprise for
you. A large man came into the kitchen with questioning look on his face.

"Hello, I'm Michele," he said, and held out his hand to shake his.

"Michele, fighu de me frati Lorenzo di America," she reminded
him.

"America," he said in a low slow voice then he realized who he was
and reached out and gave Mike the biggest bear hug he had ever had. Mario
took a few steps back just in case he was next.

"This is my friend, Mario Delarosa," he told his uncle. "he came
with me to Sicily to see our families before we go back to New York. "

"Contenti de conoshire," Filippo told him.

"Glad to know you too," Mario said in return. There seemed to be a
lot of hand movements, Mike was glad charades were a favorite in the
Winston household, it came in handy tonight. Angelina was glad to hear
that Filippo got a job today with the city of Palermo, cleaning up the mess
the war left behind. At least a pay check was coming in and they didn't
have to depend on Lorenzo or the few lira their daughter brought home.

"Anna Maria, she come now. We have one child. God give me one,"
and she shrugged her shoulders like she still couldn't believe it.   "She
smaller than you," she told him. "Me and Filippo we older when she born."

She was getting the hang of the English language. She never had
anyone other than her daughter to speak to, and she was enjoying herself.
Mike didn't remember anything about a child, and he didn't know his Zia
Caterina was a nun. My Pa never told me anything about his family except
that he had two sisters in Palermo. *Wow I have a cousin*, he thought, maybe
she is around Alicianna's age.

"Mama," he heard a voice,

I know that voice, he thought, *but how could I?* His back was to the
door, but by the look on Mario's face he knew something was wrong.

"What is it?" he asked his friend.

Before he had a chance to answer, Angelina said, "Michele, this is Anna Maria, your cousin. " He turned around and almost tripped over his feet Anna Maria was the girl at the shoe shop.

"I'll be damned," said Mario, and sat down in the chair.

"Anna Maria, Michele is my brother son from America."

"Yes, I know Mama," she answered her mother. "Nice to meet you," she said with a little twinkle in her eye and kissed him on the cheek. "We have met before," she said, in the sweetest voice Mike had ever heard.

"*Impossibile*," Angelina answered, "he came here today." Angelina used her hands like air plane propellers when she talked; they were swinging around like crazy.

"No, Mama, he came to *la potia de scarpi* this afternoon, but I didn't know who he was, he left as fast as he came, like a *vento leggero*."

It made Mario laugh to think of Mike that way.

"What's so funny?" Mike asked a little confused.

"She said you were like a light breeze," he answered him, but continued to laugh.

"Excuse me, Anna Maria, I'm Mike's friend Mario Delarosa," and shook her hand.

"Nice to meet you Mario, I hope you excuse my English, I'm self taught."

"Sounds fine to me, hope you excuse my Italian," he said in return, "I'm from the Bronx."

Mike was still awe struck. How could she be his cousin, this gorgeous girl. "How old are you, Anna Maria?" *Anna Maria--What a beautiful name,* he thought.

"Seventeen, why?" she asked.

"Your mother made you sound like you were a little girl, like my sister Alicianna."

"Oh, Mama, she thinks I am still her little girl," she replied, "I'm all she has."

"Mike, I hate to break up this happy reunion, but we better get going before it gets too dark and we don't know the territory."

"I guess you're right," he agreed. "Zia, I will be back tomorrow and we can go to the convent if that is alright with you?" he asked.

"*Si, dumani,* Anna Maria will come too?" she said.

"I hope so," he said, and looked her in the eye. "*Si, dumani,*" she said. Mario left the box of candy he bought earlier and thanked Angelina for the meal.

Filippo drew a better map for him to get them to *Isola Dele Femmine* quicker. They all got kisses and hugs good bye, but when Mike kissed Anna Maria his lips lingered a little longer on her cheek. It made her feel a little uncomfortable, especially in front of her father. She kept her hand on her cheek for a long time before she dropped it to wave good bye to the soldiers. *What just happened,* she thought?

"What just happened ?" he asked Mario.

"You got it bad, my friend, and that's not a very good thing, she is your *prima cucina,* man, your first cousin. Any ideas you have, get rid of them, I'm warning you," Mario demanded.

"Tell me honestly, have you ever seen a prettier girl? My mother is a beautiful woman, but Anna Maria is so striking. She is taller than my mother, but then the Rizzo's are a tall family. My dad and I are over 6 feet and that's tall for Italian men. Have you ever seen eyes that color green before? Her fingers, oh my god her fingers are almost as long as mine. She fits me perfectly Mario, she's perfect," he babbled on.

"She's trouble, Mike, I promise you. She is everything you say, but use your head, man, use your head."

"Have you had a lot of girlfriends, Mario?" he asked.

"Hundreds," he admitted. "I've been told a few times that I'm kind of cute," he said with a satisfied grin. "Yeah, you're a doll," Mike told him. "I have never really had a girl friend, not one that I could take home to meet the family. I've always had Larissa, she has been by best friend since we were three or four years old," Mike said.

"Was she like a sister to you then, or what? Did you play around and try to discover each other at least?" he added

"Good God no, it was nothing like that."

"Well then, what was it?" Mario asked.

"She was my dad's sister and we were always together, I love her, but not in a sexual way."

"No relation then?" he asked.

"No," Mike answered.

"But this girl is," Mario said, "see the difference?"

They argued all the way to the town they were looking for.

"Now, let's see what surprises we have in store for us here?" Mario wondered. The town was almost like a peninsula jutting out into the sea, the views were spectacular. "Wow, no wonder my family missed this place so much, it's so beautiful," Mario said with a surprising tone to his voice. The sun was beginning to set and it gave off an orange glow to the rows of homes in the seaside community.

"Do you see any addresses?" Mike asked him.

"No," Mario said.

"Let's stop and ask these kids if they know your family," Mike suggested.

"*Scussa, conoshe la famigha Delarosa?*" Mario asked a group of boys hanging out on the street.

"*Si suno Angelo Delarosa,*" one of the boys announced.

Mario smiled and pointed to himself, "*suno Mario Delarosa de America.*" A round of cheers went up from all the kids gathered, 'America, America,' they chanted! Mike and Mario looked at each other and laughed.

"What are the odds?" Mario said, "I bet there are a hundred Delarosa's in this town. "

"Come my house," Angelo said in broken English. The American soldiers stationed near by taught the children in the area a few words to get by on. Angelo and his friends loved the American soldiers and would do menial jobs for them during the war. Angelo at the age of 12 was a quick learner. Mike and Mario followed while he ran along side of the car a few houses down the road. He pointed to the door where he lived and called for his grandfather to come out.

"*Nonnu, surdati Americano, Mario Delarosa,*" he announced to the old man. An older man in his late 60's appeared in the doorway, wiping his glasses with the tail of his shirt. He looked at the boys and pointed at Mario and said, "*tu si Delarosa.*" His gesture was more of a statement than a question.

"*Si suno Mario Delarosa, fighu de Salvo,*" he told his uncle.

"Fighu de mi frate Salvo de la Bronx?," he asked.

"Si Ziu," Mario replied, and the old man started to cry. Augusto Delarosa never saw his brother again after he left for America. He was against his leaving the family and wanted him to stay and work on the fishing boats with the rest of his brothers and cousins. Salvatore wanted more for himself and his young wife and set sail for the United States.

"Nazarina, veni, fighu de me frate Salvo," he told his wife. His aunt Nazarina came to the door with about a dozen people in tow. There was hugging, kissing, crying with pure joy.

Mike thought what a wonderful people these Sicilians were, they took to him like his Zia Angelina took to Mario, no questions asked. His uncle seemed to know who Mario was by the shape of his face. The first thing they did was feed the soldiers. Fish was the menu of the day because they were naturally fishermen, living on the edge of the Mediterranean. They talked all evening with a lot of hand movements and Angelo as interpreter. A photo album was brought out and Mario saw pictures of his father and mother when they were young. He was a small boy when they died, but he was thrilled to see them again even if it was in a picture. Mario was so happy to have found his family and they in turn were happy to meet him. Angelo and his brother Salvatore gladly gave up their beds to make the soldiers more comfortable.

"Tomorrow you tell me about America?" Angelo asked Mario.

"I'll be glad to," he answered him and they all went to bed exhausted by the events of the day. Mario fell asleep right away, but Mike could only think of Anna Maria. He tossed and turned all night and felt an overwhelming sense of loss without her. *Mario's right*, he thought, *I've got it bad.*

"Will you be able to find your way back to Palermo?" Mario asked Mike before he left that morning.   "I'm sure I'll be fine," he answered. The Delarosa family invited him to come back any time and sent a package of fish caught earlier to his aunt. The fishermen went out to sea before the sun came up to get the best catch.   He thanked them and started on the twenty miles or so trip to Palermo. He couldn't wait to see Anna Maria again. Mike traded his army uniform for a crisp white shirt and a pair of brown linen slacks. He thought he looked pretty good, but he was still feeling anxious. It occurred to him that maybe Anna Maria had a boyfriend already. Why not, she was gorgeous. The boys in that town must have noticed her. What if she just wasn't interested in him, he thought? If that's the case he would have to put a little pressure on her and she would crumble like a cookie in his hands. *What an idiot you are Mike Winston*, he said to himself, you don't know anything about these people and how they are going to react to you. Suddenly he was mad at his Pa and Zia Maria for not telling him about his family; why were they keeping them from him?

What's the big secret anyway, he wondered? Before he knew it, Mike found himself at his aunt's doorstep. He knocked on the door and waited for someone to answer. He was leaning his back against the door jam with his right hand over his head leaning against the other side. He was quite a daunting figure with his six foot plus body looking so self-assured. Little would anyone suspect that he was jumping up and down inside. When the door opened, Anna Maria was standing in front of him. She was more beautiful than the day before if that was at all possible.

"*Caio Bedda*," he said to her looking into her eyes. She felt her face blush and lowered her eyes.   "Hello," she said, and reached up to kiss his cheek. Mike turned his head just enough to kiss her pouted mouth. His kiss lingered longer than they expected. At that moment his anxiety left him. Just as he was reaching out to hold her in his arms, he heard his aunt calling out to both of them.

"Michele, Anna Maria, *veni, veni,* we be late."

The girl pulled away quickly" *si* Mama," she said and tried not to look like she had just been kissed.   "Oh, I almost forgot," Mike said, "I have fish from the Delarosa's." He went back to the car to retrieve the package and delivered it to the hands of his aunt.

"*Ah, che bedda pesce, mangare pi sta sira*", as she thought about that night's dinner.

"We better go," Mike said, and the three of them got in the car. Anna Maria sat between Mike and her Mother. Angelina nudged her daughter to get in the car first; she had a plan going on in her head since last night. She might be an older lady, but she recognized sparks when she saw them. She saw the way her nephew looked at her daughter and she knew this was Anna Maria's chance to get out of this war torn country. Mike would give her chance to a better life and maybe one for her husband and herself. The sacrifice would be enormous and it would take an act of God for her husband to allow it, but Michele and Anna Maria must marry before he goes back to America.

The trio drove across town to the church of the Most Blessed Sacrament to find Lorenzo's sister, Caterina.

"Zia Angelina," Mike asked, "why didn't my Pa say anything about his sister being a Nun?"

"*Sapiddu*," she said, "only he knows? He has always sent her a few dollars along with my sister Maria," she added.

"You know, now that I think about it," Mike said, "I was so busy growing up Mike Winston, I never paid attention to Italian conversations." Anna Maria tried to translate his responses the best she could.

"Michele," she asked, "are you not a Rizzo like my mama?

"I'll explain it to you later," he said, and gave her a wink. Anna Maria blushed again and her mother smiled.

Apollinia   ------   Evangeline's Destiny

NINETEEN

When they arrived at the convent Mike was amazed at the amount of young children meandering around the building.

"They don't seem to have anywhere to go," he told Anna Maria.

"These poor babies, they wait around until the convent doors open so they can get food and a place to sleep," she said.

"That's horrible!" Mike responded. He thought of the spacious rooms at Hunters Point and a kitchen that always had plenty of food in it. "I'm going to do something about this when I get home," he promised. "My mother will know what to do and how to get it done," he said, "that's her specialty."

Angelina knocked on the door and a small elderly nun let them in. "*Bon giorno,*" she said and asked for Sister Caterina. When the women walked into the room, Mike knew immediately that she was his relative. She was a handsome woman in her long black gown and white habit. She was very tall and straight as an arrow.

"Wow, she looks just like Zia Maria," Mike whispered to Anna Maria. She was surprised to see Angelina and Anna Maria, but when she saw Mike he could tell she was taken aback.

"Lorenzo?" she asked. It was the same reaction Angelina had when she met Mike.

"No, Zia, *suno Michele,*" he said with pride. She thanked God and embraced her nephew.

"Forgive me," she said, "you look just like your Papa the last time I saw him." She asked him to thank Lorenzo and Maria for the money they always sent to her. Her Italian was much more refined than the local Sicilian and Anna Maria had to interpretate again. Sister Caterina had to excuse herself for prayers. She put her hands on the young ones shoulders and promised to pray for them.

"Si Dio voli e compamu dumani nni videimu."

"What did she say?" whispered Mike.

"If God wants, and we will live, we will see each other tomorrow." Caterina gave her sister a look of, *what's going on here?* Sisters can read each other's mind even if one belongs to the church. Angelina shrugged her shoulders and gave her a wide smile. They all kissed the nun and Mike handed her a box of chocolates that he bought the day before. In a flash she was out of the room with assurances of seeing each other soon.

Mike asked if he could go into the church and light a candle for his dad, Chance Winston, and the rest of the family. They walked down a long corridor of arches that was built in the Arabic architecture and entered in the side door of the church.

"This is so beautiful," he said, "I'm glad it wasn't bombed in the war."

"Me too," said Anna Maria, "I always thought I would get married here and baptize my babies over there," as she pointed to the baptismal font.

"How can I make that wish come true?" he asked her, with a twinkle in his eyes.

"Michele, Mama will hear you!" She looked so pretty, the scarf she wore around her waist was now covering her head in church.

"Let's light the candles," she said, as she directed him past the statue of the Blessed Mother to a wall of half lit candles. He dropped some coins in the little metal box attached to the wall. The noise, as they dropped, made a loud clink, clink, clink, in the quiet church. They each took a taper and lit their own candle. They knelt down and prayed for their intentions. Mike prayed for the soul of Chance Winston. Anna Maria prayed for the life God had planned for her and wondered if Michele was a part of it. Angelina used her intention for her daughter and a wish that Michele will take her to America and give her a better life.

As they walked out of the church, Mike asked Anna Maria, "What do you think the other lit candles were for? Did people pray for lost loved ones or a job or just enough to survive?" he wondered.

"Everyone prays for what's important to them and if they have faith, their wish will be granted in some fashion," she said.

"How did you get to be so smart?" he asked her.

"My mother is a Rizzo," she said, and swatted him with her scarf. She ran ahead to the car and he ran after her *Things are going very well,* Angelina thought to herself.

When they left the church grounds, Mike announced that he was hungry. Against Angelina's argument about cooking at home, Mike found a lovely little outdoor café and treated the women to lunch.   "What an extravagance!" Angelina protested. "Tonight I cook the fish for us and Filippo," she announced. "Don't eat too much Mia," she instructed her daughter. Mike laughed at her and her worries about how expensive everything was. He also liked the nickname Mia that she used when she talked to her daughter.

"Don't worry Zia, you deserve it just for putting up with me," he told her.

"You are my brother's son, how could I do differently?" Anna Maria interpreted.

"Tomorrow," he asked, "will you show me where my mother and grandparents are buried? I would like to put some flowers on their graves," he asked his aunt.

"*Si, dumani we go to Santa Fara,*" she agreed. On the way home he asked Angelina how she met Filippo.

"Oh," she said, with her hands flying again. " We meet at the festa for the Blessed Mother in Santa Fara."

"You're kidding?" he said.

"Why no," she said, "that's how boys meet girls in my day."

"My Pa told me he danced with my mother, Evangeline at the festa one year."

"Yes," she said, "that was a long time ago, not mentioning the things she knew about that night. Her brother could have been hanged for what he did to his mother, he was lucky her parents didn't pursue it.

"Do they still have the procession?" he asked.

"Now that the war is over I'm sure they will start again," she said.

"Didn't you know Filippo from Santa Fara?" he asked.

"No, his family was from Palermo, I never saw him before."

"How long did he wait before he asked you to marry him?" Mike asked.

"I think it was about three or four days before he went to my Papa," she answered. "Why you ask so many question?", she wondered.

"Just curious," he said. Wow, three or four days, how could he deny me his daughter when he asked for Angelina after only a few days, he thought to himself.

When they arrived home, Angelina shoed the children outside on the small patio that consisted of the entire back yard. "You go talk about what young people talk about," she told them. "I have to make the food for tonight. Filippo will be home soon."

There was a two seated swing that was supported by an ancient tree limb that they found to be quite comfortable.

"Can I hold your hand, Anna Maria?" Mike asked her.

"I suppose so," she told him, and her heart started to pound.

"Your mother calls you Mia, isn't that right?" he asked.

"Yes, it means mine," she said.

"Can I call you Mia, too?" he asked her and bent his head closer to her.

"You could if I belonged to you," she said.

"I would love it if you belonged to me," he added.

"Please Michele, don't tease me that way. I haven't been around many boys to know if you mean it or not."

"So it's true, you don't have a boyfriend?" he asked.

"No, I was a very young girl when the war broke out and all the young men went to fight. I was too young to have a boyfriend then and then they were gone. I don't know what my Papa has planned for me, he won't talk about it."

"I'm glad to hear it; maybe I can convince him to consider me for a son-in-law. What would you say to that?" he asked.

"You don't know me, "she said, "and I really don't know you," she told him. "Besides we are *primi cucini,* and that sort of thing is frowned upon."

"I bet half of Sicily is related to each other," he argued. "I'm falling in love with you Anna Maria, I don't care if we are cousins or not." He tilted her chin up and kissed her gently on the lips.

"Michele, my mama is in the house, she will see us," she said with a little fear. "What if Papa comes home?" she gasped. At that moment they heard her father announce his arrival.

"Where are the children?" he asked his wife.

"In the yard," she answered. "Filippo," she said in her own language, "I have something to tell you. I know you don't ever want to discuss this subject, but I think Michele has intentions towards our daughter."   "NO," was his answer, "Don't speak of it again," he warned her, shaking his finger to the point of it falling off. His temper could become furious when he was provoked on the subject.

"What do you think Filippo, there are hundreds of young men in this town?" she asked. "They have come home crippled or not at all. Who is left," she said with her hand on her hip. "Michele could make her life a joy and give her all she wants. You know how my brother lives in America," she insisted.

"Angelina," he put his face in front of hers, "I said no! I am not going to lose my baby to the first soldier who comes to our door and steal her away from me to lure her to America! She is all we have in the world and you want to give her away?" he asked in disgust. "Besides, they are first cousins, it can't happen."   "Your grandparents are first cousins," she retorted. His face was beet red and his hands were shaking.   "What did he say to you?" he asked.

"Nothing, I just can read the signs, remembering how you treated me when we first met," she said.   "That was different," he said, "your father had three daughters."

"Oh, so you wouldn't have bothered with me if I was an only child?" she accused him.

She folded her arms over her white apron and tapped her foot on the floor looking everywhere, but at him. She thought if she tossed the ball back at him, he might relent a little until she could talk some sense into him.

Filippo loved Angelina with every fiber of his being. There was a thin line between love of a daughter and love of a wife. They were his entire existence and he couldn't draw breath without them.

"Oh, don't do this to me." he begged her and tried to grab at her breast. "We'll talk about this tonight in bed when we are alone," he said to her and tried to make up.

"You can sleep with Michele tonight," she informed him. "I only want what's best for Anna Maria and all you can think about is yourself," she wiped the fake tears away with the edge of her apron. She knew she usually got her way with him if she used that card. Angelina was still a good looking woman for her age and she was using her slight figure and large breasts as an advantage against her husband's stubbornness. She also was crazy about Filippo, but this was important, her daughter's best interests were at stake.

"Go outside and say hello to our guest," she demanded and pointed to the backdoor. When Anna Maria heard her father's voice, she let go of Mike's hand and moved as close to the edge of the swing as she dared without falling off.

"Hello," Filippo said in English. He wasn't in a very friendly mood after his argument with his wife. "Anna Maria, why are you setting there, don't we have enough chairs on the patio? I have a job. I can buy more chairs if you want more room." he was rambling on now. He pulled a straight backed chair away from a dining table that was in the yard. "Sit here, there is more room," he said.

Anna Maria was mortified by her father's actions. She felt like a little girl who was being punished for being bad. Mike smiled at her and nodded his head to do as her father asked.

"I'm going to wash up before we eat," he told them and went in the house.

"I'm sorry," she said.

"It's alright, I think I understand him, he's jealous," Mike realized. He remembered the feelings he had when Larissa went to the Debutant ball and he didn't want her on display for all of New York to gaze at. Mike explained those feeling to Anna Maria.

"Who is Larissa,?" she asked, a little jealous herself.

"She is my dad's sister," he said.

"Oh, she is your Zia?" she asked somewhat relieved.

"No, Chance is Evangeline's husband, I mean was," he corrected himself.

"I don't understand," she said.

"It's a little complicated." he said and proceeded to enlighten her.

"My, that's some story." she told him when he finished. "How old is this Larissa?" she asked him. "She is a few months older than I am," he said. She stopped and thought about it.

"Michele," she asked, "are you in love with this Larissa?"

"I love her very much," he told her. "She is very beautiful and smart." Anna Maria could feel her face flush again.

"She is a very lucky girl," she said, and stood up. "I have to help my mother in the kitchen," she said curtly and attempted to walk away.

Mike grabbed her arm, "Mia," he said, "I love her as a sister." He looked around to see if anyone was watching and took her in his arms and kissed her. "I love you," he said, "and want you, only you, for my wife."

"I don't think Papa will let us," she said, in tears.

"He will, I promise you," and let her go to help her mother.

Small talk was the subject at the dinner table. Angelina said very little to Filippo and he tried in vain to talk to her. She never mentioned to anyone the conversation she overheard between Mike and Anna Maria about Larissa.

Mike talked on and on about the events of the afternoon. He couldn't get the children of the streets off his mind. "I'm not going to wait until I get home to do something about this," he announced. "I'm going to write to my mother and have her take a million dollars out of my trust fund and build an orphanage for these kids," he said.

Filippo almost choked on his fish when he heard this news. He blamed it on a fish bone, but did these Americans really have a million dollars in American money to spend any way they want? Angelina just sat there looking like the cat that swallowed the canary.

"Do you have a million dollars?" Anna Maria asked him.

"Yes, Mia, I have many millions of dollars, I think I can help these children and then I can sleep better at night," he told her.

Angelina didn't know if she was more impressed to hear about the money or the fact that he called her Mia.

"Zia, do you think we can talk to whoever is in charge at the convent tomorrow?" he asked.

"Yes, we will go there before we go to Santa Fara."

"My mother supports the convent in Santa Fara so I know the poor are taken care of there. I would like to see Mother Superior there tomorrow too," he told her.

"Whatever you want, *fighu mio*," she said.

"After the epidemic, the nuns took my mother and I in so we wouldn't be alone. Evangeline was eighteen at the time and I was three. Eventually my Ziu Antonino Como sent us to be with my Pa in New York," he said, "I don't remember any of it. While I'm in Palermo, I want to look up my cousins here too," he said eagerly. "My Ziu has two sons with families, I know their daughters and love them very much, I'm sure I will like their brothers as well," he told them.

"We can't do everything in one day, slow down," his aunt suggested.

"I'm just so happy to be here, I can't tell you how I feel," Mike said, and looked at Anna Maria.

"I think I know," Filippo grumbled while eating his dinner. "Finish your meal and you can tell me how happy you are later," he said.

After the dinner dishes were put away and the kitchen cleaned, Mike gave Anna Maria a lesson in English. Mostly phrases like, do you have the time, or how much is the fare or can you tell me how to get to the Empire State Building? A few things she might need when he takes her to America, he thought.

"He's teaching her English," Filippo told his wife.

"That's a good thing," she responded, "no?"

"I want to go to bed, tell her she can sleep on a cot in our room and he can have her bed, tell her now," he demanded. Angelina threw her hands up in the air and proceeded to tell the young people their sleeping arrangements.

"I don't want to put Anna Maria out of her bed," Mike protested.

"I think we better listen to what Filippo asked of us," she told them.

Filippo didn't trust Mike any more than he would have trusted himself at that age. He wanted his daughter at arm's length during the night.

"He's not an animal you know," Angeline argued with him.

"Yes he is," he said remembering his youth, "I know him."

Anna Maria kissed Mike on the cheek and said goodnight. The mother set up a bed for her daughter like her husband demanded.

"Zia, may I have paper and pen to write to my mother tonight and we can mail the letter tomorrow?" he asked her. She showed him where her stationary was and bid him goodnight. Mike sat at the dinner table and wrote to his mother. He told her he was sorry for not writing sooner, the short note that told her he was going to Palermo wasn't considered a letter. He told her about going to visit his Zia Caterina and the street children. He said he was going to see the Monsignor at the convent tomorrow and wanted to take the money out of his trust to build an orphanage for these little ones. He told her he was staying at his Zia Angelina's but didn't go into detail. He also told her he planned to visit with his cousins in Palermo when he had the time.

"Tomorrow, Mama," he wrote, "I am going to go to Santa Fara to put flowers on my mother's grave like I promised I would do. I know she is your sister and my birthmother, but I cannot think of her in my heart that way. You, Evangeline, are my mother in every way. I love you so much. I want you to know how proud of you I am, and always have been. You saved my life when I was a baby and I belong to you until I get married and have my own family. I will be home in a month or so. I also have made a new friend, Mario Delarosa from the Bronx, whose family lives in Isola Dele Femmini. Please talk to John Lee to get the wheels moving on my request. He might have to go through Rome to get permission. Tell my family I love them."

He signed the letter and addressed it to Hunters Point with his aunt's address in the return corner of the envelope. He decided to jot a few words to Lorenzo and tell him how wonderful his sisters were. "They are just like Zia Maria," he wrote, "giving and loving." He didn't mention Anna Maria, he didn't know how to tell them about her yet. "Give my love to Elsie and Elena. Kiss Zia and Ziu for me, I miss them so much." He signed that letter too and put it in an envelope that his aunt gave him. He went to Anna Maria's bed and slept like never before, he soaked in the fragrance of her pillow and dreamed of her lying next to him.

"Michele," he heard his aunt call him in the morning, "wake up we have a lot to do today."

"Si, Zia," he responded. He washed the sleep out of his eyes, not wanting to wash the fragrance of his beloved off his body.

"Good morning,"   Anna Maria said, when he came down for breakfast. "Can you tell me how to get to the Empire State Building?"she teased.

"That was perfect," he said quite amused. "The next thing I'll teach you is, 'I love to shop at Macy's.' "

"What is Macy's?" she asked him.

"Don't worry Mia, you will find out," he assured her.

"Zia, why was Ziu so angry last night?" he asked her.

"Michele, he is a normal Sicilian man, can't you guess?" she said in Sicilian.

"He is jealous towards me, am I right?" he answered in English.

"Maybe you should tell me what your intensions toward my daughter are, so I can soften the blow somehow," she boldly asked him.

Anna Maria was mortified that their feelings were so evident to her father. Her father had been the center of her universe until Mike came into her life.

"Mama," she said, "is Papa angry at me too?" she asked, "I can't stand the thought of that."

"No, Mia, he just loves you so much he is afraid of losing you to another man and another country."

"I love her," Mike confessed, "and I want to marry her if she will have me. I have enough money to take care of her and a family that I'm sure will love her as much as I do. I can't wait to take her to New York as my wife."

"You will want to take her soon?" she asked. Suddenly the reality of not having her baby at her fingertips overwhelmed her and she started to cry.

"No, Mama, don't cry I can't bear it," Anna Maria begged. Mike now had two sobbing women on his hands. This was supposed to be a happy occasion not a funeral.

"Zia, if you want we can get the papers ready for you and Ziu to come to America too." They both looked at him like he was some sort of magician.

"Yes Michele, that would be wonderful," Anna Maria agreed.

"Wait, what if he doesn't want to leave Palermo?" Angelina said, "His family is here."

"I think his family is here," and put his arms around the two women. "I'll talk to him tonight," Mike said, not having a clue what he was going to say to the man.

Mike drove the ladies to the local postal station. He wanted to mail his letters before the daily mail went to Rome to be distributed.

"I'll take them in for you," Angelina volunteered. "I have to check on my mail too."

Mike was glad to be alone with Anna Maria even if it was just for a few minutes."Mia, what do you suppose she carries in that huge purse?" he asked.

"Everything," she giggled, "my mother is always prepared for an emergency." Mike stole a few kisses in the short time they were alone.

"It's a good thing they don't leave us alone for long periods of time," he told her.

"Michele," she scolded him, but truth be known she didn't know exactly what he meant.

"*Bon giorno*," Angelina told the clerk, "mail for Filippo Noto?" she asked. When the clerk returned, he had a stack of letters for Michele that the army returned to his current address.

Michele must have given the army her address before he left, she thought. There must be a dozen letters here and her curiosity got the best of her. She flipped through the return addresses, some were from Evangeline, some from Lorenzo, but most of them were from a Larissa Winston. I know he doesn't have a sister named Larissa, she thought. *What if Larissa was his girlfriend in America after all,* her imagination ran away from her. Why did she send him so many letters in such a short time if she wasn't his girlfriend?   Angelina couldn't take a chance, getting her daughter out of Sicily was her only mission. She decided to give him the letters from his mother and father, but she was going to hold on to the others. She slipped the letters from Larissa out of the pile and put them in the bottom of her very large hand bag. When she returned to the car, she handed Mike the letters from his parents and told him she mailed the others, but the guilt of not giving him all his mail was gnawing at her. *Remember,* she said to herself, *your daughter comes first.*

"Good," Mike said, "I should hear back from my mother in a couple of weeks." He opened the letters from his father and laughed. "My pa is a man of little words," he said. "How are you, we are fine. We miss you. Love Pa. The other letter will probably be the same," he said.

"He uses little words because he never went to school," Angelina remembered. "He would go to the sea and swim all day instead of going to school."

"I don't know how he does it, but my Pa is a very shrewd business man," he said in defense of his father, "he sells and repairs cars for Mr. Henry Ford. He has a lot going for him, he is a very rich man already and has a great future ahead of him," he bragged.

"You are right, Michele, I too, am very proud of him. I'll read my mother's letters tonight." he said and put them in his pocket.

The morning drive went the same as it did the day before. Angelina knocked at the rectory door and asked permission to speak to Monsignor Cyprian. They were directed to his office and waited for him to meet them. When he entered the room, he seemed to radiate warmth that put Mike at ease.

"My name is Mike Winston, you already know these lovely ladies," he said. "I came to Palermo to meet my family before I return home from my tour of duty in the Army."

"Thank you for your support of our country," the priest said.

"When I was here yesterday to visit my aunt, I noticed the children in the street who were orphans or displaced, I'm here to offer a solution to this problem. I have directed my mother to send through our lawyer a million dollars to build an orphanage for these children," he told him. It took a few minutes for the priest to digest what Mike just told him.

"I have prayed so long for these babies to have a place to rest their tiny bodies in a home like environment."

Mike said, "I will give you the name of this man and if you can, get the papers ready to commence this dream of mine. My mother is benefactor of the poor in Santa Fara. I would like to give these children the same safety net. Do I have your permission to start on this venture?" he asked.

"You are a wonderful young man," he said. "God will bless you for this effort," he was sure.

"He already has," and Mike took Anna Maria's hand.

The priest wasn't sure what he was doing at first, then he said, "but you are first cousins."

"Yes, we are also in love," Mike added. "Can you help me with this also?" he asked a little sheepishly. He felt that he was blackmailing the priest with the orphanage.

"You can't help who you fall in love with," Monsignor Cyprian agreed, and cupped his hand under Anna Maria's chin. "God doesn't condemn you, but society will. Do you have the parent's permission?" he asked, and looked at Angelina.

"We have to work on her father a bit longer," she told him, "but I hope he will come around to our way of thinking. I only want for my daughter's happiness," she said.

"Come back with your father and I will consult the four of you, don't worry, it will all work out." The young lovers were so happy when they left the priest.

"He did say not to worry?" he asked his future bride.

"I'm not worried, God will help me if I put it in his hands," she said.

"Oh my gosh," he told her, "my mother says that all the time."

The ride to Santa Fara was lighthearted for the three of them. The views were magnificent and the little village appeared like a diamond in the rough. The houses were mostly attached, but the streets were irregular in the way they terraced up and down hills. The yellowish orange color of the stucco with their tiled roofs gave them a feeling of more Spanish than Italian. Angelina said the Spanish lived on the Island along with a multitude of other nations that invaded the land over the centuries. She was told when she was a child that her great grandfather was French.

"I think Lorenzo has those tendencies," she said, with his straight nose and angular face, "what do you think?"

"They say I look so much like my Pa. Do I have the same look?"he asked his aunt.

"I would say yes, but your face isn't as long. Don't forget I haven't seen my brother in almost twenty years," she said with a sigh.

"We are going to fix that problem Zia, as soon as possible, I promise."

"Stop over there, Michele" she pointed to a little shop. "We can get some flowers for the grave there," she said. Angelina knew the shop owner and introduced Mike to the woman.

"Vita, this is my brother Lorenzo's son Michele from America," she said.

"I am pleased to meet you, I knew your mother, Evangeline when she was a little girl; she saved a lot of lives with the help she gave through the convent. Give her my respect," she implored him. "I remember your father too, he was a little hellion in those days," she remembered and both women laughed.

It was a lovely little shop that was more of a general store. It seemed to have a little of everything in it.   "Did the war affect Santa Fara much?" he asked the women.

"The bombs weren't here, but the soldiers were, they took whatever they wanted including our beautiful young girls. They stole what they wanted and left them to die. There is much hatred here and sadness."

"I'm sorry to hear that, my mother will be saddened too," he was sure. "Mia, did the soldiers hurt the girls of Palermo?" he asked.

"Yes, my father hid me and Mama in an old bakers oven for days when they invaded our city," she said. "It wasn't until America came into the war that it was safer for us."

"I remember my Ziu Antonino saying that one of the reasons he came to America was to protect Mona and Mariella, but I didn't understand what he meant in those days," he said. "I'm so glad you weren't hurt," he said and he kissed her hand. The shop keeper noticed the affection Mike showed his cousin and it made her curious.

"Signora Vita, may I see this necklace in the case?" he asked her. It was a lovely little gold heart with laurel leaves making the heart shape. "Do you like it Mia?" he asked her.

"Oh yes, Michele, it's beautiful," she said happily.

"It's yours," he said as he clasped the chain around her neck.

"Mama, may I have it?" she asked permission.

"*Si Bedda*," you may, was her response. Signora Vita gave the mother a look of surprise.

"What's going on?" the lady asked Angelina, in a whisper.

"We shall see," she whispered back with a wide grin on her face. Mike paid for the necklace and the flowers and on they went to the cemetery.

"Look Michele, this is the house your grandfather Como owned."

"What a pretty balcony," he commented; the house seemed so tiny compared to Hunters Point. He couldn't imagine his mother living anywhere else, especially not in this house.

The Church of the Sacred Heart was only a few blocks away and the cemetery was across the road. Mike parked the car and the three of them walked into the cemetery. Some of the headstones were ancient and some were new. In fact a lot of new ones had soldier's pictures on them. It gave him the creeps to think if the bullet that hit him was only a few inches in one direction or the other, he could be lying in one of those graves. The limp he had was all but gone now and only hurt him when the nights were cold. He could only imagine how New York winters were going to be for his injury. But he wasn't complaining.

"There it is," Angelina pointed to the largest moseleum in the cemetery. It read Como on the top and inscribed Georgio, Alicianna, and Felicia Rizzo across the bottom. It was strange to see his sister's nameengraved in that fashion, and it gave him the creeps too.

Mike knelt down and said a prayer. "Mama, I don't remember you, I'm sorry. Your sister has taken very good care of me all my life," he said. "I wanted to bring you flowers, I was in Italy for the war and it was my chance to come here. My mother Evangeline said Nonnu Como made her take me to the mountain so I wouldn't get the sickness. He saved my life too. Evangeline makes sure you are never forgotten. My sister Aliciana has your name, Nonna. You would love her. She is pretty as a picture." He took Anna Maria's hand, "Mama, this is the girl I want to marry. I know you would approve. Isn't she lovely?" he said. He put the flowers on the graves and signed himself with the sign of the cross. "Where are your parents?" Mike asked his aunt.

"Just a few steps over, see the stone that says Rizzo? "

"Oh yes." He knelt down and said a prayer. "Grandparents," he said, "if you have any power to help me with Filippo, I would appreciate it. I love Anna Maria. she is your granddaughter, too. I want to take her to America and give her a wonderful life. She is the most perfect girl I have ever met," he said. "You have another granddaughter in America. Her name is Elena, like you, Nonna. Please help if you can." He crossed himself again and stood up.

"What were you saying?" Anna Maria asked.

"Oh, I asked them for just a little divine intervention, that's all," he told her.

It seemed strange to come all this way to have just a few seconds with them. He expressed his feelings to his aunt.

"Before the war, I use to come here once a week on the bus to sit and talk to my mother and father. The war kept me from traveling, it was too dangerous. I found I could sit on my swing in my own back yard and talk to them just the same. Because you don't stay long or don't visit the graves at all, doesn't mean you love them less. My parents were poor. The shack they lived in has collapsed for lack of use. Scavengers stole the wood to keep warm during the war. God bless them, I hope it kept their children alive. The land is still there, I don't know what to do with it. If it has back taxes or any kind of lien on it, they can have it," she said.

"Do you mind if I look into it?" Mike asked her.

"My father only had three grandchildren, you, Anna Maria, and Elena. I don't think Maria has any notion to keep it and Caterina will have to give it to the church. Your father never asked about it, so I guess it's up to you." Anna Maria was having a hard time explaining to Mike what her mother was saying.

"Do you want to keep the property to build on?" Anna Maria asked Mike.

"No, but its Rizzo land and I would like to keep it in the family." The three of them walked across the street to the convent. Mother Superior greeted them with much affection. Angelina was one of her favorites when she was a child.

"Mother," she said, "this is Michele Winston."

The woman couldn't believe her eyes, she hugged and kissed him, "Michele," she cried. "I haven't seen you since you were three years old. How is your mother?" she asked.

"I haven't gotten a letter since your step father died. I'm sorry to hear about his long illness," she said. "I suppose she is fine, I got a letter from her this morning, but I haven't had a chance to read it yet. I like to read her letters when I'm alone," he said.

"Please send her my regards when you see her." The Mother Superior referred to Chance as his step- father, how odd it was to have him known as that, he thought, *I just called him Dad.*

The nun showed him and the ladies around the convent. Mike remembered his mother telling him they slept in a little cubby hole of a room while staying with the nuns. Mother Superior was glad to show him the room where they kept cleaning supplies now.

"It was a very bad time then," she explained, "people were dying everywhere. Evangeline was so special to us, her sweet attitude toward life and her faith in God was enormous. I hope age hasn't spoiled that for her?" the nun asked.

"No, not at all, my mother is the salt of the earth, she takes it as a duty to care for the poor and hungry, I hope I can emulate her goodness," Mike said. "I want to build an orphanage in Palermo for the needy, myself."

"God will bless you Michele, for your act of charity," she insisted.

"Good bye Mother Superior, I hope we meet again," Mike said and embraced her.

TWENTY

"Mama," Anna Maria, said, "I don't know about you, but I have had enough churches and graves and nuns to last a long time. I want to have some fun and show Michele we do more than pray around here," she insisted.

"Sounds good to me," he said, "I think I have all my commitments met for a while."

"Let's go to la mare and get our feet wet at least," she said.

Mike drove to the coast and found a good spot to park.

"Go children," Angelina said, "take your shoes off and enjoy yourselves. I'm going to sit on this rock and enjoy the water in my own way." They left their belongings with Angelina and ran towards the sea holding hands. Anna Maria let her hair fly in the wind that had started to pick up a bit.

"Have I told you before, how beautiful you are?" Mike asked her.

"Yes," she said, "a few times," and started to giggle.

"Mia, I want to get serious for a minute," he said. You do want to marry me, don't you?"

"Yes, I do," she confessed.

"You don't want me just as a ride to America?" he asked.

"I hope you don't think that my love," she said. "I have never been as happy as I am right now with you at my side," she reassured him. "Marriage was never on my mind, American or Italian, there were so few men around my age. I always thought I was to be happy with my mama and papa, I am their whole life. Michele, I know we are first cousins and we shouldn't have these feelings towards each other, but I can't help it, I love you," she cried. "Look at our hands, they match isn't that funny," she said.

"I know, we definitely will be as one," he assured her. "I think your mother fell asleep," he said, as he held her in his arms and kissed her. The water splashed on the shore and woke them out of their dream. "We better get home before your father gets there, I have a lot of talking to do to get him to understand," he said.

Filippo Noto spent a fitful day cleaning up the mess the war inflicted on his home town. *I'm getting too old for this kind of work,* he admitted to himself. The events of the night before were weighing heavy on his mind. Was he being stubborn for the sake of being stubborn, he wondered. He wasn't crazy about the cousin thing either. True, his grandparents were first cousins, but that was in the dark ages as far as he was concerned. His worst fear was that she would go to America and he would never see her again. The idea made him sick to his stomach. Did Michele Winston really have all the money he claimed to have? How could it be? He was just a kid. All of Via Fellini couldn't have that much money if they pooled it all together for the rest of their lives, he was sure. If that was the case, he could give Anna Maria everything she wanted or needed for ever. He had a headache and he still had half a day to work. The only resolution to this problem would be to sell everything he had and buy tickets to America for him and his wife. He wished he knew more people who lived in America, all his people lived in Palermo. Maybe they changed their mind today and life could go on as usual, he hoped.

When Mike arrived back at his aunt's house he needed a few minutes alone to read his mother's letters. He went out to the patio and sat on the swing and opened the letter with the oldest postmark first.

My Darling Mike,

I am writing this letter to enlighten you of the events of the past few months. I know the Red Cross contacted you on the death of your Dad which I was grateful for.

I want you to know he had a peaceful death with your sister, Larissa and I at his side. There are many things you need to know that led up to his death, as he spent more than a year in bed. I will wait for you to come home so I can give you the details in person. We love you, miss you and need you home desperately. I pray that this war will be over soon.

Mother

Mike had no idea what she was referring to. No one wrote to tell him his dad was bedridden. The details she was talking about sounded very mysterious to him. He got a sudden pang of homesickness, and tears welled up in his eyes.

The crazy illusion he and his friends conjured up in their minds about how they were going to solve all the problems of the world if they enlisted seemed so foolish now. He was needed at home during that time and he wasn't there for his family.

"Is everything alright?" Anna Maria asked him. She was worried something was wrong.

"No I feel a little homesick right now, come sit with me while I read the next letter." He was feeling conflicted. He wanted to jump on the next boat headed for New York, but he couldn't leave this girl either.

My darling Mike,

I have news that I hope you will think is as wonderful as I do. After many years of sadness and Illness surrounding our loved ones, I have finally found happiness. Mike, I married Joe Cross yesterday. We are deliriously happy. I hope you can be happy for us too. We decided to celebrate the Armistice and elope. The family gathered at Hunters Point this morning to celebrate with us. The only thing missing was you. Please let me know when you are coming home. We are going to Mass today to thank God for this wonderful peace in the world.

Mother

Mike read the letter to himself and when he came to the part that said she and Joe got married he gasped.

"What is it my darling?" Anna Maria, asked.

"Well, it seems my mother got married again," he said.

"Is that a good thing,?" she questioned.

"I don't know, he said, "she married a wonderful friend of my dad's. It seems the family is happy about it, they celebrated with her and Joe," he said confused.

"Did she do something wrong by marring this man?" she asked.

"No, not at all," he answered her.

"Then be happy for her, my love," Anna Maria suggested.

"It's just that my dad hasn't been gone very long," he said, "it's going to take a little getting used to that's all."

Larissa asked Evangeline soon after the war ended if she had heard from Mike lately.

"No, I'm thinking the Armistice has caused the mail to back up and people are hard to find," she imagined.

"I must have written him ten letters with no reply," she told her. "Evangeline, now that my mother is gone, I have only you to tell my hopes and dreams to, I think you agree," she said.

"Yes, my darling ,what is it?" she asked.

"Well it's Mike, he keeps popping up in my dreams and daily thoughts again. I had hoped I was through with that when I accepted Alan's ring, I must have been wrong. I promised to put him in a corner of my heart and only take him out once in a while and return him safely back there so I can go on with my life," Larissa cried.

"My son has been thoughtless and careless with you for years, I had hoped you found your soul mate with Alan, we love him so," Evangeline said thinking, what in the world Rosalyn would do at this moment.

"I love Alan too, he makes me laugh and paints a beautiful picture of our future, what more could a girl ask for?" she said. "But then Mike sticks in my head and I get anxious again. I'm afraid that when he does come home he will realize I'm the girl for him and I will already have gotten married."

"Oh, my dear, I wish Mike were more mature in this case, I hope the army has seasoned him a little bit. Has Mike ever treated you as a lover or talked about a future with you,?"she asked.

"No, never," she admitted.

"Then I'm afraid he never will," Evangeline said and took her by the hand. "Come on, Larissa, you are a sensible girl. I will tell you a secret," she said. "I have been in love with Joe since the first time I laid eyes on him," she confessed. "I was in an unloving situation with my husband, he had another woman, but I was a catholic and wouldn't act on it. One day we did make love and I felt guilty and actually confessed to the priest. Joe was persistent in my affections and he was very hard to resist. Larissa, I was a good wife to Chance, I stayed with him to the end. I made sure his every need was taken care of, but you know what happened, I cheated myself and Joe out many years of happiness. I can't get them back, but I'm going to make the best of the years I have left.

"Alan is like a bulldog when it comes to you. He will stand on his head to make you happy, don't abuse it. Love him for it, my dear, don't trade a good life for a bad one, believe me. Mike is my son and I adore him as much as you do, but nobody is perfect. Think about what I have said to you." Evangeline kissed her on the forehead and went to the garden to find Joe.

"Dinner is ready," Anna Maria, announced. It was one of the new phrases Mike had taught her. "What did she say?" her father asked Angelina.

"Come and eat," she repeated in Italian. This American influence in his household was getting on his nerves.

"How are your parents?" Angelina asked Mike while they were dining.

Mike kind of laughed. "Well," he said, "my Mother just remarried."

"Oh my," she replied, "didn't your father just pass away a few months ago? I'm sorry Michele It's none of my business," she said realizing she might have said the wrong thing. She knew she sounded judgmental, she faced a lot of judging herself if Larissa's letters were ever found.

"I think this war has taught us that life is too short to worry about old fashioned protocol," Anna Maria exclaimed.

"You are right, my daughter, don't you agree, Filippo?"

"What are you getting at?" he questioned his wife.

"Well, when you find the right person to marry you should act on it and not let it slip away," she said. He gave her a scowl knowing exactly what she meant. The ice was cracked enough for Mike to make a stand.

"Ziu Filippo, I love your daughter and want to marry her as soon as possible. Yes, we will live in America, but I want you and Zia to come too.

This work you are doing is not fitting a man like you. There are plenty of jobs in New York to satisfy you, I'm sure. I can get the papers drawn up sooner than later to get a visa for the two of you to come with us."

Filippo said he needed more time to think about it. Think about what-- the job or the wedding, Mike thought?

Angelina assured Filippo that, "Monsignor Cyprian was going to consult with the four of them whenever we want to go to him."

"The priest knows about this before I do?" he hollered. " I am the father in this house. I demand the respect of being asked first." His face was getting red again and Angelina reminded him that his first answer was no.

"Ok, we go to the priest," he said, not looking at anyone. "Pass me another piece of bread," he said, and finished his dinner.

Mike spent the next few days searching out his Como cousins in Palermo. The address his mother sent him many months ago was an abandoned apartment house. The bombs had been especially damaging in that neighborhood. Mike asked around the area to see if anyone knew the whereabouts of Nino and Paolo Como. He finally found an old man selling papers on the corner who knew the family. There was a camp for displaced families set up in an old soccer field on the edge of town. Most of the people in these houses were taken there for safety, the old man told him. Mike easily found the place; he was getting good at finding his way around Palermo.

Oh, my God he thought, if Luna knew her family was living like this she would surely die. There he found a makeshift office and they directed him to his cousins. People lived in barrack style tents in perfectly straight rows. Each row was lettered alphabetically and each tent had a number. He was looking for row F number 15.

"Hello," he said when he approached the open flap of the door. He saw two young women seated at a small table and four children sleeping on cots. "Permiso?" he asked.

"Si," one women answered.

He asked for Nino and Paolo Como, to make sure he had the right place. "I am Mike Winston, from America," he told the ladies. "Nino and Paolo are my cousins, Antonino Como is my uncle," he said. "Do you speak English?" he asked them both.

"Yes, we both have been educated with some English, we just don't have a chance to use it," one lady said. "Excuse us." she continued, "I am Concetta Como. I am married to Nino, this is Rafaella Como, she is married to Paolo. These are our children, hopefully they will sleep for another hour at least," she added. "Welcome to our house," she said, and shrugged her shoulders as she looked around. "You are our first guest since we have been here," Concetta said.

"I'm so glad to have found you," Mike said. "Where are your husband's?" he asked.

"They go out in the morning before the sun comes up looking for work, they usually get laborers jobs for a few lira and come home before dark," she said.

"How can I help you get out of here?" he asked with concern, looking at the poor conditions. "Antonino and Luna will not be happy to know this is what happened to their children," Mike assured her.

"I got a letter from Mariella today saying the paper work is coming soon for the family to leave for America. We are safe here, the children have a place to play and we know most of our neighbors. The people here look after each other, the war has brought out the best and worst in us," she told him.

"Well if anyone can get the paper work done fast, that would be Mariella, she is one of the most intelligent women I know," he told her.

"Please stay until the men come home, they will be so happy to meet you," Rafaella said.

"Thank you," he said, "maybe you could tell me a little more about yourselves, I don't know much, other than I had two cousins in Palermo."

"I'll make some fresh coffee," Concetta suggested, "we just got some grounds from a job Nino did yesterday. We do a lot of bartering these days. Mike, tell us about New York," Concetta asked, "we were just talking about how little we know about where we are going.

"Mariella thought America was velvet drapes and gold staircases," he said, "we always tease her about that, although my mother Evangeline does live like that. She was a little disappointed to find herself in an apartment over the bakery, but she worked hard and married my uncle Matt. They now have a beautiful apartment uptown and are going to build a home on Long Island soon," he said.

"What is uptown?" they asked almost in unison.

"It's a place in New York City." he told them. "Mona has a baby now and she and Roberto live in an area of New York called Bensonhurst," he informed them; "they live over their bakery and are doing very well. They are crazy about each other, wait until you see them and how happy they are. Ziu Antonino and Zia Luna still live in their apartment in Little Italy and they have hundreds of friends and family around them. I am sure Luna is counting the days until you are all together again," he told them.

"I know I can't wait to see my family again." He told them about Anna Maria and the problem he had with her father.

They both started to laugh, "Sicilian fathers are very hard to let go of their daughters," Concetta told him, "don't worry if you put it in God's hands it will happen."

"Do all the women in Sicily believe that way?" he asked, "that's the answer every one of them have in common," he said. "We are first cousins," he confessed, "what do you think of that?" he asked.

"This Island has been invaded so many times in the last thousand years by so many different countries," Rafaella explained, "our blood is very mixed. The thing society is afraid of, is the children being born to cousins may have deformities or maladies of some kind. My friend wanted to marry her first cousin and her family was totally against it, so they eloped to Rome and got married there. Now they have six of the most beautiful children you ever saw. Each one smarter than the next," she said.

"If God wants you to marry Anna Maria that's how it should be," Concetta added.

"Who is this?" Nino asked, surprised to see his wife and sister-in-law drinking coffee with a young man. Paolo followed with the same look on his face.

"Hello, I'm your cousin, Mike Winston from America," he reassured them.

"*Fighu de me Zia Evangeline?*" Nino asked.

"Yes," Mike answered and got a bear hug greeting from both men.

"*Tu si surdatu?*" Paolo asked.

"Not any more, cousin, I am going home," he joyfully answered.

Their English was pretty broken, but they got their message across as well as Mike did with his Italian.

"Nino," Concetta said, "a letter from Mariella." She handed it to him and he rejoiced when he realized they were all going to the Unites States soon. The children woke up from all the commotion in the close quarters.

"Papa," the oldest boy said, "we are going to America!" and gave out a yell. The others followed suit and Mike felt at home immediately. The men sat and talked for an hour or so, the women prepared a meager dinner for them and they planned to meet again in New York.

Mike thanked them for their hospitality and slipped an American one hundred dollar bill in each of his cousin's hands. The men were startled by the large amount, but Mike wanted them to use it for the children to make their voyage pleasant.

"God bless you," was heard as he got in his car and drove off to see Anna Maria.

"Did you find your family?" Anna Maria asked as he walked through the door.

"Is your Papa home?" he asked her.

"Yes," she said, "did you find them?"

"Yes and they can't wait to meet you," he said. "Where is your Papa, Mia?" He looked around.

"On the patio with my mama," she answered.

"Good," and he held her tight and kissed her without anyone spying on them. "I've wanted to do that all day," he confessed.

"Me too," she agreed.

"Michele," he heard her mother call out.

"Coming Mama," they both said and giggled at their response.

"Did you eat?" his aunt asked him.

"Yes. I found my family living in a tent city in an old soccer field at the edge of town, they fed me," he answered.

"How terrible," she said, "I am so grateful we still have our home," and blessed herself. "How long do they have to stay there?" she asked.

"My cousin Mariella has the papers ready for them to leave soon," he told them.

"Angelina, make the coffee. I want to talk to Michele, man to man, and he led him to the living room so they could talk in private. Mike's heart was leaping out of his chest. what was this man going to say to him?. He didn't look happy, so he wasn't sure if it was good or not.

"So you think you can be good husband for my daughter,?" he grilled him. "Can you stop her tears when she is crying for her mama, a million miles away,?"he asked. "What about other women, are you sure you are done with that business?" he said, as his voice grew louder. "Just who do you think you are, walking into my world and turning it upside down?

"She is my life, my little flower, I watched her grow, and I nurtured her since her first breath. How do you think I can just turn around and give her to you? Dio mio, her mouth still smells of milk," he prayed to the heavens. Filippo put his hands to his face and the tears started flowing like a little child.

"Ziu, sit down," Mike suggested, he felt like a heel all of a sudden. Mike wasn't sure if he understood all the words he said, but he certainly got the idea. He was right, he did all those things, but he also fell in love.

"I see how my Anna Maria looks at you, she is enchanted with you. She has never shown an interest in a man before, are you the right one? Who has those answers for me?" he wondered. He was wiping his face with a kitchen towel he found on a door knob. He had never cried like that in front of another man before and he felt a little foolish, but his emotions got the best of him.

"I also have never had a girl that I could bring home to my mother," Mike told him. "I can't wait for her to meet her and love her as much as I do. When I look at her I see my whole life before me. She is good and pure and kind and will make a wonderful mother and wife," he said. "Please Ziu; give us a chance to make that life a reality. Don't send me away broken hearted or your daughter will never forget what you have done."

"Don't threaten me," he stood up with his hand clenched, and Mike knew he was a goner. Miraculously he lowered his fist, "Okay; tomorrow we go to the priest after Mass. If he tells me what I want to hear, I will give my blessing."

Anna Maria and Angelina were on the patio swing; they could hear the men arguing, but couldn't hear what was being said. Anna Maria was in her mother's arms sobbing. The two men she loved most in the world were at odds with each other and she was beginning to fear for Mike's life. Angelina knew her husband was all bark and no bite, but in this case, she couldn't be sure.

"Mama, do you hear anything?"

"No, wait one more minute," she said.

"Let's go into the house," Anna Maria said quietly. The two women entered through the back door holding on to each other. Sitting at the kitchen table, were Filippo and Mike drinking a glass of the wine from the bottle that Mike had brought home for dinner.

"What's wrong with you?" Filippo asked his wife.

"We heard the argument from the yard and we were afraid you hurt each other," Angelina cried.

"Don't be silly," he said. "Tomorrow after Mass we go talk to the priest, we see what he says, okay? By the way daughter, you sleep on the cot, again tonight.

After Mass the next morning, the Noto family and Mike along with Sister Caterina, had a sit down conversation with the priest.

"Filippo," Father Cyprian asked, "what problem do you see ahead for this couple that you have such doubts about a union between them?"

Filippo started counting on his fingers his reasons." One, she is so young, father, she has all her life to find a husband," he complained. "Two, they have only known each other a few weeks. Three, he is going to take her away from her mama to America; a young girl needs her mama. Four, they are first cousins." He stopped and pondered the next reason when he started to cry, " and I will miss her so much."

"There, there, Filippo," the priest tried to comfort the big man, "your daughter will always be your daughter where ever she goes, I have seen it a hundred times." Angelina and Anna Maria hugged Filippo and the three of them were crying again.

Mike looked at Sister Caterina with a look of helplessness on his face. "Help me Zia," he asked her. "Filippo," the nun said, "I think at least four of your reasons are concerning you, not the children. You don't want her to leave no matter who she marries. Remember how my Pa cried when I went to the convent, I was his first born and he said he couldn't part with me. Ma was so happy for me, she knew this was my vocation and I couldn't be happy anywhere else. I think Angelina feels the same way. If you don't agree to this marriage Anna Maria will carry that cross on her shoulders all the rest of her life, I promise you."

"But Caterina, they are *primi cucini*."

"I know, this country is full of them. We don't travel outside of our perimeter too often, we stay with people we feel comfortable with and that is our families," she said.

"He came from America to find her," he insisted!

"That's the point," she said, "He found her. All roads lead to her. You don't think God had that planned for him?"

Father Cyprian sat back in his chair, Sister Caterina was doing a good job and he let her have the floor.

"What about their children? They will be idiots or deformed!" he announced.

"That happens to people who aren't related also," she informed him.

"Remember your grandparents, *primi cucini*," Angelina reminded him. "They had twelve children and each one of them, perfect. Your grandfather delivered every baby too," she added.

Mike thought he needed to say something, so he told them of a friend of his whose parents had two deformed children and they were of different nationalities. "Besides," Mike said as he took Anna Maria's hand, "we will never be happy with anyone else, we belong to each other, right Mia?" he said.

She nodded her head; she was so distraught she couldn't speak. Her life was in the hands of other people and she had no say in the matter. Her father and Mike were pulling her in different directions. She understood her father and she understood Mike. It's not that her decision to marry Mike was changing, she was just overwhelmed.

"Ziu," Mike said, "I will call for the two of you as soon as you can come to America, and I know Anna Maria will need you too. There are good jobs for you in America if that is what you want to do. Please give us your blessing," he begged. The priest smiled at Filippo and suggested it was the right thing to do.

"Okay," he said in English, "you win."

"Thank you Papa," Anna Maria said, and the happy couple embraced him. Hugs and kisses were given by all and the weight of the world was lifted off Mike's shoulders.

"Thank you Zia," Mike told Sister Caterina, "I don't think we would have won him over if you had not helped me."

"Like I said, Michele, it is God's plan." and she kissed him on each cheek. They thanked Monsignor Cyprian and Mike gave him an envelope with some cash in it for the poor.

"I have one favor to ask," Filippo said as they were leaving the building, "please wait until after Natale." He wanted one more Christmas with his baby and he wanted his mother to give her blessing like she had for all her grandchildren before.

Mike asked his aunt Caterina if she was free for the day He wanted to take Anna Maria to Isola Dele Femmini to introduce her to the Delarosa's. He needed a chaperone and it would give her a chance to see some of the seaside too. She jumped at the chance, but had to be back for vespers that evening. It was a plan. Mike felt like he had just opened his Christmas presents and got everything he wanted. Anna Maria was all smiles sitting next to Mike on the trip to see Mario.

"I haven't been out this way since before the war," the nun said. "We had and old uncle who lived near here and my Pa took us in his donkey cart to visit him several times when I was a little girl," she said. It made her sentimental to think of those days.

The town was getting ready for the Christmas holidays. It was the first time in several years, since the war started, that there would be a festa in the church courtyard. It was the first week in December and the festivities were planned to continue until the first of January. The fishing boats were successful in the bounty they dragged in with their nets and the economy was starting to show a little upturn. The people who had a few extra pennies helped the ones who had none. The pomegranate trees were bursting with fruit and olives were plentiful. People were so grateful for the little they had and the festa was a good way of thanking God for it.

"Looks like we came at a good time," Mike told the ladies. "It's the festa of St. Peter, the patron saint of fishermen," Sister Caterina explained. "The people here take their parties seriously, it lasts for about three weeks," she said.

Mike pulled up in front of the Delarosa's home. He honked the horn and Mario, followed by several family members, appeared at the door. The two men hugged and Mario welcomed them to the house.

Mario noticed Anna Maria and started to laugh, "I see you didn't get away fast enough, my friend," he said.

"We're engaged," Mike said proudly.

"She's beautiful," Mario told him, and reached in to help her out of the car. "Did you have a good trip over here?" he asked, and kissed her on both cheeks.

"Yes, thank you," she replied, "I love to come here, the water is even more beautiful than in Santa Fara," she admitted.

"Mario, this is my aunt, Sister Caterina," he introduced her to his friend.

"God bless you, sister," he said, "We are honored to have you as a guest."

"Thank you my child. Michele has told us how happy he is to have you as a friend." Soon Ziu Augusto and Zia Nazarina came out of the house to welcome the visitors. Mike handed them a basket Angelina prepared for them, with homemade breads and pasta. She even added some fresh herbs she was growing in pots in her patio garden. Mike brought some candy and a box of cigars for Ziu Augusto.

"Thank you," Nazarina said, "you shouldn't have put yourself out."

"My mother was so grateful for the fine fish Michele brought to her, she wanted to do something for you. My mother is the best bread baker on Via Fellini. The neighbors smell the bread and beg for a loaf," Anna Maria bragged.

"Mike, wait here a minute, I have a surprise for you. You are going to love this," Mario said excitedly. Mario ran down the street and into a house two doors down. He came out with girl in a white linen dress with sandals on her feet and a red scarf tied in her hair.

"Mike, this is my wife, Gina," he said with a wide grin on his face.

"I told you Sicilian girls are dangerous, except this one, she is an angel," Mario beamed with pride. Mike slapped him on the back and kissed her on both cheeks.

"Congratulations you old dog," he said,

"Gina, this is Michele Winston and this is Anna Maria."

"Hello," Gina said in English: Mario had been teaching her a few words.

"When did you have the time to get married?" Mike asked his friend?

"Two days ago," he answered. "I felt as silly as you the first time I saw her. Her parents live two doors down and it's a party here all the time. They were singing and dancing in the street one evening and I asked her to dance. I felt like electricity shot through me when I touched her. I knew she was for me, that was it," Mario confessed.

"I guess I wasn't the only one," Mike laughed. "I just got the okay from her father this morning. It took an act of God to get his approval," Mike told him.

"I know," Mario replied, Gina's dad wasn't so keen on the idea of us going to America, but her mother smoothed it over. I had to promise to send them tickets to America every five years so they can see her again," Mario said.

"That's the least you can do," Mike agreed, "she is really beautiful." Gina and Anna Maria had already taken a liking to each other. They were talking fast and furious about Gina's wedding and Anna Maria told her their wedding would be after Christmas. They were comparing notes and they had the same mind set on a lot of ideas.

"Look, Mario said, "they are getting along already."

"I'm glad, Mike agreed, "She will have a friend in America when we all get home."

"When are you planning to sail back?" Mario asked him.

"After Christmas, I can't wait to get home. This place is wonderful for a while, but I need to see my family, it's been two years," Mike reminded him.

"Me too," Mario agreed, "What do you say we sail back together? The girls seem to be getting along and it will make the trip more fun."

"That's a great idea," Mike said. "I'll book four tickets to New York between Christmas and New Years. It will be my wedding gift to you and Gina," he added, "Let's tell the girls!

"Oh, the reason I came here was to ask you to be my best man, what do you say?" Mike asked.

"Just show me the way to the church and my wife and I will be there," Mario agreed. The girls were pleased to know they would be sailing to America together. Secretly they both felt afraid to sail away from home to a strange place. Having another couple to travel with made the idea of it easier.

Gina felt she could go to the ends of the earth with Mario, she was so sure of his love for her. He was her lover and his strength and assuredness made her comfortable. They had spent the last two days in a little fishing cabin owned by her brother-in-law. It was the only place they could have some privacy. She'd been completely in the dark as to what to expect on her wedding night, but her three married sisters calmed her fears and filled her in on how to accept her husband. At first she was shocked, but he was so gentle with her, that she soon began to enjoy his lovemaking.

Mario admitted to Mike that he had been with a lot of girls, but never one he was in love with. This time it was different, she was everything he could imagine a lover should be and yet so innocent. He hit the jackpot as far as he was concerned and he had never been so happy.

"This is the last letter I am going to send Mike," Larissa told Abigail. "I have laid it all on the line. I told him exactly how I feel. I told him I was still in love with him, but I have given my heart to Alan. If I don't hear from him in the next several weeks, I am going to forget about him and marry Alan like we planned next June," she told her friend.

"I can't believe you, Larissa Winston. All these years of banging your head against the wall over Mike, you still give him an option. Throw that letter in the East River, come to your senses girl and marry that wonderful man you are engaged to."

"No Abigail, this is it, do or die, no more skirting around the issue.

He tells me he wants me or we are done," she said.

"I think you were done a long time ago, Larissa," Abigail said. "But you do what you want to do, it's your folly if it fails, I'm tired of this conversation."

Everyone was tired of that conversation. Evangeline constantly told her to forget about Mike. The Winston sister-in-laws told her the same thing. Mona, the compassionate one of the bunch told her she was nuts. She was losing allies fast and she knew it. She held on to the letter a little longer than she should have when the postman took it from her to mail.

"Are you sure you want to send this, Madam?" he asked her when he practically had to pry it out of her hand.

"Yes, of course," she told him, thinking even he thought it was a bad idea to mail it. Larissa was coming in and out of little bouts of depression. When Alan was in town, she was fine and they were making wedding plans all the time. As soon as he returned to Boston, she would get in a mood that caused headaches and she was short with people. Her job at the school was in jeopardy because she didn't have enough patience with her students and she was often absent with headaches. Joe and Evangeline were getting concerned with her moods and tried to get her to visit Dr. Stein for some help. She refused to believe there was anything wrong. Elsie was sure she suffered from separation anxiety, because she lost her father, mother and Chance in such a short time. Add to the mix she missed Mike so much, Elsie was sure she was in deep trouble. Evangeline felt helpless against this malady. Larissa was a grown woman and had the right to her privacy as far as seeing Dr. Stein was concerned. They just watched her very carefully and forgave her mood swings.

"Alan was her only medicine," Evangeline told Elsie, "and he will be home for Christmas soon."

Evangeline received Mike's letter just before the holidays. He told her he wanted to take the money out of his trust to build an orphanage in Palermo.

How proud she was, she told Joe. "My son is not as selfish as I thought he might be, "she said. "I get mad at him over Larissa and then he does something as wonderful as this."

"Does he have that kind of money, Evangeline?" Joe asked.

"Yes he does, and a lot more. Chance left him a very rich young man. He never short changed him because he really wasn't a Winston. He doesn't have the assets like Ali, she inherited all his assets in England. Mike got his money every year deposited into a trust since he was three years old. It was a sizeable amount the last time I looked at the papers with John Lee, and it has almost doubled in size with the interest. It should be around thirty million by now," she said.

"Joe gave out a long whistle. "Does he know how much he has?" Joe asked.

"Yes, he always kept a close watch on his money," Evangeline answered him.

"I'm going to talk to him about buying real estate when he gets home," Joe decided. "I hear talk about the market skipping a few beats lately. I hope it's just rumor, but land is something they can't take away from you," Joe informed her. "Hopefully we won't have to worry about that for several years," he said. "I'm glad we bought the property next to Lorenzo and Elsie in Grosse Point. By the way, we have to talk to the architects next week to finalize the house plans he told her. I hope Mike gets home before we do, I want him to look them over too."

"I don't even know if he will want to go to school in Detroit or not," she said, "but he will have his own room there anyway."

"Mike will be a man when he gets home and he may not want to live with his mother," Joe teased her. "Well in this letter, he said he belonged to me until he gets married and has a family of his own. Hopefully that won't be for many years down the road"

TWENTY ONE

Christmas with the Noto family was as fun as the Christmases at Lenox Hill and Hunters Point. The brothers and sisters of Philippo got together, with their children in the country on some land that belonged to their mother. So many of them lost their homes and there was nowhere they could put so many people, it was the logical place for all of them to meet. The families brought food and drink to a small cabin that had a large patio area. There were many chairs, benches and tables for people to sit and enjoy the foods that were prepared for them by the women of the family. Singing and dancing in the style of their ancestors went on all day. This was a large, loving family that had escaped the tragedy of the war and all their soldiers came home alive. Some of them lost their homes, but no one lost their life.

The highlight of the day was the blessing Nonna Anna Noto was going to give Anna Maria. It was a bittersweet event, especially because the old women was in her late eighties and would probably never see her granddaughter again. Anna Maria was the last grandchild to get married in her family. There were many other children, but they represented another generation. A huge arm chair was set in the middle of the patio. The grandmother was helped over to sit in it. Filippo and Angelina escorted Anna Maria and Mike to her like she was the Queen of the family and she was. They knelt down in front of her. She told them she had a hard time seeing them, but in her eyes they were the most beautiful site she could behold. The crowd was silent so they could hear every word the Nonna had to say.

" Anna Maria, my precious, youngest, granddaughter," she said, "I am so happy your father gave his blessing to you and Michele on your wedding tomorrow. I would now like to give you mine. I have given it twenty five times before and was proud of all my grandchildren and their spouses.

"Michele, I hope you treat your wife with love and respect, that is the secret to a good marriage. I pray God gives you many children that will be your ticket to heaven, as you can see I will have a good seat there." Everyone laughed at the sense of humor their grandmother still had.

"I love you very much and I know my pride shows. Anna Maria, I have never given my grandchildren, anything like this before, but I won't need it soon and I want you to have it." The old lady took her wedding ring off her finger and handed it to the girl. A loud sound of air being sucked in among the crowd was heard. "No Nonna," Anna Maria said, "Nonnu gave this to you."

"Yes and I want you to have it, I have always loved its simplicity, yet the importance it represented was powerful. "

The plain gold band had Lilly of the Valley engraved all the way around it. The seventy years she wore it had worn down some of the flowers, but it was still beautiful.

"I am going to be with him soon and I want him to know you have it."

"Thank you Nonna," she said. Mike took the clasp off the chain around her neck and slipped the ring through it. It hung next to the little heart with the laurel leaves Mike gave her in Santa Fara.

"I will cherish it forever," she told her grandmother.

"Now I bless you in the name of the Father and the Son and the Holy Ghost, amen." Amen was heard throughout the crowd and a loud cheer was given. The family converged on the couple with best wishes and Filippo cried again.

Sister Caterina made all the wedding arrangements with Monsignor Cyprian. The papers for their nuptials were ready so they could be married in the church. The next day they had to go to the city offices to be married legally in the court. Mike thought it a little strange, but that was the custom of the country Mario told him. Mario and Gina were going to sign them as witnesses. Mike purchased the four tickets to New York, and everything was in place. The week before Mike, Angelina and Anna Maria went shopping for traveling clothes so she would look presentable at the Captain's table for dinners and the New Year's Eve party the ship hosted on the journey. Mike bought her a winter coat, because January in New York was freezing.   He took Anna Maria's advice and purchased a few gifts for Gina and Mario too.

"Mario will look quite dapper in this suit of clothes," Mike said, as he held up a pinstripe navy suit.   "Yes, he will," the girl agreed. "I hope Gina will like these dresses too," Anna Maria said.

"We will have a wonderful time," Mike assured her. Angelina couldn't help herself; she counted all the price tags and almost fainted. He really does have a lot of money, she said to herself. It reinforced the despicable act of keeping Larissa's letters from Mike. In her mind, she was protecting her daughter's future and that's all that mattered. She received another letter this morning and tucked it safely away with the others.

The wedding day, a crisp winter morning in Palermo, was all the bride could hope for. The Christmas party the day before was a pre-reception for the newlyweds. The only people at the church were her parents, Sister Caterina, and the Delarosa's. Anna Maria wore a beautiful white wool suit imported from France that Mike purchased on their shopping spree. It had real pearl buttons on the jacket and it fit her like a glove; the short skirt made her curvy body look especially alluring. She wore a flower in her hair and a little white veil that covered her face as her father walked her down the long aisle.

Mike looked extremely handsome in a cream colored cashmere suit that was a stark contrast to his suntanned skin and dark brown hair. His tall thin body in that suit made him look like a star from the theatre district in New York City. His mother would be proud of him, he thought, and couldn't wait to see her. The altar boy rang the bells and the Mass began. When it came time for the vows, Mike promised to love honor and cherish his new wife all the rest of their days, Anna Maria did the same. He held her hand throughout the ceremony for fear she would change her mind and run back to her Papa. He was gladly mistaken, this girl was head over heels in love with him and he had a life partner forever. Mike slipped her grandmother's ring on her finger and the priest pronounced them husband and wife. He kissed his wife in front of God and her father with no fear of being reprimanded. What a lovely feeling it was, to now call her his wife. They walked down the aisle past the angels and saints lining the church walls as Mr. and Mrs. Mike Winston. Mike wished his mother and his family could have been there this morning, they were always there for him for all his achievements and this was the grandest yet. Two more weeks, he thought, and they will be so surprised.

Mike took everyone out for breakfast to the little café where they had their first outing just a few short weeks earlier. "What a whirlwind," he confessed to his best man, "a few months ago I was in a fox hole and now I think I have gone to heaven."

"Tell me about it, *compare,* I feel the same way."

"Anna Maria and I are going to spend the night at the Hotel de la Mare near the beach. Tomorrow we go to the court house and we will meet you and Gina there," he said, "sometime around ten o'clock. Then we all drive back to Naples and it's U.S.A., here we come."

"It's a plan," Mario said. They said their goodbye's and went back to Isola Dele Femmini to pack their belongings and bid farewell to the family.

"In a few short hours we will be sailing for America, and you will be a signora Americana," Mario teased Gina.

"I can't wait to be a real American wife to you," and she kissed him. She wished it with all her heart and prayed she could make him happy.

`Mike and Anna Maria arrived at the hotel in the early afternoon. The desk clerk gave them the key to their room and told them to let him know if there was anything else he could do for them. This man was paying in American dollars and he wanted to make sure everything was perfect.

"Thank you," Mike said, and escorted Anna Maria to their room.

It was beautiful, she thought, although she had nothing to compare it to. The French doors led to a balcony that over looked the Mediterranean.

"Do you want to go swimming?" she teased Mike.

He looked at her stunned, then realized she was making a joke and said, "Yes. " He grabbed her around the waist and kissed her for the first time as a husband should kiss his wife. She pushed him on the bed and started to undo her pearl buttons.

"Are you sure you haven't done this before?" he asked her.

"Dozens of times," she said with a smile. She unbuttoned her skirt and let it fall to the floor, still smiling at him. She put her stocking foot on the bed and let him roll the hose off her leg. She did the same with the other. She pulled the straps of her slip down and took a step toward him.

"Don't move." he said and stood up and slid the slip off her body. "You are the most perfect thing I have ever seen," he said as he started to kiss her neck. She unbuttoned his shirt and he helped her with the rest. They made love for the first time, without coming up for air.

"Mia, I love you," he said, "I'm so happy I found you."

"God sent you to me, I'm sure of it," she said. They made love again and fell asleep in each other's arms. Mike woke up thinking he was having a wonderful dream, to his surprise Anna Maria was still asleep next to him. The sheet was draped lightly around her and her body was mostly exposed. He couldn't believe how she responded to his touch; she was innocent yet naturally seductive. *What a women he married!*

"Mia," he shook her slightly, "are you awake?" he asked. She yawned and stretched her tall body across the bed.

"Hello, my husband," she said, and they made love again, this time slowly and methodically.

The papers at the court house were signed and Anna Maria had her passport in her hand.

"We are truly married in the eyes of God and the government of Italy," Mike announced. Mario and Gina got a ride to Palermo from his cousin. They transferred their bags from his cousin's truck to Mike's car. They felt like the happiest four people in the world, they were on their way to their new life in America. The girls jumped in the back seat because they had a lot to talk about, while the men sat in the front.

Gina coyly asked Anna Maria, "How are you this morning?"

"I'm fine," she answered her, and they both started giggling. Gina whispered something in her *comari's* ear and they roared with laughter.

"Calm down back there," Mario, warned them, "don't distract the driver. I'm so glad they get along, Mario said to Mike. Mike just smiled. "You seem pretty happy today, what did I tell you about those Sicilian girls, wasn't I right?"

"And then some," Mike added. "Where are you going to live Mario?" Mike asked, "I mean when you get to New York?"

"I haven't thought that through yet, but I'm sure we will think of something. When I sent my sister a letter telling her that I got married, I asked her to look around for a small apartment for us. I don't know if she has found anything yet. I have been sending money to the New York Bank and Trust the whole time I was in the army," he said, "I think I can find a place for us in the city."

"Where are you going to work or haven't you figured it out yet?" Mike inquired.

"My brother-in-law will get me a job at the docks," he said, "at least that's what my sister wrote the last time I got a letter," Mario answered.

"I haven't gotten a letter in a long time," Mike said, "that's unusual. My mother and my Pa wrote a few words, did I tell you my mother got married again?" he asked Mario.

"Didn't her husband die recently?" he asked.

"It's just been six months," Mike told him, "Joe, her husband, is a great guy and she has had an unusual life with my dad. There is more to that story and I will find out about it when I get home," Mike assured him. "I wish I paid more attention to my family when I was home, I was so wrapped up in myself and my plans for my future, I didn't see things that went on right under my nose," he admitted. "I usually get something from Larissa," he said thinking out loud. "There is something odd there too," he surmised, "I'm not sure how she will react to my wife, I hope favorably. Whatever they think, that's fine, I have the best girl in the world for me."

"I feel the same way," Mario agreed, "but the difference is nobody will care."

Angelina stoked the fire in the stove. She had a handful of letters from Larissa that she needed to be rid of. She couldn't read them because she couldn't read English. Her conscience wasn't bothering her too much anymore. Her daughter was safely on her way to America with her American husband. She dropped the letters on the hot coals and watched as they burned to a crisp. She spread the ashes so no one could find a trace of the paper. It won't be long before she and Filippo will join her baby in America and life will be good again.

When the newlyweds arrived on the dock, the girls were amazed at how large the vessel was. Gina grew up on the water, but never saw a boat so grand.

"It's called a ship, Cara mia," Mario corrected her.

"A ship," she repeated. She wanted to learn the language before she arrived and her husband told her she would learn in time. The couples had rooms on the same floor, but several doors away from each other. Mario thanked Mike for the gifts and hoped he could do something nice for him someday.

"Don't think twice about it, if you wouldn't have come with me I wouldn't have had the nerve to go to Palermo alone," he said, "and we would be sharing a room together today, think about that my friend."

"That trip was our destiny, Mike," Mario believed.

"Have you been talking to my mother?" Mike asked him. Mario just shrugged off the question, he didn't understand what he was talking about.

"Have you had a chance to try on your suit?" he asked.

"Oh yes, it makes me look like a New York banker," he said, "but did you think you were going to borrow the pants?" Mario asked.

"Why do you ask?" Mike wondered.

"I'm a good four or five inches shorter than you and the pants were too long."

"I'll have the ship seamstress alter them for you," he said apologetically.

"No, don't worry, my wife shortened them this morning before we left. Isn't she a charm?" he bragged. "Well my friend," Mario said "you will have to excuse us. We have business to attend to," and he took Gina's hand and pulled her to their room. She waved good bye to her friends with a smile on her face and disappeared into the cabin.

"Well, Mrs. Winston, do you want to go swimming?" he asked.

"Absolutely," she said, and he carried her over the threshold. They didn't hear from the Delarosa's until the next afternoon. The Delarosa's didn't hear from them, either. They explored and enjoyed each other and soaked in the celebration of wedded bliss. Their cabin had a shower that was big enough for two and they let the water fall on them like rain from heaven. They washed each other with the fragrant soap and went back to bed.

Mike told her all about Hunters Point and Lenox Hill. He told her of his grandparents and how much he adored them.

"It's going to be hard to go home and not find them there waiting to hear about my day," Mike told her. He got tears in his eyes thinking of what life was going to be like without Chance also. "I can't believe my mother and Joe Cross are married," he said.

Anna Maria cradled him in her arms. "Please my love don't be sad. This is our honeymoon. We are going to think of ourselves on this voyage, not our families. When we get home, we can allow a little sadness in, but very little. We love each other and that's all that matters," she insisted.

"How did you get so smart?" he asked her.

"My mama is a Rizzo," she answered. They both laughed and made love again.

On December 31, 1919, the ship was hosting a grand New Years eve party and celebration of peace. The Winston's and Delarosa's were dressed in their finest when they entered the dining room. Decorations from Christmas were still adorning the tables and walls, but they had flags that read 1920 in all the centerpieces. Party hats and horns were laid on the tables to be used at the stroke of midnight. It was the first time any of them had been to a party that wasn't hosted at a relative's home. It was very exciting for them all, to say the least. They were seated at a large table where many important people from the American and British government were placed. Sir Malcolm Darcy was introduced to Mike by the captain. He was an ambassador to the U.S. from England.

"Winston, that name is familiar to me," he told Mike. "Do you know a Chance Winston from New York?" he asked.

"Yes," Mike said, " was my father." Sir Darcy was sorry to hear of his passing and expressed his sympathies to Mike.

"What were you doing in Italy?" he asked.

"I was with the American Army," he answered," after the war, I went to Sicily to see where I was born. I met my wife there and we were married a few days ago."

"Seems to me, you struck gold," Sir Malcolm commented, "she is a beauty."

"Thank you Sir, I think so too," he said proudly.

"Will you be working at Winston Steel when you get home?" the older man asked.

"I'm not sure what I'm going to do. I should finish school because I want to go into politics someday. But I have a wife now and maybe I should go back to work. My dad was going to help me make up my mind, but he passed before I could get home," Mike explained.

"Politics is a tricky life for anyone, be very sure you want to go down that road. It can be fulfilling and also corrupting at the same time, my boy."

"I know I have a lot to think about, Sir Malcolm," Mike confessed. "My friends and I joined this war because we were going to make a difference and save the world. It didn't work out that way," he told him.

"Mike, don't second guess yourself. What you and your friends did was most commendable, you may never know the difference you made in someone's life. Just be proud of yourself, I'm proud to know you."

"Thank you, Sir Malcolm," Mike said, as he shook the ambassador's hand.

"Call on me if you ever need anything, I should be glad to help in any way. Your father was a good business man, he was fair in all his dealings and he helped the cause immensely."

"Thank you, I will," Mike agreed. Anna Maria excused herself and asked her husband to dance. "Please dance with your wife," Sir Malcolm laughed; "I'm sure you would rather be with her than talking with me."

"It is our honeymoon," Mike said, and took Anna Maria's hand and walked to the dance floor. He took her in his arms and was amazed how her body melted into his and they danced like they had been partners for ever. The orchestra leader suddenly started to count down the seconds: five, four, three, two, one. Happy New Year! Everyone wished everyone else a happy new year, with kisses and hugs.

Mike kissed his wife and told her every New Year from now on will be a happy one. "I love you Mia," he said.

"I love you, my darling," she answered.

Several days later, early in the morning, the ship sailed into the

Verrazano Straits. The two couples stood at the ship's railing waiting for the Statue of Liberty to appear.

"There she is," Mario yelled, as he pointed to the Lady with the winter sun shining on her copper crown.

"We're home," he exclaimed to his wife. Gina waved profusely as if she was sure the statue would wave back.

"Look," Mike ordered Anna Maria, "the Lady is there to welcome you to America." Anna Maria buried her face in Mike's shoulder.

"I'm afraid," she said. At that moment she wished her Mama was there with her.

"Don't be afraid, Mia, I'm with you always. My family will welcome you too, just wait and see." After the ship docked and their luggage was collected, the couples said goodbye with the promise of seeing each other soon and went their separate ways. Mike didn't wire ahead to let the family know he was arriving because he wanted to surprise them. He hailed a taxi cab and went directly to Hunters Point.

It was the custom lately, after mass, that everyone gathered at Hunters Point for brunch. They were always starving by then, because they couldn't receive communion if they had eaten anything after midnight; the night before Mass. Elsie and Lorenzo wanted to know if Evangeline had heard any more news from Mike.

"Did my son say when he was coming home" Lorenzo asked Evangeline.

"No, he only told me to get the lawyers to prepare the papers to build the orphanage in Palermo," she answered him.

"I guess I miss him so much I'm getting very impatient," he said. "Sam has been home over a month now and he has been asking about him. I hope he doesn't get too attached to Sicily," Lorenzo sighed.

"Don't worry, Lorenzo, he will be home soon," Evangeline told him.

The family was busy with chatter of the week's happenings. The twins and their wives were talking to Larissa and Alan about wedding plans. Matt told his brother that Larissa looked so thin and pale to him, he was worried about her. Mark assured him Dr. Stein had been looking after her and had just prescribed a new medication to help her relax. The death of her parents and Chance was too much for her to handle. Alan was the only one who seemed to calm her fears and he was at her side every chance he could.

He was staying at Hunters Point for a few days because they had appointments with the priest at St. Mary's before their wedding. These meetings were called Cana Conferences and were designed to help young couples with expectations of the marriage. Maria and Nicolo were making sure everyone had enough to eat when they heard a familiar voice.

"Did you save enough food for me?" Mike asked. He had walked in the house undetected and told Anna Maria to wait in the hall with their luggage. He wanted to surprise the family. Everyone started to yell and scream when they saw him. Evangeline and Lorenzo ran to him and embraced their son with all the love they had saved up for him. Joe stood back not knowing what kind of greeting he would receive from Mike.

Mike noticed him and extended his hand and said, "Congratulations Joe, I'm so happy for the both of you."

Larissa was frozen in her chair, she didn't know if her eyes were deceiving her. Mike looked different to her in some way. He wasn't the young man who left two years ago; now he was a man. He was taller, she thought and much more muscular. Alan shook his hand and welcomed him home. Mike bent down to kiss Larissa on the cheek and she sat there like a statue.

"Hello, darling," he said to her. "I've missed you." Aliciana and Elsie jumped on him with kisses and hugs. Everyone was crying.

"Where is my darling Elena?" he said, and the little girl peeked out from behind her father's legs. She knew who he was because everyone talked about Mike, but she had a hard time remembering him. They were asking him questions about why they didn't meet him at the docks and how he enjoyed Sicily and if he was wounded and things like that.

Finally he said, "Wait a minute, I have a surprise for all of you." He left the room for a second and reappeared with Anna Maria on his arm. He went to Lorenzo and Maria and said, "This is Zia Angelina's daughter, Anna Maria."

Maria started to cry, "Mike, you brought her to us from Palermo, how wonderful. Welcome my niece, you are so beautiful," she exclaimed, and kissed her on both cheeks. Lorenzo looked at Mike for the rest of the story. He was glad to see the girl, but somehow he thought there was more to it.

Mike took Evangeline's hand in his and said, "Mama, Pa, Anna Maria is my wife." Complete silence. No one said a word. They were all in shock for several reasons.

Finally Elsie broke the ice. "Welcome my dear. I'm Elsie, your mother-in-law. We are so pleased to meet you, this is Alicianna, Mike's sister and Elena, Mike's little sister. Lorenzo, say something to her," she insisted, giving him a stern look.

"I'm so sorry, Anna Maria. It's just that I didn't know, I'm so surprised and happy of course." He embraced her and said, "Do you call me uncle or papa?"

"We can figure that one out later," Mike suggested.

Evangeline sat in a chair that Joe pushed under her before she fell down. Tears were running down her face, "I can't catch my breath," she complained.

"Bring her a drink of water." Joe asked someone.

Mike was a little disappointed at his family's reaction. He thought they would all jump for joy at his announcement. "Mother, are you alright?" he asked her.

"Yes darling, give me a second to pull myself together. You are full of surprises today," she said. "Anna Maria, come here darling, I want to properly welcome you to our family." She extended her hand to her and embraced her. What a beauty she was, Evangeline thought, no wonder, my son was enchanted with her. Anna Maria couldn't say a word, she wasn't sure if the family truly welcomed her or not. She knew Mike wanted to surprise them, and he succeeded she was sure.

"Mother," Mike asked, "is my room ready for me?"

"Yes, it's been ready for you for weeks," Evangeline assured him.

"I'm going to take my wife there so she can freshen up and we will come down in a little while, if that is alright?"

"Your wife," she repeated, *how strange that sounds*. "Yes, of course, go right ahead, we will be here when you return," Evangeline told him.

"What's the matter with them?" he asked his wife. "I didn't expect total silence when I introduced you to them," he said.

"Michele, what did you think they were going to say?" she asked him. "First you surprise them showing up without a word and then with me. I would feel the same way if you were my son."

"Do you think that's all it was?" he asked her.

"I'm sure," she lied. She didn't know what to think. They seemed like nice people, so she decided she would forget the welcoming party and give them another chance to like her. He took her to his suite of rooms where she could wash up and change her clothes. She had never seen anything so magnificent as Hunters Point before in her life. She certainly didn't know if she fit in or not.

"What's the matter with him?" Lorenzo asked anyone who would answer. "He made us all look like fools in front of that poor girl."

"He just wanted to surprise us," Elsie said. "Can't you see how in love he is with her? He is absolutely glowing when he looks at her," she continued.

"I think so too," Evangeline said, "he has always wanted to please us, he thought he was doing just that."

"But they are first cousins," Maria cried.

"Since when has that been a problem in Sicily?" Lorenzo asked.

"Alan," Larissa said, "I have a terrible headache, I think I need to lie down for a while."

"Has the new medicine made you feel worse?" he asked.

"Maybe it has," she answered, knowing exactly what the problem was.

"Mariella, will you help me to my room?" she asked her sister- in – law.

"Yes, darling, I will," she said and proceeded to walk along with her. "Are you alright, Larissa?" she asked her, "I know what a shock it must have been to you."

"I want to scream my head off right now, but I know I have to remain calm for everyone's sake," she said. Larissa was glad her room was on the opposite side of the house. She couldn't stand sleeping in the rooms near Mike's suite. Larissa took one of the sedatives Dr. Stein prescribed for her. Mariella stayed with Larissa until she fell asleep, she had an uneasy feeling about her and told Matt of her fears.

"I think we should stay at Hunters Point tonight so we can keep an eye on her," Mariella said.

"I'll tell Evangeline," Matt said, "I'm worried about her too."

Mark and Mary decided to stay also and Hunters Point was bursting with relatives, just the way Evangeline liked it. Larissa slept most of the day with Alan checking in on her every half hour.

"It terrifies me when she gets like this," Alan told Mariella.

"Mike's surprise was another shock to her system," she told him. Everyone else felt the same way. "Larissa is in a delicate state of mind lately with all the loss she has endured, she naturally was more vulnerable."

"I suppose so," Alan agreed, "I hope she feels better when she wakes up," he said.

After Mike and Anna Maria changed their clothes, they came back downstairs. Mike explained how he and his friend Mario traveled to Sicily after the war. He tried to describe his grandparents and his mother's mausoleum to Evangeline. She seemed happy to know he visited with Mother Superior and that the nun sent her regards. He told the family exactly how he first saw Anna Maria in the shoe shop and later discovered she was his cousin.

"I swear to God" he said, "It was love at first sight," and it made the girl blush.

"I can see how that happens," said Joe, "I fell in love with your mother the first second I saw her."

"I didn't know that," Mike admitted, and felt a connection with Joe. "We had to go to the Monsignor in Palermo to get counseling and to allow her father to give his blessing to the marriage. Her grandmother blessed us too, and gave Anna Maria her wedding ring. See," he said, and raised her hand to show the proof.

"Mike," Zia Maria asked, "you are first cousins, aren't you afraid for your children?"

"No, Zia, bad things can happen to anyone, not because they are related. We were married in the church and later in the court house. So we were married twice," he bragged.

"Where did you get married?" he asked his mother.

"We also were married in the courthouse," she confessed. "But we plan a trip to Rome and will get remarried in a church there," she told her son.

"That sounds wonderful," Anna Maria chimed in. It was the first words she spoke to them since she arrived.

"Ah, she speaks!" Lorenzo teased. "You are a true Rizzo," he said to her. "Your features are very much like your mother's were at your age."

"Look at this," Mike said and held their hands against each others, her smaller version were the copy of his. "Isn't that something?" Mike asked.

"Pa, we have so much in common, and I love her so much."

"I love your son too," Anna Maria said, "please give us your blessings, that will make everything perfect."

"Well, you have mine," Elsie said, "and I think you have Joe's, we both know what it's like to love someone unconditionally and want everyone to be happy about it." Joe nodded his head in agreement and kissed the couple, with tears running down his face. He felt a little foolish, tears were always left for Lorenzo to shed at a time like this, but his emotions were high and he couldn't help it.

"We have always tried to make Mike happy," Evangeline said, "he has been a wonderful son. We give our blessing freely, isn't that right, Lorenzo?" she asked.

"Certainly, my dear, I just want you to promise to love and take care of my son always."

"That goes without saying," she said In Italian.

"What a relief!" Mike felt the weight of the world taken off his shoulders for the second time.

"What is the matter with Larissa?" Mike asked with concern, "she looks so pale and thin?. I haven't heard from her in ever so long," he told them.

"She wrote dozens of letters to you," Elsie said, "I wonder what became of them all."

"Well, it was war time Elsie, maybe they got lost or something," he answered. "I got several letters from Mother and Pa while I was in Palermo, but nothing from Larissa," he added. "Alan is here, does that mean they are serious about each other?" he asked.

"Yes, I'm sure she would have told you in one of her letters had you gotten them. They are getting married next June," Evangeline informed him. "Mike, I have to tell you, she wasn't sure until you came home," his mother said. "I hate to say this without her being here, but she hasn't been herself lately."

"What do you mean?" Mike questioned.

"She had it in her head that when you came home, you might realize that she was the girl for you and marry her."

"Oh, my," said Anna Maria, "what will happen now?" She latched on to Mike's arm for dear life.

"I told you Mia, I never had those feelings for her. If I had I would have told her so years ago. This puts me in a terrible position," he told his parents," Alan knows of this?"

"No, he thinks she is in mourning for her parents and Chance. Dr. Stein is taking care of her and has prescribed a new sedative for her," Evangeline tried to calm his fears.

"Mike," Lorenzo asked, "why haven't you made yourself clear with Larissa before now?"

"I didn't know, the subject never came up, I swear. " He was getting upset now and felt a knot in the pit of his stomach. "I knew Alan was in love with her and they had my blessings. I have been jealous of her many times in our lives because I didn't want boys hanging around her with no intentions, I would have the same reaction if it was Alicianna. She is like my sister and I love her dearly. We hadn't been that close the year or so before I went into the service. She was at that fancy school in Boston and I was at NYC Prep.

" My God, what will I say to her, Mother?" he asked. "I wanted her to love Anna Maria the same as I want all of you to love her, she is my wife and my only love ever!"

Mike was emotional, but Anna Maria was level headed in this situation. This girl, who was obviously unstable, was making her husband feel like he did something wrong. She knew he loved her and only her and no one was going to change that.

"Maybe I can speak to her," Anna Maria requested. The family looked at her in amazement. This little girl from Palermo, Sicily, who didn't know much of the world, knew her husband was troubled and she was going slay all the dragons that got in their way.

"That's very admirable my dear," Evangeline said," and I love you for defending Mike, but let's give her a little time to digest what happened today. Alan is with her and he always takes her pain away, he is so in love with her. Let's give her a few days, if you don't mind, and they all agreed."

Cook was so happy to see Mike that she made all his favorite foods for dinner. She wanted to celebrate his homecoming with his new bride in a special way.

"Dinner is served," the butler announced. The family entered the dining room except for Alan and Larissa.

"Where is my sister?" Mark asked.

"She and Alan are dining in her room tonight, she had just awaken from her nap and felt a little light headed," Mariella told them. "I told her to relax and that it would be fine if Alan stayed with her, I'm afraid the new medicine might be too strong for her," Mariella announced.

"I'll call Dr. Stein tonight," Elsie volunteered, "and have him check on her tomorrow."

Mike and Anna Maria looked at each other with sympathy. "I hope she will be alright," Anna Maria, said to Mark.

"I'm sure she will. Time heals all wounds, they say," he assured her.

"Do you have any plans? Mike, now that you are home," Mark asked him. "Winston Steel always has a place for you, I hope you know that Mike."

"So does R&W Motors, son," Lorenzo added, "or are you going back to school? Do you know that we are moving to Detroit as soon as our homes are finished?" Lorenzo asked him.

"Who is moving to Detroit?" he asked in amazement? "I knew the representatives from Ford wanted you to head up a salesroom there, but I guess I didn't think about you moving permanently," Mike said.

"Your mother and Joe purchased land on Lake St. Clair next door to Elsie and I, we are going to be neighbors. I'm having a cottage built on the property for Maria and Nicolo too. We are very excited about it."

"When is this going to happen?" he asked.

"Late this summer after Alan and Larissa's wedding," he answered.

"I know you are happy about the move," Matt said, "but Mariella and I are very sad about it."

"You can come to Detroit by train any time you can get away," Lorenzo invited him.

"Between the two houses, there will be plenty of room," Evangeline said.

"There is a steel plant that is for sale in an area they call Down River," Joe told them. "I was thinking of looking it over for Winston Steel to purchase. I was going to start it up again, but if you want, Mike, I can use the help to get it going again."

"Maybe he does want to go back to school," Evangeline retorted, "he is still very young and he has his whole life in front of him."

"I have a lot to think about," Mike answered his family.

He looked at his wife and she shrugged her shoulders, "My home is where you are, where you go, I go," she said.

"You are a lucky man, Mike," Joe announced, "to have found your soul mate so early in life and she is beautiful too. "

The evening went on with news about their lives in the past two years, and Mike told them about the war and the times he was wounded twice.

"Don't worry Mother, I have healed very nicely," he said, after he saw the look of fear on her face. "By the way Mariella, have your brothers arrived yet? I met them in Palermo," he told her.

"Yes, just the other day, it's wonderful to have all my family in one place, safe and sound. Did you see the children?" she asked, "My mother and father are walking on clouds to have them in America.

"I'm glad, they weren't living in very good conditions when I found them," Mike said, "but they were making the best of it. Your brothers are very nice and their wives are great girls, I'm glad they are here," he said.

"Look at the time Elsie," Lorenzo informed his wife, "I have a meeting early tomorrow morning. I can't tell you how relieved I am that you are home, son, stop by tomorrow and see me in the office, I'll take you to lunch," he suggested.

"Sounds great Pa," Mike said, "see you then." Lorenzo scooped up a sleeping Elena and he and Elsie gave kisses all around. Mike and Anna Maria walked them to the door and watched as they drove off in his Model T Ford Torpedo.

"Your father is wonderful," Anna Maria told Mike, "and his wife made me feel very much welcomed this morning."

"I'm glad you think so, Mia," he said, "I want you to like them all."

Mark and Mary, Matt and Mariella all turned in early as Monday was a work day for them and they wanted to check in on Larissa before they went to bed. They said their goodnights and best wishes for the newlyweds, as they still felt like newlyweds themselves. They went up the stairs towards Larissa's room and knocked gently on the door. Alan opened the door and put his finger to his lips.

" She fell asleep after she ate," he said, "I was just going to my room myself".

"Did she eat anything tonight?" Mariella asked.

"Barely, you know how she just pushes her food around the plate," he said.

"Elsie called Dr. Stein and he'll be here tomorrow. He suggested not giving any more sedatives tonight," Mariella said.

"I didn't, she fell asleep before I had the opportunity to do so," Alan told her. "I'll check on her around two o'clock again," Alan said, "I probably won't be able to sleep anyway."

"I'll check in at five, I have to get up early tomorrow," Mark volunteered.

"I'll take the seven o'clock shift," Matt agreed.

"Good night everyone," Alan said, and went to his room. The couples went to their perspective rooms not knowing what doom they were going to experience in a few hours.

Ali hugged and kissed her brother a few dozen times before she went up to bed. "Thank you for bringing him home to us Anna Maria," and hugged and kissed her too. "I know we are going to be good friends as well as sisters," she said, "and by the way my name is Ali now. I'm a big girl and Aliciana is such a long name," she insisted.

"Good night Ali, my sister, I'm so happy to have one," Anna Maria told her.

"Good night Mike, God answered my prayers," she said.

"He answered mine too," he agreed, and watched her go to her room.

Evangeline was alone with her daughter-in-law while the men poured themselves a drink. She still didn't believe Mike was married. "Anna Maria, I hope I didn't act like a crazy mother-in- law this morning?"she asked the girl. "I was so shocked first by Mike's showing up like he did and then introducing his cousin as his wife; can you put yourself in my shoes?" she asked her.

"I told Michele the very same thing when we went up to change. He didn't think it through very well, but he wanted to surprise you and show you how happy we are." They spoke in their native language so no mistaken words would be said. "Michele feels very badly about Larissa, but don't you see it wasn't his fault," she told Evangeline.

"I agree," Evangeline said, "I have been telling Larissa for months to forget about him, especially since she has a wonderful man who adores her. Somehow she can't forget Mike, even though he never gave her any encouragement. She mistook his love for her as a lover not a sister. We all have been telling her, even her best friend Abigail," Evangeline said. "I hope this is the jolt she needs to place her priorities on Alan."

"I hope so, I do want to be friends with her," Anna Maria replied.

"Mother," Mike interrupted, "will you please tell me the big secret about my dad? I didn't understand your last letter about his death," he said.

"We can save it for tomorrow, darling, I think we should all get a good night's rest and clear our heads. I don't know about you, but I'm exhausted," she confessed.

Joe agreed and finished his drink. Come my dear, I'll walk you up to bed." Mike felt a little pang of jealousy when he heard that, we all have a lot of getting used to, he thought.

"Good night my darlings," Evangeline hugged them both. " I'll see you in the morning."

Mike and Anna Maria snuggled up in front of the fire in the

drawing room. "Well, what do you think of my family?" he asked her.

"I think they are wonderful," she said.

"Really?" he asked.

"Yes, they are all extensions of you, you are the hub of the wheel," she said. "They care desperately about each other and look out for each other's welfare. Look how everyone is worried about Larissa," she said.

"How did you get so smart?" he asked her.

"My mother is a Rizzo," she replied, and ducked out of the way when he threw a pillow at her.

"Let's go to bed wife," he insisted.

"Gladly husband," she replied. Anna Maria caressed the gold banister as she walked to her room. "Gold staircases," she said, "Mama won't believe it."

TWENTY TWO

Larissa awoke from her sleep still in a state of light headedness. She saw the bottle of pills on the bed table and decided she should take her medicine. She poured the pills in her hand and swallowed at least six of them. Before she knew it she was sound asleep again. *She was having the most wonderful dream her mother and father were in the garden cutting long stem roses and making grand arrangements with the other flowers in the garden. Her mother walked like she was on a cloud, her dress flowing on the ground around her. Come my darling, come with me, she told Larissa. Her father was still cutting flowers and had such a happy look on his face. He was layering long stem roses in a May basket; do you like them he asked her? Yes Daddy, they are beautiful, she said, it made Larissa so glad to see them again. Wait mother, she told her, I can't catch up with you, slow down please. Larissa, Larissa, her mother kept calling out to her. Where have you gone Mother I can't find you? Larissa, she kept hearing Rosalyn call to her. Tears were falling down her face. Mother where are you, Larissa was getting desperate to find her again. Clouds of fog were circling around her and she had trouble seeing. Larissa come with me my darling, she heard her again. Suddenly she spotted her mother in among the clouds, don't move Mama, she begged her. I'm coming, I'm coming, she screamed! Somehow Larissa felt the hem of her nightgown getting heavy. It was weighting her down and she couldn't run as fast. What is happening, she thought. All she wanted was to run into her mother's arms and feel safe again.*

Evangeline couldn't sleep. What had her son done, she thought? Does this girl really love him like she says she does? Did she marry him just to come to America? All those questions were running around in her head.

"Come to bed Evangeline," Joe insisted. "You are ruining the carpet with your pacing."

"Oh Joe, I can't sleep."

"Come, I'll rub your back until you fall asleep," he offered.

The moon was full that night and Evangeline was looking out the window. She saw a white figure walking on the pond toward the center where the ice wasn't frozen. She looked again to make sure she wasn't seeing things and she recognized Larissa.

"Joe, Larissa is walking on the pond!" she screamed. She ran out of the room screaming for Alan to run after her. She naturally woke everyone in the house and they didn't understand her ranting.

"Larissa!" she kept saying. "She is walking on the pond!"

Alan flew out of the house and the twins ran after him. Mike looked out the window and saw what his mother saw.

"Take the blankets," Anna Maria told him. He scooped them up and ran after the men. Joe called the police and sent for an ambulance. He knew this wasn't going to end in a good way.

"Get more blankets for the men." Anna Maria instructed the women. Alan ran through the snow that was more like slush the closer he got to the pond. His feet were bare just like the rest of them. No one had any time to put shoes on, Larissa was in trouble. Alan could see her walking and called out to her.

"Larissa, stop, stop!" he cried.

All she heard was the sweet sound of her mother's voice calling her to come with her. "I'm coming mama," she called out. *Why is she calling her mother?* Alan thought. Alan reached out to grab her and the ice cracked and down she went into the freezing water. First she went straight down and bobbed up again.

She felt nothing because of the affects of the drugs. She went down again before Alan could reach her, this time she didn't come up.

"Larissa!" he screamed and jumped into the icy water after her. He couldn't find her: it was dark and he was losing his way fast. Suddenly her white gown brushed up against him and he grabbed for it. He pulled her to him and Matt and Mark were there pulling them to safety. Mike wrapped the blankets around them and started to give her mouth to mouth resuscitation like he was taught in his basic training class.   Larissa came to and a lot of water came out of her mouth. She started to cry. "Mother where are you, I can't find you." She started punching Mike to let her go. "My mother wants me, can't you hear her calling me?" she insisted. Joe carried her back to the house to wait for the ambulance.

"Joe," she said, "my mama is calling me, let me go." Mercifully she
fainted and the ambulance arrived just in time. They transported her to the
hospital, where Dr. Stein had been notified and rushed to meet her. Joe put
Alan in the ambulance too, he was suffering from hyperthermia, but
amazingly Larissa had no signs of the malady. The twins drank a glass of
brandy that Evangeline forced down their throats. They wanted to get to
the hospital as soon as they could. Their wives made them change into
warm, dry clothes first. Joe sat next to Mike who was looking into space.

"Are you alright?" he asked him.

"I don't know yet," he said. "I've seen young men blown to bits and
loose limbs, but this is Larissa." He put his head in his hands and rested on
the table and cried like a baby. "Joe, did I do this to her?" he cried.

"She was asking for her mother, not you, my friend. Evangeline
found about six of her pills missing from the bottle, she obviously
overdosed herself," he said, "we'll see what Dr. Stein has to say about it
first."

Dr. Stein stepped out of her hospital room to meet the frantic
family.

"She will be fine," he assured them. "It's a miracle she was found
so quickly, we would have had quite a different outcome if she had not been
seen. We pumped her stomach so she will feel sore for a few days. She took
about half a dozen pills, but I don't think she meant to do it. If she had, she
would have taken them all. I will meet with her daily for a few weeks to try
to help her cope with her losses. Some people are strong enough to handle
death and separation, and some are not," he told them. "Larissa is lucky to
have such a close family to support her and very lucky to have Alan
Mason," he added.

"Thank you," Joe said as spokesman for the family, "we love her
very much. Can she come home tonight?" he asked the doctor.

"No, I would like to keep her a couple of days, after all she was in
the freezing water for several minutes; although her body doesn't show any
signs of it. The human mind and body work together in strange ways," he
said. "Her brain was focused in on her mother and father and the chemicals
seemed to protect her body. We don't know how it works, much study has
yet to be done on the subject," he admitted. "It's like when a person is

drunk and they fall down, seldom do they get hurt. It's a mystery still," he said shaking his head. "Go home everyone. Get some rest, she is in good hands. Alan is spending the night here too, he won't leave her anyway," he announced.

The family went in to see her for themselves and kissed her goodnight. She still wasn't sure what happened to her, but she was very tired.

"We'll be back tomorrow." they all told her.

As they were walking away, she called out," Mike, come back! " Everyone just held their breath not knowing what she was about to say.

"Yes, Larissa?" he asked. He walked back to her and held her hand.

"Congratulations," she said with a smile.

"Thank you darling," he cried, "You don't know how much that means to me." He hugged her and pulled the blanket up to her chin. "Get some sleep and we will be back before you know it," he demanded.

"Yes, I will, I'm very tired," she said, and she was asleep before they all left the room.

When they gathered in the hall everyone was relieved at her reaction.

"I think she will be fine now," Evangeline said with a sigh.

"I think she needed Mike's help to get through this," Mariella agreed.

"I'll do whatever I can," Mike assured the family, "Anna Maria and I want her to be well again."

"With the help of all of us and God, she will be fine," Mark said.

"I'm going to give Alan a big kiss when I see him," Matt said.

"Give the guy a break and save the kisses for Larissa to give him," his twin suggested. Everyone laughed and went home happier than when they arrived.

The next morning breakfast was a little later than usual. Everyone slept in a couple hours longer they were so exhausted from the night before. The first thing Evangeline did was call the hospital for an update on Larissa. Larissa was sitting up and having her breakfast with Alan.

The nurse said, "She had a good appetite and was asking for more."

"How wonderful," Evangeline said, and assured her she would be there that afternoon to see her.

"It seems she has jumped over another hurdle this morning and actually ate the food on her plate," she told Joe.

"That's great," he replied, "now we need to concentrate on the newlyweds. I wonder if they are up yet?"

When they went into the breakfast room, Mike was sitting there with a huge dish of scrambled eggs and sausages. Evangeline felt like it was a mirage seeing him like that.

"Good morning," he said, "I'm starved I hope you don't mind that I didn't wait for you."

"Not at all," Joe answered, "where is your wife?"

"She is in the kitchen teaching Cook how to make biscotti like her mother makes, they are my favorite. I like to dunk them in a cup of coffee," he told them. Joe and Evangeline looked at each other with surprise.

"She certainly got on the good side of Cook early enough," Joe admitted.

"Good morning," Anna Maria said joyfully. She had a tray of the delicious confections in her hands.   "Let me try one of those," Joe asked, and poured himself a cup of hot coffee from the buffet table. "They remind me of my mother," he said after reaching for another one. Evangeline had to laugh at the two men she loved most in the world eating biscotti and having a good time doing it.

"I hope you don't mind that I invaded your kitchen,"   Anna Maria said to Evangeline.

"Don't let Cook hear you say that," she said, "she considers it her kitchen. Anyway my darling, this is your house now, you may use it at your will."

"Mother," Mike asked when she sat down with her coffee, "can we have our talk about dad now."

"Oh my darling son, it pains me to tell you the events of the past year."

"I think I'm man enough to understand," he said.

"What about Anna Maria?" she said, as the girl pulled up a chair next to her husband.

"We have no secrets from each other," he told his mother.

"Where to start?" she said putting a lump of sugar in her coffee and stirring it until it dissolved. "Your dad was a wonderful man, he kept your best interests first, always; I want you to remember that."

"I have no doubt," Mike answered her.

"His shortcomings were of a personal matter. It seems he had a mistress in his life from the first day of our marriage. I knew about her after we were married a few months, and had her investigated. I never brought her up to Chance, because I didn't want to upset the life we had carved out for ourselves and I couldn't bear the thought of hurting Edward and Rosalyn, I also didn't want you to go without, either." "Mother, how awful for you," Mike cried. "I had no idea," he added. Anna Maria couldn't believe any man would want another woman if he had Evangeline for a wife; she felt so sorry for her.

"He gave me everything I could want and more, most of all, he gave me Ali," she admitted. "Mike, he took you as his own son, like Edward took him. He admired his father so much he wanted to emulate his goodness.

"This woman, had known Chance years before I came along and they were lovers back then," she said.

"But he married you not her," Mike said confused.

"He loved me too Mike, honest he did, but I wasn't enough for him. He kept this woman in the back of his life for years and when Rosalyn died she had enough."

"What do you mean?" Mike asked her.

"On the day of the funeral, she showed up in a red dress and a large red hat with a huge feather on it. She had been hidden out of our lives for so long, she decided to make a stand and show up outside the church dressed for attention and she got it. The newspapers went wild with false stories about your grandmother. They said she was her love child or that Rosalyn belonged to some kind of cult, crazy things like that.

"What are you talking about?" Mike said in disbelief.

"I'm telling you it was a circus around here for a couple of days. To make a long story short, everyone in the family attacked Chance. Your grandmother had requested a small family funeral, but because of all her social charities, her friends naturally showed up at the church, she was so loved.

"This woman wanted Chance to divorce me and when he wouldn't, she came to me with her sordid stories of their affair. She wanted to get back at Chance so she came to the funeral dressed like that. The twins were angry with him, Larissa started to show signs of her illness after that and Lorenzo almost killed him. I let him have it too, I had many years of disappointment pent up in me and he heard all about it.   "Chance went to her later that night and pounded on her door, she wouldn't let him in and he laid on her stoop in the rain for hours. A police man found him and sent him to the hospital in an ambulance. He never really recuperated from the gunshot wound in his lung and he got sick again. I kept him here with his family for over a year until he died."

"That was generous of you Mother," Mike said, "after all the heartache he gave you."

"He was my husband, Mike. I couldn't leave him to his own devices or put him in a sanitarium. He was, after all, Chance Winston of Winston Steel and I had to protect my children's reputation and that of Larissa. Ali, Larissa and I were at his bedside when he passed away, we told him how much we loved him and forgave his indiscressions. He died at peace knowing he was forgiven," she added.

"I should have been there with you," Mike cried. "I joined this war with a head full of foolish intentions. I should have stayed home." Anna Maria looked at him with hurt in her eyes

"Mike," his mother said, "then you wouldn't have your wife; she was your destiny, my son."

Mike took Anna Maria's hand and kissed it, "forgive me Mia, I didn't mean it the way it sounded." She kissed him and told him not to worry everything was going to be fine. The girl knew he was hurt by the story he was just told. Who wouldn't be hurt by such a thing? Her papa would never do that to her mama, she would kill him.

Evangeline took Anna Maria upstairs to her room, she had some pretty things that she hadn't worn yet that might fit her daughter-in-law. Anna Maria jumped at the chance to have time with Evangeline and look into her closet and see all the fine pieces of clothing she had to give her. Evangeline was becoming a shining star in her daughter-in-laws eyes and the respect she had for her was enormous.

"Chance all but gave me permission to marry your mother," Joe chimed in, after Evangeline finished her tale and went upstairs. "He knew I was in love with her and would always take care of her," he added.

"My mother," Mike said, "has always had good men looking out for her. Chance, you, Lorenzo and me. I'm glad you married her, Joe, I've always thought the world of you." he told him.

"Thank you, Mike that means a lot to me," Joe assured him.

"What else hasn't she told me about my dad?" he asked Joe.

"Your mother has her pride, I'm sure it was all she could do to tell you what she did. If she wants to tell you more, she will at her own time and you won't have to ask," Joe said. There has to be more to the story, he thought as they were still drinking their coffee, he was sure.

When the women came back to the breakfast room, Anna Maria had an arm full of dresses and pretty things to show Mike. "Look Michele, your mother is so generous look at all the pretty things she gave me."

"You can have anything you want Mia," he laughed. "I'll take you to Macy's tomorrow."

"No you won't," Evangeline said, "that's woman's work. Ali and I are going to take her and that's that," she insisted.

"I'm looking for private first class Mike Winston," Sam Genoa said as he came into the breakfast room.

"You won't find him here, only private citizen Mike Winston." Mike arose from his chair and got a big bear hug and hand shake from his friend Sam.

"It's good to see you my friend," Mike said, "how long have you been home?"

"Going on two months," Sam figured, "long enough to realize what I left and know I'm not leaving again."

"I hear you," Mike said, "Where's Abigail anyway?"

"I dropped her off at the hospital to see Larissa, I'm sorry to hear of the events of last night," he said.

"It was sheer terror, Sam, I wasn't that afraid in any battle in Italy. Sam I want you to meet Anna Maria, my wife."

"Your wife?" Sam repeated his words. "So nice to meet you," he said, "I'm shocked."

"We met in Sicily after the war and the rest is history," Mike said in a nut shell.

"I can see why," he said, "you are beautiful!"

"Thank you, Sam," Anna Maria said, "I hope we can become good friends too. I understand I owe a big thank you for pulling my husband out of that fox hole and saving his life," she said.

"What foxhole?" Evangeline exclaimed.

"Oh it was nothing, I was just at the right place at the right time, that's all," Sam explained.

"The right time," Mike said, "he saved my life!"

"What else do you do for your friends?" Sam laughed.

"My son has more secrets than the government," Evangeline cried.

"That's ok mama, we still have two years to catch up on." Mike laughed and put his arm around her.

"Got room for one more?" a voice shouted out' Dean McCall came into the breakfast room with Ali tagging along behind him. "Ali called me this morning to tell me Mike was home," he said.

"It's great to see you," Mike greeted him, "you look wonderful. Don't you use a cane anymore?" he asked.

"No, I've been doing a lot of physical therapy and helping out at the veteran's hospital in my spare time," he answered.

"Are you still in school,? Mike asked.

"Yes, my political science classes have taught me a lot, I enjoy them, but not as much as helping the soldiers learn to walk again. I was getting pretty far with your dad before he got sick," Dean said, "he was walking without a cane too. He had a lot of determination, I miss him very much," Dean admitted.

"We all do, I can't imagine this house without him," Mike said. "Dean, I want you to meet my wife, Anna Maria." He took her by the arm and introduced her to his friend.

"I have heard so much about you, I am happy to meet you," Anna Maria said.

Dean was in shock. "Did you say your wife?" he repeated.

"I told you I had a surprise for you," Ali reminded him.

"I thought maybe he got taller or has shorter hair or something like that," he answered her. "When did this happen?" he said still unbelieving.

"Almost three weeks ago in Palermo," Mike answered. "I took a trip with my friend Mario Delarosa after the war and we both came home with wives, I still can't believe my luck."

"She is breathtaking," Dean told his friend, "Congratulations."

"How did you meet her?" Dean wanted to know.

"Actually I saw her in a little shoe shop and it was crazy, I actually fell in love with her that minute. Mario dragged me out of the store, because he said Sicilian woman were dangerous. Later I went to see my father's sister and in walked Anna Maria, you could have knocked me over with a feather."

"Who was she, a neighbor or something?" Dean asked.

"No my friend, she is her daughter."

Dean was silent for a few seconds, "Do you mean she is your cousin?"

"Yes, first cousin," Mike confessed.

"How is that going to work with your political future, Mike?"

"I don't care, she is the only girl for me as far as I am concerned, and if the political world doesn't like it then so be it," he said.

"I hope we will see a lot of each other," Dean took her hand and kissed her cheek, still a little in shock. "Isn't it wonderful?" Ali said gleefully, and hugged them "I'm so happy." Evangeline was happy to know Ali was so taken with her new sister-in-law. Things are going to change again at Hunters Point and change was good.

Abigail walked into the hospital room to find Larissa visiting with Alan and his parents. She embraced her friend and scolded her that she scared the life out of everyone.

"We are just happy to know she is alright," Mrs. Mason told her. "Now that you are here, we are going to insist that Alan come home for a while and get a few hours rest, come along my dear." Mr. Mason and Alan said their goodbyes and Alan vowed he would see her in a few hours.

"No Alan, you need your sleep. You have been my nursemaid much too long, it's about time I start looking after you," Larissa begged him.

"I'll do it for you as long as Abigail keeps you company for a while longer," he said.

"Don't worry Alan, Sam is at Hunters Point and I'm sure they have a ton of things to talk about." The Mason's expressed their love to Larissa and went home to take care of Alan for a change.

"What in the world happened to you?" Abigail asked first thing.

"I wish I knew," Larissa said, "I was dreaming of Mother and Father and she was calling me, the next thing I knew I was in the pond and Alan was holding on to me. Matt and Mark pulled us out and Mike gave me mouth to mouth resuscitation. The next thing I remember is Joe carried me to the ambulance and here I am. The crazy thing is I have never felt better in my life. I have my appetite back and I don't feel like crying at all."

"That's wonderful my darling, I hope I have my old Larissa back," she said.

"Did you hear about Mike?"

"Yes. Sam is so happy he is home, I can't wait to see him," Abigail assured her.

"That's all you know?",

"What do you mean Larissa?"

"He brought along a little souvenir from Palermo," Larissa teased.

Abigail was getting annoyed with her friend. "What kind of souvenir, like Italian pottery or something?" "No, a wife," Larissa shouted out!

"Oh, my God Larissa, is that why you are here?"

"No, I don't think so, Dr. Stein prescribed a sedative for me and it was too strong and it made me feel sick. I took too many and ended up in the pond," she said. "It was quite a shock when he presented her to the family I will admit and it took us all by surprise. The worst part is that she is Lorenzo's niece, his first cousin. The best part is that she is absolutely the prettiest girl I have ever seen," she declared! "Wait until you see them together, Abigail, he is so happy. I never saw him like that before. And she adores him too. I thought I would be jealous and hate her and him, but I'm happy for them. Alan and I are both happy for them.

" Something snapped in me last night, I can't explain it, maybe it was the realization that he is married and my little girl dream is over. I have a real man who loves me like everyone has been trying to tell me. His mother cried when she came in here today, she was so worried about me. His dad gave me a little gold bracelet with a heart charm on it. He said I was his little girl, look how pretty it is and she picked up her arm to show her friend. I have a family of my own with the Masons and Alan and I can't wait to give them grandchildren. I know Evangeline, Joe and Ali are going to Detroit with Lorenzo and Elsie. Mark and Mary are going back to London soon too. I have Matt and Mariella as my anchor in New York and the Masons of course. Alan and I will be in Boston until he finishes school and then he will be back in the city as a partner with John Lee's firm. You and Sam aren't going anywhere are you,? So I am going to be just fine. My mother raised a strong daughter, not the insipid little thing I was becoming and I intend to make her proud"

"Larissa," Abigail said, "have a drink of water, you have been talking nonstop since I got here," as she handed her a full glass. The best friends laughed and talked about their upcoming weddings.

"We have a lot of things to do before June, so I better get out of here fast so I can become Mrs. Alan Mason," she assured herself.

"Make sure your bags are in the hall by eight o'clock," Evangeline shouted out to Ali. "The chauffer is going to take them to the station early, so we don't have to worry about them later," she told her daughter. She was busy picking up things and putting them down to make sure she didn't forget anything. Evangeline was nervous with excitement. Their trip to Detroit was the first time Evangeline and Joe were going to view their new home in its finishing stages. Lorenzo and Elsie left the day before to meet with the builders and decorators.

Joe was so excited he could hardly stand it. This house belonged to him and his wife, no ghosts of Winston's will be haunting its halls. No one made him feel like Hunters Point wasn't his; but deep down he knew his marriage couldn't be real in Chance Winston's house. Detroit was going to be the start he and Evangeline needed, even if Lorenzo was going to live next door. Honestly, the men had become fond of each other over the years and looked forward to long talks in the garden while they fussed over their tomato plants and pots of sweet basil. They spoke in their native Italian at these times and it made Evangeline laugh when they rolled the bocce balls and swore at each other if their ball missed the target. Ali wasn't so easy to persuade to come to Detroit, she knew Dean had no reason to go there and she will miss him terribly. Evangeline thought it was a good thing for her to meet new people and she had plenty of time to dwell on Dean McCall. Evangeline decided to keep Hunters Point for a while until her children knew what they were going to do with their lives. She needed a place to come back to when she and Joe visited New York and Mike and Anna Maria were going to live there for a while. Angelina and Filippo were going to arrive soon in New York and Evangeline was going to employ Filippo as caretaker of the grounds and household. Everything was working out beautifully and she was so relieved.

The train ride was pleasant enough for a cold January day. When they arrived at Michigan Central a car was waiting for them. Lorenzo sent a driver ahead to pick the family up at the station. They arrived at the hotel and Elsie and Lorenzo welcomed them and showed them to their suite. Elsie was so excited she could have jumped for joy.

"Evangeline," she said, "wait until you see our homes, they are fantastic! Not as big as Hunters Point, but plenty of room and out buildings for all the family. The lake is frozen, but it is a sight to behold, Lorenzo is thrilled with it. The picture window you wanted turned out to be beautiful and the Grand Piano Joe ordered arrived today. Your house is very art deco with tons of moldings and open spaces. My house is Mediterranean design with tiled roof and arches all over the place. They are both so beautiful I don't know which one I like best," she said. "Tomorrow we pick out drapery and carpets and floor tiles and paint, isn't it exciting?" she gasped for air.

"Slow down, Elsie," Evangeline told her. "We have lots of time to shop for things, I'm just happy to see you both, I've missed you." Lorenzo laughed at his wife, it gave him much pleasure to see her so enthusiastic about the move. Lorenzo walked across the room to the window where Evangeline's daughter was looking down at the traffic on the street.

"Ali, what's the matter?" Lorenzo could see the child wasn't happy.

"I don't know if I will like this Detroit very much, I miss my friends and family already," she said with a pout.

"Oh, you mean Dean McCall, don't you?" he teased.

"Oh Uncle Lorenzo, don't make fun of me, you know I have a crush on him."

"Don't worry my darling, he will come to see you soon, I promise."

"I love you, Uncle Lorenzo," she said and gave him a big hug.

The next morning was sunny and bitter cold all at the same time, but it couldn't dampen the excitement the families felt as the limousines pulled up to the beautiful estate Joe and Evangeline envisioned in their mind. It was just as they had hoped and even Ali was impressed.

"I told you it was fabulous," Elsie said. When they walked in the front door, a vast entry hall welcomed them in.

"Turn around." Joe told Evangeline. Over the front door was a balcony that housed the Steinway and in front of that was the picture window Evangeline asked for. The picture frame paneling on the walls and the art deco stair case was a far cry from the baroque gilded design of Hunters Point. The huge dining room was to Evangeline's liking, because she always had a house full of people for dinners. The sitting room had a stone fireplace and large windows on each side that over looked Lake St. Clair. Joe was particularly impressed with that room.

"We can throw a rug in front of the fire and watch the boats come and go, as we snuggle up to each other," he told his wife.

"I can't wait!" she told him, "Who needs furniture?" she teased. The six bedrooms upstairs were ample for the needs of the family. The bathrooms were tiled in black and white marble and the fixtures were the latest in fashion. The breakfast room, which also overlooked the lake, was a wall of windows. The huge French doors opened to a very large patio where stone grills were built. Joe wanted to cook outdoors when he entertained, weather permitting.

"We are going to put in a built-in swimming pool," Joe told Ali. "This way you can invite your friends any time you want to in the summer and we can cook outdoors and have a wonderful time."

"Thanks Joe," she said, "you're the greatest."

"Let's go to my house now," Lorenzo invited their first guests. "We are having a gate and pathway built between the houses so we don't have to walk so far to visit," he showed Evangeline.

"That will be good for Elena," she said, "you won't have to worry about her then."

"That's what I was thinking," Elsie answered.

"Welcome to my home," Lorenzo waved his guests in the front door. It was a massive wooden arched door with brass hinges.

"Very impressive" Joe said. They walked into a grand entry with arches and pillars every twenty feet all the way down the long hallway. Their dining area rivaled the Cross home, but when they got to the end of the hall, the stairway split in two directions to the second floor where the six bedrooms and sitting rooms were located. Each bedroom had its own bath and balcony.

"There will be no rose trellis on Elena's balcony," he whispered to Evangeline. She gave him a pinch in response. He had the walls plastered in the Venetian fashion with rubbed paint to show off the highs and lows of the plaster. There were murals of the Sicilian towns and coves of his boyhood.

"I just love this house," he told his family,

"Me too," Elsie agreed, "it reminds me of you, my love," she said.

"Wait until Maria and Nicolo see their house," he pointed to a lovely cottage down the lane. "I had the walls finished in the same plaster as the main house, but it is so cozy in there and she has a first class kitchen so she can bake to her heart's content and give it all away." They all laughed because they knew how she loved to feed the homeless and less fortunate.

"Mike is a lot like that," Evangeline said "his orphanage is already being built in Palermo."

Soon Mr. Collins, of the House of décor, arrived and the ladies had a million questions for him. It took all the rest of the day to satisfy them that their requests would be granted and allowed him to go to his office to get the job done.

"We want to move in at the end of July," they told him. "Larissa and Alan will be on their honeymoon in London and Ali will start school in Grosse Point in September."

"I'm sure we will have everything done by then," he assured them.

On the way back to the hotel, Lorenzo took them to the showroom that was being built for him to manage. It was on Jefferson Avenue just a few miles from their homes. All the latest in designs for the showroom and repair shop were put in place. A huge glass window where people could see the new Ford automobiles from the road was just installed.

"This is my office," he told them, "pretty executive looking, don't you think?" he bragged.

"It's great, Lorenzo," Joe told him and slapped him on the back.

Life was going to be good for all of them in Detroit, Joe thought to himself. It's a fresh start for Evangeline and himself. Elsie was going to have the home she dreamed about and Lorenzo was going to be somebody important. Ali will conform to her surroundings like all teenage girls and find hundreds of friends. He couldn't wait to get started.

Back in New York, the wedding of Sam Genoa and Abigail Norton was a grand affair. His parents rented the grand ballroom of the Waldorf Astoria for the reception. Larissa was her Maid of Honor and Mike was his best man. Sam couldn't contain his happiness in finding Abigail and made a speech at dinner.

"First of all, I want to thank everyone for attending today; it means the world to us. I just want everyone to know how lucky I am to have found Abigail, although she claims she was under my nose all along. She is a kind, caring, intelligent young woman and I am so proud she is now my wife. I love you, my dear," he proclaimed. Everyone raised their glasses to them and said cheers!

Larissa was in tears after his speech.

"What's the matter?" Mike asked her.

"Sam couldn't say two words together in front of a crowd when we were growing up, and look at the beautiful speech he just gave," she said.

"That's what happens when you find true love," he said to her. "Your heart is so full you have to tell people about it," he said as he pulled one of her blond curls. "Your turn is in a few months, you will see what I'm talking about. Alan tells people he loves you all the time, he has proclaimed it for years," he said.

"Mike," she said, "I love you with all my heart, but now I know the difference. Alan is the love of my life he makes me laugh, he never makes me cry. He has been there for me every step of the way," she said.

"Even at the debutant ball?" he asked.

"Even at the debutant ball," she laughed. "I should have known then," she said, "but it took a long time for him to get through to me." I

"'m sure he thinks it's worth it," Mike replied. "I better steal my wife away from him, before he works his charm on her," he teased. Mike and Larissa broke in on them and the proper partners finished the dance.

Joe and Lorenzo took several trips to Detroit before the big move to make sure things were going along on schedule.

"This crew better have the work done before Elsie gets a hold of them." He pointed his fingers to the sky like he was praying for them. "She is obsessed with this move, she is driving me crazy."

"Evangeline has Larissa's wedding to keep her busy," Joe told him, "I bet she will get excited after the wedding."

Lorenzo's decorator Mr. Collins had ordered an antique fireplace from Rome and it hadn't arrived yet, so he had to go to the office to find out what the problem was. "Are you coming with me Joe?" Lorenzo asked.

"No, I think I'm going to stay at the hotel for the afternoon. I'm feeling a little tired," he told his friend. Lorenzo thought he looked a little pale so he agreed he should stay in and he would meet him for dinner later. When Joe didn't show up for dinner, Lorenzo went to his room to see what was wrong. After knocking on the door several times, Joe finally answered.

"Gee, Lorenzo I didn't realize how late it has gotten, I slept through the whole day," he confessed.

"Are you alright?" he asked Joe.

"Yes. I'm good now, I guess I'm working too much at Winston Steel and trying to get this house together, you know how it is," he told his friend.

"I'll tell you what," Lorenzo said, "I'll have some dinner brought to the room and we can eat here, how does that sound?"

"That's great, I'm sorry I messed up your plans."

"Does Evangeline know how you have been feeling?" Lorenzo asked.

"No and please don't tell her, I don't want her to worry."

"You have my word, my friend," Lorenzo said.

June was here before they knew it. Larissa married Alan Mason on a beautiful June morning at St. Mary's Church on Long Island. Evangeline had the ballroom transformed into a flower wonderland. Every color of the rainbow filled the centerpieces and the walls and garland draped across the bridal table. The bride and groom said their vows and Larissa took her bouquet of flowers to the statue of the blessed mother and she prayed for a long life with Alan and many children to make his parents happy. She wished her parents and Chance were there to see how happy she was, but she knew they were looking down on her from heaven.

Mike asked Alan if he could give the speech and Alan complied. "First of all," he said, "I want to congratulate Alan on his most superb choice of a wife." Everyone cheered. "Larissa and I have been raised together since we were three and four years old respectively. I don't remember a time until I was eighteen years old that we weren't together. Although we don't share blood, we couldn't have been closer than if we were siblings. Larissa my love, my wife and I want to wish you both the best life has to offer: you deserve it. Alan, I love you like a brother, but don't you ever make her cry." *Don't ever make her cry like I did*, he thought to himself feeling guilty. The crowd of family and friends gave a cheer and enjoyed the rest of the evening.

Larissa stood at the top of the staircase dressed in her Chanel going away outfit and tossed her bouquet into the crowd of single women. It seemed to bounce around a few times before it landed right in Ali's arms.

"Oh, no!" shouted Evangeline, "She is too young!"

"Come on my darling," Joe said as he pulled her away from the crowd, "let her have her moment of glory." While they were walking away, he nudged Dean in the ribs. "You better watch out," he teased with that famous Joe Cross grin on his face. Dean smiled at him, but didn't understand what he meant.

That Sunday morning, Evangeline had a hard time getting Joe up for Mass.

"Do you think God will forgive me if I begged off today?" he wondered.

"Too much wedding?" she asked him.

"Must be," he said, "I just can't seem to keep my eyes open."

Joe was showing signs of fatigue more and more often lately. He had an appointment to see a specialist the next day, without Evangeline's knowledge. When the family returned from church, the house was put back together as if a wedding had never taken place. The catering company was the best in New York and the traditional buffet brunch was ready for them. Joe was sitting in the garden getting some sun when Evangeline found him.

"Are you feeling better Joe?" she asked.

"Yes, I am, did you pray for me?" he asked.

"No, I prayed for us," she said. "We are a team, everything we do, we do together or not at all," she insisted.

"Good girl," he said, and escorted her into the dining room for something to eat. The crowd was even larger than normal since many stayed over after the wedding.

Joe asked for everyone's attention by banging his spoon on a glass. "I have something to say," he said," this is the last traditional brunch we will be having a Hunters Point. Next week we leave for Detroit and the traditional brunch will be eaten overlooking Lake St. Clair. You are all welcome anytime you can get away and Evangeline and I look forward to seeing your happy faces there. We hope, along with Lorenzo and Elsie, that you can come for the last week in August for our house warming parties, there is room for everyone there. Your hosts from now on at Hunters Point will be Mr. and Mrs. Mike Winston until further notice." Mike and Anna Maria stood up and waved at the diners. Everyone laughed at his joke, but Joe was happy to hand off the baton to someone else.

Joe walked into the doctor's office in the Riddle Building on 5th avenue the next day. Doctor Martin was recommended to him by Dr. Stein. Joe told the man of his fatigue lately and how it was getting worse. Dr. Martin took some blood tests and gave him a routine physical.

"You seem to be in good shape, Joe," the doctor told him. "Are you having any dizziness with your fatigue?"

"Yes, a little," he admitted.

"I'll call you when the tests come back and then we can treat the ailment when we know more about what we are dealing with," he assured him.

"My family and I are leaving for Detroit next week," Joe mentioned to him.

"We will know what to do by then," he said. "I wouldn't worry too much, but I am glad you came in to see me," he told Joe.

"Thank you Doctor Martin, I'll wait for your call," he said.

Mark wondered what was keeping Joe. They had a meeting with the Pittsburgh office by telephone in an hour and he didn't notice Joe through the glass windows that separated the rooms. He got up to see what was keeping him and check his office to see if he was there. When he walked in the door he couldn't open it all the way and found Joe lying on the floor passed out. He yelled for help and checked to see if he was breathing, he was. Immediately a secretary called for an ambulance.

"Come on Joe, wake up," Mark pleaded. Matt opened the door for the ambulance attendants and in a matter of minutes Joe was on the way to the hospital. Matt called Lorenzo who was at the Long Island office to pick up Evangeline and take her to the hospital.

"What happened?" Lorenzo asked, with total fear in his voice.

"We don't know," Matt said, "Mark found him on the floor of his office when he didn't show up for a meeting."

My god, what am I going to say to Evangeline, he prayed. "We will be there as soon as I can get to her," Lorenzo told Matt.

Lorenzo found Evangeline packing her Waterford Crystal goblets and giving orders to the movers she hired to help her pack. "Come Evangeline, we have to go to the hospital right now," he said. By the look on his face she could tell something awful had happened.

"What is it?" she screamed.

"Joe," he said, "he was found on the floor of his office." She dropped the vase she was wrapping and ran out of the house with Lorenzo. Not a word was said all the way there, she was terrified. When they got to the hospital she met her brother-in-laws at the lobby door.

"Where is he?" she cried, "Where is he?"

"He is being treated by the staff Doctor and Dr. Martin has just got here too."

"Then he is alive?" she asked.

"Yes, darling, he is alive, but they have to examine him so they can find out what happened," Mark said.

"Did he have a heart attack?"

"We don't know," Matt answered her visibly shaken.

"This can't happen," she said, "he is so happy. Dear God this can't happen!" She broke down in tears. Evangeline did what she does best she gave the problem to God. She ran to the chapel down the hall and closed the door. She had a few things to say to God and didn't want an audience. She threw herself down in front of the cross that was perched on a pedestal. She was reminded of the day she lay on her parent's grave and asked for guidance in her time of need. The tears were stinging her eyes and her face was blotched and red.

"Please, help Joe" she said as she lay on the floor. "He is so happy, now dear God. I can't help him, only love him. Give him the strength to pull through whatever he is facing." The words were getting hard to say, she could hardly breathe for the pain in her chest. "I can't live without him, sweet Jesus. Please give us the chance for a good life. You have given us the means, now give us the time. Joe is such a wonderful man, everyone loves him. My children will be devastated, please let him live." Evangeline was sobbing now uncontrollably.

Lorenzo's hands were on her arms pulling her up to him.

"Is he dead?"

"No, No, my darling, he is sitting up in bed and asking for you. There is no way I'm going to take you to him looking like this, you will scare him to death!" he laughed. Lorenzo asked a nurse to help her get herself together. She washed her face and combed her hair and took a deep breath.

"I'm ready to see my husband now." she told the woman. Evangeline walked into Joe's room and immediately threw herself on top of him and cried all over again.

"I'm alright my darling, honestly, don't cry or you will make me cry too."

"I can't live without you Joe," she said, "I was so scared."

Elsie met Lorenzo outside Joe's room. "What happened? Is he going to be alright?"

"Yes, the doctors said he had some blood work done this morning and the tests were rushed because we are leaving next week. It seems Joe has some sort of anemia and with the stress of the move, the wedding and trying to tie up loose ends in New York his body couldn't take it and he passed out," Lorenzo told his wife.

"Can they fix him?" Elsie asked with great concern

"Yes, he has to take some iron pills and some kind of tonic to build his blood back up. Dr. Martin has already given him the name of a doctor in Detroit to follow up with. I hate to be him," Lorenzo said, "Evangeline will be following him around with that bottle of tonic and iron pills for weeks."

"Thank God," Elsie said, "I know how happy he is about the move, he can't wait to have his own home. What about you Lorenzo, how do you feel? Are you stressed or anything like that? I'm getting worried,"

"You know I don't get stressed," he told her.

Elsie rolled her eyes and said, "let's go home husband, we have a lot of packing to do." They walked out of the hospital with their arms around each other, thankful that they were together and in love.

"*Che bedda, Lake St. Clair,* "Lorenzo said as he and Joe stood on the dock that would soon house his new boat. Everything turned out pretty good, Joe thought as he turned around to look at the two estates. The workers were putting the finishing touches on the in ground pool on his property.

"Ali will be happy when it's finished. She has already made friends with a girl in the neighborhood and they can swim all day if they like."

"How do you feel, Joe?" Lorenzo asked his friend, "You gave us such a scare."

"I'm feeling fine now, the doctor said my blood count was at a normal level when I went to see him the other day," Joe said.

"That's great, by the way do you know how many people are coming from New York next week for the house warming?" Lorenzo asked.

"I have no Idea, probably forty or so," he figured. "Both guest houses will hold a couple of families each and we have so many bedrooms plus Maria and Nicolo's cottage. We will do just fine." Joe said, "if I know my wife, she will throw mattresses on the living room floor to accommodate her guests."

"That's the truth," Lorenzo laughed.

On Thursday of the last weekend of August the guests started to arrive. Mike and Anna Maria came with Dean McCall and Ali introduced him to her new friend Natalie. She had told her she had a crush on her brother's friend and couldn't wait for her to meet him. Natalie decided she should have a crush on Dean too, which irritated Ali. She was learning the games little girls played and didn't know she would someday be a master at them.

The entire Como family took the train on Friday. Antonino and Luna were excited to be in Detroit because they had a lot of friends who immigrated there and wanted to visit them.

Mark and Mary came on Friday, too. They had packed up their apartment and stored everything at Hunters Point. They were leaving for London the following week and wanted everything ready before they left for Detroit.

Nick Jackson was back in the states and his job with the government assigned him to Ann Arbor, Michigan to work at the University. Mike was very anxious to see him and invited him to the festivities.
Sam and Abigail were going to be there and so were the Mitchell's.

Since women had the right to vote this year, Mrs. Mitchell was at loose ends and looking for another cause to keep her busy. The President was going to sign into law any day, the 19th amendment prohibiting state and federal agencies gender based restrictions on voting. She was looking toward the temperance movement, but she didn't know that much about it. Mr. Mitchell forbade her to even give it a thought, he loved his brandy much too much to give it up. She was very fond of her evening toddy and thought prohibition was too much for her to handle. Maybe she could find something a little calmer to fight for: after all, she was getting up in years.

John Lee and his wife with their children accepted the invitation. Andrew Lee had two more sisters to add to his sibling list after his brother Richard was born that Christmas of 1914.

Evangeline was in her glory and Elsie was anxious to show off her new home. Elsie's sister Greta and her family lived in Detroit and she was a big help to Elsie. Her sister's children were mostly grown and so happy to have their aunt nearby. They doted on Elena and adored uncle Lorenzo, Elsie had never been happier.

People were playing all over the grounds. Some were swimming, some were playing ball, others were taking walks or sunbathing on the dock. Joe was cooking steaks on his grill and he was as happy as he could be. Evangeline, wearing a sun bonnet and huge sun glasses, was sitting beside Lorenzo. They were in oversized lounge chairs enjoying her large stone patio.

"I love watching the children playing in the pool," she said. Elsie had Elena learn to swim before the company came and she was supervising her daughter with her new found love of the water.

"Look Lorenzo," Evangeline said, "Elena comes by it naturally, she is just like you."

"I hope not darling, I was a devil as a child." Lorenzo lay back with his hands behind his head.

"This is what my sister Maria called the American Dream. Look all around us," and he waved his arms. "I fell in love with a beautiful girl when I was 18 years old. Who would have thought then that the two of us would accomplish this much," he said, and took hold of her hand.

"I was 15 years old when I fell in love with that boy. Who would have thought that after all we have been through, that this would be our destiny," she said. She squeezed his hand, *Pensa La Salute*, Evangeline said under her breath, *Pensa La Salute*.

THE END...